Other Novels of the Darkyn

Praise for the Novels of the Darkyn

Evermore

"The plot is full of exciting twists and turns. Viehl tells a self-contained, page-turning story."
—*Publishers Weekly*

"Viehl knows just how to liven things up: by adding danger, treachery, and betrayal to the mix."
—*Romantic Times*

"*Evermore* [is] an immensely satisfying read for even the most demanding paranormal romance fan."
—LoveVampires

"*Evermore* is a delightful and engaging book that continues the tale of the Darkyn people. The book is exciting and multifaceted. The craftsmanship is excellent. . . . Impeccable world building, complex characters and a great plot."
—Paranormal Romance Writers

Night Lost

"Viehl continues to weave an intricate web of intrigue in this contribution to the amazing series. . . . I became completely engrossed in this compelling story. Lynn Viehl had me hooked from the first page. . . . Exceptional. . . . I definitely recommend this marvelous book."   —Romance Junkies

"Fast-paced and fully packed. [Viehl] does an excellent job of world building, and provides characters who continue to be explored book by book. You won't regret spending time in this darkly dangerous and romantic world!"   —*Romantic Times*

continued . . .

"Fans of the series will agree that Lynn Viehl is at the top of her game." —Alternative Worlds

Dark Need

"An exciting book and a must read . . . thrilling. . . . What makes the Darkyn novels so compelling is the dichotomy of good and evil. *Dark Need* has a gritty realism and some frightening and creepy characters that will keep you awake late at night. Balancing the darkness are the searing heat and eroticism . . . generated between Samantha and Lucan." —Vampire Genre

Private Demon

"Lynn Viehl's vampire saga began spectacularly in *If Angels Burn*, and this second novel in the Darkyn series justifies the great beginning. Indeed, it is as splendid, if not more so, than the first one." —Curled Up with a Good Book

"Strong . . . a tense, multifaceted thriller . . . Fans of Lori Handeland's Moon novels will want to read Lynn Viehl's delightful tale." —*Midwest Book Review*

If Angels Burn

"Erotic, darker than sin, and better than good chocolate." —Holly Lisle

"This exciting vampire romance is action-packed. . . . The story line contains terrific characters that make the Darkyn seem like a real species. . . . Lynn Viehl writes a fascinating paranormal tale that readers will appreciate with each bite and look forward to sequels." —The Best Reviews

TWILIGHT FALL

FALL

A NOVEL OF THE DARKYN

Lynn Viehl

AN ONYX BOOK

ONYX
Published by New American Library, a division of
Penguin Group (USA) Inc., 375 Hudson Street,
New York, New York 10014, USA
Penguin Group (Canada), 90 Eglinton Avenue East, Suite 700, Toronto,
Ontario M4P 2Y3, Canada (a division of Pearson Penguin Canada Inc.)
Penguin Books Ltd., 80 Strand, London WC2R 0RL, England
Penguin Ireland, 25 St. Stephen's Green, Dublin 2,
Ireland (a division of Penguin Books Ltd.)
Penguin Group (Australia), 250 Camberwell Road, Camberwell, Victoria 3124,
Australia (a division of Pearson Australia Group Pty. Ltd.)
Penguin Books India Pvt. Ltd., 11 Community Centre, Panchsheel Park,
New Delhi - 110 017, India
Penguin Group (NZ), 67 Apollo Drive, Rosedale, North Shore 0632,
New Zealand (a division of Pearson New Zealand Ltd.)
Penguin Books (South Africa) (Pty.) Ltd., 24 Sturdee Avenue,
Rosebank, Johannesburg 2196, South Africa

Penguin Books Ltd., Registered Offices:
80 Strand, London WC2R 0RL, England

First published by Onyx, an imprint of New American Library, a division of Penguin
Group (USA) Inc.

First Printing, July 2008
10   9   8   7   6   5   4   3   2   1

For my brother, Robert.

We can learn to see the world anew.

. . . There where the vines cling crimson on the wall,
And in the twilight wait for what will come.
The leaves will whisper there of her, and some,
Like flying words, will strike you as they fall;
But go, and if you listen she will call. . . .

—Edwin Arlington Robinson, *The Children of the Night*

Chapter 1

As Diane Lindquist touched up her lipstick, fluffed her bangs, and dabbed Allure by Chanel under each earlobe, she smelled urine.

Behind her, her brother, Daniel, lay in his hospital bed, the wisps of his thinning blond hair neatly combed, a nasal cannula hissing oxygen through his swollen nose into his wasted lungs. Six months ago a stroke had dragged half of his face toward his square chin, where it still drooped. His cloudy blue eyes, identical in color and shape to Diane's, wandered restless in their sockets, alert but not aware, searching but unable to find.

In age he was forty-six; in appearance he looked sixty-four.

I'll always be older than you-hoo.

She turned her head from side to side, using her fingers to rub some excess blush from one cheekbone. One of the nurses had said that *he* would be here tonight, and she had to look her best. But even at $250 an ounce, her Allure *parfum* wouldn't mask the stink coming from her brother's bed.

She pressed her lips together to even out the color on her lips. "I hope you didn't do something bad again, Danny."

"Die-uh," her brother crooned, responding to the sound of her voice. "Die-uh."

Diiiiiiiaaaaaaaaaaaaaane. Daniel, eleven years old, standing beside her bed in the dark. *Wake up, Diiiiiiiiii-aaaaaaaaaaane.*

The stroke that had destroyed a good portion of Daniel Geoffrey Lindquist Jr.'s brain tissue could be called many things, depending on who you asked. Lindquist Industries' executive board felt it was a minor setback that the young Mr. Lindquist would quickly overcome. Country-club buddies called it "bad luck" but were sure that Dan would soon get back "up to par."

Those who were not close personal friends of the Lindquist siblings, or who were not obliged to keep shareholders from panicking, used the standard, socially accepted expressions of sympathy. "Horrible tragedy" topped the list, followed by "undeserved tribulation" and "unbelievably sad turn of events."

No one mentioned the drugs, the booze, the sex, or any of Daniel's other self-destructive amusements. Wealth had its privileges. While he was alive, even old Mr. Lindquist had been philosophical about his son's various addictions. When someone had the bad taste to mention them, his usual comment was something along the lines of, *Boys will be boys*.

If asked about her brother's stroke, Diane would only offer a sad but courageous smile while she remembered her brother peeing on her bed.

She could still see him there in the dark, opening the front of his pajamas, taking out his ugly snake thing, and aiming the stream at her narrow pelvis. The smell and heat of his urine would wake her up, but it always soaked through her sheets and into her pajamas before she could roll out of the way. *Look, you wet the bed again, Diane. I'm going to teh-hell. You wet the be-hed, ha, ha, ha.*

Their father had adored Daniel, of course. Had doted on his only son. Had believed every word out of his angelic mouth.

See, Daddy? Danny, standing at the foot of the bed, pointing a righteous finger. *She did it again, just like I told you. I can smell it all the way in my room.*

Daniel Geoffrey Lindquist Sr., with the stoic calm of a parent resigned to performing a highly unpleasant but necessary task, patting his son on the head. *You're a good boy, Danny. Now go back to bed.*

Diane knew exactly why her brother had had a stroke. Like an indifferent leech, he had attached himself to family, friends, and life, and sucked them all dry. That included their parents, three wives, several mistresses, innumerable hookers, and a daughter. All of them were dead or gone now. All except Diane, the only one who really understood Dan, and who had stood by her brother.

Diane endured it all, and in the process made herself indispensable to Danny. She was the only one Dan trusted to supervise his household, pay his bills, clean up his post-high puke, pay off his prostitutes, and, of course, purchase his drugs. And because Daniel had been a lifelong user, no one had been surprised that he had overdosed, as he had done so several times.

Nor had anyone bothered to check out the exact chemical components of the narcotic cocktail he had snorted moments before the first seizure hit.

I'm disappointed, Diane. Daddy, sitting behind his desk, rolling a fat Cuban cigar between his fingers. *You were supposed to find a husband at that college, not fill your head with useless nonsense.*

Magna cum laude, she'd graduated, with a sterling degree in business. *But, Daddy, don't you see, I can help you run the company—*

I have Daniel for that.

In Diane Lindquist's opinion, the stroke that had transformed her brother into a six-foot-two drooling carrot was simply long-overdue justice.

It had cost Diane a small fortune to arrange her brother's admission to the Lighthouse Rehabilitation Center. Small, exclusive, and insanely expensive, Lighthouse had an admissions waiting list a mile long—assuming you were first approved to be placed on the waiting list. But appearances had to be maintained, and a very generous donation from Lindquist Industries had finally convinced Dasherz Corporation, which owned the facility, to allow Dan to have the next available bed.

No one would ever say that Diane did not love her brother.

The doctors had been very clear about Daniel's chances. He would never leave the nursing home again, and his condition would continue to deteriorate until such time as would be appropriate to bring him home to die.

Clean, quiet, and classy—that was the Lighthouse. A discreet haven where old-money Chicago families could stick their demented, disabled, and dying relatives, owned by one of the nicest, kindest European gentlemen Diane had ever met. Not at all the sort of place her brother should have been stinking up by peeing in his bed.

Daddy, lighting his cigar, puffing on it until the end glowed bright red. *If you're going to have a nervous breakdown, I'll pack you off to that high-priced nuthouse where I put your mother. Stop sniveling and go make me and Danny some lunch.*

Diane could have summoned a nurse to deal with the mess. The well-paid staff behaved as if they doted on their patients. But now that her father was dead, it was her duty to see to her brother's needs.

Danny, drinking and reeling as he staggered in from a night of whoring. *Just get me the coke, you stupid twat.*

Diane took her duty to her brother very seriously.

She capped her lipstick and placed it back in her purse before she removed her jacket and went over to the bed. The odor grew stronger with every step she took toward him.

"Poor Danny. You were such a good boy." She stroked her hand over his skull, tugging playfully at the pathetic cobwebs of his hair. A few small beads of blood appeared on his pink scalp, which she blotted away with her handkerchief. The strands of hair she had pulled out she tucked between his curled fingers, another trick Danny had taught her when they were kids. "How could you do such a baby thing like wet your bed?"

Saliva wet Daniel's lips as his mouth worked and he stared up at her, but nothing came out.

"There's a bathroom right over there, so you don't have any excuse." She pulled back his bed linens and examined the wet, dark yellow stain that had soaked his pajama bottoms and blotched the white sheet under his bony hips. "Oh, look at the mess you made. I'm so disappointed."

At first the nurses had tried to keep Daniel on a catheter, but his physician had ordered them to remove it after it had caused several nasty urinary tract infections. After that, the adult diapers they had put on Daniel had given him a terrible rash. As Diane had told the staff many times, her brother was perfectly capable of getting up and using the toilet.

All he needed was a little reminder.

Diane yanked the urine-stained sheet out from under her

brother, grunting a little as she worked it free before she balled up the damp section and shoved it under his nose. "Do you smell that? What is that? Where does it go?"

"Uuuuuh." Daniel cowered and turned his head away. "Eeeeee."

"You're a disgusting, dirty boy." She scrubbed the urine-stained sheet all over his face before stuffing a fistful of it into his mouth to muffle his squeals. "Look at these pants. They're ruined."

Diane stripped off her brother's pajama bottoms and white cotton briefs, tossing them aside. She considered letting him live a little longer—torturing Danny these last few weeks had been surprisingly satisfying—but some of the nosier nurses had been giving her odd looks, and she couldn't afford to fail again. Until Danny died, she wouldn't inherit a dime; their father had left him in control of everything.

Women can't handle important business, Daddy had said. *Your brother will look after you when I'm gone.*

She re-dressed Danny, and then straightened his bed before she pulled on a pair of latex gloves from the box by the sink. She smiled as she removed the syringe from her purse. The drugs had been expensive, but her supplier assured her that they wouldn't show up if some fool doctor ordered an autopsy. She unbuttoned her blouse as she went to the heart monitor, and pulled up a chair beside her brother's bed. He was crying.

"Stop sniveling," she told him as she tore the monitor lead from his chest, and quickly pressed the patch to her left breast. "You're going to see Daddy." She'd given her brother enough injections over the years to know how to hide the needle mark. "Open wide, Danny. Diane has some nice drugs for you."

Daniel looked at her with his bleary eyes and, responding to the one word she mentioned that promised relief and pleasure, opened his mouth.

Diane pushed his tongue up with her thumb and looked for the right spot. The acrid reek of urine seemed to burn in her nostrils, but in a few minutes it would all be over. Then the syringe slipped out of her hand, and as she reached for it, something seemed to make time slow down and thicken.

"Miss Lindquist."

She couldn't smell her brother's pee anymore, only flowers. Such a pretty scent, but so odd. It made her arms and legs feel so heavy, and her head light.

"Miss Lindquist," repeated the low, courteous voice with a soft European accent. "Release your brother, if you please."

"Yes." Once she had, she felt a wonderfully strong, cool masculine hand rest against her hot neck. "I was hoping to see you."

"Look up." When she did, he said, "That is a security camera we installed last week after your visit, when we found three of your brother's fingers broken. It has recorded everything you have done to him today."

"I don't mind if you watch me," she told him, almost purring with pleasure. "Would you like to help? I'm going to be so rich."

"Did you intend to harm your brother?"

Part of Diane, the sly, careful part, wanted to deny it. Money was a private matter, Daddy had always said. Something to be kept in the family. Like Danny's drugs. Like Danny's whoring. *Boys will be boys will be boys will be boys will be boys . . .*

The other part of her was lost in the sweet, soft fragrance

of the flowers. The perfume grew stronger, and then she couldn't help herself.

"I have to do it," she told him, her voice rising to a childish octave. "Daniel was bad and wet the bed. He has all the money. I can help run the company. I had a business degree. I don't want a husband."

The hand moved to her shoulder and turned her. Diane smiled at him as she fell into his eyes, so beautiful and clean, like cool, pure water.

"What else have you done to your brother?" he asked.

Diane breathed in, and in a dreamy voice she told him everything. She began with the cocaine she had bought and carefully doctored to induce Daniel's stroke. Then she told him why she had done it and everything else.

It took a very long time.

Two men in uniform came into the room, and one of them pulled her hands behind her and put cold metal bracelets on them. She almost laughed at the careful way they handled her, their hands gentle and kind, as if she were the sick one. Couldn't they see that she was fine, now that he was here?

One of the uniformed men told her something about her rights, and asked her if she understood them. She knew she had never had any rights, not as far as Daddy was concerned, but said she did, and they walked with her out of Daniel's room.

Diane frowned when she couldn't smell the flowers anymore. She turned to see *him* watching her from the doorway.

Such a beautiful man, but he never smiled. "Can't I stay with you?"

His golden hair gleamed as he shook his head.

Diane understood why he didn't want her. She had told so many lies. She knew why it hurt so much, too.

Women can't handle important business.

"Don't worry," she said to him before they took her away. "Danny will look after me. Daddy said he would."

Liling Harper carried a basket of pale apricot roses into the staff room, where half of the afternoon shift took their dinner break.

"I *knew* there was something wrong with her," Nancy O'Brien was saying to two other nurses. She shook three packets of sugar into her coffee mug and took a miniquiche out of the microwave. "Nobody that rich comes to visit a brain-dead brother three times a week."

"She give me the creeps, that lady," Sonia Salavera added as she reached into the lounge fridge for a Diet Coke to go with the sandwiches she'd brought from home. "You ever look straight in her eyes?" She mimed a violent shudder.

"You can't tell that someone is a killer by looking at them, Sonia." Martha Hopkins, head nurse of ward seven, poured a dollop of skim milk to lighten the strong black tea she favored. "She is such a beautiful woman, and so devoted to Mr. Lindquist." She sighed. "Now we know why."

Sonia blew some air over her top lip. "Does she still get all the money when he dies?" She looked over at Liling, who had busied herself with replacing the wilting flowers in the table vases. "Hey, Lili, do you know? About Mr. Lindquist's sister? They took her away last night in handcuffs. She want to murder him, right here in the hospital."

Liling had noticed the beautifully groomed woman who had strenuously avoided even the most casual contact with any other person. She had never guessed that Daniel's sister had been the source of his pain, or she would have done something to stop it.

Guilt still pulled at her. "Is Mr. Lindquist going to be all right?"

"He will be now that they've locked up that crazy bitch sister." Nancy glared at Martha. "Don't look at me like that, Marti. She had the heart monitor hooked up to her own chest so that we wouldn't know he coded." To Liling, she said, "That nice Mr. Jaus walked in and caught her in the act. Apparently he got her so rattled she confessed to everything, right in front of the police."

Liling had been rattled by the nice Mr. Jaus enough to believe that much. But as much as she wished she could talk with the other women about the mysterious European and how he had saved Daniel Lindquist, she knew administration would not want the staff openly discussing the incident.

"Joe from security told me that earlier today they caught some reporters who signed in under false names so they could question some of the patients about the Lindquists," she told the nurses. "You should be careful what you say, even when you think no one is listening."

Martha nodded her agreement. "We have to protect the privacy of the patients and their families." As Nancy began to argue, she added, "Remember the terms of your employment contract, honey. They can fire us for gossiping, if they want."

"Can we gossip about Mr. Jaus?" Nancy's eyes twinkled. "He *is* the best-looking visitor we get on the ward."

"*Dios mío*," Sonia breathed. "Now, that man, he make my heart race like Jeff Gordon driving it."

Liling smiled at Martha before she left the lounge and pushed her flower cart down the hall to the patients' rooms. Along with tending the facility's grounds and landscaping, she took care of the houseplants in the lobbies and waiting rooms, and restocked vases in every room with fresh flowers twice a week. She was no doctor, and had no formal training in patient therapy, but bringing a little nature indoors helped lift everyone's spirits. Some of the nurses often joked about how calm and happy the patients were after Liling made her "rounds."

She also had to thin out the beds frequently, or someone would notice just how good she was at gardening.

Liling reached her last stop of the evening, a private room somewhat secluded from the rest of the ward. It had once been a treatment room that administration had specially converted for the use of the current occupant. An armed security guard sat on a folding chair outside the door, but he knew Liling, and only looked up once from the *Sports Illustrated* he was reading to give her a nod as she went past.

Liling knew how special Luisa Lopez was. A poor girl from the inner city, Luisa had struggled through dozens of operations to repair the horrifying injuries she had received after being attacked, beaten, raped, and nearly burned to death three years ago. Officially she'd come to the Lighthouse to begin an extensive regimen of physical therapy; unofficially she was being carefully protected. No one knew why, but the staff assumed it had something to do with her injuries. Whoever had been responsible for hurting Luisa had wanted her dead.

Liling had never felt strong connections to people, even other Chinese like herself. Yet from the moment they'd met, she'd felt an instant, inexplicable attraction to Luisa. As if the girl shared something with her that had no name.

" 'Bout time you got here," Luisa said as Liling came in with an armful of camellias. "I been waiting on you."

The doctors kept the girl's head shaved to allow the many skin grafts to her scalp to heal, but recently they had given her back eyebrows that arched black and sleek against the seamless grafts of her dark chocolate skin, as well as thick, curly black eyelashes that made her large, hazel eyes look like emerald cabochons with hearts of pure amber.

Liling smiled at her friend, whose hands were newly bandaged from the latest operation to separate and restore function to her burn-fused fingers.

"You have been waiting on me," she said, gently correcting Luisa's English. "Or are you grumpy because your other friend has not arrived?"

"Him." Luisa scowled. "He always . . . he is always late."

A few weeks after Liling had met Luisa, the girl had made a gruff request for Liling to help her learn to speak better English. To keep her charade intact, Liling had to suggest that an American would be a more suitable tutor, but Luisa had been adamant.

"I like the way *you* talk," she told Liling. "I doan wanna ax nobody else. Jes tell me when I mess up how I should say it."

Liling arranged the flowers in Luisa's vase before she drew a chair up to the side of the bed and took a copy of *Sense and Sensibility* from a drawer in the bedside stand. Corneal transplants had restored Luisa's vision, but she still struggled with reading, which she claimed gave her severe headaches. Liling had offered to read to her, and selected Jane Austen for the formal but beautiful English she had used to write her novels.

Liling looked for her bookmark, but it was missing from the pages of the novel. "Can you remember where we left off the last time?"

"Willoughby was supposed to propose to Marianne, but he made her cry," Luisa said. "She ran out the room."

"Out *of* the room."

Luisa sighed. "She ran out of the room. You sure? That sound like she ran out of Kleenex."

"*Sounds* like. Yes, I'm sure." Liling opened the novel to chapter fifteen and began to read out loud:

> "*Is there anything the matter with her?*" *cried Mrs. Dashwood as she entered.* "*Is she ill?*"
> "*I hope not,*" *he replied, trying to look cheerful; and with a forced smile presently added:* "*It is I who may rather expect to be ill—for I am now suffering under a very heavy disappointment!*"

"Ha." Luisa made a rude sound. "Marianne is so in love with him that she would never say no. I bet Elinor had that Colonel Brandon chase him off 'cause he's too poor." When Liling started to reply, she shook her head. "Don't say it. I know it's 'because' and I have to say the 'be' part."

Liling suppressed a smile as she continued reading.

An hour passed as the twilight deepened to night, glossed silver by a ghostly full moon. No sound alerted Liling, but she knew the moment he arrived. He waited silently, listening along with Luisa as the charming Dashwood sisters had their hopes destroyed and their hearts broken.

The scent of the camellias grew stronger, as if the flowers she had brought Luisa wished to personally welcome the fair, blue-eyed man standing just inside the doorway.

Liling finished out the chapter and returned the book to the drawer before she greeted Luisa's only other visitor. "Hello, Mr. Jaus."

"Good evening, Miss Harper." The mellow voice, with its eastern European accent, brushed against her ears like velvet.

Valentin Jaus was of average height, not towering over Liling's petite five-foot frame, but the broad shoulders and powerful build under his exquisitely tailored clothes mocked anyone who might label him as small.

Then there was the matter of his spellbinding, unearthly good looks. A Prince Charming mane of golden hair framed features strong and handsome enough to make the heart of any breathing female skip a beat. Rather than making him look sickly and wan, his pale skin bestowed an unearthly quality on him, as flawless as a god, as alien as a star traveler.

Liling tried not to stare openly at him—handsome people, she imagined, disliked being gaped at—but she often wondered if he even had pores, veins, or mortal flaws.

Jaus also projected an unapproachable aura for other reasons. His mouth, hard-lipped and very male, never gave away his emotions. He had beautiful white teeth, judging by what Liling could see when he spoke, but he never smiled. She couldn't tell if he was in pain; she had never had occasion to touch Jaus. She sometimes imagined she could feel it anyway. The man seemed surrounded by invisible walls; had he built them to keep himself in, or the rest of the world out?

The nurses speculated endlessly about Jaus, but no one seemed to know anything about him. The man never talked about himself at all, and neither did Luisa. It didn't bother Liling, who had enough secrets of her own to appreciate the desire for privacy. That her hands itched whenever she shared the same room with him was only a minor annoyance. She never tried to touch him, not even casually. Jaus was not the sort of man to whom casual things happened.

She saw no indications that he was dangerous in any way, but his eyes, a blue so light they looked like glass, sometimes made her slightly uneasy. She had never seen a man with eyes that might have been carved from some iceberg found at the ends of the earth.

The uneasiness came whenever Valentin Jaus regarded her directly. His eyes changed, not in color, but in intensity. His gaze took on a piercing quality, so unequivocal and merciless that Liling felt as if he could see into her soul.

As he did now.

Jaus went to stand on the other side of the bed and removed his coat. He had some difficulty, as apparently he could use only one of his arms; the other barely moved at all. "How are you feeling, Miss Lopez?"

Luisa shrugged. "They been walking me like . . . I have been walking three times a day, and I've not yet fallen. Still won't let me go outside, though."

"Your physicians tell me that your skin grafts are still healing," he reminded her as he draped his coat over his good arm. "You cannot be exposed to sunlight just yet."

Luisa muttered something grammatically incorrect under her breath.

Jaus took pains to hide his disability, but Liling wondered what could have been responsible for crippling his arm, and if that were the source of his steely aloofness. She thought he might have been badly burned, as Luisa had been. It would explain why a rich, white European businessman came to visit a poor multiracial girl from the projects.

Jaus caught her staring at him. "Do you suggest that Luisa go outside, Miss Harper?"

"Not if it will harm her," Liling said, trying not to cower under the crystalline gaze. "I could put in a request to administration to allow me to install some spotlighting around the garden paths and flower beds. That way patients like Luisa could enjoy them in the evening, after the sun sets."

"How kind of you." He turned back to Luisa and began

discussing the physical therapy she was having to help build up the muscles in her legs, which had become atrophied during her long hospital stay.

Liling sat quietly as the two talked, but she soon forgot to follow their conversation. Watching Jaus even from across the room made her imagination go off in wild directions, taking her to other places that were not so modern or civilized. She could easily picture Jaus as a marauder at the helm of a Norse ship, or issuing orders from the throne of a barbarian king, or even riding at the front of an ancient army of warriors as he led them into battle. Whatever he did, he would be in charge—he had the self-control and watchfulness of a leader.

Something inside Liling responded to that, too, but not with unease or fear. To combat her loneliness, Liling fantasized a great deal, and over time Jaus had come to figure prominently in her most private daydreams.

She gave herself to Jaus in her fantasies, but she made herself different women. An innocent taken from her village by the marauders and claimed by Jaus as his thrall. A slave girl made to dance naked before Jaus at a victory feast. The princess of a defeated land, brought bound and helpless to Jaus's tent . . .

She fell back onto cool, soft furs. Among them his slaves had scattered talismans of gold and copper, all etched with his profile. Sleeping with himself, was he? Not this night.

Sand shifted under the furs, under her palms, as she tried to brace herself for the weight of him. She couldn't see his face, but she could smell the wine on his breath and the lust on his skin.

He did not jump on her, still watching, still looking for weakness. She sensed that although he didn't trust her, he still wanted her, the beautiful, traitorous harlot princess who had come to him begging for mercy. He had accepted her, but only after his men had stripped her veils away from her countenance. She intended to use her prettiest words to plead with him.

His tent was his throne room here in the desert, so she knew the guards would not disturb them. They had already staggered off to their bedrolls, half-drunk on the sweet, heavy wine taken from the last raid on her lands.

He did not fall upon her, but lowered himself to recline at her side. He did not grab; his big hand moved only to cup and caress her shoulder.

"You please me." His voice wrapped around her, indulgent, perhaps to mask his suspicion.

She knew that after three months in the desert with no woman to relieve his need, he was hungry for sex. She saw him breathe in the scent of her skin, the sight of her half-bared breasts. She longed to touch him with her cool hands and offer him her ripe lips.

He pulled back her head, covering her mouth with his. She opened to the press of his tongue, feeling soft and helpless as he gathered her close and feasted. He took her mouth as a starving man ate, greedy and desperate, the sound from his chest like the throb of his heart under her fingers, deep and heavy, and when he lifted his head she gasped his name.

Master.

She gave herself to his hands and mouth, holding nothing back. She wanted him to ravish her, to treat her not as a princess, but as a lowly body slave. She wanted his tongue in her mouth and his hands on her breasts and his thighs pushing hers apart. Deep inside her barren belly, she wanted to feel the thrust of his flesh, the clench of hers around him, the rush of his release.

He was her enemy, and yet he was beautiful to her eyes, a man carved from the whitest, rarest stone, as remote as the snow atop the mountain that cannot be climbed, as chilling as the frost upon the winds, as potent as the seed spilled by the high priest's hand on the altar stone. Only then did she understand that his need was not born of months alone in the desert but of a lifetime alone and wandering. His hunger was her hunger, and—

"Lili?"

"Hmmmmm?"

"You falling asleep over there?" Luisa asked.

Liling opened her eyes to see Luisa and Jaus both looking at her.

Thank God he can't read my mind.

"Just daydreaming again." She made a show of checking her wristwatch. "It's time for me to go home. I'll be back to see you on Friday."

"Don't forget," Luisa said, closing her own eyes. "I got to . . . I'd like to know what happens next." She drifted off into a relaxed sleep.

Jaus followed her to the door. "Thank you for visiting Luisa, Miss Harper."

He hardly ever spoke to her other than to offer a greeting, so she wasn't sure how to reply. "I enjoy reading to her, Mr. Jaus." Did he want her to stop? "I hope I'm not intruding on your time with her."

"Not at all. There is a leaf in your hair. Hold still." He lifted his hand to her hair, moving his fingers through the straight black strands before resting his hand against her neck.

A garden of unseen camellias surrounded her, paralyzing her by wrapping her in layers of soft white silken petals. Jaus always smelled of camellias, as if he had them hidden under his beautiful suits, just out of sight. . . .

"What is the real reason behind your visits to Luisa, Miss Harper?" he asked.

"You asked me to bring fresh flowers to her room each day," she said truthfully. "Luisa wishes to speak better English. Administration approved the time I spend with her."

"I know these things," Jaus said. "Why do *you* wish to visit her?"

"Luisa is lonely," she heard herself say. "So am I. She is the only friend I've made since I came to Chicago."

He brought his hand up to her cheek. "Why did you suggest taking Luisa outside to see the gardens? Have you made arrangements to have her removed from the Lighthouse?"

"I've made no arrangements. I don't want to remove her. I want her to see my gardens." She smiled. "It's spring, and all the flowers are beginning to bloom. Luisa loves flowers."

He was silent for a long moment. "What is your first name, girl?"

"Liling."

The pad of his thumb made a gentle circle against her temple. "Forget the questions I have just asked you, Liling. If you are ever in need of help, you will come to me first."

"Forget." Liling nodded. "Need. Come to you."

Jaus took his hand away. "Here it is." He handed her a stray laurel leaf and opened the door. "Do you need a ride into the city, Miss Harper?"

"I don't . . ." A waft of air from the hall made her catch her breath. She felt foggy, as if she had somehow drifted off in the middle of their conversation. She had to stop fantasizing so much about this man. "No, sir, thank you. I, ah, drove my car to work."

He bowed to her. "I will say good night, then, Miss Harper."

Surprised, Liling returned the bow. "Good night, Mr. Jaus."

Chapter 2

Valentin Jaus drove his Jaguar up the long drive to the black-granite-and-gray-slate medieval manor he called Derabend Hall. A dozen guards in dark suits stood at their posts around the mansion, which was a replica of Schloss Jaus in the Austrian Alps.

During his human life in the fourteenth century, Jaus and his home would have been referred to as the master and his castle, his guards the garrison. Now the master of Derabend Hall was a major metropolitan entrepreneur, guarded at his lakeshore estate home by private security.

Names and locations changed; life remained the same. So it was for all of the immortals known as the Darkyn.

The men nodded in deference to their suzerain as he followed the path out to the gardens. There he found the old man sitting in the gazebo, his head bobbing as he dozed beside a bottle of bloodwine and an exquisite Baccarat crystal goblet.

Like all *tresori*, Gregor Sacher had been trained from birth to serve his immortal Darkyn lord. He had been Valentin's human servant for more than fifty years now, long past the age he should have retired. His grandson, Wilhelm, had been at his side since leaving high school, and was now more than ready to take up Gregor's post. But Gregor had so far refused to step down, always finding some excuse to avoid the comfortable retirement he had earned. Neither Wilhelmn nor Valentin had the heart to force the issue.

A slim, dark-haired boy whose features were a younger version of the elderly man's came out of the shadows and walked to the steps of the gazebo. "I tried to persuade him to come inside, my lord, but Grandfather insisted he was not tired."

"He is a proud man, Wil," Jaus said as he gazed at his most devoted servant and oldest human friend. "We must allow him his dignity." He came down the steps. "What news?"

Wil updated him on the day's events and various business projects concerning the *jardin*. "The district attorney's office called in regard to Miss Lindquist. They are accepting the plea agreement our attorneys offered. She will be incarcerated at an appropriate psychiatric facility for the term of her sentence."

Jaus felt satisfied. The confession he had compelled from Diane Lindquist had included the details of the emotional and sometimes physical abuse she had suffered at the hands of her brother. "What of the media?"

"Our contacts at the newspapers, periodicals, and broadcasting companies have been successful in suppressing the story," Wil said. "No more reporters will be sent to the facility. There has been a limited amount of exposure on the Web from independent sources, as usual, but our Internet contacts are now working to eradicate it."

The Internet caused more trouble than it was worth. "Did you see to the video of Miss Lindquist's confession?" He could not allow it to remain in human hands, as he appeared on the tape while compelling the human female to confess. To protect their identities and keep their immortality from being discovered, Darkyn never allowed themselves to be filmed or photographed.

Wil nodded. "The copy given to the police has been erased, and the original placed in our vault."

The old man stirred, murmuring in his sleep, "The vault. Must not . . . forget . . . secure . . . vault."

Jaus went up and woke him gently. "You are issuing orders in your sleep, old friend. Why are you not in bed?"

"I cannot rest when you go out alone, master." Sacher sat up, wincing a little as his arthritic joints protested the movement. "Wilhelm said that you went to the Lighthouse. Did you find Miss Lopez well?"

"I did." He glanced at Wil, who came to take Gregor's arm after Valentin helped the elderly *tresora* to his feet. "We will talk tomorrow. Rest now, *mein freund.*"

Jaus watched until his *tresora* and his grandson were safely inside, and then poured himself a goblet of blood-wine. He drained it quickly, refilling the glass and taking it with him down to the seawall.

Light from the full moon turned the lake water black and fathomless, and plated the pebbles onshore in pewter. He knew his guards would watch over him from their various vantage points, but they would not intrude on his privacy. Nor would Wil, no matter what matter of *jardin* business became pressing.

No one came near the suzerain of Chicago when he walked down by the water.

So many times Jaus had come here to think, to worry, or to brood. It had first become his habit after he had noticed his young neighbor, Jema Shaw, walking down by the lake at night. Jema, his first love, his only love. He closed his eyes, remembering her

A love doomed from the very beginning.

Jaus climbed over the short seawall and made his way toward the rocks. Despite all his caution and longings and endless inner debates, this was when he felt most ridiculous. He had come to this country to acquire power. A man in his position had thousands of responsibilities, and no time to indulge such useless pursuits. He also knew nothing would come of going to the rock and speaking to his lady. He never dared to do anything else.

Still, he went to her, as helpless as a storm-tossed ship driven to shoals.

"Good evening, Miss Shaw," he said as soon as she noticed him approaching.

"Mr. Jaus." She turned and smiled. "How have you been?"

"Very well, thank you."

Their conversations rarely varied from the polite, impersonal greetings exchanged by passing acquaintances. Before and after such meetings, Jaus often thought of many clever remarks he might have made, but whenever he spoke to Jema, none of them would come out of his mouth.

It would help if she gave him permission to use her given name, but she never had, and the rigid manners he had been taught as a boy prevented him from using it without her leave. Thus they had remained Mr. Jaus and Miss Shaw. It made Valentin want to dash his own head against the rocks. No, that was not precisely true. It made him want to scoop her into his arms and carry her back to his house. . . .

Jaus swore softly as he banished the memory of that night from his mind.

He could never have had her; he had known that. Aside

from the fact that Jema was human, an illness believed to be juvenile diabetes had been slowly stealing her life away year after year. Valentin had been well aware that her sickness had meant that they could never be together, and still he lost his heart to her. So he had watched her from afar, pining in silence, or walked down on the shore with a schoolboy's hopes of exchanging the occasional polite greeting with her.

Ironic that he had thought words were all that they would ever exchange.

Jema had not been stricken with diabetes, but by Valentin's own blood. A simple accident in his gardens during her infancy had caused the exposure, when he had removed a sliver of glass from her tiny hand, and had somehow cut himself in the process. Although they would never know for certain, Jema had probably ingested a few drops of his blood by sucking it from her thumb. It should have poisoned her, as Darkyn blood had been fatal to humans for the last five centuries. Somehow it hadn't. That in part may have been due to the Shaws' family doctor, a crazed man obsessed with Jema, who had used powerful drugs to keep her alive while trying to acquire the secrets of immortality.

The mad doctor was now dead, and Jema had completed the transition that had started in her infancy to finally become Kyn. But it was not Valentin's love or blood that had saved her. That honor belonged to Thierry Durand, the Kyn lord with whom Jema had fallen in love. Thierry, who had made Jema his *sygkenis*, his woman, his life companion.

Thierry, who had cut off Valentin's arm while dueling with him over Jema.

Each time Valentin came down to walk beside the lake, he thought of his loss. It was impossible to escape his memories of Jema, so he embraced them, as he would never embrace her. They were all that he had left, the last spark of feeling in his frozen heart. He had already accepted what had happened to him as his penance, for none of these things would have occurred if he had not tainted Jema as a baby with his own blood.

Luisa is lonely. . . . So am I.

The gardener's pitiful confession slipped into Valentin's thoughts so quietly that at first he thought the words his own. Absently he flexed his good hand. He had not fed on nor had any physical contact with human females since losing Jema. What blood he needed he took from males, or from the supplies the *jardin* kept stockpiled for their use.

That explained why the brief contact with the Asian girl had produced such unfamiliar sensations. Abstinence had made him forget how warm and alive mortal women felt to touch.

The gardener, the Asian girl, the human. He scowled. Why did he avoid naming Liling Harper, even in his remembrance of her? Her name might sound like some sort of exotic music on the tongue, but she was simply another of the humans who served his *jardin*.

The girl did not know it, of course. Only humans whose families had served the Kyn for generations were entrusted with the *vrykolakas*'s dangerous secrets. Only they knew that the Kyn were immortal, dependent on the blood of humans, and maintained secret communities and compounds in every part of the world.

Liling Harper remained ignorant of his nature and how much influence he had over her existence. She did not even realize that she owed her only friendship to him, in an indirect sense.

After installing Luisa Lopez at the Lighthouse, Valentin had asked that fresh flowers be brought to her room every day. As the facility gardener, Liling had been given the task. His security guards logged her visits, which grew longer each week, until the two were spending hours together.

Initially Liling's interest in Luisa had worried Valentin, who had ordered an investigation and background check. Through that he learned that the gardener was twenty-six, single, and lived alone in a one-room apartment near the Navy Pier. She had immigrated from Taiwan to the United States at the age of sixteen, and through a series of very fortunate sponsorships by prominent Chinese-American citizens had been naturalized.

Liling had no criminal record or outstanding debts, and lived simply and frugally. She had to; her annual salary roughly equaled what Valentin spent during one visit to his tailor.

"She's diligent and punctual," the chief administrator at the Lighthouse reported over the phone. "Never late, never calls in sick or asks to leave early. She keeps the grounds immaculate, of course, and the gardens have become a showcase. The nurses adore her."

Valentin learned that Liling was not only a favorite of the staff, but had become very popular among the most seriously ill patients at the facility.

"Some of them have said that her touch removes their pain," the administrator said, his voice growing wry. "Of course, sir, you have to realize that these are the same patients who regularly talk to Elvis and are convinced that aliens steal the chocolate pudding off their dinner trays."

Valentin suspected the patients were responding to the girl's interest and kindness. The sort of attention she gave them also had some bearing. How could you dislike someone who brought you flowers?

Doubtless Liling's stature and appearance likewise con-

tributed to the many favorable opinions of her. Barely five
feet tall and built as slender and delicate as one of her flowers, Liling Harper seemed as fragile and vulnerable as she
was exotic. Small women often brought out protective instincts in others, as their diminutive size made them seem
more childlike and helpless. Her skin, sun-kissed to a bur-
nished gold, enhanced the natural drama of her ebony eyes
and full, curved lips.

Liling kept herself as tidy and well-groomed as her gardens. Her thick black hair, always neatly confined in a pre-
cise French braid, hung down from the back of her head to
the very end of her spine. Two plain gold hoops adorned the
lobes of each small ear; a waterproof watch encircled one
wrist. She also wore a silver chain around her neck, but kept
it tucked inside the collar of her staff polo shirt. She used no
cosmetics, and kept the nails on her slim fingers short but
neatly manicured.

To Jaus she seemed almost painfully shy and reserved,
more interested in her own thoughts than in the world
around her. He had seen her drift off into a daydream more
than once. He wondered what she thought about during
those moments when her eyes took on that faraway look.
Probably her gardens.

Valentin acknowledged that she was the only human female who—despite a similar petite form—did not remind
him of Jema Shaw. Jema was American; Liling was not. The
gardener spoke excellent English, but her accent and hesi-
tancy with some words made it obvious that it was not her
cradle language. Jema had been wealthy even before she became Thierry Durand's *sygkenis*; Liling worked hard, possessed little, and lived a modest life. Thus, the fact that he
could not banish the image of her face from his thoughts was
meaningless. Jaus knew that if he took her and fed from her,

the temporary and highly annoying attraction would die. Just as it had with every other human female except Jema Shaw.

As he thought of how it would be to take Liling Harper's blood, his *dents acérées* emerged, full and sharp into his mouth, while his cock stiffened against his fly.

His cell phone chimed, and when he flipped it open the screen displayed a small brown bird perched on an arrow. Valentin tapped the answer key and held it to his ear. "What is it?"

"Good evening to you, too, Lord Jaus," Robin of Locksley, the suzerain of Atlanta, said with good-natured cheer. "I can call tomorrow, if I have interrupted something."

"No, forgive me." Valentin breathed in deeply, reaching for the iron control that had never failed him. "My mind was elsewhere. How may I be of service?"

"I have been trading with the Kyn who have recently come from France and Italy," Robin said, "and I acquired a blade that may be of interest to you."

Valentin felt the weight of his dead arm drag at his shoulder. He could not hold a sword anymore, much less use one. "I thank you, Rob, but I have enough blades."

"This one is a two-handed sword with a very unique hilt," Locksley continued as if Jaus had said nothing. "It is solid, handworked silver, with two rubies, four star sapphires, and eight black diamonds inset in the grip. I believe you can guess the letter they form."

"That cannot be my grandfather's sword," Valentin told him. "The Nazis looted the church where it was kept on display when they invaded Vienna."

"As it turns out, my friend, the night before the Nazis arrived, the blade was smuggled out of the country to France. It was hidden there, along with several other important pieces, for safekeeping," Robin said. "The *tresori* responsible never revealed the location to anyone and were later killed during the occupation. Kyn using the same tunnels to flee the Brethren only just discovered the cache last year."

Valentin had little left in the way of personal effects from his human life: a few daggers, his father's hauberk and spangenhelm, a tattered banner. His grandfather's sword, wielded in so many wars of state that his men had referred to it as the King Maker, had been his family's most prized possession.

"I can ship it to you next-day air, if you like," Robin said. "UPS does not pick up here at the compound until five thirty."

"No." The idea of humans handling his grandfather's sword made Valentin's gut knot. "With your permission, I will come to Atlanta to see it. If it is authentic, you have but to name your price, my lord."

"I already have your friendship, and Scarlet claims I have too many automobiles as it is. Let me think." Locksley made a *hmmmm* sound. "I have several men who wish to move up in rank, but Will is likely to outlive all of us. Would you consider one of them to serve as your seneschal?"

Valentin had not had a seneschal since the night he had dueled with Thierry. "That sounds more like the sort of trade Cyprien would propose."

Robin was silent for a moment. "There is no deceiving you, is there? You know Michael. He worries."

Michael Cyprien, the American seigneur who ruled over all the suzerain and their *jardin*, had been a friend of Valentin's for centuries. He had also spent much of his human life as Thierry Durand's ally and closest friend. The duel and its aftermath had created a rift between Michael and Jaus, one that they never acknowledged but that existed just the same.

Jaus had not cared, but Cyprien had never been a man to leave well enough alone.

"Do your men know that I executed my last seneschal for betrayal?" Valentin asked.

"They do. I believe if you accept an oath from one of them, he will do everything in his power to avoid a similar fate." Robin's tone changed, grew more persuasive. "I would give you the sword for nothing, Val. But I think Michael is right about this. It is time for you to . . . move on."

Valentin had no desire to replace Falco or change the status of his household. Nor did he wish to be micromanaged by the seigneur. But he could not walk away from the chance to regain possession of his grandfather's sword, and his pride would not allow Locksley to make a gift of it. "I will agree to consider them, but that is all."

"Excellent. I await your arrival."

Jaus ended the call and checked his watch. Five more hours until dawn. He needed something to do, something to fill up the time. Something to keep him from thinking about Jema.

He walked up to the gardens, where Wilhelm was waiting for him. "Bring me the file on Liling Harper."

The boy stood. "At once, master."

After making a small dinner salad for herself, Liling wandered restlessly around her apartment. The thought of watching television or reading didn't tempt her, and it was too dark to work in the tiny garden she had planted in the back of her building, so she pocketed her keys and went out into the night.

It was a short walk from her apartment to the Navy Pier,

one of the main reasons she had rented the place. She liked seeing the lights of the enormous Ferris wheel from her windows; she had probably ridden it herself a thousand times now. Walking among the tourists and suburbans who came to enjoy the pier's attractions made her feel less lonely.

There were places at the pier where she could be alone, too. She walked past the family pavilion and the Navy Pier Park, pausing for a moment to watch the laughing, shrieking children riding the Ferris wheel before she continued down the walkway. She liked this side of the pier, where the long line of boats waited to ferry visitors out onto the lake; if she didn't get seasick the minute she stepped foot on a boat she'd take a cruise every night.

She intended to stop at the Häagen-Dazs Café for ice cream, but an odd sensation on the back of her neck made her keep walking. She glanced around several times, but no one strolling along the pier paid any attention to her.

At Festival Hall, she walked into the lower-level terrace and entered the Smith Museum, her favorite place on the pier.

The long, quiet galleries of the museum housed 150 stained-glass windows, with access provided at no cost for public viewing. The first stained-glass window museum in the United States, Smith showcased some of the most spectacular secular and religious windows in the country.

Liling loved the hushed atmosphere of the museum as much as the glowing, magnificent displays. It seemed more like a cathedral of light and art than a tourist attraction; to walk through the galleries and see the jewel-bright colors fed some nameless hunger inside her. Her childhood had been so dull and gray; here she could commune with the genius of John La Farge and Louis Comfort Tiffany, and see the world through their eyes.

As magnificent as Smith's collection of important glass-
works were, Liling's favorite piece was *Seated Woman in a
Garden*, a stair-landing window created by an unknown
artist at the turn of the twentieth century. She always went to
that one first, to stand in the gentle white, copper, and
turquoise glow and study the woman in the glass.

The artist had used hundreds of tiny pieces of glass in vibrant colors, so that sunlight shining through would cast
beautiful light on the landing of a staircase. But it was the
figure of the woman, not the unusual colors, that drew
Liling. With her white gown slipping from one shoulder, and
her fiery red hair echoed by the delicate, intricate glass flowers growing all around her, the woman in the window sat
alone, but seemed serene and happy.

"She looks as if she is waiting for her lover."

Liling turned, amazed to see Valentin Jaus standing just
behind her. "Mr. Jaus. What are you doing here?"

"I am stalking you."

Her chin dropped. "Pardon me?"

"I make a poor joke. Luisa told me that you often come
to the pier at night," he said. "I have never visited it, and I
had some spare time tonight, so thought I might do the same.
When I arrived, I saw you walking ahead of me and followed you here."

No wonder she'd felt that odd sensation of someone
watching her. She'd never have guessed in a million years
that it would have been Luisa's wealthy friend, however.

"It's so strange to see you outside the hospital." She
couldn't believe she'd blurted that out. "Not that there is
anything strange about your coming here. You can go anywhere, of course. It's just, uh, very unexpected."

"I was equally disconcerted to see you," he admitted. "I
did not wish to appear untoward by approaching you, but I

felt curious about this museum, and it seemed the polite thing to do." He watched her face carefully. "Perhaps I was wrong."

"Oh, no. I'm glad you came here. This is a beautiful museum. I come to see the windows here at least once a week." Which officially made her the dullest person in Chicago. "I hope you enjoy the displays, Mr. Jaus."

"As you are far more knowledgeable about this place, would you tell me which gallery houses the Tiffany collection?" he asked. "I find his work especially riveting."

"It's right through here." Liling led him to the gallery, where the displays had been placed strategically in deep wells of shadows and startling theatrical pools of light.

The Tiffany windows were magnificent examples of stained-glass art in its most evolved form. Liling told Jaus about the different types of glass the artist had used to create his windows, and the often daring techniques he had developed to bring a sense of movement and life to each piece.

"How do you know so much about this man?" Jaus asked.

"I bought a book about Tiffany at the gift shop," she said, glad for a reason to think about something other than his shoulders, and how his suit fit them. "It has all the facts about the windows, and some pretty interesting trivia about the artist, too. For example, Tiffany specialized in designing religious and memorial windows, but he preferred depicting flowers and landscapes rather than people and icons. He felt nature was much more divine than man. He also used the symbolism of flowers in much of his work. The poppies and passionflowers in this piece represent the Resurrection and the Crucifixion of Christ."

"Whatever his intentions, he created glorious art." The artificial light shining through the window cast Jaus's face in red and gold. "Although I would guess that you prefer the window of the woman in the garden."

"There is something about her that is so mysterious," she admitted. "As if the artist knew that she had a secret. Sometimes I think that if I keep looking at the window, I'll discover what it is."

He didn't smile, but he seemed amused. "You must tell me if you do."

He never asked; he commanded, Liling thought. Like a general . . . Oh, she was not thinking about that while he stood right next to her. "This next window is very pretty, too."

As they walked slowly through the thirteen displays, Jaus mentioned the particular reverence Chicagoans had for stained glass.

"I imagine it all began shortly after the Great Fire, while the city was rebuilding," he told Liling. "Immigrants drawn here by industry and the opportunity for work began decorating their churches, businesses, schools, and homes with the stained glass they once had known in Europe. Many of our old buildings have been carefully preserved, which is why Chicago itself is like one enormous glasswork museum."

"I can believe it," she told him. "In my book, it says they even put stained-glass windows in some of the old railroad cars." She gave him a curious look. "You seem to know a lot about the history of the city. Have you studied it?"

He nodded. "I know it as well as if I had lived through it."

A security guard stepped into the gallery. "Folks, the museum is closing now."

Liling felt startled. Had she actually been talking to the poor man for an hour? He must be bored out of his mind. "Well, it was very nice running into you, Mr. Jaus."

He followed her out of the museum, but as she turned to go he caught her arm. "It is late. Permit me to escort you home, Miss Harper."

Not a question, but another command.

"There's no need," she said, feeling embarrassed again at the thrill she felt in response. "I live only a couple of blocks away."

A large family leaving the pier passed by, obliging her to move closer to Jaus to make room for them. The scent of camellias came over her, making her feel warm and a little sleepy.

She didn't want to go home anymore. "Do you have to go now?"

"I can spend more time with you," he said, "if that is what you wish."

Her head bobbed up and down as she caught the edge of his lapel between her thumb and forefinger and leaned in to breathe his scent. "You always smell like your flowers. Why is that?"

"I spend a great deal of time in my gardens." His voice had changed, some of his words slurring, and his crystal eyes shifted down to look at her throat.

"Then why are you so unhappy?" she heard herself ask.

He drew back. "I don't know what you mean."

"You can't be unhappy in a garden." Her head began to clear, and she pulled her hand back, appalled at the way she had touched him and spoken to him. "I shouldn't have said that. It's none of my business."

"Perhaps that is the secret of the woman in the window," he said, putting more space between them. "I will not detain you any longer, Miss Harper. Until we meet again."

"Good-bye, Mr. Jaus." She turned and hurried away.

*   *   *

Chicago City News photographer Boyce Kinney picked up his latest batch of proofs from production on his way to the morning editorial meeting. He'd tried to get a shot of Daniel Lindquist in his room at the Lighthouse, but security had grabbed him before he could set foot on the ward.

His editor was philosophical about the missed opportunity. "No one is running anything about Lindquist or his sister trying to kill him; it's dead in the water. Yesterday it seems our fine, upstanding state senator Ryan Litton was arrested downtown for soliciting an underage prostitute."

"Oh, yeah?" Kinney perked up. "How old was she?"

"*He's* fifteen," the editor said, grinning. "I want you down at the courthouse; Litton will be arraigned at noon. They've shut out the media from the courtroom, so get me all the close-ups you can outside. Anything showing him in cuffs or being handled by the cops."

"Hang on." Serena, the Lifestyles editor, plucked one of Kinney's photos off the table. "Who's this?"

Kinney glanced at the photo he had taken of the Asian girl in the gardens outside the Lighthouse. He'd snapped it only to check his lens adjustment. "Nobody."

"What's this mark on the back of her shoulder?" Serena used a magnifier to inspect the spot, and then answered herself. "Looks like a tattoo of a bird of some kind."

"Everybody's got a tattoo these days." Kinney stretched and yawned. "Who cares?"

"I'm running a front-page piece on the next generation of nursing homes," Serena told him. "These are great colors, and the gardens are amazing. I could mention Lindquist, since he's a patient there, maybe work in a paragraph or two about the sister."

The senior editor shook his head. "The powers that be

aren't interested in raking Lindquist over the coals. They were very specific."

"Old golfing buddies never die." Kinney made a jerking motion with his closed fist. "They just keep their circle of friends happy."

"So I don't utter a peep about Lindquist; got it." Serena studied the image again. "I still need a color shot for this piece. Her back is to the camera, so we don't need a sign-off. Mind if I use it, Boyce?"

Lifestyles ran only feel-good stories that rarely did anything but take up space, so there was nothing in it for Kinney. "It's okay with me."

A day later his editor clapped him on the shoulder. "You're not going to believe this. AP picked up that garden shot of yours. We've had reprint requests from a dozen agencies overseas, too."

His first big break, Kinney thought, and it had to be a throwaway shot he'd taken only to check his camera settings. "Too bad I didn't get the girl's face. She'd be famous."

Chapter 3

The twenty-first century had not been kind to the Catholic Church. Numbers were down and scandals were up; a worldwide shortage of ordained priests had grown from severe to desperate. Atheists and prochoice groups hounded the Church, pouncing on any opportunity to smear its good name.

Even in countries where Catholicism had controlled the population more stringently than the petty dictatorships that rose and fell from power with monotonous regularity, the newer generations had lost touch with the faith. Young Catholics went through the motions only on holy days, primarily to please cantankerous, elderly relatives.

No one feared the wrath of God anymore. Allah and the crazed jihads formed in his name had become the big bogeymen of this century.

In Chicago, cost-cutting measures taken by the archdiocese had required nearly half of the city's churches to curtail their expenses. Some were even shut down, their parishioners sent to attend Mass elsewhere. The archbishop of Chicago had suffered the indignity of being packed up and transferred to St. Luke's, one of the humblest parishes in the city.

It was a punishment handed down from Rome, from a cardinal who had as little to do with the Catholic Church as August Hightower did.

"I found the paper, Your Grace," Mrs. Clare Murphy said as she brought in his afternoon tea tray, the latest edition of the *Chicago City News* tucked under her plump arm. "Why that Shaughnessy boy has to throw it in the hedges every morning, I'll never know." She set down the tray and removed the newspaper from the plastic bag. "Looks as if that Senator Litton's got hisself all over the front page again."

"The sins of the flesh are not merely visited upon the meek, Mrs. Murphy." August suppressed a smile as he took the paper and unfolded it. The media was having its usual field day with the sex scandal. "We will pray for him."

"I'm praying for his wife," the older woman said, her careworn face wrinkling with distaste. "God help her, but who knows what sort of diseases he's inflicted on the poor thing."

Senator Litton hadn't slept with his wife since impregnating her with their only son twenty-five years ago. Hightower didn't bother to pass that bit of intimate information along to his housekeeper. Nor did he need to read the articles printed under the headlines to know that the boy prostitute the senator had been fellating just before his arrest had been transferred from police custody to a halfway house for runaways run by the archdiocese. He had, after all, personally arranged the transfer.

Now that the annoyingly liberal atheist senator had been permanently labeled a political leper, and would be forced to resign his seat before the end of the month, the order could move forward with plans for his replacement. Three strident, impeccable conservative candidates who actually did have sex regularly with their equally dull and unattractive spouses were presently under consideration. Once backed by other prominent political figures under the control of the order, the worthiest and greediest of the trio would doubtless move gracefully into the U.S. Senate.

All as it should be.

Hightower happily munched his way through three cream puffs and a napoleon by the time he finished the news section, and had just began delicately devouring a fruit tart when he took out the Lifestyles section. Seeing the photo on the front page, that of a girl working in a beautiful garden, made him smile. Until he saw the tattoo on her shoulder and began to choke. Bits of kiwi and strawberry spattered his desk blotter and the paper until he cleared his throat and was able to take a breath and a closer look.

The image showed only the young woman kneeling with her back to the camera. A jacket had been tied around her waist, and the sleeveless shirt she wore had a T-back, which showed off her smooth shoulders. She could have been anyone, Hightower thought, and then took the magnifying glass from his desk drawer and held it above the image.

The photo was grainy, but not enough to blur the tattoo of a red swan.

"It can't be."

August sat paralyzed until Cabreri came into his office without knocking, a copy of the Lifestyles section crumpled in his fist.

"Your Grace, have you seen . . ." He looked at the paper Hightower held. "Then you know."

"That the red swan still lives? No, Carlo, I did not know. No one knew." Hightower flung the paper aside and jerked the napkin out of his collar. "Certainly not Rome."

As members of *Les Frères de la Lumière*, both Hightower and his assistant were obliged to pose as members of the Catholic Church. In the Dark Ages, their secret order had been created and charged with protecting the Church and humanity from a group of cursed priests turned into demonic vampires who called themselves the Darkyn. Their work required them to play certain roles within the Church's infrastructure in order to carry out their mission.

Now this girl, a girl everyone had sworn had died during a catastrophe that she herself had caused, could expose one of their most closely guarded secrets.

"I read the reports ten years ago," Cabreri said. "They indicated that she was killed during the storm with the other children. They would not have done so unless they had seen her body."

"Of course they said she was dead," Hightower snapped. "They were covering up their own incompetence in handling that disaster. They would not dare tell Rome that the red swan had escaped into the general population."

"But they must have known . . . an elemental . . ." Cabreri looked ill. "Your Grace, the risk to the innocent is too great. We must inform Rome immediately."

Hightower braced his hands against his desk and rose, his heavy body trembling with the effort. His assistant's loyalty to the order, something August had used over the years to control him, would prove the greatest impediment. "D'Orio has been looking for any excuse to remove us from our positions. We will take care of the girl first, and then we will decide how much Rome is to know about the business." He snatched up the paper and read the caption. "This photograph was taken at a nursing home outside the city. You will go there immediately and begin surveillance."

"Assuming she has not already run." Cabreri's Adam's apple bobbed. "I cannot take her alone."

"You are not to touch her. Only locate and follow her." He glared at his assistant. "You will report to me on the hour."

Hightower's phone rang, and Cabreri flinched. The light on it indicated it was his private line, the number only members of the order knew.

The archbishop picked up the receiver slowly. "This is Hightower."

"Have you read the paper today, August?" Cardinal D'Orio's voice grated over the line.

He sank back down into his chair. "I have, Your Eminence. In fact, I was just preparing to call you—"

"Thou shalt not bear false witness. You do remember that from your days in the seminary, don't you?" The cardinal inhaled sharply. "Tell me how it is that the red swan, whom our California brothers reported burying ten years ago with several hundred of our best researchers, is still alive and working in your city."

"All I can think, Your Eminence, is that those who were in charge of cleaning up the disaster falsified their reports to Cardinal Stoss," Hightower said, sinking back down into his chair. "The girl survived, obviously. Since we were not aware that she had, she has been able to live off the grid, so to speak."

"Obviously. So to speak. You sound like Miss Carolina, you idiot," the cardinal said pleasantly. "Do you have her current location?"

"We know where she was working at the time the photo was taken, Your Eminence, but there is no guarantee she is still there. This level of exposure would likely cause her to flee. Then there is the more immediate problem of the danger she presents." He eyed Cabreri. "I wonder if I might request one of your trackers to help us with the situation."

"That is the other problem I am dealing with today, August," D'Orio said. "Kyan has left China. He gave no explanation to his cell chief and has avoided using the usual travel routes. He also removed his tracer and withdrew ten thousand dollars from our banks in New York last night. I wager he'll be in Chicago by this evening."

Hightower schooled his expression. "May we be of assistance in this matter?"

"Even you aren't that stupid, August," D'Orio said. "Get to the girl before Kyan does, capture her alive, and transport her to Rome directly."

A thousand possibilities rushed through his mind. "Is that wise, Your Eminence? Given the girl's, ah, nature, I think it would be more prudent to terminate her."

"I don't care what you think," the cardinal said. "You'll do exactly as you're told. Because if you fail me this time, I'll transfer you to a church so far into the Congo that the only tongues you'll be pressing communion wafers on will belong to mountain gorillas."

After he ended the call, Hightower consulted with Cabreri.

"The cardinal wants her alive and brought to Rome, so we must move quickly," he said. "Call our people at the bus and train stations, as well as the airport."

"You believe she will try to leave the city?" Before Hightower answered, Cabreri added, "Your Grace, perhaps it is best that we do not pursue her at this time. We could instead intercept Kyan and prevent him from finding her."

Cabreri often had moments of brilliance, even when he was as wrongheaded as he was now.

"I will do whatever is necessary to protect the city," he told his assistant. "Go now."

Hightower waited until his assistant departed before he placed two more calls.

Michael Cyprien found the woman he loved busy at work in her lab. "Are you making something for me, *chérie*?"

Dr. Alexandra Keller adjusted the flame on the Bunsen burner and eyed the bubbling, dark contents of the beaker she had placed over it. "If you're in the mood for a hot vampire-blood toddy, I am."

Michael took a moment to appreciate the sight of his *sygkenis*. She had gathered her long, thick chestnut hair into a loose ponytail, from which a few corkscrew curls had escaped. A stained white lab coat covered the dark green silk dress she wore, and the emerald-and-diamond earrings he had given her the night before sparkled in her ears.

"I think I will pass." Michael inspected the impressive array of laboratory equipment she had assembled and was working over. "This looks very complicated."

She drew a sample from the boiling beaker with an eye-dropper and placed a drop on a glass slide, and then added a drop of clear liquid to it. "It is."

In her human life, Alexandra Keller had been a reconstructive surgeon devoted to restoring the ruined faces of accident victims and abused children. Along with the talent of an Old World sculptor and the determination of a zealot, Alexandra had the gift of speed—no other doctor in the world had been as fast as she with a scalpel.

Michael had inadvertently taken much of that away from her when he had brought her against her will to New Orleans to restore his face, which had been obliterated during his imprisonment and brutal torture by the Brethren. After some resistance, Alex had operated on him. Michael had never intended to infect her with his blood, which should have poisoned her. Instead, Alexandra had become the first human in five hundred years to survive the change to Darkyn.

Outraged by both the deliberate and inadvertent interference in her life, Alex had despised him, eluded him, and fought him with all the righteous fury of an innocent wronged. Then, to make matters much worse, she and Michael had fallen in love with each other.

Cyprien had lived many centuries as a Darkyn lord, and had resigned himself to never finding a life companion. Now that he had this brilliant, beautiful, driven woman as his *sygkenis*, he wondered how he had survived for so long without her.

Michael came up behind her and slid his arms around her waist. Bending close to her ear, he murmured, "Are you in the mood for a hot vampire?"

"As you've told me a zillion times, we're not vampires; we're *vrykolakas*." Alex covered the slide with a small clear square and placed it under her scope. She peered at it and adjusted the magnification. "I'll be damned, if I'm not already."

"I am sure there are sins you have never imagined, *mon coeur*." He brushed her hair away from the side of her neck to place a kiss there. Smelling her aroused him, but touching her made him go hard. He removed her lab coat and glanced down to see the stiff points of her nipples denting the emerald silk. One of the many advantages of having a *sygkenis* were the delights of their physical bond, which had enslaved both of them. "I could help you commit them."

She shimmied her hips against him, but in an absent fashion, and made a vague, affirmative sound.

Michael frowned. "What is this that is more interesting to you than me and sin?"

Alex stepped back and gestured toward the scope. "Have a look and tell me what you see."

He gave the instrument a wary glance. "I will not know what it is."

She folded her arms. "Guess."

With a sigh Michael peered into the instrument. "I see tiny black spots floating in red-spotted liquid. None of them are . . ." He lifted his head, frowned, and looked again. "They are not floating. They are swimming, and . . . sucking up the red spots. And now they are dark red, and splitting in two. No, four." He turned to her. "What did you put in here?"

"A sample of your blood, after I heated it to five hundred degrees Fahrenheit." She grinned at his reaction. "Now you're wondering why."

"Among other things," he agreed.

"The pathogen infecting your blood cells—they would be the black things that turned dark red, ate the lighter red spots, and started replicating—is not destroyed under conditions of extreme heat. It actually becomes dormant." She reached over and turned off the burner. "When the heat is removed and the pathogen is immersed in human blood"—she poured a small amount of fresh blood into the beaker—"it wakes up, regenerates, eats, releases that really nice euphoriant we all love into the bloodstream, et cetera."

Michael looked into the eyepiece again and watched the blackened liquid turning slowly red. "But fire kills us."

"Not necessarily." She picked up a chart and opened it. "I got curious about the effect of heat after I talked to some of the new guys at the Realm about a *jardin* in southern France that the Brethren torched last summer."

"You talked to them?" While he and Alexandra had attended the annual tournament held in central Florida at the Realm, a medieval-themed tourist attraction run by the Kyn, he had not noticed her conversing with the refugees. "When? Why?"

"It was while you were busy being the seigneur, and I didn't feel like chatting with Lady Harris about her dumb dog. Don't be jealous." She patted his arm. "Anyway, according to the survivors, whom you very kindly allowed to immigrate to America, some of them came out with extensive third-degree burns. After finding a few willing human blood donors"—she gave him an ironic look—"they all healed."

"I know about the incident," he said. "Burns are not enough. To kill us, our bodies must be completely charred. Then they crumble to ash."

"Sorry, sweetheart, but even in crematoriums, bodies don't crumble to ash. There are always bits of—" Alex's desk phone rang, interrupting her, and she reached around him to push the speaker button. Before anyone spoke, she said, "Yes, Phillipe, I know, I've been playing in the lab too long again. The boss is here, trying to lure me away from my boiling beakers of blood."

"Alexandra?" The voice did not belong to Michael's seneschal, Phillipe.

"John." She went over and snatched up the receiver, cutting off the speaker. "Mind telling me where you've been for the last three weeks, big brother? I've been worried sick." She listened for a moment. "As in Monterey, California? What are you doing there?"

Michael, who suspected John was calling to report what he had found, reached over and pressed the speaker button so he could hear the other half of the conversation. Alex was so agitated she didn't notice.

". . . from the brothers I helped relocate," Alexandra's brother was saying. "They gave me only very general directions, so it took more time than I thought. But I found it. I need to speak to Cyprien, Alex. It's important."

"John, I'm here," Michael said before his *sygkenis* began ranting at her brother again. "What did you find?"

"Everything exactly as they said," John told him. "It's under an abandoned Catholic mission in the hills. They didn't remove anything. They only sealed the entrances and exits."

"They intend to use it again someday." When Alexandra opened her mouth, Cyprien shook his head. "How many were they keeping down there?"

"I don't know." John sounded frustrated now. "They have security guards patrolling the property around the clock; one of them almost caught me last night. I can't do this by myself."

"We will come to you." Cyprien checked the caller ID display. "Will you be at this number in an hour?"

"I can be."

"I will call you back with our travel arrangements." Cyprien disconnected the call and saw Alexandra's eyes narrow. "I can explain."

"I'm sure you can," she said smoothly. "Start with why my brother, who hates your guts for turning me into a vampire, is talking to you like you're pals."

"You are not a vampire, and John does not hate me," Cyprien corrected her. "In fact, he came to me with information he had received from the former Brethren he helped escape the order while we were in Fort Lauderdale."

"Came to *you*." She sounded skeptical. "Did he have a little help, *l'attrait*-wise?"

L'attrait, the pheromone-like scent the Darkyn's bodies naturally produced, had a powerful effect on most humans exposed to it. By using it the Kyn were able to hypnotize and compel humans to do almost anything they wished.

"I did not force him to do this, *chérie*," Cyprien assured her. "He came to me of his own free will."

"If I find out differently, I'm kicking your ass," she said. "So what did they tell him?"

"The friars involved related how the Brethren acquire new members for the order, and directed him to one of their secret facilities," Cyprien said. "I told him if he could locate it, I would help him expose what they have been doing."

"So, just like that, John goes scampering off to California to look for some religious nutcase training center?" She threw up her hands. "John's already been imprisoned and tortured by the Brethren once. Wasn't that enough? And now he's out there alone, playing private fucking eye? My brother doesn't know how to do this stuff. He was a priest, for God's sake. Why didn't you send anyone with him?"

"He asked if he could go alone, and I said yes." Cyprien could see she didn't like hearing that. "This is very important to John. You know that he is not yet comfortable with accepting our help. He also knew you would be concerned about his safety if you knew he was pursuing this alone. I agreed."

"I love how you guys just *decide* these things for me. What am I, twelve?" She saw his hand move and stepped out of reach. "Don't even think about it."

"I only thought to spare you the worry," he told her. "You have been through enough."

"I'm not made out of glass," she snapped. "And I don't

care where the Brethren train their new morons. John is all the family I have left, and even though most of the time *I'd* like to kill him, he needs the protection. Not me."

Cyprien took her hands in his. "These facilities are not being used for training new Brethren. They are for breeding them."

"Training, breeding, who cares what they . . ." She stopped and stared at him. "Wait a minute. You mean *breeding* as in the livestock sense of the word?"

Cyprien nodded. "We've known for some time that the young women they recruit have children with members of the order. These children are kept secluded and not permitted contact with the outside world until they have been trained accordingly. Male children, of course, become Brethren. There are only male Brethren, so we believe that any female children are used to produce the next generation."

She processed this. "That's disgusting."

"That is how a successful cult keeps its numbers healthy and controls the absolute loyalty of its membership." Cyprien wondered if he should tell her everything he and her brother had discussed. "Your brother told me that some of the young women used by the Brethren in these breeding facilities may not have been born into the order. The priests he helped spoke of runaways and addicts brought in from the streets and made into willing participants."

Alex swore viciously and at length. When she calmed enough to speak coherently again, she demanded, "What happened to the unwilling ones?"

"Those who caused trouble or resisted were killed." He took her hands in his. "That is why I promised your brother I would help. We have contacts in the media, Alexandra. Once we have proof, we can expose what they are doing."

Alex nodded slowly, but her eyes never left his. "You're not telling me everything. Your eyes always turn that pretty turquoise color when you're withholding information. What else?"

Michael knew how much she loved her brother, and had no desire to invoke her wrath by pointing out the obvious: Ever since he'd been tortured by the Brethren, and then learned that his sister had become Kyn, John's emotional state had been deteriorating. "Your brother is torn between his beliefs and his knowledge, and he cannot reconcile them. He is deeply troubled."

Her mouth twisted. "That's the story of his life."

"You know how sensitive we are to humans. Some of us can tell a human's emotional state by shifts in their natural scent. Since he came back from Ireland, John's has changed." Cyprien looked into her eyes. "I fear he is becoming unstable, Alex."

"I'll pack the Armani suits and the bagged blood." She headed for the door. "You have Phillipe warm up the Learjet."

Chapter 4

Liling was used to people smiling at her, but it did seem odd that the entire staff of the Lighthouse seemed pleased to see her that afternoon. Several nodded and congratulated her, and one young nurse gave her a heartfelt hug.

"It's *so* wonderful," the nurse gushed. "You must be over the moon." Before Liling could ask what was wonderful, she hurried off to answer a patient's call button.

Confused, Liling retreated to the gardens, where she weeded the primroses and bluebell beds, and replaced the fading snowdrops with a number of bleeding heart plants she had picked up at the garden center.

Next year, she decided, she would plant some clusters of purple iris around the moss-covered rocks she had arranged in between the flower beds. The irises looked bold and beautiful against the feathery green moss, and as they matured she could pot them for some of the patients' rooms.

Then Liling remembered she wouldn't be working here next year, and sighed. One year in one place, and then she had to move on; that was the rule she had lived by since leaving San Francisco. Still, it would be difficult to leave this job.

Especially when it meant never again seeing Luisa and her fascinating friend.

Valentin Jaus. Now his name seemed to make her heart beat a little faster.

Liling knew she was being ridiculous, fantasizing about a man like Jaus, who until last night had barely noticed her existence. That was what had made him safe: Like a movie star or a famous musician, he was beyond her, completely and utterly unattainable. And what a woman couldn't have, she could daydream about.

Only, the daydreams had taken an unexpected turn, and now Liling was actually dreaming about Jaus. After meeting him at the Navy Pier, she'd gone to sleep last night and found him waiting for her in one of her fantasy tableaux. She'd found herself in a medieval castle, chained naked to the foot of the lord's bed, where she huddled until he came into the room.

She took in a quick breath, remembering what had happened next.

"Stand up, girl."

She cowered at the sound of his voice, and then cried out as he dragged her to her feet.

"You're a lovely wench." *He walked around her, pushing his cloak from his shoulders. It fell in a heap of indigo-dyed wool to the floor. "Why have you not served me before tonight?"*

"I w-w-work in the g-g-garden, m-my lord."

"Not anymore." *He stopped and leaned so close that the tips of her breasts brushed the cold surface of his iron hauberk. "What are you called?" He ran his hard, calloused hand over her buttocks, the leather of his glove rasping over her delicate flesh, and then slapped her sharply. "Give me your name, girl."*

She couldn't open her mouth or make her tongue move.

Jaus sat down on the bed and used the chain hooked to her slave collar to tug her over to him. "Bend yourself over my thighs."

She shook her head, too frightened to move, and he used the chain again to pull her across his lap. His thigh muscles felt like stone against her belly, and she hung there, her long hair spilling over her face.

His hand slapped her bottom hard enough to sting. "I am your lord," he said. "You will answer me when I speak to you." He swatted her bottom again, but not quite as hard as before. "What is your name?"

"L-L-Lili."

He brought his hand down a third time, softer still, and let it rest against the plump lips of her little mound. "What is this?"

The touch of leather made her body slicken and open.

"If you are afraid of me, why are you making my glove damp?" he asked, rubbing his leather-covered palm against her with slow, deliberate pressure.

"I don't kn-know."

He slapped her again, but it was hardly more than a tap before he slid the glove between her legs. "Very damp." He pulled his hand away and removed the glove, tossing it to the floor.

She saw the faint spot on the palm and closed her eyes. "Forgive me."

"'Master.'" His hand caressed her bottom before he slapped her once more. "'Forgive me, master.'"

The feel of his bare hand on her skin made her moan the words he wanted to hear, and then she stiffened as his fingers went where his glove had been.

"You are wet for me."

She shook her head, crying out as he spanked her again, and then his fingers probed, pushing into her. "Please, master."

"You please me." He lifted her and turned her, holding her on his lap as he slowly fondled her breasts. "Pretty." His head bent and he suckled one nipple, pulling on it until she arched against him and his hand moved down her belly. . . .

It still disturbed her how real the dream had seemed. So real that she had woken up as aroused and needy as if Jaus had been in bed with her, making love to her while she slept. She'd put her hand down between her legs, shocked to feel the wetness, and had further stunned herself by climaxing against her own fingers.

You can't have sex with a fantasy.

Liling didn't practice promiscuity, and she could never risk staying in a relationship longer than a few weeks, but she was practical about her own needs. Jaus was completely out of her league, and the sole reason she had dreamed about him was because he was the only man besides the people she worked with whom she saw on a regular basis.

That was it. She hadn't dated anyone since coming to Chicago; what she needed to do was to find a nice, normal man to bring to bed. Someone who didn't want love forever, but would be amenable to fun for right now.

Finding a boyfriend wouldn't be that difficult; there were always plenty of available men in the city. She never dated people she worked with, but Martha or Nancy might know a single man who wouldn't expect a blind date to look like Scarlett Johansson or act like a nymphomaniac who had just been rescued from a deserted island.

She never imagined any man would ever fulfill her private fantasies. Sharing that level of intimacy with someone she intended to see only for a month or two seemed unlikely.

Even if she tried, men were so politically correct these days that none would know how to play a bedroom game like master and slave girl.

Except Valentin Jaus. He had exquisite manners, and he was the kindest man she'd met in Chicago. There wasn't a single complaint she could make about his demeanor or how he spoke to women. But he would not bother with being politically correct in his bedroom, she sensed, or anywhere else. Jaus would take what he wanted.

Liling felt herself go wet between her legs, and she stood up, stripping off her weeding gloves as she silently cursed her wandering thoughts. She had to stop thinking about Jaus like this, or she'd never be able to look at the man again without cringing.

Martha was actually waiting for her in the staff lounge when she took her dinner break. "There you are, you rock star, you. I brought a copy for you to autograph for me."

"Rock star?" Liling echoed, bewildered.

"You know," Martha said, nudging her shoulder playfully. When Liling shook her head, her smile became a gape. "Oh, my God. You don't know, do you? Nancy said you never breathed a word about it, but we all know how quiet you are."

"Martha," Liling said, "please tell me what 'it' is."

The nurse took a folded newspaper from her tote bag and spread it out on the table. "See? That's you, right there. They wrote a lovely piece about the facility, and how much you've improved the gardens. Well, they don't name you specifically, but we all know whose hard work it is."

Liling stared at the photo. It showed her from the back as she trimmed the yew hedges surrounding the foxglove beds. The dramatic pale pink, rose, and purple spires of flowers all around her made the image particularly striking. So did the fact that she had taken off her jacket, exposing her shoulders. It had been so warm that day that she had taken off her staff polo and worked in the cooler, more comfortable T-back shirt she wore instead of a bra.

The shirt that plainly showed the red swan tattoo on her shoulder.

She picked up the paper with a trembling hand. "Who did this?"

"It says, 'Photo by B. Kinney.' He's one of those photographers who were nosing around here after Mr. Lindquist the other day, I guess. But it's such a lovely shot that I thought for sure you had posed for it." Martha touched her hand. "Lili, honey, you're shaking like a leaf."

"I'm surprised." *No, I'm dead.* She licked her dry lips. "Is this today's paper?"

"The morning edition. Lili, it doesn't show your face. If you're worried about being deported . . ." Martha grimaced. "I'm sorry, I know it's none of my business, and with all the hatred being directed at you people these days it must seem terrifying. But, honey, I'm sure administration will help you get a green card or whatever you need to stay in the country."

Martha thought she was an illegal immigrant. If it hadn't been so tragic, Liling might have laughed.

"I am an American citizen, Martha." She straightened her shoulders. She *was* an American, even if her birth records and papers had been falsified to make her appear Chinese-born. She had rights that were protected by their laws. If they tried to take her or hurt her again, she could go to the authorities. And then they would want to know why she was being hunted, and she would have to tell them. The government would protect her. They would. . . .

This way, General.

Once, at the facility, the priests had brought a man in a military uniform to watch her during testing. He had said nothing, but his eyes had never left her. After the tests were over she was led from the room. That was when she heard the general talking to one of the doctors.

If she fails to reach her potential, the general said, *we will take her for one of our test groups.*

Liling hadn't reached her potential; nor had she known the full extent of what she could do until after she had escaped the priests, for which she was grateful. If they had had any idea, they would have killed her, or worse, locked her away so that she never saw the sun again.

In the beginning she had thought about going to a hospital, a real one, and asking for help. But her mentor had assured her that the doctors would never let someone with her ability roam around freely.

They see what you do, Mrs. Chen had said, *they call the police and lock you up.*

"It's only a picture. As you said, it doesn't even show my face." What were the odds that the priests would see it? "By tomorrow it will be birdcage liner and fish wrapping."

"You really don't know. Lili, this picture is in every paper in the country. *Lili*." Martha caught her elbow as she staggered and guided her to a chair. "It's all right; you're all right. Put your head down between your knees, honey, and breathe." She pressed her forward. "That's it. Just breathe."

Liling breathed, and gradually the faintness receded. When she felt sure she wouldn't pass out, she sat up slowly. Now she would have to tell this woman something to explain her reaction, and then she would go.

"I'm sorry," she said to Martha. "This . . . honor . . . is so astonishing, and I think I forgot to eat something today." She forced her lips into a smile. "It was so warm outside, I must be dehydrated."

Martha was a good nurse, and insisted on checking Liling's pulse, eyes, and temperature.

"You're fine, but I think you should go home early for a change," Martha said as she went to the fridge and brought back a cold bottle of soda. "I've never seen anyone turn so pale so fast. I thought you were going into shock. Here, drink this; it'll settle your stomach."

Liling allowed the older woman to fuss over her for a few more minutes, until she was able to convince Martha that she was steady enough to make the trip home. She thanked her and went directly to the employee locker room, where she kept her purse and car keys.

For the first time since she had begun working at the Lighthouse, she also removed the small carrying bag she had kept in her locker at all times. In the bag were three changes of clothing, three sets of identification, and three wigs. She checked the large roll of money she had stashed in the side pocket—five thousand dollars in twenties and tens—before putting the strap over her shoulder and going to the shower room.

Quickly she stripped and washed, drying off to change into a pair of jeans and a dark T-shirt from her bag. She checked the folded map she had marked with her route from Georgia to Texas; it would be a long drive from Atlanta, but she would be filmed by airport security cameras getting off the plane, so she couldn't risk staying in Georgia even for a day. Her braid had gotten wet, but there was no time to dry her hair. She considered cutting it off to further change her appearance, but it would be wiser to do that when she changed her clothing again in a restroom at the airport.

Liling had never been forced to move this quickly, but

she had always been prepared for the possibility. Chen Ping, the ninety-year-old woman in San Francisco who had taken her in and saved her life, had believed her story. It was Mrs. Chen who had taught her to always be ready to go.

"These bad men think you are dead," the old lady told her. "We can hide you here in Chinatown until they stop looking, but you not go outside."

Mrs. Chen told her many friends that Liling had come to America to escape being imprisoned for protesting against the Chinese government. The people of Chinatown revered the old lady, so they had gladly provided Liling with a number of identities and documents. Others had relatives working as translators for INS, and in a few years they were able to arrange foreign birth documents and secure approval for her to become a citizen.

Liling had stayed with the elderly woman, caring for her home and tiny garden until Mrs. Chen died one night, very peacefully, in her sleep. After the modest funeral, Liling discovered the old lady had left her entire savings to help Liling begin a new life.

"Chen Ping told me that you were the daughter of her heart," the lawyer told the astonished Liling as he handed her the certified check. "She asked me to tell you not to grieve for her, but to be happy."

The money had been a final gift, one that provided her with the means to take responsibility for her own life. It had been difficult for Liling to bid her friends in Chinatown good-bye and set out on her own, but without Mrs. Chen to conceal her presence, she knew she would only endanger them.

Liling deliberately kept only cheap housewares, thrift-store furniture, and minimal clothing at her apartment—nothing she needed to retrieve and take with her. She had split her inheritance up between three national banks, and had also put large sums of cash in safety-deposit boxes in several different states.

As she did with every car she had owned, she had bought her Ford Focus with cash and had registered it under a false name; when they found it abandoned at the airport they would not be able to trace it back to her. As part of her preparations, she had already obtained a license and papers using the next identity she would assume. When she arrived at her destination, she would no longer be Liling Harper, but Lian Hart.

No, she reminded herself, she would have to purchase her plane ticket as Lian Hart. Liling Harper had to die in Chicago.

She went out to use the phone at the nurses' station to call the airport, but stopped at the sight of a dark-haired man in a long black garment.

"I understand that Ms. Harper has left for the day," he was saying. A distinct Italian accent colored his cold voice. "Did she indicate her destination?"

Liling silently backed out of sight and hurried down the hall to Luisa Lopez's room.

"You're late today," Luisa said as Liling came in and quickly closed the door. Her hazel eyes shifted to the carry-on. "You planning on going somewhere, girl?"

"Luisa, do you remember when I told you that I might have to leave someday?" Liling went over to the bed. "I have to go today."

Luisa looked stricken. "What?"

"I'm sorry." It broke her heart to see tears well up in the girl's eyes. "I would stay if I could."

"But you can't go yet," Luisa protested. "I don't talk well

enough yet. I need more practice. We haven't finished the story. I don't know what happens to Marianne."

"There are bad men who are looking for me," Liling said. "They know where I work now. They are going to try to take me, and when they do they might hurt you and the other people here."

"We got security guards, don't we?" Luisa gestured toward the door. "You can take mine. He'll kick their asses all over this hospital."

"He can't help me." She sat down on the edge of the bed. "I'm going to miss you so much. Thank you for being my friend." She bent over and kissed her forehead.

"He won't stop," Luisa whispered, her eyes fixed on the wall behind Liling. "Not until you're dead." She seemed to come out of the trance as quickly as she went into it, and awkwardly pushed at Liling with her splinted hand. "You have to go. Don't waste time sitting here and crying on me. Hurry."

"I have to use your phone." Liling heard the boom of lightning and looked out through the window. Huge thunderclouds had erased the sun and were swelling up all around the facility. "To call the airport."

"Then what you—what are you waiting for?" Luisa wiped her face on the sleeve of her hospital gown. "Damn new eyes."

Liling kissed her friend's cheek before she picked up the phone and dialed nine for an outside line. Once she had a dial tone, she quickly put in star-sixty-seven to conceal the number she was calling from, and then dialed the number for the airline she had used to come to Chicago.

The reservations clerk who answered didn't bother to check for unreserved seating.

"I just sold the last available seat to Atlanta through tomorrow morning, Ms. Hart," she said pleasantly. "I can get you a seat on a flight in the late afternoon or early evening."

"No, I have to leave now. Can you check the other airlines?"

"Yes, ma'am, I'm doing that right now." The clerk fell silent for several minutes, and then said, "All of the flights out of Chicago to Atlanta are full."

Liling tightened her grip on the phone. She would have to abandon her plans. "I'll take a flight to any major city in the country, as long as I can leave in the next hour."

"You're very flexible. Just a moment, ma'am." The clerk put her on hold, and then came back on the line a minute later. "Miss Hart, I'm terribly sorry, but all the flights out of Chicago International are booked solid. If you'll give me a number where I can call you, I'll let you know the moment there is a cancellation."

Liling hung up the phone. She had been on the line for only a few minutes, but that might have been enough time for the call to be traced. She would have to risk driving out of the city until she found an airport the priests did not control.

The scent of fresh-cut camellias filled the room.

"Good evening, Luisa." Valentin Jaus came in. He wore his usual trench coat and carried a black umbrella, which he propped by the door. "Miss Harper."

"Hello, Mr. Jaus." She smiled quickly at him before she bent down and gave her friend one last gentle embrace. In a whisper, she said, "I'll try to call you when I can."

"You do, or I'll come looking for you," Luisa whispered back.

Jaus stopped Liling from leaving simply by blocking the door with his body. "Miss Harper, what is the matter?"

She felt a strange tugging sensation in her chest, as if

Jaus were a magnet for fearful hearts. "I have to travel to Atlanta tonight, but all the flights are booked. I'm going to have to drive down. Excuse me, sir."

"I am flying to Atlanta tonight, and I have ample room on my plane for a passenger," he told her. "You will fly with me."

Wealthy men did not offer gardeners rides on private jets, Liling thought. Not that he was offering; the way he sounded it was more like he was ordering her to come along. But instead of feeling afraid or intimidated by Jaus, she felt immediately better. If only she could confide in him. Something inside her whispered that he would be a friend she could go to for anything.

"You can trust Valentin, Lili," Luisa said. "He'll look out for you."

Liling gnawed at her bottom lip. She had no more time, and leaving Chicago on a private plane would virtually guarantee that no one would track her. "I would be so grateful, Mr. Jaus, thank you. When are you leaving?"

"I only stopped in to say good-bye to Luisa."

"Good-bye, so long, farewell, and off-weeder-stain, or whatever it is your folks say, Valentin," Luisa said. "Now go on and get out of here, both of you."

Jaus opened the door and gestured toward the outside hall. "Shall we?"

By now, Kyan thought, his masters would know he had left China without their permission. He doubted the priests would send anyone after him—they would have the proof that she lived, and would wish her dead almost as much as he did—but he was taking no chances. They had lied to him, claiming she had been killed during the storm, but deep inside he had known she still lived.

Not for long.

"I'm so sorry you missed your cousin," the nurse said, her gaze roaming his face with somewhat dazzled admiration. She had touched the girl recently; her scent was all over her hands. "Liling wasn't feeling well, and had to go home early. Do you have her address?"

"Yes." Kyan never needed an address. "Thank you."

He tracked the girl's scent from the nurses' station to a shower room at the back of the hospital, where he put his hand against the still-wet tile in one stall. Among other things, the water told him that the girl had been the last to use it.

He stood in the shower for several minutes, his head bowed, the veins on his arms popping out as he flattened his hands against the tile walls and absorbed everything he could about her.

Kyan saw a bag she had carried with her for many years. Inside he knew there were three changes of clothing. Three sets of identification. Three wigs. Money. Keys. A book. Between the pages, a dried, pressed pink flower with brown-spotted leaves. That was all she had thought about while washing in here. She must have known that he was coming for her.

Of course she knew. Who else would she hide from?

When the walls and floor of the shower were bone-dry, he stepped out and inspected the locker room. On the floor in front of the lockers he found a folded map of the United States. She had handled it just before leaving; he could still smell and feel the faint, damp impressions her fingers had left on it. She had taken a red pen and traced a route to a city called Atlanta in the southern part of the country.

As Kyan left the shower room, he followed the girl's trail to a room guarded by an armed man sitting and reading a magazine. Some rainwater had been tracked across the waxed tile floor, and Kyan glanced down at it as he walked past the guard. Infinitely tiny beads of water streamed toward the guard, running up the side of his shoe and sock and sinking into his skin.

Kyan watched from the corner as the guard grimaced and adjusted his belt, and then stood, his hand pressed to the crotch of his trousers. He made as if to use the radio clipped to his belt, but then his eyes widened and he ran into a restroom a few doors down from the patient's room.

The amount of water Kyan had sent into the man's body wouldn't harm him, but he would spend at least ten minutes emptying his painfully full bladder and bowels.

The patient sleeping inside the room was a bald black female with bandaged hands and dozens of scars on her face and head. She opened her eyes and watched him as he locked the door and approached the bed.

"You're too late." She regarded him with damp, hostile eyes. "She's gone, and I won't tell you anything."

"I know." Kyan gently put one finger against her cheek, following the path of her last tear. "This will."

Chapter 5

Alexandra Keller hated flying. Even in this luxurious, leather-upholstered pit of decadence her lover called his private plane, she was all nerves. After they were airborne, she paced the length of the cabin until she knew she was getting on Michael's and Phillipe's nerves. Finally she sat down and fiddled with a small glass of white wine.

"I can't even eat peanuts anymore," she said to no one in particular. "I really liked those honey-roasted ones in the little packets. Being a blood-dependent immortal with an atrophied digestive system sucks."

"We need a lab on the plane, don't we?" Michael turned to Phillipe, his seneschal. "See to it."

The big, brutal-looking Kyn nodded. "As soon as we return, master."

"Hey. I don't have to be working all the time," Alex informed them airily. "There are plenty of other things that make me happy besides medicine."

Phillipe leaned forward, the yellow eyes in his scarred face intent on her face. "Are any of these things on the plane?"

"Well, him." She pointed at her lover. "And you, when

you're not slaving for him. I like lots of things, you know. Like . . ." She looked around the cabin. "All right, God damn it. We need a lab on the plane." She got up and went back to pacing.

Cyprien came after her. "Alexandra, you cannot do this for six hours. Come and sit down."

"You're right." She grabbed his hand. "Excuse us, Phil." She dragged Michael back to the rear sleeping compartment and closed the door. "Just how unstable did John smell to you? Slightly depressed unstable, bipolar unstable, incoming-psychotic-episode unstable, pending-suicide-attempt unstable, what?"

"I cannot compare it to anything else." Michael shook his head. "I have never encountered such a scent change. I think I could also be wrong, Alexandra. It is why I did not wish to say anything to you. Your brother is not like other humans. He is . . . a complicated man."

"A complicated pain in my ass." She went over and flopped on the round bed, staring at the ceiling.

"It could be an effect of what happened to him in Ireland," he continued. "Elizabeth did feed on him. She may have had sex with him."

"Michael."

"I know you do not care to hear that, but John is no longer a priest—"

"I just have one more question for you."

"Chérie?"

She tilted her head and watched her reflection do the same. "Has that mirror *always* been up there?"

"Oui." He walked over to the bed.

She studied how she looked on the bed. The round mirror, fixed to the ceiling above her, reflected the entire mattress. "Funny that I never noticed it before now."

"Merci." He knelt in front of her, his long fingers gently sliding the skirt of her dress up her thighs.

Alex lifted her head to glare at him. "That's why you like me to be on top when we fly. So you can watch. You pervert."

He smiled a little. "That is *one* reason." He pulled her panties down to her knees and pressed her thighs wider.

"Wait a minute." She tried to sit up, and then her spine dissolved as he put his open mouth against her sex. "Wait. God. *Michael.*"

Her lover did not wait, but used his tongue to part her labia and lick the sensitive, more delicate flesh within. When she bucked against the explicit kiss, he took hold of her hips and held her in place.

"I don't want . . . I'm not . . . damn it." Alex couldn't catch her breath, not while she was watching him in the mirror, his long, white-streaked dark hair painting her thighs, his mouth moving against her as he licked and sucked. "I am not coming." She was going to come any second.

Michael raised his head to look at her, the amber rings in his eyes wide, his pupils slits. His fangs elongated, and then he brought his mouth down sharply, sinking them into her mound, dragging his tongue over her clit as he bit down.

Alex screamed as she came, convulsing, and shook uncontrollably as she felt him feed from her sex, his tongue working over her, forcing her back up and over again, and then he stood, his cock in his hand, and crouched over her, feeding the long, blunt shaft into her body, pushing and grunting as he took her, his lips covering hers, her blood and fluids on his tongue as he fucked her mouth and her pussy.

Alex forgot about the mirror and the rest of the unimportant universe until some time later, when Michael rolled away to lie panting and sweaty beside her.

"I like that mirror," she said, groping with her hand until she found his. "Thank you."

"My pleasure, *chérie.*"

They cuddled for a while. Alex usually liked that part—neither one of them had ever been cuddlers, except with each other—but even the afterglow of unexpected sex couldn't hold her in its dreamy grip for long.

Michael watched her as she pulled up her panties and straightened her dress. "I could tie you to the bed, you know."

"No, you can't. It's round and you don't have any rope." She left him there and went out to the cabin. Phillipe looked at her, his expression diplomatically bland. "Sorry about that. Cyprien has got to soundproof that compartment."

He shrugged. "I used the headphones."

When Michael came out, he made her sit down with him and his seneschal. "No more pacing. Phillipe has collected some research on the history of this mission John found. You may find it interesting."

"Historical research. Terrific." She yawned. "Buckle me in if I get too excited."

Phillipe opened his laptop and turned it so Michael and Alex could see the screen. "This is a map of the hills of Monterey that I took from Google Earth." He pointed to a secluded spot that appeared to be empty land hemmed in by acres of trees. "This is where your brother says the Brethren were."

"According to the records Phillipe found, Franciscan friars established a mission there in the late eighteenth century," Michael told her. "They dedicated it to Saint Francis, the founder of their order, and worked to feed the poor, take in orphans, convert the local Indians to the faith, and start the first school in the area."

"They sound like saints." Alex closed her eyes. "Wake me when we hit the Pacific."

"That is the *official* account of their activities," Michael said. "Unofficially, the brothers of St. Francis defied the local grandee and the army he had stationed at the Presidio by giving sanctuary to rebels and criminals, stealing shipments of gold bound for Mexico City, and redistributing it to other missions serving the humble poor."

"Really." She eyed him, intrigued in spite of herself. "Rebels in robes?"

"One of their brothers, a handsome young man of noble birth, worked as a friar by day and a leader of the rebellion by night," Michael told her. "He was reputed to be the best swordsman in California."

"Oh, I've seen that movie." Alex nodded. "But Antonio Banderas wasn't a priest. He was like a petty thief or something. He played Zorro version two. Anthony Hopkins was Zorro version one. What?"

Phillipe pressed his lips together. Michael gave her a familiar look.

"What do you want from me? I was working hundred-hour weeks. I was tired. It was easier to sit and eat a pint of Ben and Jerry's and watch a movie." She scowled at Michael. "Until they put pictures of Antonio Banderas, preferably half-naked, in the real history books, I'm sticking to DVDs."

"With respect to the film version you have seen, the friars of St. Francis continued their gentle reign of terror for several years, until they were betrayed by one of their own and arrested." Michael nodded to Phillipe, who pulled up an image on the screen. It was a very old painting depicting a group of monks being burned at the stake in the center of a crowded courtyard. "None of them would confess to their crimes. Even when the grandee offered to douse the flames and set them free as soon as they confessed."

"John would do something noble and stupid like that." Alex felt her heart twist as she studied the painting. "What happened to the mission after they got torched?"

"After the friars were executed, the grandee burned it to the ground." Michael tapped the keyboard and brought up an image of a crumbling adobe structure, its walls blackened and nearly obscured by weeds and brush. "This is what the mission looks like today."

"I found a story about military girls who went into the hills," Phillipe said. "They saw their spirits."

Alex's eyebrows rose. "Military girls?"

"Two air force linguists who were stationed at the Presidio in the eighties," Michael said. "The two went hiking while they were off duty and came across the ruins of the old mission. The girls told police that they saw a fire burning in the old courtyard where the friars had been put to death. One of them, a handsome young man, smiled at them."

"Typical ghost story," Alex said, dismissing it. "They probably saw a couple of campers and let their imaginations go wild."

Michael gave her a shrewd look. "Those two girls disappeared a week later from their barracks, apparently in the middle of the night. The only thing military investigators found were ropes hanging from their windows. The two girls were never seen again."

Alex shivered. "Now that? Is truly creepy."

"I think those girls saw something more than ghosts at the mission," Michael said. "It's possible that they saw Kyn being killed by the Brethren. It would explain their disappearance. The order does not leave witnesses."

"Kyn being killed by Brethren burning them at the stake?" Alex knew the religious fanatics could be unbelievably brutal, but they were still modern men. "Isn't that a bit medieval, even for these guys?"

"They use only fire both then and now," Phillipe said. "Everywhere they attack the Kyn, they burn them."

"Arson destroys a great deal of evidence, and there is no Kyn with a talent that combats fire," Michael added. "All of the Kyn who were recently driven out of France and Italy were burned out."

"But that doesn't make sense," Alex protested. "You just can't go around setting fire to people, not in this day and age. Even in Europe, every kid has a cell phone that takes digital pictures, right? Something like that would be all over YouTube."

"Kyn prefer to live on large estates in remote areas," Michael reminded her. "That gives the Brethren room and privacy to do as they wish when they attack."

Alex shook her head. "I'm still not buying it. Fire is too random, and smoke doesn't incapacitate the Kyn."

"Fear does," Phillipe put in. "We remember how it was after the trials, when they began burning our leaders. We all have a terrible fear of fire."

Alex knew the obscene ordeals the Templars had suffered in the fourteenth century, after the church ordered them rounded up, imprisoned, and tortured. Until learning of the Kyn, she had thought the warrior priests had been mere men. According to what Michael had told her, by the time the pope disbanded their order, all of the Templars had become *vrykolakas*, the "dark Kyn" of humanity. As the inquisitors learned during long months of torture, the virtually indestructible bodies of the Kyn made them very hard to maim and almost impossible to kill.

"There weren't any copper weapons in those days, were there?" Alex asked Michael.

He shook his head. "Copper was used for other things, at least until the Brethren discovered that the metal poisons us."

"What about 'off with his head'?"

"Beheadings were only for the royals," Phillipe told her. "Too good for common people."

She tapped a finger against her lips. "So the only way to kill the Kyn in those days was to burn them alive. Interesting." She saw how they were looking at her. "Just FYI, if I wanted to kill you, I'd go with decapitation every time. Fast, no smoke, easy cleanup, plus a nice trophy for the wall."

While the two men laughed, images of fire and blood began dancing in her head and forming a vague theory. Alex had only begun studying the effects of heat on the pathogen, so her knowledge was limited, but there were other tests she could perform. All she needed was . . .

"Phillipe, can I borrow your laptop for a while?" The seneschal handed it to her. "I need to make some notes for when we get back."

Alex opened a Word document and began outlining her theory and what she would need to prove it.

Some time later, Michael touched her shoulder. "*Chérie,* can you stop for now?"

She looked over at him absently. "What for?"

"The plane has landed."

Alex checked the screen. The few notes she had intended to make took up seventy-three pages of text. "Yeah. Okay. Sorry."

"Do not apologize." He tucked a stray chestnut curl behind her ear. "You are beautiful when you type."

*   *   *

As he never traveled with humans, Valentin had not taken into account how the confines of the plane would affect his senses. Although she sat at the back of the cabin, he could almost taste the girl's terror.

He had been happy to assist her in her moment of need, but he did not want to feel this supremely annoying curiosity. It had been a mistake to seek her out last night, and he had been resolved not to repeat it. As soon as they landed in Atlanta, he would never have to see her again. As for her reasons for leaving Chicago so quickly, they were none of his concern.

Another wave of her scent came to him. If she did not soon cease projecting so much fear, she would rouse other feelings in him.

Valentin saw that Liling had lifted her carry-on bag onto her lap and was searching through it. She then looked all around the floor, as if she had lost something. "Is anything wrong, Miss Harper?"

She glanced up. "Not really. I had a map tucked in the side of my bag, and it's gone now. I must have dropped it in your car. I'll just buy another one when we land." She put the bag down. "I didn't mean to disturb you."

He inclined his head and went back to pretending to read the prospectus he had not been reading. Her scent intensified as her anxiety increased, teasing his nose. Unable to concentrate, he finally rose and walked up to the galley section at the front of the cabin. Although he had no use for it, he had it kept stocked with food and drink for his human pilots.

He would put together a meal for her; that should calm her and give her something to do besides drive him into a blood frenzy, as she had nearly done last night.

Gregor would be outraged to see his Darkyn lord preparing a pot of tea for a mere human, Valentin thought as he

heated the water and placed the tea bags in the small Royal
Doulton china pot. Certainly if this surge of philanthropy
continued, he would have to consider hiring an attendant to
travel with him.

He inspected the contents of the small refrigerator and selected a few of the sandwiches and fruit he found there for
the tray. Then, adding the pot and a cup and carefully balancing the lot with his good hand, he walked slowly out to
the cabin.

"Miss Harper," he said, "would you be kind enough to assist me?"

Liling was there in a moment, taking the tray for him and
placing it on the console table beside his seat. She smiled at
him before turning to go back to her seat.

She thought he had made the refreshments for himself.
"This is for you, Miss Harper."

"Me?" Her voice squeaked on the word as her black eyes
filled with dismay. "I'm not . . . You don't have to feed me,
Mr. Jaus. I'm fine."

"Then this will only go to waste, as I despise tea," he informed her. "Fruit gives me indigestion, and I find little
sandwiches especially annoying."

"I'd be happy to make something for you." She glanced
past him to the galley. "Anything you like."

He would like to unravel that thick braid of hers, Valentin
thought, and see if she could sit on her hair. Then he would
wind it around his fist and use it to tug her head back, exposing the delicate golden length of her throat. . . .

She was staring at him now.

"Nothing, thank you. I never eat or drink . . . on planes."
He gestured to the seat across from his. "I would, however,
enjoy your company."

The girl sat down gingerly, as if she expected the seat to

explode, and carefully poured tea into the cup. She added no cream or sugar, but took a small sip of the steaming liquid and winced.

Her embarrassed gaze met his. "Very hot."

"I used boiling water." Next they would be discussing the uncertainties of the weather. "Tell me why you've chosen to work at a rehabilitation facility. It seems an unlikely choice of employment for such a talented gardener."

"Gardens are like little havens away from the troubles of the world," she said. "Nothing seems impossible when you're surrounded by flowers and green, growing things. Most medical buildings have professional landscaping, but I noticed that few do anything more than that. I guess that's what first attracted me to working at hospitals and nursing homes. I'm not a trained therapist, but I know my gardens and flowers help the patients, even if they only lift their spirits."

Valentin studied her face. "What you say is true. I find I am most at peace in my garden." It was not the happiness she had claimed last night that he should feel, but it suited him.

"Luisa told me that you raise camellias. The bouquets you've brought for her room are so unusual." She looked as if she wanted to say more, and then she glanced away.

Somehow he was making her feel more uncomfortable. "The camellias I raise are called Daijohkhan, or the castle camellia. They were originally bred at Castle Nayoga in Japan, but they are little known outside their native country."

"I couldn't find them in any of the flora books I've checked." Her smile came and went, quick and shy. "They're so white and perfect. How do you get such large blooms to grow?"

"I strip all but one bud from each branch," he said. "Camellias are like roses in that they are egotists: The less competition they have, the more they blossom. You have planted some camellias at the Lighthouse that I didn't recognize."

"They are *Hakutsura*," she said. "I found several pots of them at a specialty convention last spring. I worried that the winters here were too cold for them, but the grower told me they originated in Asia, and that they would thrive—and they have done very well."

"Ah, the White Crane." He nodded. "I remember when they were brought over from Japan."

She looked bewildered. "I'm sure that you weren't growing camellias in 1930, Mr. Jaus."

"Of course. I must have them confused with another specimen." He would have to watch his tongue; she knew more than he thought about his favorite flower. "I was curious as to why you planted violet beds at the front of the facility. I don't grow them myself, but I had thought that species was partial to shade."

"Those are dooryard violets," she told him. "They're native to Illinois, and they're very hardy and will grow in any light. I thought violets would be more welcoming to incoming patients and visitors."

He was amused. "You speak as if flowers have personalities."

"I think they do, in their own way," she said. "Violets smell sweet and look restful, while zinnias with their crayon colors seem more energetic and showy. And you can't show me a rose that is humble and retreating."

He found her fancies charming. "What of camellias? What is their personality?"

"Elegant and passionate. Resolute," she added. "There is nothing hesitant about a camellia. It brings a certain presence into every garden where I plant it."

"Tell me about your very first garden."

"It was in Chinatown, at the home of a friend. There's hardly any room in the city, so I used containers and placed them around this tiny patio and a horrid rosebush she was trying to keep alive." She shook her head. "I chose all the wrong plants, and half of them died in a few weeks. Still, it made Mrs. Chen very happy. She spent hours out there, sitting and watching the birds and butterflies that came."

"How did the horrid rosebush fare?"

"Beautifully, although you'd never know it to look at it," she said. "The first time I saw it, I thought it was dead; it was all ugly, gnarled brown canes. Mrs. Chen insisted that it would bloom, so I waited all spring. It grew a few leaves, which immediately became covered with brown spots. I trimmed one cane and it died. I think it did that deliberately."

Valentin was amused. "I have never heard of a suicidal rosebush."

"Mrs. Chen said it didn't like being touched," she told him. "It was summer by the time it finally budded, and it produced only two small blossoms."

"Did they become covered in spots as well?"

"No. They were apricot-colored blooms, with the merest hint of yellow at the base of the petals. The sort of heirloom rose you can't find anymore. They budded so slowly they took almost two weeks to open, and their scent was unlike any rose I'd ever grown." She thought for a moment. "I can't describe it adequately, but it was strong and soft and so delicious. Not like the scent of roses at all; more like silk and fruit and the way sunlight warms the air after a rain shower. It made you want to keep your nose buried in them for hours."

Her lips framed her words in such fetching ways as she spoke, he thought idly. And the rose scent she described sounded exactly like how her body smelled to him. "Did your friend plant the rose?"

"No, she claimed that she inherited it from the previous owner of her house. She liked to blame a lot of things on the previous owner." Her eyes gleamed with mischief. "She bought the house in the late thirties, so that would make it the oldest rosebush in the city."

Valentin wondered why Liling spoke of her friend as if she were a parent, but made no mention of her own family. "Were you born in San Francisco?"

"No." Her gaze remained direct. "I am from Taiwan."

In spite of her body language, Valentin knew at once that she was not being entirely truthful. His Kyn abilities made him aware of the subtle changes stress caused in the scent of a human, and he had learned to detect the shift that occurred whenever they were not being honest.

But why would she lie to him about where she had been born?

"I've since learned to cultivate many heirloom flowers over the years," Liling said. "But I still miss Mrs. Chen's garden, and that ugly, cranky, suicidal apricot rosebush of hers."

A sudden jolt of turbulence made Valentin frown, and Liling wrap both hands in a protective gesture around her teacup.

Chapter 6

Liling peered through the window. "The clouds out there look very dark." Lightning flashed, and she drew back with a visible flinch.

"I had thought the weather would be clear for the flight." Valentin pressed the intercom button on the side console. "Is there a problem?"

"We've encountered an unexpected storm, sir," the pilot replied over the cabin speaker. "We're ascending to avoid the worst of it. You should keep your seat belts fastened until we're clear."

"Thank you." He didn't care for how the pilot's voice had quavered, as if he were as nervous as Liling. He looked across to her and noted how her color had changed and her lips were pressed together. "It should be over in a few minutes."

Liling nodded, but her eyes stayed fixed on the window.

The turbulence increased until the jet bounced as if it were on springs. Liling lost her grip on her teacup, which flew across to smash against Valentin's chest.

"Mr. Jaus." She fumbled with her seat belt before she knelt in the space between their seats. She brushed away the broken bits of porcelain and pressed her linen napkin against the quickly spreading stain. "Did it cut you? Are you hurt?"

"I'm only a little wet." Seeing her like this, on her knees in front of him, made his *dents acérées* ache.

"That tea was so hot." She pressed her full lips together as she lifted the napkin to look beneath it before her anxious gaze moved up to his face. "It must have scalded you."

Oh, he was burning, but the tea was nothing compared to her touch, her scent, the midnight delights beckoning to him from the darkness in her eyes. Just as it had last night, the tantalizing perfume of her skin, like sun-warmed peaches, filled his head, his thoughts, his blood. He bent, wondering if her lips would feel as soft and sweet as her breath against his skin.

"Valentin?" Liling's lips parted on his name.

If you kiss her, this time you will *take her.*

"It's nothing, Miss Harper." As Valentin rose, he reached down and gently lifted her, placing her back in her seat. "I keep a change of clothing in the back cabin," he told her as he fastened her seat belt over her lap. "Please excuse me for a moment."

Valentin focused on regaining control as he walked into the back cabin. He felt nothing for Liling, just as she felt nothing for him. The turbulence must have triggered his defensive instincts; his shedding so much scent in such a confined space would have bespelled any human. By the time he changed and calmed himself, the effect of *l'attrait* on her would wear off, just as it had last night outside the museum. Liling would never realize how close she had come— twice—to being ravaged by his endless, cursed hunger.

He didn't bother with the lights; like all Darkyn he didn't need them to see. Shrugging out of his jacket, he pulled off his tie and reached for the first of the buttons. As always, they resisted his one-handed efforts to unfasten them. It infuriated him to be so clumsy, even as he knew there was nothing to be done about it. He might be a cripple, but he would be damned if he would be reduced to having someone else dress him.

The shirt was new, the fabric around the buttons stiff and unyielding. Viciously he tore at the front of it, sending buttons flying as he ripped it from his body.

"Mr. Jaus? I found a towel and a first-aid kit in the restroom." The door to the cabin opened, and a small shadow blocked out the light shining in from the center cabin. "Do you need some help? There's some burn cream here."

"I am not burned." He didn't want her to see the flash of his fangs, which had sprung into his mouth the moment he had heard her voice. "Thank you, Miss Harper. Please go back to your seat before we encounter more turbulence."

"This was my fault." Liling looked down at the buttons on the carpet around his feet and stepped inside, closing the door behind her. "Please let me help you." She put her hand on his useless arm. "It's the least . . . I can . . ." She went silent as her fingertips brushed over the long, narrow recess in his flesh.

The place where Thierry Durand had brought down his blade and severed Valentin's arm from his body.

The towel fell from Liling's other hand as she gently traced the length of his scar, following it all around his arm. "How did this happen to you?"

"It was an unfortunate accident." He turned his head so he would not see the pity in her face. "There was only so much the physician was able to do to repair it."

"When did you have the reattachment surgery?" Her voice sounded thin and strained.

"Some time ago." He hated her seeing him like this, only

half a man. He did not want to face her sympathy or her revulsion. "I am partially paralyzed, Miss Harper, not helpless. You may leave me to deal with this."

Instead of hurrying away, Liling stepped closer, bringing her other hand up to the scar, spanning it with all of her fingers. She bent forward and brushed her lips against the recess of flesh.

Valentin went still. "What are you doing?"

Her lips moved against his scar, but whatever she said was lost in the accompanying rush of sensation. Human warmth, effortless and beautiful, wrapped around his cool flesh and sank into him, until he thought he could feel it seeping into his very bones.

No lover, human or Kyn, had ever touched him like this.

The subtle curve of Liling's cheek brushed his shoulder as her small hands slid down to become the gentlest of bracelets. She looked up at him, tears making her black eyes wet.

"I'm sorry." That was what she was saying. "I'm so sorry."

Sympathy had always angered him, but hers only made him wish she had been there the night he had lost the duel with Thierry. Her touch might have saved him then.

It was too late now.

Valentin tried to move away from her, but discovered that he didn't want the moment to end. Before she could speak of her pity again, he brought his good arm up around her narrow waist, curling it to pull her closer.

"No," he murmured when she stiffened. "Stay."

He closed his eyes as Liling relaxed and rested her hands on his chest, where the warmth followed and lingered, surrounding the cold stone of his heart.

He held her for as long as he dared, until the need to taste her became a beast clawing and writhing inside him. Then, very carefully, he took her hand and brought it to his lips.

That her compassion aroused him as much as her beauty made him even more disgusted with himself. "You should be careful. You don't know what you do to me, *mein Mädchen*."

"I'm touching you," she said, her voice low and shy. "I wish I could do more."

Valentin despised himself for using his talent, but it didn't stop him from asking her, "What more do you want?"

"I'd like to kiss your mouth." Her fingers turned in his, pressing against his lips. "And put my hands on you, and move them all over you. I want to be naked with you. I've thought about how it would be. How you would make me feel. I've dreamed of you with me, in my bed, and then I wake up all alone and shaking."

"You cannot desire me." He could not believe her words. *L'attrait* compelled her to make such claims, not her heart. "Tell me the truth, Liling. Now."

"I've wanted you since the first time I saw you," she answered, the words leaving her lips with halting reluctance, as if she fought saying them. It was the same with every human he compelled to tell him something they considered a shameful secret. "It was when you brought Luisa the camellias for the first time. I saw you and thought you were a prince out of a fairy tale. Then you spoke to her, and I knew that you were better than a prince. You treated Luisa with such kindness and respect." She swallowed. "I envied her your friendship."

Valentin's hand trembled as he slid it over her hair to cradle the back of her head. "Why did you never say anything to me?"

"You're an important man," she whispered. "I'm only a gardener. I knew I could never be with you."

"Liling." He kissed her forehead, the bridge of her nose, the curl of her upper lip, the curve of her jaw, and breathed in the luscious scent of her. "You were wrong."

Liling felt time stop, as if she would spend the rest of eternity held there, against Valentin's bare chest, her mouth tingling from the touch of his breath. She had just told him things she never wanted him to know, heard the words pour from her lips without hesitation. As if it meant nothing to confess her most private fantasies to a virtual stranger. How could she have done it? The weight of the humiliation alone should have crushed her.

But it was what he had said that smashed through the glass walls of her shame.

You were wrong.

He wanted her. Somehow, some way, this man felt the same attraction, the same longing.

"I don't believe it," she said, more to herself than him.

"Why not?" he murmured, tugging at her braid. "Each time you looked at me, *mein Mädchen*, I looked back."

"But I know who you are." She couldn't fit herself into this puzzle. "Luisa told me that you own the Lighthouse, and that you live in a mansion on the lakeshore. You own corporations, and you have chauffeurs and servants, and you—" She stopped and shook her head. "You could have any woman in the city. Any woman you want. Why would you even notice someone like me? I'm a gardener, I have no family, no money, I'm not American, I'm . . . I'm not even white."

"So?" He sounded amused. "I am not Chinese, and you

noticed me. I will tell you a secret." He bent his head. "I am not American, either. I am Austrian."

Liling couldn't help the laugh that escaped her. "This is not happening. People like you and I don't . . . This is crazy."

"Is it." His fingers deftly worked her hair free and smoothed it across her back. "I adore this hair of yours. It feels like a cloak of black silk."

Her hand went to her hair as if to hide it. "I keep forgetting to trim it."

He caught her chin with his hand. "Never cut a single strand."

"It grows very fast." She caught her breath as his hand encircled her throat. "It would end up dragging on the floor. Mr. Jaus—"

"You are in my arms, *Mädchen*," he said. "My name is Valentin." When she didn't reply, his fingers tightened. "Say it for me."

Her mouth went dry. "Valentin."

His body vibrated against her, as if something inside him was breaking loose, and then he hoisted her up, his arm under her buttocks, and turned, taking her to the back of the cabin. She hadn't realized there was a bed until he laid her down upon it. The surface of the coverlet, something incredibly soft, teased the back of her legs as he stripped her jeans and panties from them.

"If you do not wish me to tear your shirt," he said, reaching for the front of his own trousers, "you must take it off."

Lost in a haze of passion and camellias, Liling found herself pulling her T-shirt over her head. He didn't wait for her to unfasten her bra, but yanked down the cups. They pushed her small breasts up higher, making them into an offering.

She didn't think he could see her, the cabin was so dark,

but he stared down at her as if there were a thousand candles around them.

Lightning flashed, illuminating the cabin for several seconds. In the harsh white light, Liling saw Valentin's body. Broad, tight muscle and thick ropes of tendons bulged under his pale skin, which the storm gave an almost luminous glow. If he had been a statue, chiseled by a master's hand from a single block of flawless moonstone, he could not have been more perfect.

He was not a statue, however, but an aroused male, hard and eager for sex. His penis, thick and erect, testified to the fact as it strained in a swollen arc against his lower belly. A shiver went through her at the thought of being impaled by him, and then the folds between her legs ignored her fear and went damp as they throbbed and ached, as if he were already there, pushing himself inside her.

As much as she wanted that, shame swelled inside her heart. After they arrived in Atlanta, she would have to leave immediately for Texas, and have no contact with people who had known her as Liling Harper. She would never see him again.

This could be only a one-night stand.

His fingers caressed her cheek. "Don't be afraid of me, *Liebling*. I will never hurt you."

Tired of her own doubts, Liling pushed herself up, reaching for him as he came down for her. He lifted her from the bed just as the plane jolted, standing up with her, and she wrapped her legs around him, clinging instinctively to his powerful frame. Only after a moment did she feel the satiny dome there, nestling against the delicate recess between her thighs.

Liling turned her face to his, seeing that the pale blue eyes she had always thought so cold had changed, becoming lustrous and piercing, the pupils elongating. Bathed in the heady perfume of a thousand unseen camellias, she loosened her grip on his neck, sinking against him, enveloping the blunt head of his shaft, saturating it with the silky wetness seeping out of her slit as he stretched her wide.

He supported her weight, going no further than she had taken him, keeping her poised on the very tip of his sex.

"Is this what you want, Liling?" His voice had gone so deep and thick the words sounded slurred. "For me to fuck you before I even kiss you?"

His language and his question didn't frighten her; they freed her. She had taken lovers—she was no stranger to sex—but the men she had been involved with had treated her like one of her flowers, as if she might break if they did anything more than cuddle and pamper her. For once she wanted to be treated like a real woman instead of a doll.

To be like the women she was in her fantasies.

His strength and size excited her on a level so deep and hidden she hardly recognized her own longing. She needed him to be strong for her, to take instead of ask, to hold on to her and take control by making her his. They had only this night, so she would let him do anything to her that he wished. She also suspected that if she tried to explain her feelings that the words might repel him.

She had to show him with her body.

Liling brushed her lips over his in a brief, sweet touch that made him inhale sharply. Then she slid her hands down to his shoulders, allowing the weight of her body to say what she could not, to surrender to him what he would not take.

This was what she had wanted, but even her secret desires had not prepared her for what followed: for blasting through the boundaries of polite sexual conduct, for how his penis stabbed into her softness, so deep and hard that there seemed no space left inside her body that he did not claim with his own. The intimacy of his penetration, of taking him so ferociously, was every bit as stunning as the power of how it felt.

"Wait, please." She bit her lip, trying to adjust both mind and body as her muscles clenched around him. The fantasy of surrendering herself to a powerful man had never included so many new sensations. The wanton slickness of her sex seemed to melt into the rigid spike of his shaft, but the neglected muscles inside her body quivered, still unsure of handling such a union.

"Forgive me." He rested his forehead against her shoulder for a moment, and then lifted his face before bringing his open mouth down on her flesh.

Liling felt twin points of fire pierce her skin and cried out, writhing against him, before the flowers closed around her and her hand came up of its own volition, stroking his hair and urging him closer.

Watercolors of pale blue, violet, and green shimmered around her, washing away the pain and the fear. She and Valentin lay together on a bed of white fur, on their sides, facing each other, bodies entwined. All around them stood tall, wide stained-glass panels, each containing gardens of glass.

Liling glanced down and saw that they were still joined, their body hair meshed in a tangle of gold and black. The light shining through the glass on them made other patterns of color on their skin. "Where are we, Valentin?"

"A better place for this." His hand cupped her breast, massaging the weight of it before plucking at the small brown nipple. "Tell me what you want me to do to you, Liling."

Real flowers began to grow up around the edges of the fur. Lavender-hearted morning glories opened at their feet;

red poppies lifted their scarlet faces out of the lacy fern near their heads. And on the stained-glass panels, elegant, passionate white blossoms of camellia appeared and flowered in the glass, until the light bathing their bodies turned opal white.

Liling rolled onto her back, wanting him on top of her. Valentin came with her and braced himself on his good arm, moving against her just enough to keep their bodies joined. Only then did she realize how rigid he was, and she saw the set of his jaw, as if he were grinding his teeth together.

Over his shoulder she saw a gap between the stained-glass panels, showing another place beyond them, a place as shadowed as the panels were radiant. The dark place reflected their naked bodies like a brooding mirror, but in that place they were not on furs surrounded by flowers. They were back in the cabin of the plane. Liling saw herself on her knees in the dark, her hands clasped behind her, her head flung back. Valentin stood before her, his hands caressing her hair.

Part of her understood. His needs were like hers, hidden and denied. "Take me there."

He looked over at the dark mirror and then down at her, his eyes narrowed. "You can't want . . ."

Liling kissed him, and then looked into his eyes. "I've kissed you. I've taken you inside me. Now give me what you want, Valentin."

The panels of stained glass turned dark, until only streaks of lightning painted the world. Then they were in the plane, on the bed, Valentin pressing her thighs apart with his hips as he drove into her.

"You wanted me," he said, "then take me."

She took him as he forced his way into the narrow ellipse of her flesh, bracing herself as he recoiled to thrust again, faster and harder, until Liling's back bowed and she cried out, the pleasure drenching her, drowning her in the storm of his lust.

Valentin jerked her to the edge of the bed, holding her down with his hand as he stood and wrenched himself out of her body. He pulled her up, guiding her face to him.

"Take me in your mouth," he said, wrapping her hair around his fist.

Reality was not the same as the image in the dark mirror. None of Liling's lovers had asked her to do this for them. She had no experience, no knowledge.

Valentin tugged on her hair. "Open for me, Liling. I want it."

He wasn't asking. He wanted her submission, not her doubt. He demanded it. Dark delight rocketed through her as she parted her lips for him, surrendering, taking the full thrust of his cock into her mouth. She tasted herself on him before she began to suck. Valentin pushed against her tongue, forcing her to take more of him, until her mouth stretched wide and his body hair brushed the tip of her nose.

No man had ever treated her like this. Not even her fantasies were this hard, this rough, this real. Liling thought she might climax from the sheer excitement of it.

His fist snarled in her hair as he urged her closer, stabbing deeper, filling her mouth as completely as he had her body. "That's it. Deeper. Take me deeper. Yes. Like that."

Liling moaned around him, her thighs tightening as the notch between them pounded, empty and hungry, unbearably aroused.

He came without warning, in silence, in long, thick jets as cool as cream. She drank from him, greedy for the taste of his semen.

Valentin gave her no respite, but pulled out of her mouth

and put his fingers between her legs, cupping her and working the heel of his hand against her swollen mound even as he lifted her.

"Now you," he demanded, pushing her back onto the bed and fucking her with two fingers, pushing and stroking and stabbing until she twisted, unable to escape the rasp of his palm as it dragged over her clit. "Give me what I want. Give it to me. *Liling.*"

The storm outside the plane was nothing to the one he raised inside her. Terrifying pleasure seized her and flung her into the dark, where nothing mattered but the heat and the bursting light and the harsh voice of her lover demanding everything she had, taking everything she was.

Liling collapsed, pleasure-blind, and rolled bonelessly against the damp vault of his chest. She couldn't speak, and nothing wanted to move. She might have to stay forever right there where she was. Only after a time did she feel the motion of his hand, gentle and steady, stroking up and down her back.

She opened her eyes to see him watching her face. It was impossible to read his expression, to know if she had pleased him. "Is that what you wanted?"

He nodded, brushing the hair back from her eyes.

"Good." She closed her eyes, satisfied beyond belief, and happy that she was able to make their one time together perfect. "So did I."

Chapter 7

John sat in the stone courtyard in front of the hotel, waiting for the sun to set and his watch to tell him it was time to meet Alexandra and her lover up in the hills.

He had not checked into the hotel, but had parked his rental car down by the pier in an all-night lot and slept in the backseat. He knew he was being paranoid, but he felt safer not using the credit card and phony ID Cyprien had given him. He might have to use the vampire's resources, but he didn't want to give him the means to track his movements.

A small collection of exclusive shops had been built on the west side of the hotel courtyard to cater to the whims of the guests. John watched stressed-out parents herd their children into the ice-cream shop, while pretty girls with bored boyfriends in tow idly browsed the clothing boutique.

The scents of sunshine, expensive perfume, and engine exhaust dwindled as John smelled something less civilized.

A young, grungy-looking man dressed in dirty clothes and a knit cap and carrying a sagging backpack passed by John as he went to a garbage can outside the small designer sandwich shop. The drifter took the protective green hooded lid off and bent down, rummaging through the trash before he straightened and with eager hands unwrapped a crumple of paper. He grinned and bit into the half-eaten sandwich inside.

John remembered doing the same thing when he was a kid on the streets. Sometimes he had staked out certain garbage cans in particular so that he could get the food thrown in them just after it was discarded. He had never stolen or begged for food for himself, only for his little sister.

Alexandra had hardly ever complained, even when he couldn't get the milk she always craved. She'd been just a baby, but somehow she'd known.

A man in a white apron with his sleeves rolled up stepped out of the sandwich shop. He smelled of Calvin Klein and cheap mayonnaise. "Hey," he shouted at the drifter. "Get out of there."

Rather than taking off, the drifter stuffed the discarded sandwich into his mouth, making his cheeks bulge, and bent over the garbage can again, reaching for something inside.

"Hey." The aproned man came over and shoved him away from it. "You deaf or something, you bum?"

John got up and strode over, stepping in front of the drifter. "Knock it off."

"He's eating out of the fricking trash can," the man complained. "It's making my customers sick."

John looked at the avid faces watching them from inside the shop. Two girls were openly laughing. "They don't look so green from here."

"Now look," the aproned man said, glowering at John from under his brows. "This is private property. We got city ordinances against vagrants."

"You fucking hypocrite," John said, the rage coming over

him so fast he didn't even think to resist. "You probably waste enough food in one day to feed fifty people."

"Yeah, well, this ain't no soup kitchen." To the drifter, he said, "You got two minutes to clear out of here before I call the cops." He stabbed a finger at John. "Same goes for you, asshole." Muttering to himself about bleeding-heart liberals, the aproned man stalked back into the shop.

Hatred ballooned inside John. He felt like going in after him and grabbing the self-righteous bastard by the throat, and shaking him until his false teeth popped out of his mouth.

A dirty hand touched his arm.

"Let it go, man," the drifter said. "He ain't worth spending a night in the drunk tank." He sized up John with a speculative glance. "There's some good places to sleep down by the dock, if you're looking."

"I'm not drunk, and I have a place to sleep." Still glaring at the windows of the sandwich shop, John reached into his pocket and took out his wallet. "Here." He gave the drifter Cyprien's credit card. "You can use this at any ATM. The pin number is seven-four-one-two. I think it's got a five-grand limit."

"You for real?" The drifter took the card as if it were made of solid gold. "It ain't stolen, is it?" He immediately tried to hand it back. "I don't want to get busted."

"It's not stolen." John felt better, lighter. "My sister has a rich boyfriend. He gave it to me, but I don't need or want his money."

"If you're sure." The drifter stuffed the card down the front of his grimy trousers, and then offered his hand. John shook it. "Thanks, man. You're a walking saint." With a quick glance at the sandwich shop, the man reached into the garbage can and retrieved a partially eaten slice of pizza. He grinned at John. "I can't resist pepperoni and mushrooms. My favorite." He began to munch on it as he wandered around the side of the building.

John heard a siren drawing close and walked down a block to where he had parked the rental. He ducked inside and waited until the patrol car passed, and then started the engine and drove off.

John went down to Cannery Row and parked the rental by a small movie theater. He had enough money left in his wallet to buy a ticket, and went in to sit in the back row of the theater. When the film started, he slouched down and closed his tired eyes.

Back when they lived on the streets in Chicago, John had learned how to sneak into movie theaters. He'd stand out of sight by the ticket booth and wait until a large family bought tickets. He would scoot out, leading Alexandra by the hand, and walk in right behind them. Nine times out of ten the usher wouldn't check the number of tickets given to him, and would assume he and Alex were part of the family group.

Movie theaters were good, safe places to sleep. In between shows, John would take Alex into the restroom, and keep her there until the ushers were finished cleaning the aisles. Then he would return for another two-hour nap.

Sometimes just before the show started, he pretended he'd left something in the front seats, and scout around for any buckets of popcorn or boxes of candy wedged in the seats; the ushers always missed those. Once he found an unopened box of SnoCaps, Alex's favorite candy. He would have let her eat the entire box during the next showing, but by then Alex had learned that treats were precious. She'd carried the box around for a week, eating the candy one or two pieces at a time.

Sweet, sweet boy. Thin, bloody fingers caressed his cheek, his chest, his cock.

He opened his eyes to look up at the petite blond woman. She had returned to the bedroom they had locked him in, but now there were no guards to stop her.

Did you miss me? She had changed out of her ball gown and now wore a yellow silk negligee that did more to reveal her body than conceal it.

John knew what she wanted. *Leave me alone.*

I don't believe I'm going to do that. Elizabeth smiled as she fingered the bandage Alexandra had put on the side of his throat, and then ripped it off. *They say you were a priest. I find that very arousing.*

She had taken the thin braids out of her golden hair, the ends of which brushed against his chest as she straddled him. She rubbed herself against him, her smooth brow furrowing when his body didn't respond.

You deny me?

The stink of mildew and damp wood filled John's head, promising to take him back to the alley behind the produce warehouse. Where he had slept with Alexandra one night when he was eight years old, in a small fortress he had fashioned out of moldering fruit crates. Where the rats had prowled after dark, furtively looking for any fresh meat.

No. John couldn't go back there again.

Then give me what I want. She ground her crotch over his.

She repulsed him, but he feared the memory of the rats more. He seized her waist and rolled over with her, yanking up the transparent nightgown and baring her pelvis.

Elizabeth scowled and pushed at him. *Get off.*

John knew she had Kyn strength, and in the next moment fully expected to feel himself flying across the room. But she didn't use it against him as she pushed. She was only going through the motions; her eyes gleamed with excitement.

John felt his blood turn to ice as he realized what she wanted him to do. It didn't arouse him, and it didn't frighten him. It enraged him.

His hands wrapped around her neck. He shook her like a doll. *You think you can make me rape you?* he shouted. *I'm not an animal.*

Oh, but, sweet boy, you are. Elizabeth undulated beneath him, her lips pouting. *We know everything you've done, how you've forced yourself on other women, and you loved every moment, didn't you? Shoving yourself into them, making them take it, making them do those dirty, dirty things to you.*

He slapped her. *Shut up.*

The blow split her lip, spilling blood onto her chin before the cut instantly healed. She gave him a gory smile. *Those things you wanted* her *to do to you.*

No. John shook his head, releasing her and desperately trying to scramble away, but her hands became manacles around his wrists.

She smiled. *Didn't Alexandra want to do them?*

Horror destroyed the loathing and lust inside him, and then Elizabeth was pulling him down, her bloodied mouth wide, her lips peeling back from her fangs—

Mister.

"Mister."

"Mister."

John jerked awake, startling the usher standing over him.

"Theater's closing, mister," the young boy said. He looked at John's face and retreated a few steps. "You gotta go now."

"Sorry." John pushed the sweat-soaked hair out of his

face and forced his tired body out of the folding seat. The usher followed at a safe distance until John staggered out of the theater and into the night.

John didn't dare go to sleep after that, but drove around the empty streets of Monterey for hours, the radio in the rental car turned up loud enough to keep him from thinking.

Fog slowly rolled in from the bay and swaddled the apartments and cottages and mansions in damp, white mist. John passed an ancient VW Bug, its battered, rusting body still bearing some faded remnants of the psychedelic art a stoned hippie had hand-painted on it forty years ago. In the space next to it a red Maserati gleamed, a sleeping demon on wheels, its vanity plate reading, 2FAST4U.

That made curious sense to John. Everything was happening too fast.

He drove up to the small military base on the hill above town and parked outside the gates. In a few hours, a lone bugle would pierce the air at oh-six-hundred, rousing the soldier-students from their dorm rooms. Some would walk down the steep hill to have breakfast in town, while others wandered into the chow hall, where they practiced in low voices the tongue-twisting dialogues for their Arabic-, Russian-, Korean-, and Chinese-language classes.

But for now the linguists at the Presidio and the owners of the VW and the Maserati slept, safe in their beds, assured that all was as it should be, and the world would continue, as it always had, to spin day into night, night into day.

None of them, John was sure, would dream of rats, or rape.

At last the time came to go up into the hills. John drove up as far as he could on the dirt road, and then took his case out of the back of the rental and went the rest of the way on foot. He waited at the lightning-struck tree he had chosen as the meeting place. A few minutes later, a limousine pulled off down on the dirt road below him. John waited until he saw his sister, her lover, and their bodyguard step out before he turned on his flashlight.

"Johnny?" Alexandra called, shielding her eyes with her hand as she started up the incline.

For a moment John thought he saw a little girl, her small hand taking a SnoCaps out of the box, her baby teeth nibbling carefully at the nonpareils. Then his vision cleared, and he saw Alexandra, the woman in the green silk dress.

No, not a woman anymore. A vampire.

They came, his sister, her lover, and their bodyguard, and stopped a few yards away. Their wariness didn't make him angry, only wistful. Once his sister would have run to him to throw her arms around him and babble a thousand questions. Now, after all that had happened, she kept her distance, her hand curled around Michael Cyprien's. He didn't have to see her face to know her eyes would be as guarded, her expression as shuttered, as his own.

The scents of lavender and rose twined together, taunting him as much as seeing his sister's fingers threaded through Cyprien's.

It was the way things had to be. That John had in large part caused the rift between them, all for the sake of the calling he had abandoned as worthless, didn't make the estrangement any easier.

"The security guards will be driving by here in five minutes," he said. "We'd better move."

Cyprien said something in archaic French to his bodyguard, who returned to the limo. To John, he said, "Phillipe will see to the guards."

John didn't like Michael Cyprien. He had never wanted

anything to do with the Darkyn, not after they had taken his sister from him. But the Brethren had to be stopped, and there was no one else he knew with the power and resources to do so. Officials from the real Catholic Church would never believe him without evidence, and the order had infiltrated their ranks with so many impostors that it was impossible to know whom to trust.

"You look like shit," Alexandra said, releasing Cyprien's hand to walk close to her brother. She sniffed. "You smell worse. When was the last time you had a meal or a bath?"

He couldn't tell her that he couldn't remember. "I've been busy."

John guided them along the old trail he had found during his first visit to the place, and around the crumbling adobe to the first of the underground entrances. He pulled away the mat of dead weeds camouflaging it, and took the tire iron out of the case he carried.

Alex stepped in front of him. "Allow me." She bent down and worked her fingers into the seam of the heavy iron door, and lifted it as if it were made of Styrofoam. "Was this left open like this?"

"It was padlocked, and completely covered with branches and dead leaves and weeds. I had to rent a metal detector to find it." He directed his flashlight into the tunnel. "It goes down forty feet. There's a ladder on the side, but it's slippery. Be careful climbing down."

His sister blew a short raspberry. "Please." Without warning she jumped in.

"Alexandra." John snatched at the empty air where she had been, and then knelt at the edge, trying to see her. His light showed her standing at the bottom, gazing back up at him.

"Come on, Michael," she called up to them before stepping out of the way.

"We don't climb," Cyprien said to him, almost apologetically, before he too jumped in.

John reconsidered walking away and leaving them to it. They were the ones with the superhuman abilities, not him. This wasn't his war. He didn't belong to either side. But he couldn't trust Cyprien and the Darkyn any more than the Brethren, and someone had to stand up for the humanity caught in the middle.

John pocketed his flashlight and climbed down into the tunnel.

Below the surface, the vertical accessway opened into an intersection of four ten-foot-high horizontal tunnels that ran off in opposite directions. Here the air was cold and stale, soured by the rotting smell of mildew. Water dripped somewhere, the impact of the drops echoing through the tunnels like the first moments of a rainstorm. Scurrying feet retreated as the mice and rats that had nested nearby fled the light.

"These passages are lined in cement," Alex said, touching one wall.

"It's built like one of those old bomb shelters from the fifties," John told her, and flipped a switch next to the ladder. Light illuminated the corridor intersection by the ladder. "Another reason I know they haven't totally abandoned this place. The electricity was never cut off."

"How much have you seen down here?" Cyprien asked him.

"I didn't have time to do more than a quick walk-through of about half the facility. There are offices and records rooms down there." He turned to the opposite passage, which was gated with iron bars. "The dormitories are through there."

"Give us the grand tour," Alex suggested.

He took them first to the eight dormitory rooms, each filled with twenty single beds. "They were keeping the kids in here." He pointed to the doors, which locked with dead bolts from the outside.

"How do you know the occupants were children?" Cyprien asked. "They might have used these rooms for members of the order."

John went to one of the beds. "Too small for adults." He demonstrated by reclining, and had to bend his knees sharply to fit on the short, narrow frame.

Alex bent down to read some faded numbers and letters stenciled onto the end of the frame. "'AK-nine-one-nine-eight-one.' The last four might mean the year 1981."

"Perhaps the year it was manufactured," Cyprien suggested.

"No, there are different numbers and letters on each bed," John told him. "They probably branded them on the kids' arms after they abducted them and shipped them off here. The way the Nazis did to the Jews in the concentration camps."

"That's kind of a leap, John," Alex said as she straightened and gazed at the other beds. "Twenty per room, that's a hundred and sixty kids. No one could take that many children and get away with it."

"Thousands of children go missing every year," John told her. "Most of them are never found. The Brethren are well organized and own extensive property all over the country."

"If this is how they've been recruiting members for the order," she said, "we need more evidence than some numbers on an old bed frame."

"They weren't just recruiting kids for the order," John told her. "They were experimenting on them." Her shocked reaction made him glance at her lover. "Didn't you tell her what I found?"

"I thought it would be best if Alexandra saw these facilities first before we drew any conclusions," Cyprien said. "Young children get sick quite often. What you saw could have simply been an infirmary."

John didn't care for the way Cyprien looked or spoke to him, as if he were indulging a fretting child. "You know exactly what monstrous things the Brethren can do, and you're defending them."

"I know what they do to me and my kind," Cyprien said. "We have never known them to hurt human children."

"Well, they have," John told him. "I found a laboratory set up to perform experiments on large subjects. Too large to be lab rats."

Alex's gaze moved to Cyprien and then back again. "Are you sure they weren't experimenting on monkeys or other large primates, like gorillas? It's repulsive, but it happens."

"Other than the Brethren, I haven't seen any evidence of animals down here," John told her. The anger flared up inside him. "How can you make excuses for them? These were children."

"I'm not making . . ." She blew out a breath. "Show me this lab, John."

John took them back through the corridor and into an adjoining passage. Alex halted a few times to look through the dusty windows in some of the doors.

"These look like some sort of treatment rooms," she said.

"They were cleaned out; there's nothing left in them but the exam tables and empty cabinets." He stopped in front of a set of double doors. He hated going in, but it had to be done. "This is where they did the real dirty work."

He walked around the room as Alexandra examined the equipment.

"Okay, we've got some extremely decrepit EEG and EKG machines, a sucky treadmill, lousy endoscopes, Jurassic-era blood pressure monitor, intravenous equipment with unsafe needles—is that really a defibrillator?—a crappy ventilator. . . ." She stopped at one cart. "And what very well could be the world's oldest incubator."

"Look at the tables," he insisted. The first time he had, he'd vomited. "The straps on them."

Alexandra went over to one of the flat sheet-metal tables and inspected the perforations in the surface before gingerly unbuckling one of the leather restraints. She examined the inside of the leather before putting it down. She went to the cabinets and opened each one, pulling out some of the dusty contents.

Cyprien came to stand beside John. "The Brethren despise us, but they believe they are protecting humanity. I am not defending their methods, but I cannot believe that they would kidnap or harm human children in their mission to destroy us."

"You're right about one thing, John," Alexandra said as she closed the last cabinet. "Everything in this room indicates that the subjects who were treated here were human beings." Before John could say anything, she held up her hand. "I can't say for certain that they were kids, and if they experimented on them, they didn't do it here. This lab is set up to perform standard tests and monitor physical conditions. They have some emergency equipment, John, but nothing out of the ordinary."

She still didn't believe him.

"Why would they need to do that?" he demanded. "Test and monitor the children for what?"

"I don't know," she admitted. "I need more information. You said there were records."

John took them to the offices at the end of the next tunnel, and gestured to the barricaded doors he had been unable to open.

"I only brought bolt cutters with me the last time, so I couldn't get in." He pointed to the three steel bars at the top, middle, and bottom of the door. "These are welded in place."

Alex peered through the webbed glass at the rows of old metal filing cabinets. "They cleaned this place out pretty thoroughly before they left. Those cabinets could be empty."

"Then why seal the room?" he asked her.

"Good point." She glanced at Cyprien, who took hold of the other end of the center bar welded across the door. Together they pulled it off, the steel tearing like tin foil, and then they did the same to the other two.

John brushed past them and went to the first cabinet, almost pulling the empty drawer out completely in his haste to open it. He bent and opened the one beneath it, and the next. The entire cabinet, as Alex predicted, was empty.

"No, there has to be something in here." He moved to the next cabinet, jerking at drawer handles and finding it empty, and then the next, and the next, until a drawer flew out of his hand and hit the wall on the opposite side of the room. He stared at the small crater it made in the wall before landing on the linoleum floor. "Where are they?"

A cool, gentle hand touched his cheek. "Johnny, stop. Michael, would you give us a minute?" Alexandra waited until Cyprien left them before she guided John to a chair and sat on the edge of the desk beside it.

"I was so sure I'd find the proof in here." His eyes felt hot and dry, his eyelids lined with sandpaper. Something like a laugh came out of his throat. "I should have known they wouldn't leave any evidence behind."

"It's obvious from the dormitory that they were keeping some kids here," she said in a placating tone. "There's just not enough left to indicate why. Maybe if we can find out where they're operating from now, we can go to the media with that. Anderson Cooper just got back from filming starving Afghan farmers growing opium poppies for the Taliban, you know. He'd jump all over a story like this."

"I'll never find them." John felt defeated. "They use the Church as a front, so it could be any Catholic program, parish, or building anywhere in the country. There are hundreds of thousands of places they could be."

"Michael will help," she told him. "The Kyn have some amazing resources we can use. We'll find out the truth, John, and we'll expose them. I promise."

The truth. That was the key.

"We have to go back to Chicago." He hesitated. "There's a vampire living there, the one named Jaus. He can touch people and make them tell the truth. I know; he did it to me in Florida. If anyone knows how the order recruits new members, it's Archbishop Hightower."

Alex looked startled. "You want Val to work on Hightower? I don't know, John. We try to avoid contact with the Brethren. They do unfriendly things like torture and kill us."

"If I brought the archbishop to Jaus, would he do it?" he countered.

"He probably would for me." She looked past him as Cyprien came back into the room. "I have a favor to ask."

After she related what John said to Cyprien, he agreed to make the trip to Chicago. "After the problems we encountered with the order while tracking Thierry Durand in Chicago, I am not inclined to risk exposing Suzerain Jaus or his *jardin* again. Still, there are ways it can be done safely, and as Alexandra says, Valentin is a friend. It is almost dawn; we should go now."

Chapter 8

The figure of a man on horseback drew Liling from the red camellias she had been arranging to the window. He had stopped at their whitewashed gate and gazed up at the cottage. Surely it was one of the priests, come to take her back to the facility, and that dread expectation made her feel ill. But it was *not* a priest—he carried neither cage nor scissors.

Was it possible? Was it him? She looked a second time, as he dismounted, and saw the sunlight find itself in golden hair and fine blue eyes.

She had not been mistaken. It *was* Valentin.

Liling retreated from the window and sat down, holding a bouquet of camellias in her tight fingers, watching the petals change from red to white. His color, like the snow in his voice and the ice in his eyes. "He comes from the Lighthouse purposely to take me," she told the flowers. But why? And where? "I *will* be calm; I *will* be mistress of myself."

She had been mistress of herself for so long, though. She was so tired.

You sure, Lili?

The ghost of Chen Ping bustled around the room, trying in vain to wipe the dust-coated furniture and chase the cobwebs in the corners with her broom. She disturbed the blue cygnet that had taken up residence on the pianoforte, sending him skidding along the keys. The angry swan hissed and spread enormous wings, pecking at her spirit until Chen Ping changed substance, becoming a thing made of shadows instead of memories, and gave Liling one last smile.

Wish him joy.

As Valentin entered the room, his expression seemed bewildered, as if he had never been to such a place. But Liling had entertained him so often he should know every room, every wall, every brick of the place. How could he look upon her now as if he expected no welcome—he, the only one to whom she had ever extended an invitation?

"This is not real." Disbelief made soft his mellow tenor. "You are mortal. You cannot summon me."

"I am as surprised by your visit as I am delighted, sir." Liling went to him, commanding her countenance to remain smooth and untroubled, and offered him her hand to shake. "I wish you only great happiness, Mr. Jaus."

"Happiness." He gripped her hand and held it much longer than could be considered polite. "What do you know about my happiness?"

The blue swan uttered a wild call and flew across the room. It smashed through the window, showering both Jaus and Liling with shards before it escaped through the jagged hole. Blue feathers, stained with red blood, slowly drifted to the floor.

From the horizon, inky night streaked toward the cottage, bringing with it fiery clouds pregnant with blue lightning.

Now that the swan had fled, a terrible silence fell over the room. Liling looked at the storm closing over her little

home, and tugged at his grip. "I was to rejoice in the dryness
of the season. It cannot rain now. Please let me go."

"No." He put his hand to her throat. "How did you bring
me here, Liling? You are not my kind. You cannot be here."

Behind her, the fire began to smoke.

Not his kind. That was his opinion of her. She had never
been allowed to feel angry, had never allowed herself to feel
so. It had always been too dangerous, especially after she
had discovered what she could do.

You must not give, Chen Ping whispered. *Only take.*

"Your behavior insults me, sir," she said as harshly as she
could. "I gave myself to you. I believe that there can be no
danger in my being with you. Do not convince me otherwise."

"The danger is my own," he told her, his voice growing
tight with regret. "I am doing no injury to anybody but myself."

The smoke from the hearth dwindled. Camellias began to
sprout from the cracks and knots in the planking on the
floor. They curled around Jaus's boots and Liling's bare feet,
cool and white, soft and fragrant.

Liling covered his hand with hers. "Then cease this un-
seemly behavior, and be with me this night. Only be with
me."

Jaus tucked her head under his chin, his arms going
around her, and as Liling accepted the embrace, the cottage
faded all around them.

She opened her eyes and found herself in Valentin's arms,
on the bed at the back of his plane. There was nowhere to go,
no place for her to retreat. They had been together. They
were sleeping together.

For a time she lay watching him. He should have looked
different, more vulnerable. When they slept men seemed to

lose that animal vitality that animated them; they all went slack-jawed and limp as they snored or grumbled and talked in their sleep as they tossed and turned.

Not Valentin. He didn't move or make a sound, his stillness and silence absolute. The set of his features appeared as compelling and obdurate as when he was awake.

Liling's gaze moved down to the terrible scar around his arm, made silver by the moonlight. It hurt her to look at the permanent reminder of his disability. Everything about him was so alive, except for his arm. No doubt his pride forced him to accept the limitation it imposed on him, but it would always be a burden he suffered.

Unless she could do something about it.

Something so difficult as this she had never before attempted; she feared it might overwhelm her. She also sensed that Jaus's pain merely began with his paralyzed arm. There was much more damage, and it lay in places she could not see or touch.

Still, she had to try. Not as repayment for what he had done for her, or as a gesture of sympathy. She had made a promise to Mrs. Chen to help as many as she could in secret. And after they parted, she wanted to know that Jaus was somewhere in the world, whole and happy.

Liling had seen television programs and movies, fictional surmises of what it was to take pain from another. She had read a hundred books on the subject. Most had been wrapped in the misconception that the pain was somehow deserved by the one taking it; that the transfer involved suffering, or some other nonsense.

If she had believed that, what she did would have killed her long ago.

Liling imagined a red swan spreading its wings. It was how Mrs. Chen had taught her to focus her thoughts when she prepared to take from another. She saw her fingertips glow faintly red as she made the space inside herself, and then placed her hand over his scar.

With great care she opened herself to him. Tiny charges of the curious energy contained by the body tingled against her palm, assuring that the connection between their pathways had been made.

The doctors had always wanted her to explain how she was able to do the things she had done as a child, but they could not feel the energy as she did. To them the charges were beeps on a machine or squiggly lines on a graph. To Liling, the body's energy was a flowing liquid river of color and sound, scent and taste. Sickness, disease, and pain disrupted the flow, diverted it, or blocked it altogether.

Liling took a deep breath and began to draw on that part of his flow she knew to be blocked by his pain.

Luring pain from his flesh to hers required patience and endurance. It did not come placidly, but sizzled hot and angry along her own pathways before emptying into the space she had made for it.

It was not the pain she expected, either. This pain was something quite different, a variety she rarely encountered. At first it came in an unwilling trickle, for the arm had been lifeless for some years. But the connection spread, waking long-dormant cells with the energy flowing through it, until Liling had increased his flow to a stream, and then a channel, and then a torrent.

More came, and her hand glowed bright red as she took it, enduring the heat funneling through her body, patiently directing it where it belonged, until the torrent became a flood, and the scarlet glow turned orange and spread up to her forearm, her elbow, her shoulder.

Taking didn't hurt, but his pain filled her until she

thought it might overwhelm her, in the same way water closed over the head of a drowning swimmer. At last the pain began to slow and taper off. She kept drawing it to her, determined to have the last of it, until the glow from her skin darkened and disappeared, and the connection ended.

Jaus's pain roiled inside her like a living thing, looking for a new place to fester. She reached inside herself and closed the space. It shrank, as it always did, collapsing in on itself until it felt no larger than a single spark. She took her hand away from his body, and the spark inside her winked out.

Liling rolled onto her back, exhausted. In his sleep, Jaus murmured something and reached for her, pulling her close.

She looked down at the arm holding her and smiled before she drifted off to sleep.

Kyan didn't attempt to intercept Valentin Jaus's plane at O'Hare, but arranged with his teacher a flight on a private jet. Thanks to a minor upheaval in the weather, Kyan's plane landed in Atlanta a full thirty minutes before the girl and Jaus would.

"Jaus is a billionaire entrepreneur who owns a great deal of property in the city," his teacher had warned him before Kyan had left Chicago. "Under no circumstances is he to be approached or involved."

"He pity her," Kyan told him. "She fool him, use him, escape me. Read dark girl tears."

"Someday, my boy, you are going to have to learn to speak proper English." His teacher sighed. "When you arrive in Atlanta, go with the attendant. He will take you where you need to be in order to capture her."

Now Kyan followed the attendant of the jet across the tarmac and into a hangar where a number of other chartered aircraft were stored. It seemed empty of people, until he smelled the salt of sweat and the breath of someone who had recently drunk grain alcohol. The sweat changed, became tainted with gun oil.

The attendant stopped walking as soon as Kyan did, and looked back. Sweat covered his face. "It's just over here."

Kyan seized the man by the back of the neck. "Liar." He turned him around and glanced down at the gun barrel the attendant pressed against Kyan's belly. "Why kill me?"

"You're a traitor, a thief, and you. . . ." The attendant choked on his own sweat as it began pouring over his nose and mouth. He dragged his sleeve across his face, soaking it, and then pulled the trigger.

His gun didn't fire. Water poured out of the barrel, bringing with it a bullet that fell to the concrete with a splash and a ping.

The attendant swore, and then grabbed at his skull. His hand came away with a fistful of his own hair. "What are you doing? I am Brethren."

"I Brethren too." Kyan stepped back and lifted his hand, which began to glow with an inhuman light. "Who tell you kill me?"

The man's eyes bulged out as the skin of his scalp and face began to tighten over his bones and then split. Red powder, not blood, spilled from his wounds. He tried to speak, but his teeth began crumbling in his mouth.

"Your water tell me." Kyan lifted his other hand, and the sweat and fluids from the attendant's body flew to hang suspended, swirling in the air between his palms.

The attendant's body shrank, his flesh peeling away from his bones as Kyan stripped every molecule of moisture from his body. The man died some time before his remains collapsed into a small pile of dust, and by then the water drawn from his body had formed a small tornado in front of Kyan.

He stepped into the vortex, allowing the water to soak him briefly before he dispersed it with a flick of his hand. The attendant had been a cold-blooded mercenary, a useful man of low rank in the order who had obeyed without question the orders issued to him by his superior, another brother unknown to Kyan.

His teacher would not have flown him to Atlanta merely to have him killed; he could have done that at any time in Chicago. The hit must have been ordered by Rome, by this new cardinal with the fondness for accounting and records. No one had advised him that it would take a great deal more than a lone assassin to kill Kyan.

He found an office with a telephone at the back of the hangar, and called Chicago. "Try kill me here."

"Is the assassin dead?"

"Yes." Kyan felt another presence, but it moved away before he could fathom anything about it. "Lightkeeper send. Angry I leave China."

"I can smooth things over with the cardinal, my son," his teacher assured him. "But we have a more pressing problem now."

Kyan looked at the pile of dust that had been a man. "Rome take girl?"

"No," his teacher said. "The plane she is on has disappeared."

Valentin untangled himself from Liling's arms and carefully got out of bed to dress. The girl murmured something and rolled over, her hair sifting over her bare shoulders and back. She never woke.

She would be tired, of course. He had used her long and hard, both for blood *and* sex.

He had taken advantage of her fear and vulnerability to take his pleasure of her. Yet he would swear that the thought of having sex with her or using her for food had never crossed his mind when he had offered her a seat on the plane. He had wished only to repay her for the kindness she had shown to Luisa. To help her as she had helped so many others. And, to be flatly honest, to help her leave Chicago, and by doing so eliminate the temptation she had brought into his life.

Instead, he had helped himself to her.

This was why he had avoided human females since his duel with Thierry Durand. Without hope of love, he had become a beast. The only satisfaction he wanted was that of the ravager, taking what he wanted and satisfying himself in flesh he had rendered docile and obedient.

As Liling had been for him this night.

He could still taste her blood, warm and sweet in his mouth. He had never feared losing control of himself in blood thrall to a human—he had too much self-discipline to allow it to happen—but if any female could lure him to that madness, it would be Liling Harper.

When she woke, Valentin would compel her to forget the incident. It would be cruel to leave her with the memories of what he had done to her. He had unleashed himself and taken her like a demon, denying her the gentleness and consideration she deserved. His bitterness over losing Jema and the use of his arm had brought him to the level of a mindless animal.

Even as he berated himself, he realized that while he had been with Liling, he had not once thought of Jema or his ruined limb. In fact, he felt changed. The burden of regret and sadness he'd carried no longer crushed him; he felt lighter, even hopeful.

Had this human female somehow exorcised the ghosts of his past, and healed the wounds of yesterday?

She had pleased him enormously. Valentin had known many women, but in all the centuries of bedding females as both human and Kyn, he had never once felt the pleasure Liling had given him. It was as if she had looked into places in his heart no one knew were there, and reached for them. Even when he had offered her the tenderness modern women craved, she had refused it.

She had gone into those places with him freely. Willingly. He would swear to it that she had.

That he still felt that deep and abiding satisfaction from the sex should have disgusted him. His pleasure had been at her expense, and he had made her pay in full. But as rough as he had been with her, he had given her something back. He knew it when she had shattered under his hand, and heard it in the drowsy words she had murmured just before she had fallen asleep against him, as open and trusting as she had come to his bed.

Would she despise him for how they had been together?

He got up from his seat to check on her, and halfway down the aisle he felt the plane lurch. He reached out and grabbed the top of a seat to brace himself, but the turbulence passed as soon as it had started. He ran a hand over his face and tightened his grip on the seat.

His gaze shifted down. He had taken hold and braced himself with his other hand. The hand of his paralyzed arm, which he could not lift more than an inch or two at best.

The plane rocked under his feet, and the world spun away from him as he stared at his arm. *"Zum Teufel."*

It took a moment for him to work up the courage to relax

his grip and straighten the limb. Carefully, almost fearfully, he lifted the useless hand up. His arm bent stiffly at the elbow, his tight muscles stretching with the movement, but he was able to touch the seat again.

His bones seemed to creak as he straightened and lifted it another time. His shoulder, accustomed to the hanging dead-weight, made a ticking sound as the joint flexed.

He could use his arm.

He spread his hand, clenching his teeth as the nerves under his skin began to burn and then sent a dull ache up into his forearm. The burning and aching soon disappeared, and the stiffness followed soon after.

The arm was not as it had been—it felt weak and trembled from the strain of movements it had not made for more than two years. But it moved and bent and obeyed his will.

Valentin tore off his jacket with both arms. He put it back on again with both arms. He used his dead arm alone to take it off and put it on a second time.

His paralyzed arm was alive again. Not as strong as his good arm, but a hundred times better than it had been. In his gut he knew that if he worked it, he could bring it back even more. Perhaps not as it had been before the duel, but with enough range of motion to make it impossible to call him a cripple.

He was not a man who believed in miracles or divine intervention. He had spent too many years devoting himself to an indifferent God to believe in such drivel. There had to be a logical explanation. He turned his head and stared at the back compartment. Liling had kissed his arm, and that strange sensation of warmth . . .

A ringing sound diverted his attention, and with a wry smile he used his now-usable arm to take his mobile phone from his jacket pocket. "Jaus."

"Master, it is Gregor," Sacher said, sounding worried. "Your signal is very poor. Have you landed yet?"

"No." Being with Liling, he had lost all track of time. "Call me on the in-flight phone."

"I tried, master, but the line is not working. I must tell you that the seigneur and his *sygkenis* are traveling from California to Chicago tomorrow night. They need your assistance in a matter concerning the order."

Jaus wondered what Michael would make of his miraculous recovery. "Prepare rooms for them. I will fly back tomorrow night."

"There is another matter I must tell you, master. Your pilot, Captain Speicher, was found murdered today. He was killed in the crew parking lot at O'Hare." Gregor's voice faded out, and then back in. ". . . know the pilot who replaced him."

Jaus was sorry to hear that; Speicher had been a good man and had served as his personal pilot for the last decade. "Gregor, the connection is very bad. I will call you as soon as we land."

The signal terminated before his *tresora* could reply.

Valentin decided to see to Liling, and checked his watch for the time. It was after midnight. He frowned. The plane should have landed in Atlanta thirty minutes ago. He pressed the intercom button on his seat console. "When are we arriving at the airport?"

No answer came over the cabin speaker.

Valentin walked up the aisle, through the galley, and opened the door to the cockpit. "Is this intercom not functioning?"

"No, sir, I'm sorry, it's not," the pilot said, glancing back at him. "The storm knocked out some of our equipment. I'll have it seen to as soon as we land."

He didn't recognize the man at all. "Were you assigned to replace Captain Speicher?"

"Yes, sir." The new pilot turned back to the control panel. "He didn't show up for the scheduled flight, so the flight supervisor called me in."

"He didn't show up because he was murdered today." Valentin glanced at the copilot, a friendly man named Fisher, with whom he had flown several times. The copilot didn't look back at him or comment on Speicher's untimely death. He sat with his head cocked to one side, staring out at the night. "Fisher? Are you sleeping?"

The copilot didn't move or reply.

Valentin walked up and shook his shoulder, and watched the copilot slowly fall forward in his harness, his neck at an unnatural angle.

He turned to the pilot and grabbed him by the throat. "Did you kill him?"

The frightened man's face turned red as he choked out, "Yes . . . broke . . . his . . . neck."

"Why?"

"Interfered." Pale brown eyes bulged. "Passed . . . approach . . . point . . . to . . . Atlanta."

"Why are you hijacking my plane?" he snarled, his *dents acérées* emerging to gleam long and sharp and white in his mouth.

"The girl . . . must . . . die."

"What?" Astonished, Valentin released the pilot, who wheezed in air as he fumbled with his harness. "You mean to kill Liling Harper?"

"The girl must die." The pilot coughed, doubling over, and then straightened suddenly, producing a pistol and pointing it at Jaus. "After I kill you."

Chapter 9

Liling woke as soon as Jaus slipped out of bed, but turned on her side and pretended to be asleep until he left the compartment. She needed time to prepare, to come up with some sort of explanation for throwing herself at him the way she had, and for what she had done to him while he was asleep.

She didn't know if her taking his pain had restored any function to his arm. She had never attempted such a taking, and the type of pain he suffered was not something a doctor could detect. If she had been successful, he would hardly expect her to take credit for it.

The unusual sex would not be as easy to explain away.

Who am I kidding? I loved it. I'm not sorry. I should thank the man for ruining every sexual fantasy I've ever had. Reality is so much better.

What they had done together had been outrageous and vivid and undeniable. Nothing in her experience compared to it. She still couldn't quite believe it had happened to her.

What will he think of me now?

Liling's body ached pleasantly as she inched off the bed and searched the floor for her clothes. She found her jeans and panties wadded up in a ball in one corner, and her shirt tangled up in the sheets. It wasn't until she looked down that she found her bra, still fastened and twisted around her waist.

God, she hadn't even been fully undressed.

She pulled it around and tugged the straps up over her arms. A sore spot made her wince; she felt it with her fingers and found two small puncture wounds in the curve between her shoulder and neck.

She vaguely remembered Valentin biting her, but not hard enough to break the skin. Had she bitten him back? She ran the tip of her tongue over her lips, which felt tender and slightly swollen, but didn't taste blood. She tasted man.

He was not the only one who might be changed by this night. She'd gone into the dark mirror with him, and come out a different woman. She felt no shame, no regret. She'd loved him, and it had been better than any of her lonely, pathetic little fantasies.

Now there was only sorrow that it was over, and that there could be nothing more between them. Even if he wanted to be with her again, she had to protect him. It wasn't only her life that was in danger; the priests wouldn't hesitate to hurt or kill Valentin to get to her.

He would forget her, and she would never see him again. That was how it had to be.

She still had a few minutes before the plane landed, and she was not going to spend them hiding from him. Her head throbbed painfully—a remnant of the taking, perhaps, although it had never had that effect on her before tonight. Liling dressed and went into the small bathroom adjoining the compartment to wash her face.

As the water ran over her hands, she stared at it. Her ears felt hollow with the absence of the bells. Each time she washed or dressed or ate, a part of her felt wrong because there were no bells signaling that it was time to do such things. The priests had trained her and all the other children to respond to them like dogs, so they wouldn't have to speak to them or be present to supervise their activities.

She hated the sound of bells, and still, she listened for them.

The pain throbbing in her temples made her look in the cabinets for a bottle of ibuprofen. She instead found several lipsticks, hairbrushes, and small bottles of perfume. All of them had been used.

The jealousy withering her heart surprised her. She wasn't the first woman he'd had on the plane, and she wouldn't be the last. Valentin was an extremely sensual man; he had a bedroom built into the back of his plane. Naturally he'd use it for something more than simply sleeping.

Idly she took out one of the bottles, a wildly expensive French perfume she could never have afforded, and uncapped it to take a sniff. The heavy floral scent had an unpleasant soapy undertone to it from the chemicals and agents used to boost the perfume's intensity. Why women felt the need to spray themselves with such odors to feel beautiful confused Liling. Certainly no garden ever smelled as vile as the perfumes created to mimic them.

She carefully replaced the bottle of perfume and closed the cabinet. If Jaus preferred women who wore French perfume and expensive makeup, then it was a good thing that she would have only this one night with him. She'd bore him to death in a week.

And she'd never again meet another man like him; she knew that. It had nothing to do with his wealth, his power, or the tragedy that had stolen the use of his arm from him. He wasn't like other men; in some fundamental way that defied explanation, he was much more. In a sense most men were as simple to understand as a page from an open book. They wanted attention and pleasure and gratification; they needed ways to channel their basic aggressions.

Liling knew from the taking that was not the case with Valentin Jaus. The depths inside him had felt like some well-guarded, secret library she would never be permitted to enter. Even when the lust had overtaken them and she had surrendered herself, he had been holding something back. Not to deceive her, but to protect her.

If only she didn't have to run. If only she could be like other women. But she could not let the priests capture her again.

Liling went out to the main cabin, ready to see him and talk with him, and perhaps even give him one last kiss before they parted. She could be as civilized about this as he was, and leave him without regret.

No regret he can see, she amended silently. She had a feeling that emotionally she was going to pay for this night for a long, long time.

The cabin was empty. Liling heard Valentin's and another man's voices coming from the front of the plane, and slowly walked up to the open door leading to the cockpit.

". . . can't fire that in here," Valentin was saying, his voice cold. "Hand it to me now and I will not harm you. I give you my word."

The pilot laughed. "The word of the *maledicti* means nothing."

Liling came up just behind Jaus before she saw the gun in the pilot's hand, and froze. The pilot was going to shoot Valentin.

The scent of camellias became smothering.

"Give it to me," Jaus repeated, holding out his hand.

The other man trembled all over, and then slammed his fist into his thigh. "The girl must die." He shouted something else in a strange language as he shoved a handle down.

The plane tilted sharply forward and began to hurtle down in a steep dive.

"God does not want your death," Valentin told him.

"No," the pilot said, his face contorted with pain. "He wants hers, and yours." He fired.

Valentin didn't move, but a sharp pain made Liling stagger backward. She grabbed an overhead handle and then screamed as the pilot reversed the gun, put the end in his mouth, and pulled the trigger.

The top of the pilot's head exploded, sending a horrific splash of blood and gore all over the window behind him.

Liling's fingers and legs went numb, and she found herself on the floor. She felt something wet and tried to straighten out her leg, then curled over with a sharp cry as the pain hit her. She pressed her hand to the hole in her shirt over her ribs and pulled it back soaked with blood.

"Stay there, Liling."

Valentin pulled the dead pilot's body out of the seat and took his place. He adjusted some of the controls, and the plane leveled out of the terrifying dive.

Liling panted and pressed her arm against the bleeding wound in her side. Somehow she had gotten shot; the bullet had missed Jaus. She watched through a haze of pain as Jaus moved the body of the pilot into a storage space behind the seat. He did the same with the copilot, who also hung limp and unmoving, his head flopping. Dread filled her as she glanced at the empty seats in front of the controls.

With both the pilot and the copilot dead, there was no one to land the plane.

"Liling." Valentin lifted her into his arms and carried her

to the copilot's seat. "I have put the plane on autopilot." He looked at the blood on his sleeve and pulled up her shirt, staring at the wound. "*Mein Gott*, the bullet hit you."

She swallowed and touched the bullet hole in his jacket over his heart. "I thought he only fired one shot."

"He did. It passed through my . . . jacket and struck you." He took off the jacket, folded it, and wrapped it around her torso. "I know it hurts, but you must be brave a little longer for me."

"Valentin." She clutched his arm. "Are they both dead?" He nodded. "Do you know how to land the plane?"

"I have watched the pilots do it several times. I will call for help on the radio." He bent over and kissed her. "Whatever happens, I *will* land this plane."

He put the copilot's seat harness over her and tightened it over her abdomen before he went back to the pilot's chair. There he put on the headset, checked the instruments, and flipped some switches. He took the headset off again and looked out into the night before he turned to her.

"I can't send or receive a signal," he said. "He must have disabled the radio."

She dug her fingers into the armrest as she fought a surge of pain. "Do you have a very good memory?"

"As it happens, I do." He thought for a minute, then reached into his trouser pocket, removing a small mobile phone. "My friend Gregor called me on this a short time ago. I might be able to use it to get help." He flipped it open and dialed a number, listening and then smiling at her before he began speaking in German.

Liling wondered vaguely what airport would have air traffic controllers who spoke German. She intended to ask Jaus when he finished his call, but he kept talking, and the burning in her side spread up her chest, stabbing into her lungs and heart.

She was dying. Mrs. Chen was dead. She had to tell him, to warn him.

"They took us when we were babies," she said as quickly as she could, turning her head from side to side as the fever spread. "They changed us like the others. Separated us. So angry."

"Liling?"

She looked into the cool blue heaven of his eyes. "I knew what they wanted. I wouldn't do it, Valentin. Something happened . . . the night they tried . . . to bring us together." Lightning flashed all around her, and she reached out to him. "If he finds us . . ."

He put his cool hand over hers. "What is it, *Geliebte*?"

"If he . . . finds us"—she gasped through heat—"kill me."

Phillipe of Navarre had served Michael Cyprien for centuries as his Kyn seneschal, and before that as his villein during their human lives in rural France. He had taken vows as a priest at Michael's side, and fought at his master's right hand during the holy wars.

No one could question his loyalty, or say that he did not know his duty. Over time, Phillipe had become the standard to which other Kyn lords compared their own men.

Although Phillipe was devoted to his master, he had not always liked Alexandra Keller. From the beginning he had had a bad feeling about the angry, brilliant petite physician he had abducted for Cyprien. Although she had been reputed to be the fastest reconstructive surgeon in the world, he had argued against bringing her to New Orleans to restore his master's pulverized face. Human females, in his opinion, served their purpose best as food and temporary amusement for Cyprien.

To allow one to use a scalpel on his master, after the horrific torture he had already endured . . . Unthinkable.

Now he could admit that part of his dislike of Alexandra had been jealousy. Phillipe, who had successfully protected his master for seven hundred years, had not been able to save him from the Brethren. The torture Michael had endured during his captivity in Rome had been Phillipe's fault. He had freed Cyprien, but there had been nothing he could do about the terrible wounds his master had suffered while imprisoned.

Then Alexandra had come, and in a single night had restored his master's face to what it had been before the Brethren had beaten and burned it away. Phillipe could not admire her skills with a knife. He had resented her, a human, for doing what he could not.

Or perhaps even then he had sensed how important she was to become to his master.

Time healed all manner of wounds, even the unworthy ones Phillipe had carried in his heart. Alexandra had not usurped the seneschal's place among Cyprien's household, even after she survived making the change from human to Kyn. She had rejected Michael, the Kyn, and even the enormous changes that transition had brought to her life. She had wanted to kill Michael. And while Phillipe worked diligently to prevent that, the anger they both felt had gradually become the foundation of a strange sort of bond between them, and then a friendship. He saw past his own jealousy to the sort of woman Alexandra Keller was, a woman who reminded him of the strong-minded sister he had lost so long ago. By the time Alexandra and his master had settled most of their differences, Phillipe knew he would have killed for her.

He only hoped the life he might have to take in order to protect her would not be that of her human brother.

Phillipe said nothing when Alexandra bullied John into accompanying them to the enormous suite Phillipe had arranged at a small, exclusive hotel overlooking the bay. Cyprien had instructed him to watch John Keller closely, but to intervene only if he proved to be dangerous to Alexandra.

"Finally, I have a reason to order room service," Alexandra said after they arrived in the suite. "John, go get cleaned up and I'll order some breakfast for you."

Phillipe used his own mobile phone to call the hotel manager, and issued a set of instructions before he went into the master's room. He was glad now that he had packed some of the garments Cyprien had purchased for John, as the man looked worse than he smelled. He took them into John's room and placed them on the foot of the bed. He gathered up the pile of crumpled, odorous clothes the human had shed, bagged them, and took them to the service room at the end of the hall to throw them down the garbage chute.

Cyprien met him in the hall on his way back. "You checked his clothes? It has not changed?" When Phillipe shook his head, he glanced at the door to the suite. "She does not realize."

The scent humans shed was not like that of the Kyn; even when it was as pungent as John Keller's clothing was, it had no power to do anything except offend the nose. But most Kyn were sensitive to changes in human scent, and used them to gauge their emotional state. Fear soured their scent, and hatred turned it rotten.

Alexandra's brother had been behaving oddly since returning from Ireland, but one disturbing change had occurred, one that neither Cyprien nor Phillipe could account for.

John Keller's scent had disappeared.

"Alexandra does not hunt, and her mind is on other things when she is with her brother," Phillipe said. "She would not recognize the difference." He hesitated. "Master, could he be trying to hide it by going unwashed and wearing soiled garments?"

"How could he know to mask it?" Cyprien rubbed his eyes. "You will not leave him alone with her until I decide what is to be done."

"She loves him," Phillipe said as they walked back to the suite. "Perhaps you should tell her now, before action must be taken."

Cyprien looked at the waiter rolling an enormous cart toward their rooms. It was stacked with dozens of plates of food. "Not yet, my friend."

The long, hot shower helped revive John. As he dried off, he noticed that his overgrown, scraggly beard had begun to thin out against his cheeks. No wonder the drifter in town had thought he was a homeless drunk.

Hightower would be expecting to see him with a beard, John thought. He took a pair of fingernail scissors from the hotel's large basket of complimentary toiletries and trimmed it close to his face, and then shaved off the remainder.

He found a new suit and shirt in his size lying in a plastic garment bag on the end of the bed, as well as a pair of boxers and socks and shoes. He didn't have to check the tags to know they were designer tailored garments; Kyn didn't dress in off-the-rack. For a moment he was tempted to put on the clothes he had been wearing—they might be dirty and cheap, but they were his—until he saw that they had vanished.

Alex was pouring coffee into a delicate porcelain cup when he came out of the bedroom. "You should have been a girl. You take forever in the bathroom." She looked up and the pot wobbled in her hand. "Holy shit, what happened to the beard?"

"It was time to get rid of it." He rubbed his chin. "Feels a little strange."

"I hardly recognized you. Jesus, how much weight have you lost?" When he shrugged, she pointed toward the table. "Get over here and grab a fork, pal."

"In a minute. Were you able to contact Jaus in Chicago?" he asked as he went to the glass doors leading out to the balcony.

"Val went down to Atlanta for a couple of days, but his *tresora* said he'll be back by Friday." She came over and closed the curtains he had just opened. "If you don't mind, daylight makes my eyes itch."

"Sorry, I forgot." He went over to the dining table, then stopped in his tracks. Plates crammed every inch of it with enough food to feed an entire camp of lumberjacks. "Dear God, Alexandra, I can't eat all this."

"I didn't know what you wanted, so I ordered one of everything on the menu." She glared at him. "Don't give me that what-about-the-starving-children-in-China look, either. *You're* starving."

After what had happened with the drifter, the amount of food before him killed what little appetite John had. "You could have simply asked me what I wanted."

"True," she said. "Tell you what: I'll have what's left

over put in bags and taken to the nearest homeless shelter. Okay?"

She would, too. Alex may have changed, but she still remembered what it was to be hungry. "Okay."

She handed him the coffee. "Eat."

Liling slumped in the chair, still muttering in her delirium. Valentin knew blood loss could cause humans to go into shock, but her skin was hot to the touch, and she had said her wound was burning. The other things she had said, disjointed as they were, had sounded equally as ominous.

He couldn't worry about the man who frightened her so much she would rather die than have him find her. He had to get this plane down before she bled to death.

His mobile phone rang, and Gregor told him that he was putting Jonas Frank, one of the standby pilots, on the line.

"Talk quickly," Jaus told Frank. "I may lose this signal any moment. Tell me where the nearest airport is, and how I am to land this plane."

"Sir, if the readings you gave your assistant are correct, you don't have enough fuel to make it to an airport," Frank said bluntly. "You'll have to make an emergency landing. Let's review the procedures you'll follow to bring the plane down safely."

Jaus listened as the pilot told him step-by-step how to use the instruments to make the landing. He repeated them back to Frank's satisfaction.

"Your signal is starting to fade. Find an open, flat road or a clearing for your approach," the pilot said. "We're sending search and—" The line went dead.

Valentin tried to call back, only to discover that his battery had run too low.

Storm clouds were closing around the plane, pelting the

windows with tiny hail. He had dropped altitude to move the plane out of the commercial airline lanes, as he could not receive any radio transmissions to change course. Outside it was still night, but Jaus's Kyn eyes could easily make out the features of the land below.

Wherever the dead pilot had flown them, they were over what appeared to be uninhabited forests, rivers, and lakes. No towns or houses appeared, increasing his frustration. He couldn't land in a deserted area. Liling needed to be taken to a hospital.

The storm lashed the plane with rain and buffeted it with ferocious wind gusts at the same time a low-fuel indicator light blinked on. Valentin couldn't risk running out of fuel or being forced down by high winds. Some miles ahead, he saw a narrow but cleared area stretching out in front of a large lake, and decided that would be his landing site. He disengaged the autopilot and began guiding the plane down.

As he descended, he reduced airspeed and went through instrument procedures, methodically following the instructions that the pilot had given him. He was only too aware that one mistake would end in disaster, and looked over at Liling. She had already been seriously hurt by the bullet that had gone through his body.

He would not crash. He would not snuff out her young life.

The meadow was not meant to be a landing strip, and the plane jolted and rocked as the landing gear touched the ground. He applied the brakes, slowing the plane as quickly as he dared, seeing the lake looming in front of them.

There was not enough meadow, he realized too late, and at the last moment released his harness and lunged across the cockpit, covering Liling's body with his.

The plane gave a sickening lurch as it ran out of land and

slid over the banks into the lake. The windows of the cockpit imploded, water blasting in through the broken frames.
A support frame broke loose and slammed into Jaus, knocking him away from the girl. The surge of water flooding the
cabin swept him off into the darkness.

Chapter 10

Water filling her nose jerked Liling awake. The interior of the cockpit had flooded with dark, cold water. She tore off the seat harness and turned to see the dead bodies of the pilot and copilot floating up toward the ceiling of the plane. A glint of golden hair between them made her push off the seat and dive under the water.

Jaus floated beneath the surface, limp and unmoving, bleeding from deep cuts on his face and hands.

A torrent of air bubbles escaped Liling's mouth as she called his name without thinking. She kicked her way up to the dwindling air pocket, gasping as she refilled her lungs, and then dove under a second time. Keeping her gaze averted from his face, she tugged at the tangle of equipment trapping his body.

It took three tries before the pile of debris shifted and she was able to pull him free. She put an arm across his chest and kicked, swimming up to push his face into the air pocket and surfacing beside him.

Jaus was not breathing.

"No." She dragged him by the collar to the cockpit emergency exit. The pressure of the water had knocked out the door, and through it she saw the lake bank some two hundred feet away. She pushed Jaus's body through the open door frame and into the water. From there she swam on her back, using her legs to propel her while towing Jaus in front of her. Oily water swirled as the sinking plane completely submerged.

A few feet from solid ground Liling's heels scraped the silted bottom of the lake, and she stood and dragged Jaus's body the rest of the way out of the water.

"Help, someone, please," she called out. The land around them appeared uninhabited, but the pitch-black conditions made it hard to see exactly where they were.

She wasted no more time shouting but rolled Jaus onto a grassy section of the bank. She had to stop and pant through a stabbing pain twisting in her side, and then she remembered what had happened in the cockpit. She pulled up her soaked T-shirt to check the wound. Where there had been an ugly, ragged-edged bleeding hole in her side there now appeared to be smooth, wet skin.

The gunshot wound had vanished.

Liling looked at Jaus, who had not been so lucky. Dozens of ugly cuts and scrapes covered his face, and when she felt for it she couldn't find a pulse in his throat. She would worry about the wounds after she got his heart started and his lungs working. Thank God one of the requirements of her job at the Lighthouse had been to take a course and become CPR certified.

"You landed the plane, Valentin," she said to him as she tipped his head back. "We're safe. So you can't give up now."

Liling opened his mouth to check whether his airway was clear, and listened for sounds of breathing. His chest remained still, and she heard nothing. She pinched his nose shut, took a deep breath, and sealed her mouth over his. She blew hard, twice, trying to force her breath, into his body.

She lifted her head. "Breathe for me, Valentin. Please breathe."

She straightened, checked his throat again, and listened. Nothing had changed. She tore open his shirt and found the lower part of his breastbone, crossing her hands against it as she began to push down, performing the cardiac compressions. After fifteen compressions, she still found no heartbeat. She bent to put her mouth over his, and then stopped. At first she didn't believe what she was seeing, but she put her fingers to it. When she felt it happening, she had to believe.

The gashes and cuts on Jaus's face were closing and disappearing, as if they were erasing themselves from his skin.

No human being healed that fast, not even when Liling touched them to take from them. She shook her head, sure she was hallucinating, and pinched his nose before forcing her breath into him twice more. This time when she sat up the lacerations were only a few fading pink lines on his flesh, and his eyes were opening.

"Valentin." She rolled him onto his side as he choked out lake water, supporting him with her hands as he shuddered and cleared his lungs. He didn't gasp or make any breathing sounds, and she was about to flip him over to breathe again for him when he pushed himself up into a sitting position and turned to her.

Wet hair hung around his face, which now didn't have a mark on it.

She felt stupid, as if she had forgotten or missed something important. What she had seen on his face must have been only streaks of blood. The burning in her side flared, making her grimace as she pressed her hand to her ribs.

"Liling." She saw in his eyes the same confusion she felt. "What has happened?"

"I don't know. I must have blacked out." She tried to smile. "What do *you* remember?"

"Landing the plane." He turned his head and spit out a mouthful of water before finally breathing in. "I did not do it very well. Forgive me."

"For saving my life?" She wanted to laugh and hug him and dance around the meadow. She settled for brushing the wet hair back from his eyes. "You landed the plane, and we survived. You don't have to apologize for that." She dropped her gaze and swallowed against the tightness in her throat. "I thought we were going to die."

"I keep my promises." Valentin caught her hand and brought her palm to his mouth, placing a gentle kiss in the center of it. He closed her fingers over the tingling spot and pulled her suddenly into a tight embrace, holding her as close as he could.

Liling wanted to shriek with happiness. He was using his arm. The taking had worked.

As if he heard her thoughts, he said, "I do not know what you did to me, *mein Mädchen.*" He put her at arm's length to look into her eyes. "But now I can hold you as I have wanted to."

She started to deny it, but his touch burned strangely into her, and she couldn't find the words to lie to him. "Valentin."

He tipped her head back. "It is my turn, I think, to kiss you."

Valentin brought his mouth to hers. The kiss felt weightless, the brush of a tendril of breeze against her lips. He took her deeper, coaxing her lips apart and tracing their edges before pushing into her mouth. The slow glide of his tongue against hers made her sigh with pleasure, the sound catching and humming between their lips.

Her hands crept up his chest and stilled. She couldn't feel his heartbeat, and then she could, a single pulse. An eternity passed before the next thudded against her fingers.

Fearful again, she pulled back. "Something is wrong. Your heart is hardly beating." She touched his neck, searching for the pulse.

"I am not like other men." Valentin took her hand away before he stood and scanned the entire area.

Liling didn't understand. He had virtually no heartbeat, but he moved and talked and breathed as if nothing were happening to him. Adrenaline did odd things to people, she knew, and while he appeared fine now, he might collapse at any moment. Her anxiety doubled as she felt the pain in her side return. How could she find help for him if she couldn't catch her breath?

He crouched down again beside her. "We have to find some shelter. I think I saw a house or a barn over there, by the pine trees. Can you walk?"

"I don't think so." Liling gritted her teeth as the heat blazing across her ribs doubled. "I have a cramp in my side. You had better leave me here for now."

"I am not leaving you anywhere, *mein Mädchen*." He frowned, catching her shoulder. "Liling?"

She tried to push him away, but the pain flared up into an inferno that she thought would burn away the world, and Valentin with it.

A hammering fist made Jayr, the newly named suzeraina of the Realm, lift her mouth from the place she had been kissing on her seneschal's shoulder. She turned her head toward the sound of it outside their bedchamber. "Did you bolt that door?"

"No." Aedan mac Byrne, former suzerain of the Realm, nuzzled her throat. "But I will strangle the first man who walks over the threshold."

"Better you learn how to lock it." She climbed off his lap, pulled on a robe, and went to open the door. "What?"

Rain, a hulking bear of a man with the personality of a mischievous boy and the temperament of a kitten, grinned down at her.

"I did not wish to interrupt while you are training your new man, my lady"—he neatly caught the edge of the door before she could slam it in his face—"but there is a problem that requires your attention."

"Indeed." She gave him a pointed look. "Will someone die or the Realm burn to the ground if I do not attend to it for another hour or two?"

"Three hours," Aedan called out. "If you wish her coherent, make it four."

Rain looked innocently at the ceiling. "It is Locksley, my lady. He says it is an emergency involving Suzerain Jaus."

Robin often made jests, but not about other Kyn. She wished Byrne would let her keep a telephone in their chambers, but he had been adamant about keeping the human technology he hated out of their bedroom. "Have the call forwarded to the office. We will be there in a minute."

Rain nodded and then looked down. "Jayr." His brow furrowed. "When did you grow breasts?"

Jayr closed the door in his face before she walked over to the armoire to retrieve some clothes. Byrne reached it before her and leaned back against it.

His garnet red hair framed a strong face covered with

dark blue tattoos and a smug smile. "It is my duty as your seneschal to dress you."

"You can never seem to finish the task." She nudged him aside and reached for a shirt and trousers, pausing and taking one of her new dresses. Tall and lean, Jayr had made the change from human to Kyn in the fourteenth century, before her body had finished making its natural mortal transition from girl to woman. Now, thanks to Alexandra Keller and the treatments she had administered, Jayr had small but mature breasts, curved hips, and a more feminine appearance. "Rob would not call if it were not important."

"Aye, he would." Byrne bent down to press a hard kiss on her mouth. "Rob wanted you and the Realm for himself. He is a poor loser."

"He is our closest Kyn ally," she reminded him, "and your best friend." She pulled the frock over her head, tugged it down, and straightened the skirt. She gave her smiling lover a pointed look. "Do you need my assistance to dress?"

"No, but when we come back," he warned as he grabbed his own garments, "I am barricading that door."

A few minutes later Jayr and a scowling Byrne walked from their chamber in the private wing to the business offices. Knight's Realm, which the humans of central Florida knew as a medieval-themed tourist attraction, was run and inhabited by Darkyn men and women who had actually lived during the Middle Ages.

Jayr was proud of how well the men of her *jardin* had adjusted to the recent changes in rule. Byrne, who had been suzerain of the Realm since building the Kyn stronghold, had stepped down. Michael Cyprien, the Kyn seigneur, had named Jayr, Byrne's seneschal, to serve as the very first female to rule over a *jardin*.

Some of the more conservative *jardin* outside the Realm

still didn't approve of the notorious switch, nor of the appointment of a female to such a position of power. That Jayr and Byrne had also become lovers had been viewed as utterly scandalous by the traditionalists among their kind.

But Jayr had proven her honor and her worth at the past winter tournament to the satisfaction of everyone who had attended, and they were loud with their praise of her. As for those who still grumbled, none dared to publicly speak out against the suzeraina, not after what Byrne had done to the men who had tried to kill both him and Jayr during the annual gathering.

Harlech, Jayr's second, was waiting for them outside the business office.

"I regret that we had to disturb you, my lady." Harlech, her most loyal supporter, emphasized her title with a certain amount of relish. "But Lord Locksley was most insistent on speaking with you."

Jayr nodded, then went in and put the call on the telephone speaker. "Good evening, Lord Locksley. How may we be of service?"

"Jayr, Byrne. I apologize for the lateness of my call." Locksley, usually cheerful and charming, sounded grim. "Suzerain Jaus was flying down to visit my *jardin* tonight when his plane was hijacked by a Brethren operative."

"Have you contacted Chicago, lad?" Byrne asked.

"They informed me after Jaus contacted them by mobile phone," Locksley said. "It seems the hijacker murdered Jaus's regular pilot, took his place, and killed the copilot. When Jaus confronted him, he killed himself. Jaus called and asked to speak with a pilot who could give him instructions on how to land the plane."

"Dear God." Jayr couldn't imagine such a nightmarish

scenario. "Where is the plane now? Has he attempted the landing yet?"

"We don't know. Hold for a moment; Scarlet has just handed me a fax from Chicago." The line went silent for several moments. "The last time the plane appeared on flight-control radar, it was in the vicinity of the Georgia-Florida border. It disappeared shortly thereafter, along with the signal from the mobile phone Jaus was using to talk to the instructor pilot." There was the sound of paper crumpling. "They do not know if he was able to land the aircraft."

"What can we do now, Rob?"

"Assemble your trackers and send out search teams," Locksley said. "Monitor local news reports. Humans may find the plane before we do, so be prepared to move quickly to retrieve the suzerain. I will send twenty of my best trackers down to you to aid in the search."

"Have Jaus's men inquire as to how much fuel the plane carried," Byrne suggested, "and how far it could have flown before running out. That may narrow our search area."

"I will, thank you, Aedan," Locksley said. "Jaus's *tresora* told me one more thing: There is a human female on board with him. She may or may not be part of this attempted hijacking. Contact me as soon as you have any new information, and I will do the same. Good luck, my friends." Locksley ended the call.

"You sure you know how to handle a boat by yourself, boy?" the owner of the charter boat service asked, squinting at Kyan again. "Rivers 'round here get a mite tricky, 'specially if you've never fished 'em."

"I know river." Kyan didn't have enough English to tell the middle-aged white man how many boats he owned in

China; nor did he care to explain himself. He breathed in, the man's sweat filling his nose.

Fragments of thought and images flooded Kyan's head. *Damn economy . . . doing the best I can.* The man in the back office, a stack of invoices in front of him, worried as he talked on the phone. *Heart attack . . . HMO . . . Democrats. . . Billy.* A cluttered, dismal trailer. Portrait of a dead wife. A son in an army uniform. More invoices.

From those disjointed thoughts and images Kyan knew the man was not greedy, only struggling to keep from losing his business to his creditors. Kyan peeled off another dozen bills from his roll of the unfamiliar currency, adding it to the stack before saying the two words the man wanted to hear. "Security deposit."

"All right, then. Long as you're sure." The man scooped up the money and tucked it into his till before handing over the keys and a business card. "You call me if you can't make it back by Friday. I got this boat rented out for some weekend warriors think they know where all the bass are, dumbass fools." He chuckled. "If you're late, even ten minutes, it'll be an extra five hundred. I can't afford to lose the business."

Kyan nodded and walked out to the dock, where seven boats in various sizes and conditions were moored. He'd chartered the largest mainly because it had the most powerful outboard motor, as well as a tiny cabin with a bunk. Once he was on the water, he planned to dock only to refuel, get supplies, and kill the girl.

He spotted a pay phone and debated over whether or not to report in. This was his business, not theirs. At the same time, he had an old obligation to fulfill.

He dialed the number.

"Where are you?" his teacher demanded at once.

"In Florida, on river." He hated speaking English, but his teacher could not understand Chinese. "I track her water."

"Give me your exact location."

"Trace call." Kyan felt impatient that his teacher would use such tactics to stall him. "You no interfere. She mine."

"The plane went down," his teacher said harshly. "How do you know that she's still alive?"

"Always know." He hung up the phone.

Kyan released the mooring lines before he stepped onto the deck and checked the motor and fuel before taking the boat out the narrow channel to the St. Johns River.

Even in spring Florida was warm and humid, and the river water was muddy with runoff and pollution. Kyan didn't mind. It was the water, not the condition of it, that mattered to him. He never felt at ease on land, and the hours he had wasted tracking her from Chicago to Atlanta to this place had left him tense and irritable.

Kyan stopped in the afternoon for fuel at a small pier. He tied the boat to the dock and waited, but no attendant came out to the pumps. Kyan knew he could find the girl, but he had already tired of making himself understood to Americans. He didn't have the time or patience to read every person he met.

"It's self-serve, buddy," a fair-haired girl called from the window of a shack at the end of the pier.

Kyan didn't understand the words, so he secured the boat and jumped up onto the pier. The shack, little more than an aluminum shed with hand-lettered pricing signs, sold worms and bait for fishermen. The young girl inside was reading a textbook and writing in a spiral-bound notebook.

He took out the small book of English phrases that he had bought at the airport in Chicago.

"Dude, you are so going to get your butt kicked if you use a phrase book on this river," the girl said without looking up, and then translated her own words by repeating them in his native language.

Kyan frowned. "You speak Chinese."

"Uh-huh." She kept reading.

She was young, tanned, and hardly more than a teenager. It didn't make sense that she would speak his tongue. Did she have a phrase book? "You know Chinese how?"

She lifted her face, revealing Caucasian features and Asian-shaped blue eyes. "My grandmother taught me." Her lips bowed as she subjected him to a slow, thorough inspection of her own. "Wah-how-how."

Kyan gave up trying to speak to her in English. "I do not know what that means."

"It means, *Dude*, you are *gor*geous." She looked over him again and fanned herself with her hand. "Jet Li and Keanu Reeves all wrapped up in one great big yummy package."

People of mixed blood were considered inferior in China, and Kyan didn't care to be compared by this American to film stars. Still, the blend of East and West in her open, smiling face was somewhat intriguing, even if the Caucasian curves on her petite Asian frame were a bit too generous.

"Like what you see?" she asked, pulling back her shoulders. "Or are you like all these other guys and just want some worms?"

"I am not fishing." He inspected the shack. It looked like the sort of thing a refugee constructed out of scrap salvaged from trash heaps. It also smelled like it. "Your family, they own this . . . ?" He gestured at the shack.

She shook her head. "My parents live up north with my little brother. I just work here part-time on weekends to make some spending money." She sighed. "It's spring break, so I'll be here for an entire week. I need the money, but it's beyond boring."

Her complaints sounded childish. He had watched young women work themselves into unconsciousness on some of the collective farms in China. "You should get another job."

"But then I wouldn't have met you." She opened and closed her eyelids rapidly. "Maybe you could stop by later, when I get off work. We could go get a drink in town or something."

Her American accent made her Chinese sound very odd, but he could understand her perfectly. He might be able to use her. "Why are you here and not with your family?"

"School." She lifted her textbook up to show him the cover, revealing that it was a volume on economics. "I'm a junior at Stadlin University. It's about five miles that way." She pointed west.

Kyan didn't care for the way she spoke to him. She was too forward, too disrespectful. She gave out information too willingly. Her smile was too easy. And her breasts were definitely too large.

"Okay, so you obviously don't want to get a drink. The only other thing I've got are these." She lifted up a plastic container filled with a writhing pink mass. "The guys say the fish have been biting pretty good out in the basin. We rent poles and tackle, too."

"No, thank you." He would have to read her, and for that he would have to touch her. "What is your name?"

"Melanie Wallace." She pushed back her shoulders again. "My friends call me Mel. What's your name?"

"I am Lí Kyan." He held his hand through the open window.

The girl took it awkwardly, as if she were not accustomed

to such polite contact. "Are you, like, always this stiff with people, or is it just your first day in the U.S.?"

Kyan could not take anything from the faint sheen perspiration on her skin; she happened to be one of the small percentage of people whom he could not read. Not that the thoughts of a student would be of particular interest to him. She spoke both English and Chinese, however, and she was American-born. She would be able to speak for him and explain things to him.

"I need a translator," he said, holding on to her hand. "Will you come with me on my boat today?"

"I make six-fifty an hour just sitting here in this sweatbox." She eyed the container of worms. "Can you pay me seven?"

He released her hand and took some of the bills from the roll in his pocket, handing them to her.

"Yikes." Her eyes widened, but then she shook her head and opened the side door to the shack, coming out onto the pier with him. "Here." She handed most of the bills back to him. At his blank look, she added, "You just handed me a thousand dollars, dude. I'd have to work for you, like, forever to earn that." She fluttered her eyelids again. "Unless you want me to do something else with my mouth."

Kyan inspected her, hiding his distaste. She was perhaps a foot shorter than he was, and dressed in a thin white shirt stamped with the name of her university. The short pink pants she wore were skintight and reached only her knees. On her feet were thongs showing off toenails with yellow and pink flowers painted on them. Small rhinestones flashed at the center of each flower. Her breasts bobbed unrestrained under the shirt, and the shadows of her nipples showed clearly through it.

If they had been in China, she would have been arrested. He told her that.

"Really?" she said, deliberately striking a provocative pose. "Do you think I'd get a cute Chinese cop to frisk me? Would they strip-search me?"

"It is not funny." Neither was the fact that he would have an image of his own hands stripping the clothes from her rudely healthy American body for the rest of the day.

"Come on, dude, I'm just kidding." Her breasts shook with her laughter. "How can such a cute guy like you be so uptight?"

"My name is Kyan, not 'dood,'" he told her. "You are coming with me?"

She went back into the shack, shoved her books in a large tote bag, and came out, kicking the door shut behind her. Her fetching smile made dimples in her cheeks. "Let's go."

Chapter 11

"Richard Gere was right," Alexandra murmured as Valentin Jaus's driver skillfully drove the *jardin* limousine through the complicated mesh of downtown traffic. "If I'm going to die, let it be on Chicago concrete."

Being back in the city tore at Alex. She had accepted that she could never go back to the life she'd had as a human reconstructive surgeon, not until she found the cure for the Kyn pathogen. Assuming that there was one to be found. As her recent tests with heat indicated, the pathogen responsible for their mutation might be indestructible.

Then there was the small problem of giving up the incredible benefits of being Darkyn. She'd had them only a few years, but already she'd grown accustomed to being able to heal quickly and having the strength of ten men. Even her talent, the ability to read the murderous thoughts of both humans and Kyn, often came in handy.

Michael's long, sensitive fingers entwined with hers. "Do you still miss it?"

"Why should I? I was only born here, and grew up in this city, and met all of my friends here, and opened my first practice not five blocks from this spot." She sat back as they passed the hospital from which Michael Cyprien's men had abducted her. "What's to miss?"

John stared out the window. "We weren't born here."

"What?" Alex surged upright. "It says so right on my birth certificate—"

"We didn't have birth certificates. The church filed for the ones the state issued for us." Contempt colored his voice as he added, "They put that we were born in Chicago so it would be easier for the Kellers to adopt us."

Alex couldn't quite believe that he had never informed her of this stunning fact. "Then mind telling me where we were born?"

"I don't know," John admitted. "I was only a few years old when we came here."

"When our parents brought us here?"

Her brother's expression turned to stone. "Alexandra, I don't want to talk about this now."

"You never want to talk about it." And he wouldn't say another word on the subject; Alex knew that much from past experience. "I'm a big girl now, John, if you haven't noticed. I can handle whatever it is you've been keeping from me all these years."

John didn't reply.

"Just like the good old days."

"Alexandra," Michael said. "Your brother is tired. Leave him alone."

"Sure." Why was Cyprien defending John?

She brooded in silence until they drove past the dignified front entrance of the Shaw Museum.

"Have you heard from Thierry and Jema lately?" she asked Michael.

"I have been trying to persuade Thierry to take up suzerainty of the Carolina territories," he said. "He and Jema have bought a home there, so he may be coming around. They are staying with Locksley as they finalize the arrangements on the property."

Alex thought of the last time she had seen Jaus, standing alone in the moonlight. "Did anyone bother to warn Val that they were there before he left to go see Grandpa's sword?"

Now Michael tried to give her the stone face. "I'm certain that Locksley is aware of the tension between Valentin and Thierry."

"Oh, no." Alex groaned. "Please tell me you didn't set this up."

"I may have suggested to Locksley that it is time for Valentin and Thierry to reconcile their differences." He shrugged.

"So Robin's playing vampire peacemaker. Great." She thumped her head back against the seat.

"My suzerain are quite capable of sorting out their differences," he said. "Why does this upset you?"

"Hasn't Val been through enough?" Alex demanded. "He infected Jema, and he fought for her, and he lost her. To Thierry. Who, in the process of fighting over her, permanently disabled him. Do you have to rub his nose in it like this?"

"This is not merely about Jema, *chérie.* I need my lords paramount united. Personal resentments must be set aside for the greater good of our kind." He gave her a pointed look. "As we both witnessed during the tournament at the Realm, these old grudges can lead to disaster."

"The old grudges?" Incredulous, she stared at him. "Michael, in Kyn time, this whole thing with Jema happened, like, ten minutes ago. Val has been a mess ever since. You really think he's going to kiss and make up with Thierry for the good of the team? The guy stole his girl. The guy cut off his *arm*."

"Which you repaired."

"Which I sewed back on," she corrected. "Val can't use it. He's a walking slot machine minus the cherries. Every time he tries to reach for something, or clap his hands, or do the wave, he's reminded of that duel, and losing Jema. I'm surprised the guy hasn't completely cracked up by now."

"Jaus is a strong man."

"That's the other problem," she pointed out. "That damned Austrian pride of his. What if these little peace talks you've set up end in another duel? You guys love duels. I've never seen more duel-happy idiots. And I won't be there to sew the body parts back on this time."

"Sacher said Jaus would be returning to Chicago tonight to meet us, so there will be no time for duels, reconciliation, or anything else." He gave her a mildly exasperated look. "I know that Valentin cared for Jema, but I think you are exaggerating the situation. She was only a human female."

"*Only* a human female?" Alex echoed. "Like how I was *only* a human female when you kidnapped me, forced me to operate on you, and then infected me with a pathogen that turned me into a blood-dependent mutant who can't help reading the minds of killers?"

Michael winced. "Point taken."

"Val had Jema watched around the clock. He also had pictures taken of her every day for years. He covered an entire wall in his bedroom with them. I saw it when I went to talk to him. And I'm sure you remember the five guys he pounded into the ground when we found out the human female wasn't being treated for juvenile diabetes. We even stood there and watched him do it." She smiled at him.

"Baby, if that's not obsessive love, it's a damn good imitation."

His eyes took on an amber gleam. "Why *did* you go to talk to Jaus in his bedchamber that night?"

"He needed a friend." She saw his reaction and laughed. "Not that kind of friend. Just someone to talk to. Why are you jealous? Despite all the shit you've done to me, I love you. Val is your strongest supporter. You were there. You know nothing happened between us."

His mouth tightened. "I don't care to know that you deliberately went to be alone with him in his bedchamber."

She poked his chest with her finger. "Then you have a pretty good idea how Val feels every time he sees Jema with Thierry. And he knows a lot more than talking happens in *their* bedchamber."

Michael sighed. "Will we ever have a disagreement where you are wrong and I am right?"

"No, because I'm always right." Her gaze shifted to John, who had fallen asleep. She lowered her voice. "Before we try to do this thing with Hightower, I need to check my brother over. He's exhausted, he has no appetite, and he's lost way too much weight."

Valentin Jaus was not waiting to meet them at Derabend Hall, however, when they arrived at the lakeshore mansion. A young, dark-haired man came to the car to greet them formally.

"Welcome to Chicago, seigneur. I am Sacher." He clicked his heels together and bowed smartly, first to Michael, then to Alex and John. "My lady. Sir." He turned to Michael again. "Seigneur, we have a situation—"

"Willie, why did you not tell me they had arrived?" a gravelly voice called out from the front of the mansion, interrupting the young man.

Wilhelm grimaced. "My grandfather has not yet stepped down, seigneur. He is very proud, and my master loves him as much as I. With your permission . . ."

"I understand, Wil." Michael smiled as Jaus's elderly *tresora* shuffled out to the car. "Gregor, it is good to see you. I trust you have things well in hand here."

"Seigneur, thank God you are here." The elder Sacher bowed stiffly. "There has been a terrible incident involving my master, and we are desperately in need of your guidance and assistance. Please come inside."

Sacher and his grandson led them to a reception room that had been transformed into a command center. Several humans and Kyn were poring over maps, while others were on phones and computer terminals. The atmosphere was tense, even when all the Kyn stood and bowed to Cyprien.

Alex listened as the old man related the murder of Jaus's pilot, and the phone calls from the plane. The thought of Val alone at the controls trying to land by himself made her sick.

"The pilot who spoke to Valentin, where is he?" Michael asked.

"Here." A small, wiry-looking man in a flight jacket came around the table and sketched a bow before offering his hand. "Jonas Frank, Seigneur. I reviewed the landing procedures with Suzerain Jaus."

As Michael talked with the pilot, Alex noticed John slipping out of the conference room. She followed him outside, where she stopped him.

"Hey." She stepped in front of him. "Where do you think you're going?"

His dark eyes shifted toward the mansion. "Your friends have problems, and I don't want to get in the way. I'll have the driver take me to a hotel in town."

She glowered. "You're not leaving."

"Jaus is the only one who can force the truth about the Brethren breeding centers out of Hightower," he said. "Without him, there's no point in trying."

"It's time we talked about exactly what happened to us when we were kids. And don't give me any more of your bullshit." When he turned away, she grabbed his arm. "I saved your ass from that psychotic bitch in Ireland, remember? Even if you don't care about me as your sister anymore, you owe me."

"Alex." His expression changed from frustration to sorrow. "I never stopped caring. I've tried, God knows."

"Come on." She looped her arm through his. "Val has a great view down by the lake. Let's take a walk."

Her brother came along reluctantly, and once they reached the retaining wall he unwrapped her hand from his arm and stepped away, sitting down to look out at the lights glittering on the lake.

He was steeling himself, Alex knew, to tell her what he knew. Or shifting into priest mode while he searched for the right words to sugarcoat things. He had always wanted her to exist in some sort of Barbie-doll world where everything was pink and perfect and happy.

She might as well kick things off by cutting to the chase. "That place in Monterey didn't upset you just because it looked as if they kept children there. It reminded you of something. Something that happened to you and me when we were kids."

He looked down at his linked hands. "There are things that I don't remember, Alexandra. Holidays, birthdays, that kind of thing. I can't remember one Christmas, and you always remember those when you're a kid. There are other gaps, like where we lived before we came to Chicago, or how we ended up on the streets."

"I know I don't remember because I was just a baby." She sat down beside him. "Didn't our parents abandon us? You would have been old enough to remember."

"I don't know," he admitted. "I don't even know how we got on the streets, only that I had to protect you, and I was terrified of being found." He dragged a hand through his hair. "Before that, someone kept us locked in a room with bars on the window. I was seven, and you were two. I don't remember much about that place, just a very vague memory of you in a crib, and me sleeping in a bed like the ones in the dormitories at the mission."

Alex concentrated, but her memories of life before their adoption were nebulous at best. "How did we get out of there?"

"I jammed a bread crust into the bolt plate on the door frame." He kicked over a stone with the toe of his shoe. "I waited until lights-out, took you from your crib, and sneaked out of the room. You weren't heavy, but I was weak, sick. I had to stop and rest a few times. I got into the back of a van and hid between some boxes. Someone got in and drove for a long time. Then we were in the city. I jumped out of the back with you and ran."

Alex thought over what he had told her. "What if the place you remember was some sort of hospital or orphanage? Maybe they locked us in to keep us from running away."

"I think they sent someone after us," he told her. "A man. He found us one night in an alley."

As John told her about the man who had tried to pull him out of the crate, and whom he had beaten away with a pipe, Alex watched his eyes. He sounded feverish, almost to the point of raving. Whatever had happened to John and her before they were adopted, it had scarred him deeply. Perhaps all the facility in Monterey had done was reawaken those half-remembered terrors from childhood, many of which may or may not have actually happened.

"The day after that man attacked us, a Child Services caseworker found us and took us to the Catholic orphanage downtown," John said. "Do you remember that? They kept us there before the Kellers adopted us."

She shook her head.

"Neither do I," he said. "All I recall is the alley, and then meeting the Kellers when they came to pick us up."

"You were a severely traumatized kid, John, shoved into a strange place run by people you didn't know," she pointed out. "It's natural for a kid's mind to erase things like that."

He took her hands in his. "Alex, we were at that orphanage for six months. I don't remember a single day of it. Do you?"

"No." She frowned. "It wasn't six months. It couldn't be that long."

"It was," he insisted. "I compared the dates on the paperwork in Audra's files. The investigator's report stated that he found us in August. Audra adopted us on Valentine's Day."

She shook her head. "The dates have got to be mixed up or something."

"What I do remember is how different we were when we moved in with the Kellers." He turned her hands over and held them, palm-up. "You always wanted to play jacks like the big girls we saw on the stoops. When we were living on the street, I stole a bag of them from a toy store for you. You tried so hard to pick up a jack and then catch the ball." He smiled down at her hands. "You never could get the hang of it."

"Okay, so I was lousy at jacks."

"Mom gave you a new set when we moved in with her,"

John said. "The first day you played with them, I watched you. I watched you pick up all the jacks and catch the ball before it started coming down from the toss."

She drew her hands back. "So I must have practiced in the orphanage."

"You could write in cursive by the time you went to kindergarten. You used to sit and copy my homework assignments for practice. I timed you once. It took you only three minutes to copy a five-page book report. You started catching things you dropped before they hit the floor. Then there was that day in the garden, when you grabbed a bird that flew past your face, and Audra screamed—"

"Shut up." Alex clenched her hands into fists and turned away from him. "It's a coincidence. That's all."

"You were a normal little girl before then," he told her. "Then we went to Audra's, and your hands could move faster than I could see."

"It's a fluke, John." She threw out her arms. "Luck of the gene pool, that's all. It kicked in when we were adopted. So I'm fast. There's always somebody faster."

"No, there isn't," he said. "You're the fastest surgeon in the world. Just ask *TIME* magazine."

"You think they did something to me to make me like this." She laughed. "Fine. If that's the case, then what did they do to you? Besides make you into a religion-obsessed jerk?"

"You remember the dinner game?"

Alex shut up.

"Every day when we were coming home from school, you would ask me what Audra was making for dinner. And I told you, and I was always right."

She shrugged. "You cheated. You probably asked her every day before we went to school."

"I never asked her once. I could smell her cooking ten blocks away from the house." He came to stand beside her. "When we went to church on Saturdays, I could hear people in the confessionals, whispering their sins to God."

"Those booths were soundproofed."

He smiled down at her. "One Saturday you told Father Seamus you'd taken my baseball bat and ball and broken old Mr. Murphy's back window. You used your allowance to buy a new ball, and then you rubbed it around in the dirt to make it look like mine."

Alex gaped. "You saw me break Mr. Murphy's window?"

He shook his head. "I was at altar boy practice that day. I didn't know until I heard your confession on Saturday. I heard all of them."

"You knew all my sins."

"I knew everyone's." He looked at the first rays of light coming over the horizon. "Smell, hearing, taste, sight—all of my senses became acute. It's why I became a priest. I thought it was a gift from God, to make me more aware of the world and the suffering of humanity."

"But now you think something happened to us while we were at the Catholic orphanage? Something that made me fast, and upped the wattage on your senses?"

"I don't think it was an orphanage, or run by the Catholics." He met her gaze. "I think the Brethren took us. I think they experimented on us, the same way they did with those kids in Monterey."

Alex started to argue the point, and then grabbed her brother as he began to pitch forward over the wall. John muttered something and slid through her hands to fall unconscious on the rocks.

Chapter 12

Valentin had brought down the plane. He had not killed himself or Liling. Now all he had to do was keep her from bleeding to death.

Valentin carried Liling away from the lake and toward the woods. While he had been unconscious, she had somehow dragged him out of the water. She had assumed from the condition of his body that he had stopped breathing, and had attempted to revive him. Now he had to find help for her before she bled to death from the gunshot wound.

He felt her skin. It was wet from the lake water, cool to the touch, almost cold. He saw her slight breasts rise and fall, but he could sense her heartbeat slowing. She could be going into shock; he had to get her warm.

The structure he had seen from the air sat back against a wide swath of thin pine trees. It was a cabin, although the windows were dark and it appeared deserted. He kicked open the door and carried her inside.

Valentin placed her on a battered-looking couch, stripped off her wet garments, and checked her wound. He was astonished to see it was healed over, until he remembered the makeshift bandage he had put over it; the blood he had shed on his jacket must have sealed the wound.

He pulled the dusty quilt covering the back of the couch over her, tucking it around her body before he straightened and looked around the room. The cabin had not been lived in for some months, but he saw signs that it had been regularly occupied. There were electrical outlets, lamps, chairs, and a small radio. The fireplace was empty, but next to it was a small electrical space heater.

Liling murmured something, and when he put his hand to her brow she felt a little warmer.

There was no time to chop wood and try to light the fireplace. Something had to supply electricity to the cabin, and Jaus went through a hall to the back of the house. Outside he found a small, slat-sided shed with a large generator and several cans of petrol inside. He managed to fuel and start the generator, which sputtered into life.

He returned inside and plugged in and brought the space heater beside the couch. Liling was shivering under the quilt. He stripped out of his own dripping clothes and drew back the quilt, lifting her up and sliding his body under hers. He turned her in his arms and held her close, wishing he were a human so he could warm her better.

"We're safe now," he said, rubbing her with his hands to encourage her circulation. He felt the warmth of the space heater penetrate the quilt. "Can you hear me, Liling? We're safe."

He was lying to her; they were not safe. He had not seen a telephone or CB in the cabin; he had no way to contact anyone. They were alone in an uninhabited area. She had a bullet inside her body, and she had lost a great deal of blood, both to him and from the wound. Too much for a human. He would be lucky if he could keep her alive until morning.

No, she would live. He would keep her alive. They had beaten insurmountable odds. She was young and strong. She had pulled him to safety. They would survive this, and he would get her to safety.

He had to, because it was not safe here.

Valentin closed his eyes and held her tightly. He had taken enough blood from her to sustain him for several days, but soon his body would demand the only nourishment it could take: human blood. When he went without feeding, he would grow weak, but after a time his body would demand to be fed. That need would become voracious with every passing day, and then it would take over his every thought. When that happened, he would no longer have a choice. He would feed on any blood he could obtain.

They were not safe because there were no other humans here from whom he could feed.

Only Liling.

Liling stood by the lake to watch the swans. They glided around the glass-smooth surface, serene and content, silent as the moonlight.

"They are beautiful." Martha Hopkins came to stand beside her. "He's come for you." She gestured back at a cabin near some pine trees. In the doorway stood a man, but not the one she feared. "So will the other. Who will you choose to kill this time, Lili?"

She saw fire in the shape of her body reflecting on the surface of the lake. When the swans came too near, they burst into flames and sank beneath the water.

The same would happen to the man who stood watching for her. "I'll run away."

"As you always do." Martha nodded, agreeing with herself. "But the fire will not die."

Liling walked up to the cabin, but it seemed the man was gone. Inside, she saw a series of narrow, upward-spiraling corridors of stone, lit only by smoking torches. Blue and green ivy leaves growing around the curved block frame made a bower of it, but she saw small nets of cobwebs lacing the vines, and heard tiny things rustling in the darkness beyond the arch.

"Is someone here?" she called out, her voice echoing a hundred times.

When no answer came, she stepped inside the arch. Nothing jumped out at her. The torches here were dead, but she could smell plants, water, and flowers.

"Demon ground," Martha said, tucking her arm through Liling's. "You should recognize it. It's where they spawned you."

Liling had been called worse. "We were not demons. We were children of the wind, the fire, the water, and the earth." That was what Mrs. Chen had said.

"You hid so much from that old woman." Martha turned, looking at a bench filled with clay pots of gray plants blooming with tiny white flowers. "As you hide from him."

She thought of the others who had perished in the storm. "I didn't mean to do it. I didn't know it would happen."

"Ignorance is not an excuse." The nurse turned and walked away.

Liling followed Martha into the hothouse but saw only gray and white. The flowers became larger until they were camellias; only the blooms appeared blighted and deformed, with tiny worms crawling in and out of holes they had eaten in the petals.

"Don't you like them?" Martha asked, caressing one of the ugly blooms. "After all, they're his favorite flower."

Liling ran past the nurse to the nearest door, jerked it

open, and stepped through. Outside the door was a draw-bridge guarded by two large, unhygienic-looking guards with matching spears, helmets, and metal chest-plate things over the filthiest leather clothes imaginable. Both eyed Liling, straightened, and stared out across a rolling hundred acres or so of what might have been wheat or waist-high dead grass. The field was ringed by pine and oak forests so dense she couldn't see space between the tree trunks.

She looked back over her shoulder at soaring walls of black stone. No sound but the wind threshing grass and whistling through the gap-toothed stone of the battlements. Across the enormous field, the tree line was interrupted by something large and white that glittered like frost in the sun.

Valentin.

Liling couldn't walk to the ivory castle; it was too far away. She stepped up to one of the guards. "I need some transportation."

The guard bowed and took off at a fast trot to a big barn to one side of the castle. The other watched her from the corner of his eye, as if expecting her to take his head off.

She smiled at him. "I don't give."

"As you say, my lady." He stopped checking her out and stared so hard at the field she thought his eyes might pop out of his skull. "Everything will be as you say."

The other guard came back leading a monster-size red horse with a black-and-silver saddle on its back, and handed her the reins.

She stared up into black eyes backlit with some kind of red glow. "I don't know how to ride a horse."

"It is all we have, my lady." The guard bowed again. "Do you wish me to accompany you as an escort?"

Liling wished for some riding lessons. "No." She had seen horseback riding enough on television to understand how to mount. She shoved one of her feet into the loop thing at the horse's side and swung onto its back—which was so far off the ground she nearly had a heart attack once she'd settled herself in the saddle.

The horse shuffled under her. Feeling the moving mass of powerful muscle made her heart crawl up her throat, but her hands and legs settled themselves like they knew precisely what to do, and the horse responded to her touch as if she were a pro.

She looked down at the guards and pointed across the field. "What's that place called?"

One paled. The other gulped and said, "Brumal, my lady."

"It mean's Death's Hold," the white-faced one muttered.

I'm not going anywhere that has death *as part of the address.* Just as she decided that, the other, obviously suicidal part of her grabbed the reins and thumped the sides of the big red horse with her heels.

Liling thought she squeaked something out of sheer horror. It came out like a "ha," and the horse took off like a four-legged rocket.

Until this dream she had never ridden a horse, for the same reasons she had never played with dynamite or handled poisonous snakes: On the commonsense scale, potential pain, injury, and death always outweighed any likelihood of fun, excitement, and thrills.

Considering the way the ground and the sky were jumping around her, she expected to fall off versus ride the horse. Instead, she bent over and settled in somehow, moving her body in sync with the animal. Her jaw ached, but she couldn't unclench her teeth until they were three-quarters of the way across the field and coming up fast on the ivory castle.

What did the guard call it? Brumal. Death's Hold.

Uneven slabs and chunks of white rock covered the ground, and she tugged on the reins and slowed the horse to a walk. No need for it to break a leg, and she wanted some time to have a look before knocking.

The architecture wasn't the same as the black castle across the way, nor was everything a snowy white. Various white and ivory shades of marble, plaster, and what she thought might be quartz had been used to build it. It seemed very old, and yet showed no signs of aging. The stone appeared as if it had been quarried and cut yesterday.

Nothing moved, and no one came out to meet her.

She counted eleven towers, four in the front, with thirty-foot-high retaining walls stretched out on either side of them, encircling the main structure. The towers and turrets were narrower and taller, the stonework fussier, and nothing was symmetrical or proportionate. She couldn't understand why she couldn't focus on any single detail for more than a few seconds without her gaze jumping to something else. Brumal didn't shift or change in any sense, but it didn't want her to look at it. Finally she glanced at the ground to rest her eyes, and dragged in some air. The horse did a two-step under her.

"Don't move," she told it, and freed up her feet before swinging a leg over and dropping to the ground.

By not looking at the rest of the ivory castle, she discovered she was able to focus on the four front towers. Between them was a narrow drawbridge-type gangway behind a huge iron gate.

She led the horse over to stand in front of the quad of towers, and shouted, "Is anyone there?"

No one answered, but heavy metal cranked and the iron gate between the front towers began to lift. Blade-shaped spikes edged the bottom of the gate. It stopped midway, leaving just enough room for Liling and the horse to ride through.

Right under the spikes.

"Think if we try to go in, they'll drop it on us?" she asked the horse. The horse didn't answer. "You're a lot of help." She swung up onto its back. "Next time I'm calling a taxi."

A row of petite, dark-haired women in plain white nightgowns stood inside the tower passage. Each of them wore bridal veils over their glossy hair and pretty faces. Each of the women had the exact same face.

Ahead of Liling stood a man dressed in mostly midnight blue armor. He held a sword in each hand, and white feathers covered one of his arms, making it appear like the wing of a bird. On his golden head sat a crown made of apricot roses with brown-spotted leaves. The long, wicked thorns on the stems of the roses were cutting into his flesh. Drops of blood slid down his face, flowing red tears.

"Valentin." Liling walked slowly up to him.

He held the two swords out between them, as if he meant to attack her.

Liling held out her hands to show him they were empty. But fire sprang up from her palms, orange-red, hot and hungry. The crown of roses around his head began to wither and blacken, tightening around his skull.

He drove the two swords into the stone floor between them.

"Choose," he told her, the blood on his face turning to real tears.

Liling looked at the blades in the stone. One sword was covered in blood; the other glowed scarlet. She took a step back. "I can't."

"Choose."

"Valentin, please."

He walked past her, blind to her, his eyes filled with ice. As he passed through the rows of veiled women, their faces changed, becoming exact copies of Liling's. One by one they turned their backs to him and faced the walls.

"Valentin."

"You take away the sins of the world." He did not look at her. "Have mercy on us."

Water began to well up around her feet, covering them, creeping up around her ankles, swirling and churning, dragging at her as she tried to run, and then the water came at her from all sides, pounding her, beating her back and forth, and the world disappeared as an enormous wave swelled and curled and came down on her, swallowing her scream.

Chapter 13

Kyan ignored Melanie Wallace for most of the afternoon as he guided the boat down the river. She seemed content to sit on the deck and sun herself, alternately thumbing through her economics text and scribbling notes. That she chose to lie on her belly just in front of the helm where he couldn't help but see her was a minor annoyance. He concentrated on the scents coming off the water, avoiding shallows and navigating through dense patches of water lilies.

Occasionally he watched her as well. He justified it by reasoning that his observations of an American-raised female could prove helpful when it came to dealing with his target.

"Hey."

Kyan looked at the girl, who was peering at him. "What is it?"

"I have this assignment for my philosophy class." Melanie sat up and stretched. She had unbuttoned her shirt, and the movement made it gape open even more. "This dude Albert Einstein said, 'We must learn to see the world anew.' I have to write an essay on that."

Kyan caught a glimpse of a black mark on the inside curve of her left breast, like the edge of a tattoo. "So?"

She dropped her arms. "So what do you see in the world that could be called new?"

"Nothing."

"Dude, this counts as, like, sixty percent of my grade," she advised him. "If I turn in a one-word essay, I'm, like, totally flunking the semester."

She had the typical American attitude of seeking answers only to serve ambition. "The world is nothing new," he told her. "Everything is as it was at the dawn of creation."

She made a show of looking around. "So where are dinosaurs, and the cavemen, and shit like that?"

"They are still here. You build your cities on top of them. You dig up their bones and display them for the amusement of schoolchildren." He looked out at the river. "You burn them in your gas tanks and fight wars to control the land they once walked. They have not gone; they have only changed." His voice went rough. "Everything changes, but everything is the same. Nothing new."

Melanie gave him her full attention, her blue eyes solemn. "That is seriously fucked-up, dude."

Kyan felt amused. "Do you mean to put that in your paper?"

She muttered something uncomplimentary to native Chinese, and reclined as she returned to her reading.

An official stopped the boat once in the late afternoon to check its contents and to question Kyan. The young man, a reed-thin youth whose new uniform sat stiffly on his scrawny frame, seemed more interested in Melanie's breasts than Kyan's intentions.

The girl smiled and talked with the young official as he made some sort of awkward overture. She gave his arms and shoulders coy little touches and laughed a great deal. Kyan couldn't follow most of their conversation, but it seemed to satisfy the official, who returned to his own diminutive craft and continued down the river.

"Do you think you could have frowned a little more at that guy?" Melanie asked as she came to retrieve a bottle of water out of her bag.

"Did I not frown enough?"

"Way you were acting, he thought you were a dope smuggler." She took a drink from the water bottle before holding it out to him. "Don't look like that. It's not like I have cooties."

He didn't understand the last word she uttered, until she sighed and translated it in Chinese. "I would not have hired you if you were carrying body lice."

"I am *so* glad Granny came over here to marry a white guy," Melanie said, before she put the bottle back in her bag and returned to her spot on the deck.

Kyan watched her as he took the bottle from her bag, uncapped it, and let the water inside touch his lips. Her mouth had left traces of her taste on the water. The girl had a sweet, simple taste, like candy. He closed the bottle and replaced it, licking her from his lips.

At that moment she looked up from her book and her eyes narrowed. "You're staring at me again."

He shrugged.

"It's too hot out here." She got up and came back to the helm, shimmying her shoulders as she went past him and down into the cabin. "If you want to see more, come in here."

Kyan assumed she went to use the head, until he heard the sound of water splashing and frowned. He hadn't stocked enough water for her to waste it.

"Melanie, what are you doing?" She didn't answer. He shut off the motor and went down into the cabin. "What are you . . ."

Melanie stood in the doorway of the head, dripping wet and naked to the waist. "I'm cooling off. Is that, like, a problem?"

Kyan took three seconds to admire her too-large, perfectly round, pink-tipped breasts before he turned his back on her. "Put on your clothes."

"I'm hot." She walked up behind him, and before he could move slid her hand around his hip, spreading her fingers over the ridge of his erection. "Dude." She fondled him right through his pants. "So are you."

"Stop touching me."

"Make me." Melanie giggled and unzipped his trousers, inserting her hand in his fly. "Very nice. I thought Chinese guys were supposed to be, you know, small."

"You should not be doing this." Kyan gritted his teeth as he felt her fingers curl around him. "You are just a child."

"No, I'm not." She made a fist and began pumping him gently. "You should know; you've been staring at my boobs all day. Don't you want to touch them? They're real, you know."

Kyan removed her hand from his penis and turned to face her. Her breasts brushed his chest. "You know nothing about me. You mean nothing to me. Do you give yourself to any man?"

"Come on; it'll be fun." Melanie took his hands and brought them up to her breasts. She had a tattoo of a black rose with long, wicked thorns drawn to look as if they were piercing her breast. Realistic drops of red blood had been inked in a long trail across her belly. "There. Don't they feel nice?"

Kyan shoved her back against the nearest flat surface, which happened to be a wall. He pulled down her pants, lifted her up until he could suck on her breasts, and pushed her thighs apart. He drove his shaft into her, pushing a cry from her mouth, and began to pump.

Her breasts were soft and sensitive, and she climaxed the first time he used his teeth. It took him a little longer, as he had a great deal of frustration to expend. She didn't seem to mind that his thrusts into her body lacked finesse and were hard enough to keep her head thumping against the wall.

Kyan pinned her in place and buried his mouth between her breasts as he came, shuddering and jerking.

"Rude, crude, thank you, dude." She sounded breathless, and draped her arms around his neck as she slid down the length of his body until her feet touched the floor. "Was that, like, so awful?"

Kyan looked down at his pants and hers, both in a tangled heap around their ankles. "No. That was good."

She grinned. "Told you."

He straightened his clothes and went back up on deck. A short time later she emerged and retrieved her text, and sat quietly reading beside the helm.

Kyan glanced at her a few times, puzzled by how freely she'd given herself to him, and how little she had to say about it. Perhaps that was the way it was done in this country.

"Why do you have a black rose and drops of blood tattooed on your front?"

She didn't look up at him. "Because a flaming skull and little swastikas would have freaked out my mom."

The boat's fuel was running low by the time the sun set, and Kyan docked at a fishing pier with a sign that read, SCULLERVILLE MARINA. The few boats moored at the dock looked patched and well used; some of the outboard motors were cobbled together out of salvaged parts. Beyond the pier a road led toward a well-lit building surrounded by pickup trucks, motorcycles, and old-model cars.

"I'm hungry," Melanie said, looking up from her text. "When are you going to feed me?"

Kyan thought of the fish, vegetables, and rice he had stored in his bags. He had enough for himself, but he had not allowed enough supplies for her. Still, he could buy more farther down the river. "I will prepare a meal when we stop for the night."

She rested her chin on her hand. "We're stopped now."

"Only for petrol."

"But I'm thirsty and my stomach is growling." She stood up and peered at the well-lit building. "Let's go get something over there at that roadhouse. I'll teach you how to play pool."

Kyan had another three or four hours before he would need to eat and rest. He didn't want to spend them in a roadhouse, whatever that was. "I do not play."

"Come on," she begged. "You might actually enjoy yourself without having to get naked with me. Unless you want to again."

Kyan considered knocking her out and tossing her in the cabin, but that might attract attention. He had not picked up the girl's trail, and he had to assume she had not yet arrived in Florida. He had to focus on his target, not on having sex with the American.

"Please?" Melanie wheedled.

"I will buy the fuel first."

The boat rocked as she jumped up and down and clapped her hands. Kyan noted the way her large breasts bounced, and remembered how they felt under his mouth. He decided that as soon as he finished his work and returned to Taiwan, he would buy himself a concubine for his bed. Perhaps two.

Both would have to have large breasts, but no tattoos.

After filling the boat's fuel tanks, Kyan followed the girl across the pier to the dirt road. The feel of land under his feet again made his mouth dry and his knees unsteady, but the sensation soon passed. His pace slowed as he steadied himself and found his center.

Melanie had walked ahead of him, and now glanced back over her shoulder. "You okay, boss? You look a little green."

"I am well." He caught up to her, shortening his long strides to match hers. "Do not call me 'boss.'"

She gave him her impish smile. "How about 'Sugar Buns'?"

"I am not a cake," he said, offended.

"Okay, but you're definitely a stud muffin." She made her eyebrows go up and down.

She seemed determined to provoke him. "My name is Kyan." He climbed up the steps to the roadhouse's main entrance. "Use it."

"Kyan. Right." She cocked her head. "When did they outlaw having a good time in China, anyway? Same time as sex?"

The roadhouse seemed more like a madhouse inside, with hundreds of people crowded around a long bar and dozens of tiny tables. At one end of the building, couples danced in front of a five-man band playing primitive-sounding music. One of the men sang into a microphone about doing impossible things to a heart.

Women dressed in fewer garments than working whores would wear flirted with men in old leather, denim, and plaid work clothes. Those who were not wearing bent-brimmed hats covered their hair with caps stitched with the brand names of farm equipment or NASCAR drivers.

Melanie looked around, apparently delighted.

Kyan closed himself to the sweat, saliva, perfume, and alcohol that saturated the air, and saw two men preparing to vacate stools at one end of the long bar. He took Melanie's arm and pushed her toward them.

"Hey, I thought we could get a table near the band," she protested.

"I prefer to keep my hearing intact." He edged past the two men and claimed one stool, pushing her toward another. He lifted his hand and made a curt gesture at the fat bald man serving the patrons at the bar.

The bartender leaned over to make a remark to several men sitting near the taps before he casually moved down to Kyan and Melanie. "Ain't got no sake here for you, boy."

Kyan was often mistaken for a Japanese, so he didn't comment. "Menu."

"Ain't got none of them neither." The heavy chin jerked toward a blackboard covered with white dust and some chalked words. "Wings, skins, nachos, and my mama's homemade chili. Mama's pit bull went missing last week, so I can't really recommend the chili." He eyed Kyan. "'Less'n you one of them kind like to eat dogs."

The men at the center of the bar, who were eavesdropping, started chuckling and elbowing one another.

Melanie leaned over so that the bottoms of her breasts rested on the bar. "We'll have two Buds, a basket of wings, and double order of celery and blue cheese."

"No beer," Kyan told her. "Mineral water."

To the bartender, she said, "Make that a Bud and a bottle of water. Please."

The bartender peered at her face, spit on the floor, and went over to the open kitchen window.

"Not a candidate for president of my fan club. Tragic." Melanie sat down on the stool and spun around on it to face the band.

Kyan glanced sideways. "It doesn't bother you?" he asked her in Chinese. "The way they treat Asians?"

"I'm not Asian. I'm a multiracial American." She swayed in time with the music. "They would treat me the same way in China. Probably worse."

"You said you have never been to China."

"I don't have to go there to know how Asians feel about kids with mixed blood. I get all that crap every time I go for Chinese takeout." She propped her elbows back against the bar. "Don't act so huffy, boss. You might be okay with screwing me, but you don't like me any more than that bartender does."

"I would not look at you and spit on the ground." His gaze drifted up to the television set hanging over the bar, and the news story being broadcast. "What are they saying?" he asked her, pointing to the screen.

She watched for a moment. "A bunch of people reported seeing a UFO go down over the Ocala National Forest. The authorities are refusing to investigate because no planes are missing, and they'd have to search an area that's, like, the size of Rhode Island. Weird."

Kyan removed the girl's pamphlet from his pocket and showed it to Melanie, pointing to the map. "The UFO went down here?"

"No, that's way west of here." She hopped off the stool and stepped in front of him. Before he could grab her hands, she hooked her fingers in the belt loops of his trousers. "Come on and dance with me."

"I do not dance."

"Do you do *anything* besides drive a boat, frown, slaughter English, and stare at my boobs?" she inquired sweetly.

"Yes. But I do not dance."

"Oh, God." She seized the beer bottle the bartender handed her and carried it with her to stand by the place where the patrons were dancing.

"Don't you Jap fellas beat your women?" the fat man asked as he thumped a basket of fried bird parts, celery stalks, and two cups of some white lumpy sauce in front of Kyan.

"We not have to," Kyan told him in English he was careful not to mangle. "She American. Multiracial."

"No shit, Sherlock." The bartender scowled and stalked off.

Kyan did not touch the food, which looked as repulsive as it smelled, but drank from the bottle of water. It had been purified, so it contained no trace of anything but the machines at the bottling factory.

Melanie went out amid the dancing couples and began shaking her body by herself. Several men came to join her. Kyan watched for the next hour as the American girl danced, drank many bottles of beer that the men bought for her, laughed, and generally acted like an intoxicated child.

When she climbed onto one of the tables to dance for six grinning men crowding around it, Kyan decided she had had enough of a good time, and left his stool.

Melanie undulated as much to the calls of the excited men as to the music, and began unbuttoning her flimsy shirt, revealing the tops of her breasts. Kyan reached up before she could expose herself, clamped his hands around her waist, and lifted her down to the floor.

"We are leaving," he told her. "Now."

"I didn't get to eat my wings yet," she whined, tottering toward the bar.

He turned her around to face the exit. "I will make you food after you are finished puking."

"I'm not going to puke." She leered at him. "I know. You just want to have sex with me while I'm drunk."

It was easier to agree with her. "Yes. That is why we must go to the boat. To have sex again."

"Hold on, there, Bruce." One of the men from the bar approached them. "This little lady hasn't finished her dance."

Kyan watched as the men who had supplied Melanie with beer and the other men from the bar gathered in a loose circle around them. "She finished."

"I say she's not," a hulking boy said in a low, nervous voice. "What chew gonna do about it?" He giggled like a girl.

"Aw, he's just her boss," another man said. "Not her boyfriend. She said so."

"I don't care what the little slant-eyed bastard is," a fourth man growled. "He ain't drinking, and he ain't white, so he got no business coming in here in the first place."

"You rednecks are such pussies," Melanie said suddenly, weaving as she jabbed a finger toward the last man who had spoken. "Kyan could wipe up the floor with you. With all of you. One hand tied behind his back."

Kyan felt the mood of the men around them change from unpleasant to ugly. "Melanie, be quiet."

"I'd like to see him do that," the fat man called from behind the bar.

Kyan looked down at the floor, which was wet and sticky with spilled beer. He slipped his foot out of his deck shoe and stepped in one of the larger puddles. A crackle of blue light flashed across the floor, leaping from puddle to puddle until it disappeared under the stools.

Beer taps began popping off and soaring into the air as fountains of beer erupted. Women screamed and men shouted. The foaming ale sprayed wildly, coming down like a rain shower on the heads of the patrons. Some ran up, laughing as they tried to catch some of the beer with their mouths. The men around Kyan and Melanie scattered.

Kyan bent down and put his shoulder to Melanie's belly and lifted her up onto his shoulder. She shrieked and pounded his back with her small fists as he strode out of the bar with her.

"What are you doing? Put me down."

Kyan carried her back to the pier and set her down on her feet by the boat. He released the mooring ropes.

"You're not going to have sex with me again," she said, following him to the bowline. "Are you?"

"Not now."

"Well, I don't want to hang out with you anymore. You're mean." She whirled around and stumbled down the pier.

Kyan caught her arm from behind. "Melanie, get on the boat."

"Fuck you." She repeated it in Chinese.

"Later." He reached into his jacket and took out his weapon. "Get on the boat now."

Valentin left Liling sleeping restlessly and pulled on his damp clothes. He needed to inspect the rest of the cabin and find water. The cabin's owner had not left any fresh food in the refrigerator, as with the generator off it would have spoiled, but had stocked cans and boxes of nonperishable items in a large kitchen pantry.

The generator, Valentin discovered, provided ample power

to the house and to a well with an electric pump. He ran the taps in the kitchen and tasted the water, which was cold and clear.

Unfortunately, he confirmed that there were no telephones, radios, or anything else he could use to send a message to the outside world.

Valentin abandoned the idea of summoning help and turned his attention to what he could do for Liling with what he had. He knew she needed fluids; humans who lost too much blood quickly became dehydrated. He vaguely remembered Sacher giving his grandson sugary tea when the boy had broken his arm falling off his bicycle. After searching the pantry, he found a container of orange-flavored sports-drink mix and made a glass of that for her.

In the front room he knelt by the couch, held her upright, and coaxed her into swallowing some of the drink. She coughed, and then began to choke. He rolled her on her side as she immediately regurgitated what she had drunk from the glass. He tried two other drink mixes with the same results. Finally he gave her plain water, and that she kept down.

"I know you like tea," he told her as he gently wiped her face clean. "If I find some, I will make you as much as you can drink." He smoothed the damp hair away from her face. "Not too hot this time. With a little practice, I will find the perfect temperature."

The sound of his voice seemed to help as much as the water, and she fell into a deeper sleep.

Valentin reluctantly left her to check on the generator and bring into the cabin some of the wood that had already been split and stacked in the shed. Using the fireplace would conserve the electricity, which would run out as soon as the petrol for the generator did. When he stacked the short logs beside the hearth, he noticed that what he assumed was a wood rack was in fact a curious metal device with dials and a button.

Valentin pushed the button and smelled propane gas just before a light flickered and the gas ignited. The dials, he discovered, controlled the amount of gas supplied to the device.

A fireplace that burned gas in the middle of a forest of perfectly good trees. He shook his head in wonder.

He thoroughly searched the rest of the cabin, finding a locker-style trunk filled with old clothes and shoes, and boxes of rifle ammunition but no rifles. A fish made of resin hanging on one wall began to twitch and sing to him as he passed it. He took it down, found the battery switch on the back, and shut it off.

After looking in on Liling, Valentin felt sticky and looked down. The sugared drinks she had coughed up had saturated his clothes and were drying on his hands. He took some of the clean clothing from the locker and went into the cabin's small bathroom to wash up.

As he stripped and stepped into the small shower stall, he realized that he was using both arms without hesitation, accepting the unthinkable without question. His damaged arm felt so improved it seemed no different than it had before the duel.

I'm sorry, Val, Alexandra Keller had told him after he had healed from the surgery, and they had discovered that his reattached arm wouldn't work. *I've done what I can, but even Kyn can't heal from everything.*

He had heard that some of the patients at the Lighthouse had claimed that Liling's touch healed them. He could attribute his own miracle only to her touch. But if she could heal with her hands, why was she working as a gardener? Why hide what she could do?

She hides it for the same reason we Kyn hide our existence, he thought. *Humanity fears what it does not understand.*

If the public knew about a woman who could heal with a touch, Liling would be hounded unmercifully. The world was filled with the sick and dying, and everyone would expect her to use her ability to heal them. The wealthy and powerful would want to control her gift for their own benefit. The zealots would condemn her. Governments might even go to war over possession of her.

At best she would end up imprisoned; at worst she would be murdered.

Liling had wanted to deny that she had done anything. In that moment when Valentin had taken her into his arms, he had felt her panic. He could compel her to tell him the truth about her gift, and exactly how she had healed his arm. She could not resist his talent. But she must have a reason for not volunteering the information, something that had made her a target of the Brethren. All he would do by forcing the truth out of her was satisfy his own curiosity. He could allow her to keep her secrets until she trusted him enough to share them.

He would give her that time, but he already knew he could not let her go.

When they escaped this place, Valentin decided, he would take her back to Chicago with him. The pilot had been a Brethren operative, and willing to crash the plane in order to kill her. Jaus could not fathom why the Brethren would want to murder a woman who could heal with her hands, unless they assumed she had the talent because she was Kyn. They would pursue her without cessation if that was the case. It might also explain why she had changed jobs and locations so often; surely she had known she was being hunted.

Liling could not run from the order forever; they had found her this time and they would find her again. She needed the protection of the Kyn.

The plastic shower curtain jerked to one side, and the subject of his thoughts stood there weaving slightly on her feet, a strange look in her black eyes.

"Liling." He reached for her.

She moved before he could touch her, and grabbed the shower curtain, ripping it from its rings. Scarlet sparks swirled in the night depths of her eyes, and she didn't seem to know who he was, for her gaze had an empty, mindless quality to it.

"You take away the sins of the world." She braced her hands against the tile walls. "See how you like it."

The cold water of the shower suddenly turned hot, and steam filled the small room.

Valentin swore as he climbed out of the shower to avoid the now-scalding spray. "Get back before you are burned."

Her gaze shifted from his face to the water and back again, and recognition dawned in her eyes, along with terrible fear.

"Forgive me. I didn't mean to shout at you." He reached in and managed to shut off the shower's taps, the scalding water making his skin turn faintly red for a moment before the light burns healed. "Are you feeling a little better?"

"Not him." She brought her hands up to her head and held it, her eyes shut tightly. "I didn't do anything. Stop shouting at me." She said something in Chinese, and then she screamed the words, *"I won't."*

Valentin had to lunge to grab her as her knees buckled.

Her eyes had rolled back in her head, he saw as he lifted her up. She was babbling to herself in Chinese.

"Liling." He held her carefully. "What are you saying to me? Tell me in English."

"Take, not give." She whimpered, cringing, clutching her hair as if she wanted to tear it from her scalp. "He's coming. I can feel him. I can hear him. Take not give take not give—"

"Nothing will harm you." He caressed her cheek, and the touch seemed to soothe her. "I won't allow it. I swear this to you."

"He is coming." She groped at him, her hands clawing. "You have to kill me. Promise me. Before he finds us. Before it's too late."

Fever was making her delirious, but the fear in her eyes was genuine. Was this the reason she had run away from Chicago? "Who is this man? Why are you afraid of him? Liling, I am here. I will protect you."

She shook her head, flinging the tears from her eyes. "You can't. Not from him." She covered her mouth with her hands, and then dropped them away as her eyes filled. "He is the sea and the river and the lake," she said, almost chanting the words. "He is the rain and the snow and the hail."

She spoke of him as if she loved him, this man who terrorized her. "Who is he?" he demanded.

She frowned at him, as if she had expected him to understand. "He is the tsunami. No one can stop him. We will die. Everyone around us will die."

He held her as she wept against his chest. "Tell me of whom you speak, *Geliebte*."

"He's not a man," she whispered, sagging. "He's a monster." Tear-drowned eyes closed. "Like me."

As Lili collapsed against him, Valentin felt a burning sensation against his skin, and put his hand between them. The skin over her rib cage was red-hot in one area, over a small, unnatural bulge on one bone.

He remembered again the sensation of warmth wrapping around him when she had used her healing touch on his arm. Her body was trying to heal itself, he guessed, but the bullet inside her was somehow hindering the process. It might even be poisoning her, as copper did the Kyn. He would have to take it out.

Valentin had almost no medical knowledge, and his own ignorance frustrated him. He would kill to have Alexandra Keller here now.

He carried Liling out of the bathroom, but the couch was too low for his purpose. He picked up the quilt from it and carried her into the kitchen. The table there was small but supported her weight. He put the quilt over it and laid her down gently.

The flesh where the bullet wound had been looked flushed. Upon closer inspection he saw that the tiny veins under her skin had ruptured. He might know nothing about doctoring, but it was obvious from the pattern of broken veins that the bullet was responsible. They were in the shape of a slug.

Liling was still semiconscious, and Valentin had no drugs with which to sedate her. He feared that using *l'attrait* to compel her to sleep would only make matters worse, but he couldn't remove the slug while she was still conscious.

He would have to risk it.

Valentin placed his hand on her slender throat and shed as much scent as he dared.

"Camellias." Her lips curved and her eyelids drifted down.

"That's it; go to sleep, *Liebling*," he said softly, stroking the delicate arch of her throat. "I will care for you until you wake."

Her lips moved to frame a word, and then parted over a sigh. He waited, but she didn't stir again.

Valentin went to the counter and took the thinnest blade out of the knife block. The edge had dulled, so he took a saucer from the cabinet, flipped it over, and used the porcelain rim of the base to hone the blade.

He remembered cutting into Alexandra Keller's back to remove a copper bolt. Alex had Kyn healing ability, however, and Liling was human. He would have to cut fast and not too deep.

He went to the table and bowed his head for a moment. He could no longer trouble deaf heaven for himself, but surely his entreaty for this innocent life would be heard.

"Guide my hand, Father," he said to the God he had not addressed in centuries. "Make her well and whole again."

Valentin prodded the flesh over her ribs and located the small bulge he had felt before. The blade trembled slightly as he brought the knife to her body, but steadied as he gripped the handle tighter and plunged the tip into her skin.

He did not have to cut far; the flattened slug lay just beneath the tissue, lodged partway into the surface of a bone. It did not pop loose, and he was obliged to work the tip of the blade under it before it moved. Blood welled from the incision as he bore down, trying to remove it from the bone in which it had buried itself. Finally it came out like a rotted tooth, emerging from the tissue with an ugly, familiar red-brown gleam.

The slug was made of pure copper.

Valentin pried the slug out of the incision, barely feeling the burn to his own skin as he tossed it aside. He had to close the incision, and he had only one way to do that: with his own blood.

This too was dangerous; too much could potentially poison her. He lifted his wrist to his mouth, biting into his own flesh and turning the wound to drip over hers. The few drops of his Kyn blood were not enough to harm her, and they quickly sealed the wound.

Once he had tended to her, he looked at his hands, which were wet with the blood from her wound. He hated using it for himself, but until he could get them back to civilization, he could not afford to waste a drop. He cleaned the blood from his hands with his mouth, allowing himself a brief moment to savor her taste before gathering her up in the quilt and carrying her back to the bedroom.

Dawn shimmered in the distance.

He put Liling on the bed and closed the window blinds before he joined her. The bed had no linens, but her temperature seemed normal, so the quilt would be enough for now. Valentin pulled her body close and held her, her head tucked under his chin. Only then did he release the tight hold he had kept over his emotions, and pressed his lips to her hair.

"Come back to me, *mein Mädchen*," he murmured to her. "I will never ask anything more of you. Only come back."

Chapter 14

To her relief Alexandra discovered that Jaus had never dismantled the lab she had used during her last visit to Derabend Hall.

"Let's take him in there," she told the guard who had carried her brother up from the lake. "That'll be my infirmary for now. I'm going to need some things."

Wilhelm accompanied her to the lab and took down the list of medical supplies and equipment she needed. "I will call our suppliers and have these delivered to the hall within the hour, my lady."

"Thanks." She took her scope out of her medical case. "And call me Alex, okay? The 'my lady' stuff makes me crazy."

"Of course, Alex. I am sorry that your brother fell ill." His dark eyes strayed to John's unconscious face. "If you wish to consult with another doctor, my grandfather keeps a list of those who are our friends."

She used a penlight to check John's pupils. "Depending on what I find, I might take you up on that."

The boy nodded and left to take care of the list.

Alex knew she should have John taken to a hospital in the

city. She didn't need to use Sacher's list; this was her town, and she knew exactly where he'd get the best care by the sharpest specialists. But she wouldn't risk having the Brethren discover where her brother was, especially not while he was helpless. They had as many friends in the city as the Kyn did, and she wouldn't put it past them to abduct John or even try to kill him.

Cyprien came in as she was assessing her brother's condition. "Do you know what caused him to collapse?"

"Aside from malnutrition and exhaustion, he's running a high fever. I have to cool him down and get some fluids into him before he has a seizure." She looked up from the blood-pressure gauge. "How are things going with the search for the plane?"

"Locksley and Jayr have trackers searching the areas where they think Jaus may have tried to land the plane, but they have not yet found it," he admitted. "We have received more information from our contacts at O'Hare. It seems the pilot who was flying killed Jaus's regular pilot, a man named Speicher, and used his credentials. He looked enough like him to pass casual inspection and gain access to the plane."

"A suicide stand-in pilot." She shook her head. "I need to write another letter to Congress about airport security when we get back home. Was he just a garden-variety terrorist?"

Michael shook his head. "We are still gathering the facts, but the pilot may have been a Brethren operative, sent to assassinate Val."

If the Brethren knew the plane belonged to Jaus, and that Jaus was Kyn, it wouldn't take them long to track down his home address. "Sounds like we're going to need some reinforcements here."

"I have recalled three shifts of guards," he told her. "After

Falco's betrayal, Jaus had tunnels built under the mansion for quick evacuation. They will not take us, *chérie*, I promise you."

"I feel so much better." She sighed. "Anything else happening? Iran invade? Antarctica melt? The Cubs lose?"

The corner of his mouth curled. "There is another odd circumstance involved in this situation, although I hardly know what to make of it. It seems Jaus had a human female with him on the plane."

"Oh, really?" She smiled a little. "*I* know what to make of that. About time, too."

Cyprien's amusement faded. "She might have helped the phony pilot hijack the plane."

"Val isn't that stupid." She wagged her finger at him. "You're only thinking that because you're not a romantic."

"I strongly disagree." He bent down and kissed her. "If you need anything, I will be in the conference room."

Once Alex had taken down his vitals, she drew a blood sample from John and carried it over to the microscope, making several slides before putting a sample in the analyzer.

Under the scope, Alex saw several ruptured red blood cells and other markers that indicated that John was infected with malaria. Since he had spent years ministering to the poor in South America, she wasn't surprised; malaria ran rampant in tropical countries.

The only thing that perplexed her was the appearance of the ruptures. They had closed over, and the cells still appeared viable. That didn't conform to any type of malaria she had ever diagnosed.

"I knew I should have taken a couple of extra hematology seminars," she muttered as she changed slides.

*   *   *

Valentin woke several times during the day to check on Liling and coax her into drinking a little water. The incision mark had vanished, as had the small broken blood vessels in the flesh over her rib cage. Her body temperature fluctuated wildly, however, growing hot with fever and then plummeting until she shivered in a cold, clammy huddle against him.

He kept her clean, dry, and warm, and talked to her. Sometimes he spoke of Luisa and how over time he had come to care for her. He described the many stained-glass windows he had seen during his travels, and the castles and cathedrals and great mansions they had illuminated. At times he felt like a fool for talking to an unconscious human, but he kept hoping that the sound of his voice would rouse her, or at least comfort her.

After the sun set, he rose and prepared some clear broth, but he was able to give her only a few spoonfuls before she vomited again. Gently he bathed her with a damp cloth, then dressed her in an old, extra-large T-shirt one of the cabin's former occupants had left behind.

"The plane is going to crash," she muttered in her sleep as he put her on the old battered couch and pulled it near the fireplace. "We're going to die."

She had drifted in and out of consciousness, occasionally speaking a few words but never anything as lucid as this.

"The plane did not crash," he told her, lifting her so that he could sit with her head on his lap. Being close to him and hearing his voice seemed to calm her during these delirious moments. He stroked the tangled mess of her hair. "We are alive."

She reached, found his hand, and curled her fingers around it. His hand, which should have been useless, held hers securely. He had not held a woman's hand in years, he thought as he closed his eyes, not since the night of his Halloween masque.

Valentin gestured to the small orchestra he had hired to play for his guests at the masque, and turned to Jema. She looked like a princess in the midnight blue gown he had chosen for her. "Would you honor me with the first dance of the night, my lady?"

A line appeared between her eyebrows; she had not been expecting to be asked. "Oh." She looked down at his boots, which Sacher had polished to a glassy finish. "You don't have sensitive toes, do you? I haven't danced in years."

Charmed by her modesty, and unwilling to let her refuse, Valentin led her out onto the floor. With a nod to the conductor, who immediately struck up a waltz, he took her into his arms and spun her out onto the ballroom floor.

Jema gazed around them. "Mr. Jaus," she said in a whisper, "no one else is dancing."

"They are shy," he whispered back, smiling into her eyes. "We will show them how it is done, ja?"

Over the centuries, Jaus had danced at a thousand balls in as many courts. His accomplished partners had been lovely women, important women, women he had desired, and women he had bedded. Yet he could not remember a single dance that thrilled him as much as this. Jema was like an angel in his arms, floating along with him as the music rose and ebbed. He turned her across the floor so quickly she grew breathless. She didn't seem to mind, however, and even laughed when she stumbled.

The Kyn watched them dance, and Jaus felt their silent disapproval. A lord paramount did not single out a mere human female for such attention; it violated their customs and the sanctity of their ranks. Aware that appearances had to be maintained, some of Jaus's guests began pairing and

*joined them on the dance floor. Although they waltzed in
perfect form, they still watched Jaus with Jema, as curious
as they were condemning.*

*Valentin found that he didn't care. He held the woman he
loved, and she mattered more to him than the opinions of his
own kind.*

"Is there some dirt on my face?" Jema asked Jaus.

*Valentin returned the scrutiny of Lord and Lady Halkirk
with a cool smile before he answered her. "Not a speck. Why
do you ask?"*

*"No reason." She seemed uneasy now with the attention
being given to them.*

*He had no intention of hiding his regard for Jema after
this night, whatever the Kyn thought of them. Still, she felt
uncomfortable, and he knew how to distract her. "You have
lied to me. You are an excellent dancer. You must have practiced for years in secret."*

*She gave him one of her sunny smiles. "You caught me. I
sneak out to ballrooms five, six nights a week."*

*"You must permit me to escort you one night." He dared
to pull her a little closer during the next turn. "I get so tired
of watching the History Channel. I feel as if I know the
script for every program." As well as how often they got it
wrong, he thought with some irony.*

*"You should try the SciFi Channel. They have some great
miniseries, like* Children of Dune. *I loved that one." Jema
fell silent for a moment. "Did your friends expect you to
bring one of your girlfriends tonight?"*

*Of course—she would want to know if there were any
other women in his life. He had invited her to be with him
tonight; he held her in his arms. She had to at least suspect
that he had feelings for her. "I will tell you a secret," he said,*

leaning closer, moving his hand to the small of her back. "I have no girlfriends. I am all alone in the world, Miss Shaw."

"Oh." *Jema seemed confused, and peered at him oddly.* "You're not gay, are you?"

"I am feeling quite happy." *He saw the blood rush to her face and knew he had misinterpreted her.* "Gay . . . ah, you mean it as a lover of other men. No, I am not."

"Thank heavens. I mean, not that it would be terrible if you were, just a terrible waste." *She groaned.* "Please step on my toes anytime now."

How adorable she was, blushing and stammering like this. She was grateful that he did not prefer men. It was the sort of encouragement he had needed. Valentin had only to be sure of her feelings for him.

"It is difficult to guess what impression you make upon another person," *he said softly.* "I am not offended." *He lifted his hand and brushed a piece of hair from her cheek, and then rested his hand against the side of her neck.* "I would very much like to know your opinion of me."

She could not lie to him now, not compelled as she was by his touch, his talent.

"You're very handsome, of course, and in great shape," *she said sincerely.* "You're one of the nicest men I know. I don't know anyone who grows such beautiful flowers as you do."

A tall Kyn dressed as a golden demon brushed by him, taking Jema from his arms and whirling away with her into the falling snow. Before they disappeared, the demon took off his mask to reveal Thierry Durand's face.

Valentin stood alone in the center of the empty ballroom. She did not care for him. Jema and her lover had vanished along with the rest of the Kyn. Jaus had loved a human fe-

male for nearly all of her life, and she had given her heart to another.

"Do you see now?"

A woman dressed in black and wearing the mask of a scarlet bird walked to the edge of the dance floor. She stood there as if waiting for an answer.

"Leave me."

"Why should I?" she asked. "She is not coming back. She chose another instead of you. She will never love you. She does not even know you."

Valentin strode across the dance floor and took the jeering woman by the arms. "Who are you to speak to me of her?"

"I am everything you wished her to be," she said, her hands coming to rest on his chest, her touch so hot it burned him. "But as long as you grieve for what you could never have, you will not have me. As you can never have her."

"I don't want you." He shoved her away from him. "You are nothing like her."

"I know that." The woman's mask burst into flame. "Do you?"

As he came awake, Valentin saw fire, and covered Liling's head with his arms, until he realized the flames were still confined to the fireplace in front of them.

Memories and dreams did not become visions—at least, not for Jaus. The woman in the red swan mask had not been there that night of Halloween, when he had learned of Jema's true feelings for him. Yet he knew the masked woman; he could feel a sense of her in his bones. She was not Alexandra Keller, but she reminded him of her.

She, not Jema, had made his *dents acérées* extrude into his mouth. She had brought out the bloodlust in him, as if she were a real woman and not part of some fantastic vision.

Liling appeared to be sleeping peacefully, so Valentin eased away from her and silently left the cabin to stand outside. He knew part of his desire to feed was due to the isolation, just as a mortal denied water felt constant thirst. He considered catching and feeding on an animal—something desperate Kyn did when no humans were available for their use—but animal blood would make him ill, and he could not care for Liling in such condition. Nor would he risk leaving her alone here to walk out until he did find a human; he still had no idea how far they were from the nearest occupied area.

He would return to the cabin and brew some tea, one of the few liquids he could stomach. That was why he had prepared it on the plane for Liling, so that if she expected him to join her . . .

Valentin recalled looking into the refrigerated unit in the galley for food for Liling. There had been bagged blood stored discreetly in one of the bottom bins for his use. He walked down to the edge of the lake. The plane, fully submerged, was still intact. There was a very good chance the blood was as well.

Quickly he stripped out of his clothes and waded in to dive down.

He swam to the cockpit emergency exit and entered the plane through the open hatch. The pilot's and copilot's bodies floated faceup against the ceiling of the aircraft; he swam under them and around a tangle of debris to the galley section.

The refrigerated unit's door hung open, but Valentin found the bin and the bags of blood in it still intact. The cold lake water had flooded the bin and kept them cool; they would still be usable.

Relief eased the gnawing hunger in his belly. There were

enough bags to keep him alive and Liling safe for a long time.

He found a floating carry-on bag and opened it, placing the bagged blood inside before swimming out of the plane and up to the lakeshore. He tossed the bag up onto the bank and waded out.

After he dressed, Valentin took one of the bags from the carry-on and drank from it. Feeding on stored blood was not the same as taking it from a human, but since losing the use of his arm he had disdained using humans and had become accustomed to it. As he drank, he saw that some of the original contents of the bag had fallen out onto the grass: a sodden pile of red hair, a large, soggy roll of currency, and some cards bound with a rubber band.

Valentin carefully set aside the blood and inspected the belongings. The pile of hair turned out to be a wig, the roll contained thousands of dollars in small bills, and the cards were three driver's licenses. The latter pictured Liling Harper's face surrounded by different shades and lengths of hair. All of the names on the licenses were different.

Whatever trouble in Chicago Liling had been trying to escape, it was serious enough to have her prepare three different false identities. Now he was more convinced than ever that she had been trying to evade the Brethren. But why? She wasn't Kyn. She couldn't harm other humans with her ability to heal. Why would the zealots pursue a woman as gentle as Liling, whose power allowed her to do the same as Christ himself had done with the sick and lame and dying?

He touched his arm, which gave him one possible answer. *Because she can heal more than humans.*

* * *

"I dinnae want you stepping one foot into anything with wings," Byrne warned as they walked across the runway to the small plane hangar. "Not one."

"I wouldn't be of any use to the CAP anyway," Jayr said, and smiled at the human approaching them. "Hello, Major Stevens."

"It's a pleasure to meet you at last, my lady." The human held out his hand, on which he wore a black cameo ring. "We appreciate the support the Kyn have given to the CAP over the years."

"CAP?" Byrne asked, looking puzzled.

"Civil Air Patrol," Jayr explained. "One of the ways we have helped the local human community is by donating funds to purchase aircraft for them. They are an auxiliary of the American air force."

"We are strictly nonmilitary volunteer pilots, my lord," Stevens assured Byrne. "CAP flies primarily search-and-rescue and disaster-relief missions. We sometimes provide reconnaissance for authorities at their request, usually to track drug smugglers, and in times of disaster we help out by transporting medical personnel and relief supplies. Here in Florida, our primary mission is to search for downed planes. The men involved in this operation are all CAP-trained, but in order to avoid exposure, we are conducting this search privately, with our personal aircraft." He gestured toward the hangar. "If you'll come this way, I can give you a more comprehensive update on the search."

As they walked past a row of single-engine planes painted red, white, and blue, Stevens explained some of the odds Jaus was facing.

"The survival rate for an airliner is actually very good," the pilot told them. "Every year, only about one in twenty passengers don't make it. The problem is that once the plane is down, those who survive the impact succumb to the subsequent lethal environment. There is a window of opportunity—usually about a minute and a half after the crash—before the fuselage burns, explodes, floods, or sinks. The passengers who exit the aircraft during that time have the best chance to make it out alive."

"Jaus's plane cannot flood or sink," Byrne said, "unless he flew over the ocean."

"I have to disagree with you on that point, my lord," Stevens said. "There are over a thousand lakes in Lake County alone, along with the St. Johns River, and other significant bodies of water in surrounding counties. Many of the lakes are deep enough to sink ten planes."

The Civil Air Patrol's offices were small and cramped. Three men were marking points on a wall map showing central Florida with a grid drawn in red ink.

"We're borrowing some of CAP's equipment to use in the search. They've recently developed hyperspectral imaging sensors, or HIS, and a visual computing network, or VCN. HIS allows sensors on our search aircraft to pick up light reflected by objects on the ground. Through VCN, we can identify the spectral signatures for natural and man-made objects, which makes it pretty easy to spot something that isn't supposed to be there, like a plane."

"How accurate is this sensor system?" Jayr asked.

"Our aircraft can use it from as high as a half mile up to locate an object on the ground that's as small as three feet in size," Stevens told her. "Even if it's hidden by brush or trees. Makes it ideal to pinpoint crash sites in a hurry."

He brought them over to the wall maps to show them the search-and-rescue grid.

"So far we've covered this portion of the Ocala National Forest," he said, circling with his finger a large green area on the map. "We found no signs of the aircraft, and it's unlikely that he would have had enough fuel to make it farther south, so we're moving east."

He told them about the flights he had scheduled, and how they were coordinating their efforts with the Kyn search teams on the ground. "Your trackers have covered a lot of area, which has been helpful, but I won't lie to you: This part of Florida has hundreds of miles of uninhabited forests, lakes, and wetlands. To keep local law enforcement out of our hair, there are only a certain number of pilots we can use for the mission." He grimaced. "It could take weeks, even months."

"If you or your men need anything to assist in the search, Major Stevens," Jayr said, handing him a card with only a series of numbers on it, "call this number and we will see to it immediately."

"We will call you the moment we find any evidence, my lady." Stevens bowed.

As they walked back to the car, Byrne pulled Jayr to a halt. "What other local human community projects have we been supporting?"

Jayr thought for a moment. "Well, there are the scholarship programs, financial assistance for single mothers, the youth center, the free medical clinic, meals for elderly shut-ins—"

He held up a hand. "And why dinnae you mention these projects when *I* was suzerain of the Realm?"

"Initially I brought them all to your attention as worthy causes," she said, giving him a smug smile. "Usually when you were busy training the men, or working the horses, or gossiping with Locksley. You always told me to deal with them myself, and so I did."

"How generous of me." He bent down until the end of his nose touched hers. "I never in my life gossiped."

Jayr shrugged. "Like it or not, we are part of the human world, Aedan. We can no more ignore their troubles than we can our own. They remember what we do for them. Those men in there." She nodded toward the hangar. "They have been flying reconnaissance missions ever since Jaus disappeared. They will keep searching until they find him, or we do."

Byrne looked out at the runway and the Cessna taking off into the night. To his eyes it seemed such a small, flimsy craft, little more than a toy. "I hope it is soon."

As soon as Wilhelm delivered the medicines and supplies, Alexandra set up and started IV antibiotics for her brother, and administered a dose of chloroquine. John's fever decreased over the next several hours, and his vitals improved to the point where she cautiously decided he was stable.

Cyprien checked on them regularly, but stayed only a few minutes each time before returning to coordinate the search-and-rescue effort.

Alex was scanning through an online article on tropical diseases of the blood when John regained consciousness.

"Alex?"

She got up and walked over to the bed. "Right here." She checked his temperature and pulse. "Next time you feel like losing consciousness, big brother, a heads-up would be nice. You weigh a ton."

"You have superpowers."

"I don't have supernerves," she said, "so don't get on them."

"You always look upset when you're being a doctor," John observed idly. "Why is that?"

"Oh, no, this is my happy face. See?" She pointed to her scowl. "This is me, overjoyed."

"You're the happiest person I know, then." He looked around him. "Why are there tubes stuck in me? What happened?"

"Other than the fact that you're malnourished, feverish, and evidently in need of a good beating?" She adjusted the drip on the IV. "You tell me."

He gave her a long-suffering look. "Just tell me what's wrong with me, Alex."

"You'll have to answer some questions first," she said. "For starters, how long have you had malaria?"

"Is that what it is?" He seemed bemused. "Fifteen years, I guess."

"Fifteen years. You guess. Wonderful." Her shoulders stiffened. "Since you didn't know what it was, I assume that you never got treatment for it." She watched him shake his head. "You never once mentioned it to me, either. Any particular reason why?"

"It's no big deal. Every couple of months I run a fever, and then it goes away." He seemed totally unconcerned. "Did they find the plane yet?"

"No. John, we need to talk about this." She sat down on the bed. "Do you know how many people in the world die of malaria every year? A million, minimum. It wipes out whole villages in Africa."

He averted his gaze. "So, I'm lucky."

"No, you're stupid. You're not being treated, and when complications from malaria kick in, as they so often do, they can affect your liver, brain, and kidney function," she informed him sweetly. "When that happens, you drop dead, just like the other nine hundred ninety-nine thousand nine hundred and ninety-nine other people who die of it every year."

He looked up at the light fixture over his bed. "Alex, as you've so often said, I'm an idiot. Don't worry about it."

"You've been hiding this since I was in high school." She sniffed. "Kissing my ass now will not make it go away."

"You really *are* overjoyed with me." He sounded tired. "I mean, don't worry about the malaria. If it kills me, it kills me."

"You don't want to say that to me right now," she said through her teeth. "Not after I've been staring at your abnormal blood smears for twelve hours."

Michael came in. "I thought I heard voices." He looked down at John. "How are you feeling?"

"Fine." John sat up. "I remembered something on the flight to Chicago, and I wanted to tell you before I forget it again."

"He is not fine," Alex told Michael. "He's got malaria, and maybe something else. His blood's a mess."

John made a dismissive gesture before saying to Michael, "When Child Services turned me and Alex over to the church, they took us to a place named for one of the saints. I think it was the St. Benedict Home for Children."

"We will talk about it when you are feeling better," Michael told him.

"It can't wait, Cyprien. It was north of the city, near some factories with orange smokestacks. Do you think your people could locate it from those details?" When Michael said nothing, John tried to get up. "I'll look for it myself."

"Oh, no." Alex pushed him back. "You're staying in this bed."

"There's no point," her brother said.

Alex stared at him in disbelief. "You're having a serious health crisis, John. Whatever happened to us when we were kids was thirty years ago. It can wait another week or two."

"No, it can't." He pulled back the sheets. "I can't."

"You can if I break your legs—"

"If the orphanage is still operating," Michael said, interrupting her, "Phillipe will locate it. When he does, you can advise me on how to proceed."

She turned to her lover. "Did I suddenly acquire Jema Shaw's talent and become invisible here?"

"Excuse us, John," Michael said, and led Alex out into the hall. "Your brother is becoming very agitated. It is best that we keep him calm."

"No, it is best that I find out what type of malaria he has, so I can keep it from killing him," she said. "Stay out of this."

Michael glanced at the door. "Haven't you noticed what's happened to his scent?"

"Yeah, and I made him take a shower," she snapped. "So he was a little grungy. Who cares?"

"And did you notice his scent after he bathed?"

"He didn't smell like anything. Just fresh and clean and . . ." She trailed off and stared at the concern in her lover's expression. "And like nothing. I couldn't smell him. His scent is gone. What does that mean when we can't smell them?" She grabbed his arm. "God damn it, Michael, tell me."

"It means either your brother is dead," Michael said slowly, "or he has gone mad."

Chapter 15

Valentin brought Liling's carry-on and the blood into the cabin. He stocked the refrigerator with the blood, covering the bags with some hand towels and stacking some cans of soda in front of it. He intended to tell Liling what he was, once she felt better, but until then it was better to keep certain facts of his existence from her.

He looked at the dripping carry-on. They both had significant secrets they were hiding from each other. He wanted her to know his—he needed her to know—but would she trust him enough to tell him hers?

He went out to the front room, but the quilt lay empty, and Liling was nowhere in sight. He went to the bathroom, and then the bedroom, but he couldn't find her. "Liling?"

Valentin breathed in, ignoring the smell of the propane from the fireplace to find her scent. It was very light, the slightest trace of warmed peaches, but she was here in the cabin. He followed it back out of the bedroom and to the couch. He thought for a moment that the scent came from the quilt he had wrapped around her, until he heard the beat of her heart coming from beneath it.

Gently he picked up the end of the couch and lifted it

away to reveal her small form. She had crawled under it to hide.

"There you are." He knelt down and pulled her hands away from her face. "Why are you under the couch? I know the cushions are lumpy, but they must be more comfortable than the floor."

"I heard what the pilot said before he shot you," she said, her voice unsteady. "He said, 'The girl must die,' and I was the only girl on the plane. He was going to crash the plane because of me. You almost drowned. None of this would have happened if I'd left Chicago on my own."

Jaus picked her up and sat on the couch with her, holding her on his lap. "Did you hire the pilot? Did you give him the gun? Did you knock me out?"

"No, but—"

"But no." He pressed a finger to her lips. "You did not do any of those things. You are not responsible for this, *Geliebte*. It simply happened, and we are fortunate to have survived it."

She shook her head. "I should have known. I should have . . . expected it."

"Is that why you were carrying so much money, and disguises, and false IDs?" Before she could answer, he said, "I found your bag. What are you running from, Liling?"

She paled. "I can't tell you. It's too dangerous."

Jaus considered compelling the truth out of her, but she was shivering and terrified. He took the quilt and bundled it around her. "Very well. When you are ready to trust me, I hope you will."

He sat holding her until her body stilled and her breathing slowed. He thought she was sleeping until her hand touched the scar on his arm. The warming sensation her fingers brought to his flesh eased some of the stiffness he had acquired from using it after long inactivity.

"Does it still hurt?" she asked.

"A little." He kissed the top of her head. "I am very grateful for what you did to heal me."

She stiffened. "I didn't do anything."

He set her back and looked into her downcast face. "My arm has been useless for years. The doctor who reattached it said it would always be so. Despite that, I have tried time and again to exercise it and loosen it and force it to work, to no avail. Then you touch me—you kiss my scar—and a few hours later, I can use it again. It was you."

"I didn't heal you," she insisted. "I can't do anything like that."

"You did something."

She stayed silent for so long that he thought she would not reply. Then, in a voice so low he could barely hear it, she said, "I took away your pain."

Jaus felt puzzled. "I was never in pain," he told her. "I could not feel anything in my arm."

"Paralysis is a kind of pain. It blocks the body from feeling what it should feel," she said. "Sometimes that is better for a person, because it keeps them from suffering. There is a man at the Lighthouse who is paralyzed from the waist down. The wounds to his legs from the car accident he was in compressed his nerves. If his spine worked as it should, he would be in agony for the rest of his life."

"How could you know these things?"

"I feel them when I touch people." She looked up at him. "Like Mr. Lindquist, the man who had the stroke. He must have been aware of what his sister was doing to him. He felt it, and he can see and hear. But he couldn't tell anyone, not even me. He is trapped inside his body and he can't get out.

Many of the stroke patients are like that. Aware but imprisoned by their flesh."

"Could you heal him?"

"No, I can't heal. I can only ease their pain." She looked ashamed. "The wounds remain, and the body must heal itself. Sometimes I can help them for only an hour or a day."

Jaus looked at his arm. "So my arm will not remain like this. It will become paralyzed again."

She stroked his scar. "Not unless you want it to."

"What do you mean?"

She bit her lip. "Your arm was never paralyzed, Valentin. Your heart was."

A surge of anger made him put her aside, and he got up from the couch. "You are mistaken."

"You could always use your arm, but your mind wouldn't allow you to," she insisted. "It happens that way with some people when they feel guilty."

"I am not guilty of anything."

She came to stand in front of him, her hand holding the quilt around her. "I could feel it. Each type of pain is unique, and your heart created this one to control your flesh. Perhaps it came from something terrible that happened just before you were wounded—"

"Willst du wohl gefälligst den mund halten?" He seized her shoulders. "Be silent. You will not speak to me of this. Ever again."

"Very well." She swallowed. "In a few hours, your arm will grow numb again. You won't be able to lift it or use it. And your heart will see to it that you never again do whatever it was that caused it to be severed."

Jaus went still. He walked away from her and went to the large front windows, where he stood with his arm braced against the frame.

Liling came and sat on the window seat. She said nothing, but sat waiting and looking up at him.

"Her name was Jema," he said slowly. "She was all I ever wanted. Like a dream that you know will never come true but you can't stop thinking about it. I was well aware that it would be almost impossible for us to be together. She was frail and sick, and I had my reasons to stay away. But I couldn't. I watched her from a distance. No, I worshiped her from a distance," he corrected himself. "Jema was everything bright and beautiful and perfect in this world." He rested his forehead against his arm.

Liling pulled her knees up against her chest and looked out at the lake. "She sounds lovely."

"She was," he agreed. "But do you know, never once in all the years I cared for her did I imagine I would one day lose her. Not when I lived and breathed every moment with her in my heart. I knew her condition was terminal. I knew there was no cure. I knew all of these things, but I still held on to hope. I believed there was still the chance of a miracle happening, and she would be saved, and we could be together at last."

"Did Jema die?"

"Nothing so simple as that." He looked down at her. "I was so blinded by my own regard for Jema that I didn't see what was happening to her right in front of me. On the night that I finally found the courage to tell her how much I cared for her, she revealed her own feelings. She didn't care for me. All those years I had devoted my heart to her and she didn't care. She never even thought of me. I was no one, nothing, a nice man she barely knew."

Liling didn't say anything, but curled her hand around his calf.

"Thirty years of my life, rendered meaningless in an instant. And then I learned that she had been with another man. A man I knew named Thierry. She was in love with him."

He sank down, propping his back against the window seat and staring at the flames in the fireplace.

"I never felt such rage," he said, his voice breaking on the last word. "I think I went mad. I attacked Thierry. We fought over her, and although he was the better swordsman, I had nothing left to live for. I meant to kill him or die trying."

Liling looked at the fireplace. "Did you kill him?"

"Almost. Jema distracted him, you see, and Thierry lowered his guard for a moment. Only a moment, but that was enough. I used it. I lunged, and then she was in front of Thierry, between us." He shook his head. "It happened so fast. I couldn't stop myself in time. . . ." He closed his eyes. "After I ran her through, Thierry cut off my arm."

"Oh, Valentin." She came down from the seat to sit on the floor beside him, and rested her cheek against his shoulder.

"She survived. She is with Thierry now. I am told that they are very happy together." He ducked his head. "You think that is why I have not been able to use my arm?"

"It makes some sense," she said in a tentative tone.

He looked at his hand and clenched it. "Because the last time I did use it, I almost killed the woman I loved."

"The heart makes harsh decisions," she said quietly. "If you couldn't use your arm, then you couldn't hold a blade or hurt another woman."

He met her gaze. "Are you afraid of me, Liling?"

"No." She said it without hesitation.

"You should be." He pushed himself up from the floor and left the cabin.

Valentin walked blindly, barely aware of his surroundings. He stopped in front of a massive oak tree. Bark exploded as he drove his fist into the trunk.

"Why should I be afraid of you?" a soft voice said behind him. "I am not a tree."

He leaned against the scarred trunk, hiding his bloody hand from her. Then he turned and held it out in front of him. "Here. Here is one reason." When she looked away, he walked up to her and grabbed a handful of her hair, forcing her to face him. "Look at it. *Look.*" She took a deep breath and watched his wounds as they slowly closed and disappeared. "You see? I do not need you to heal me." He released her. "I do not need anyone."

"Valentin." She rested her hand on his shoulder and lifted her face to kiss his wet cheek. "I am still not afraid of you."

"You think I need your polite lies?" He slid his hand to her neck. "Now you will tell me the truth. Tell me that you despise me for what I am, and what I have done. Tell me how you cannot wait to be rid of me. *Tell me.*"

"I don't despise you," she said slowly, the words halting. "What happened was an accident. I know you would never have hurt Jema, just as you would never hurt me. I don't want to be rid of you. I don't want to leave you when we arrive in Atlanta. I want to stay with you. I know what you want. I can give it to you."

The place on his cheek where she had kissed him burned under his fingers. "What is it that I want?"

She pressed herself against him, her cheek against his shoulder. "My surrender."

His touch compelled her to be truthful, so she could not be lying to him. He hardly knew what to make of it. "Why?"

"Because it will please you as much as it does me." She buried her face against him.

Valentin swept her up in his arms and carried her back into the cabin. He took her to the bedroom, stripping the T-shirt from her body before placing her on the bed. He tore off his own clothes and joined her, stretching out over her. When she tried to touch him, he pinned her wrists down.

"Did you like what we did on the plane?"

Her eyelashes swept down shyly. "Yes."

His cock had been hard and erect ever since the word *surrender* had left her lips. "I did not frighten you?"

"You did, but it excited me. I felt"—she closed her eyes—"so alive, so wanted."

Valentin rolled onto his back and stared at the rough oak beams above them. He knew his own nature, and he had spent many lifetimes controlling it to a fine degree. He had even conquered it, he had thought. But being with her had caused a resurrection, brought it rising out of the darkness inside him. He *had* wanted her surrender, all of it, everything she was, for himself.

And she had given it to him. Beautifully, completely, without condition. Remembering how made his shaft swell even larger.

Few women, human or Kyn, could respond to such a need. It had been another reason he had never approached Jema Shaw. She had been too delicate, too ill. Had they managed to have some sort of relationship, Valentin could never have been himself with her; she had been too fragile. With Jema, he would never have known the dark satisfaction he craved to take, and to give.

Why had he never realized that?

"I will go." Liling scrambled off the bed.

Valentin jumped after her, lifting her and holding her as

she fought him. She was much stronger than he had imagined; he could barely hold her. "*Geliebte*, be calm."

"You don't want me," she said, pushing her hands against his chest. "Please, I don't want your pity, not like this."

Valentin fell onto the bed with her, trying to contain her struggles. "You are wrong." He braced himself on top of her. "Liling, *stop*."

Instantly she went still and stared up at him blindly. Her fists relaxed, and her legs shifted, opening, spreading. She lifted her hips, rubbing herself against the surface of his thigh. The soft black hair over her mound felt damp, and as she rubbed, he felt on his skin the slickness between her legs.

Valentin looked down at his hand, which he had somehow clamped over her small breast. He watched her face as he massaged her gently. "Do you want me to touch you like this, *mein Mädchen*?"

Liling's eyes softened, and her lips parted before she averted her face. "You don't want me. You want her."

"Or do you like it here?" He brought his hand from her breast to her crotch, cupping her.

A spasm of delight crossed her features, and she shuddered, pushing her hips up against his hand.

The scent of her arousal poured over him, the tang of hot peaches, and Valentin drew his hand away, taking hers and bringing it to his erection.

"Wrap your fingers around me," he said, guiding her with his hand. "There. Now stroke me, like this." He moved her hand in slow motion before releasing it and bringing his own fingers back to her sex. He parted her and rubbed gently. "Tell me what else excites you."

"This." She pumped him with the languid motion he had shown her. "Giving you control. Doing what you say. The surrender. It feels safe. You're the most exciting man I've ever known."

He bent to kiss her open mouth, doing with his tongue what he longed to do with his cock. She trembled against him, and he lifted his head, his body shaking with his own lust. "You want me to take you."

She nodded, her fingers tightening.

"I would very much like to," he told her softly. "But this changes everything. Do you know what it means to surrender?"

"It means being yours. Belonging to you. Giving you what you need." She bit her bottom lip and arched, digging her heels into the mattress.

Valentin closed his eyes, fighting back the ferocious need to put his teeth to her flesh. She was too weak now for him to take her as he wanted. He had to end this before he lost control.

He took her hand away and gathered her close, reaching down to seat his shaft against the top of her mound. He worked himself against her hardened clit, using the friction to bring them both to the edge.

"You will give me whatever I wish," he whispered against her ear as he pressed her hips closer. "Whenever I want it. You will do this willingly."

"Yes," she whispered.

"When we are naked together, you will let me do whatever I wish to you," he persisted, pushing his cock faster, harder. "You will trust me to see to your pleasure."

"Yes. Anything." She sobbed the word.

Valentin shifted her, impaling her wet slit with a single thrust, making her cry out.

"Then, my lady," he said against her mouth, "I am yours."

*   *   *

A large shadow and a small one inched across the table in the guards' hall. "My lady."

Jayr didn't look up from the map she was studying. "Not now, Rain."

"I would not disturb you," the big man said, "but Farlae and I wish to help search for Suzerain Jaus."

"You and Farlae?" Jayr frowned as she took in the sight of her men. Rain had garbed himself in a baggy pair of camouflage-patterned trousers and a leather vest over a striped shirt. None of it would have merited her attention, except that they were made of pink and yellow fabrics. Her wardrobe keeper, who stood next to Rain, wore his customary black turtleneck and fitted black denims. Both men were armed with sheathed daggers. "What is this?"

"Rain and I wish to help," Farlae said. One of his eyes, flawed with an enormous black mote, glittered. "Rain is the best tracker in the Realm, and I can see what others cannot. If we can search together, I think we can find Jaus."

Jayr sat back and folded her arms. "*Rain* is the best tracker in the Realm."

"Among most Kyn, too." The former court jester produced a modest smile. "Well, Gabriel Seran has a better nose." He studied her face before he turned to Farlae. "I told you she would not believe us. Now will you come and play strip Monopoly with me?"

Farlae cuffed the back of Rain's head. "We must demonstrate, my peacock. Tell her where Harlech is."

Rain scowled, sighed, and then breathed in deeply, turning as he did. "The stables, feeding a horse."

"Farlae, I don't have time—" Jayr said, but the wardrobe keeper held up one hand.

"Where is Beaumaris?"

Rain took longer to answer. "On the battlements. No. At the east tower now. Standing guard."

Farlae nodded. "And where is Lord Byrne?"

"In the suzeraina's bedchamber." Rain gave Jayr a decidedly lecherous grin. "Preparing the lady's bath."

Jayr couldn't help smiling. "I sent Harlech into town an hour ago, Beaumaris is off duty tonight, and Aedan does not draw baths for me. I shower. Now, if you don't mind, I have to coordinate the next phase of the ground search."

Farlae tossed her his radio/mobile phone, which she caught out of reflex. "Call them."

Jayr knew from the look on her wardrobe keeper's face that she wouldn't get anything more accomplished until she did, and she keyed in Harlech's code. "Harlech, when will you be returning from town?"

"I apologize, my lady, but I have not yet left," her second said. "The stablemaster asked me to give Byrne's palfrey a bit of coddling. She has been off her feed of late. How may I be of service?"

"It's nothing, Harlech." Jayr eyed the two men as she keyed in Beaumaris's code. "Beau, where are you?"

"The east tower, my lady," Beaumaris replied.

Jayr frowned. "You're not on duty tonight."

"Gawain has become infatuated with a human in town, and this is her only night off," Beau explained. "I agreed to switch duty shifts with him. Did you need me at the keep, my lady?"

"Not now." Farlae's gloating expression annoyed her, so she asked, "One more thing, Beau. Have you been on the battlements tonight?"

"I went up to check the perimeter," he admitted.

"He went up to have an assignation with the new French

girl from the kitchens," Rain whispered overloudly. "I can still smell her scent in his."

"Thank you, Beau." Jayr switched off the radio.

Byrne came in and surveyed the three of them. "Why are you two annoying my mistress?"

"It seems Farlae and Rain wish to help search for Lord Jaus."

Byrne chuckled. "I dinnae think Jaus will need tailoring or entertaining."

"Sprinkling rose petals in the lady's bath was a romantic touch," Farlae said unexpectedly. "But she favors slices of citrus or stalks of heather."

Byrne stared at him. "How did you know what I put in the bath?"

"Rain can smell it," Farlae told him, "and I can see the traces of essence the petals left on your hands."

Jayr turned to regard him with her dark brows lifted. "You drew a bath for me?"

"For us. I thought it would be romantic." Byrne glanced at his hands, which appeared clean and unmarked, and glowered at Farlae. "What color were the roses?"

"Blush pink, with reddened edges." As Byrne gaped, Farlae gave Jayr a complacent look. "Are you convinced, my lady?"

She chuckled. "I am. Very well, you two may lead the next search team."

Alexandra shoved open the door to the one room in the house where there wouldn't be any vampires—the kitchen—and stomped over to the cabinets.

"My brother isn't nuts, oh, no," she muttered to herself. "*I'm* the one who's crazy. I gave up my life for this. Not like there were any other options, but still. I could have stayed here. Opened a blood bank or something. Doesn't want treatment. 'If it kills me, it kills me.' Who does he think I am, a crisis-line counselor?" She slammed shut the cabinet and banged her head against it. "Shit. I can't do this. I can't."

"The tea canister is on the second shelf to the right," an old, tired voice behind her advised. "The chamomile will not make you sick."

Alex turned and looked at Gregor Sacher, who was sitting at the kitchen table. In front of him was a small bottle of schnapps and a half-empty glass. "Can I have some of that?"

"Even if you could keep the alcohol down, my lady, it would not intoxicate you." He gave her an apologetic smile and lifted the glass. Before he drank, he looked into it. "My doctor in the city says I should not drink. I think he is jealous, because he is not yet old enough to legally buy his own liquor." He took a swallow.

Alex came over and sat down beside the elderly *tresora*. "Please tell me that you're not suicidal. Apparently I *suck* at handling the suicidal."

Gregor uttered a sour chuckle. "Never fear, you need not handle me. I am merely old and useless. Or so I heard one of the guards telling my grandson."

"Oh, useless, my ass," Alex said. "You've got this place running like clockwork. Who is this guard? I'll go and beat him to a pulp for you."

"You are a lovely friend, but you will hurt your hands. Besides, Wilhelm agreed." He took another sip of the schnapps. "These days it seems that all I am good for is wandering around the house after him, fretting and complaining. 'Getting in the way,' he called it." He carefully replaced the glass on the table. "It is past time I retired. They are indulging me because I am old and they pity me." Before she could comment on that, he asked, "How is your brother?"

"I've started him on chloroquine, which should eliminate the parasites from his blood." She sat back in the chair. "Unless it's a strain of falciparum malaria, which is resistant to the drug. If that's what he's got, we're looking at a more serious situation. It could kill off so many of his blood cells that they'll start blocking the vessels to his major organs. His spleen will enlarge. He'll have brain-damaging convulsions and go into renal failure. And then my big brother will finally get to know for sure whether or not there really is a God."

"There is," Gregor assured her. "Nothing as tragic and ridiculous as this world could have happened by random chance."

Alex nodded. "Anyway, if it's a resistant strain, I can try other drugs. They've had some success treating patients with a combination of pyrimethamine and sulfadoxine—" She stopped and jammed her fists against her eyes. "No. I don't know what to do. I don't even recognize the type of malaria he has. I've never seen anything like it. I thought it might be a new strain of something that's come out since I stopped practicing medicine, but John says he's had it for fifteen years."

"Could it be something other than malaria?" Gregor asked.

"No, because it has the exact same symptoms as malaria," she admitted, dropping her hands. "There's something else, though—something working in conjunction with the disease— that I can't nail down. I've ruled out blackwater fever, Ebola, and AIDS. I need to run more tests. I need to run about a thousand tests." Why were her eyes stinging? "But I'll find out what it is and I'll put together a treatment plan. I'm a great diagnostician. Everything will be fine. I just have to chain my brother to the bed. Are you sure I can't beat the snot out of that guard for you?"

"Quite sure." Gregor offered her a white handkerchief.

She wiped the tears from her eyes. "His white blood cells are being compromised by this other thing. It's driving me crazy. It's not leukemia, but it's attacking his immune system."

"Is this fatal?"

"Not always," she lied. "There's radiation therapy, transfusions, and with a bone-marrow transplant—" She stopped herself. "I'll figure out something. I found a treatment for Richard, I diagnosed Jema, I sewed Val's arm back on. . . ." She gave him a guilty look. "Sorry. I know you're worried. Michael and the men will find him and bring him home."

"I do not think my master is coming back this time," Gregor said. "I think his plane crashed, and he was torn to pieces or he burned to death in it. Or he is somewhere so far from humans that he will starve or bleed to death before he can be found."

Alex's heart constricted. "Don't give up hope yet, Gregor."

He added more schnapps to the glass, but his hand was shaking, and it splashed over the rim. He put the bottle down quickly. "I wish only that I knew for certain. I can feel him when he is in the house, but not when he travels. When he is gone, I never know if he is coming back. I never . . ." He covered his eyes with his hand.

"Let me have that." Alex took the glass of schnapps and drank down the rest, coughing as the fiery alcohol blazed its way down her throat. "Good Lord," she wheezed. "Is this liquor or paint remover?"

"Wilhelm sometimes uses it to clean the chrome on the

Ferrari." The old man sniffed. "You are going to be very sick from drinking that, you know."

"I think it's my turn." She shoved the hair hanging in her eyes out of her face. "Val's not dead. My brother isn't going insane, and he won't die of mutant malaria. In a week or two all of this is going to seem pretty funny."

He gave her a sad look. "I do not think I will laugh."

"Neither do I. Which is why they will never hire me to be a crisis counselor." She felt her stomach heave, but after a moment the sensation passed. "Waiting and not knowing. How do we do that, Gregor? How do we act like we're okay and everything will be fine when the people we love are in danger and we can do nothing to help them?"

"I can't." His lower lip trembled. "Suzerain Jaus is a lord paramount, and I am sworn to serve him. I know my place and my duty. But that is not all that he is to me, Alex. I love Valentin. I love him like a son. Now, when he is in trouble, when he most needs me, I cannot go to him."

"Gregor."

"I cannot find him. I cannot bring him home and take care of him. I don't eat; I don't sleep. I cannot think of a life without him in it." He drew in a shuddering breath. "I cannot bury another son, Alexandra. This time I fear they will have to put me in the grave with him."

Alex put her arms around him and held him as he wept, making soothing sounds until he composed himself.

"You are very kind to an old man, my lady." Gregor seemed embarrassed now.

"I wish I were like you, but I hate my brother. He's a stuck-up, sanctimonious jerk." And the way he avoided looking at her was driving her up the wall. "I didn't ask for this vampire thing to happen to me. I didn't want it. But I adjusted, and I'm doing the best I can. I'm not whining or crying, even when I want to. And I'm still his sister. I love my brother. And you know, he can't even look at me anymore? Because when he does, he can't hide how much he hates me for what I am."

"Alexandra." He rested one frail hand against her cheek. "Whatever happens, he will always be your brother, and you his sister. That bond, it is forever. Nothing changes it. Not even death."

She sat back and looked into his eyes. "I think the same thing goes for you and Val."

He took his handkerchief from her and blew his nose in it. "You are wrong. You do not suck at this."

"Thanks. I feel better." She pressed a hand to her abdomen. "Except I have to go throw up now."

Chapter 16

L iling woke up at dawn, the sunlight making her squint. Jaus had rolled away from her and pulled a pillow over his head. He slept so deeply he looked almost lifeless. She got up and draped the window with the quilt they had kicked off sometime during the night.

She went to find some clothes. Her own had been left in a soggy pile, but she discovered a trunk filled with clothing and took the smallest she could find to wear: a pair of black sweatpants with an elastic waist, and a red-and-black plaid shirt.

Taking them into the bathroom, she turned on the shower and stepped inside. The deodorant soap and strong shampoo the cabin's owners had left behind made her nose wrinkle, but in the past she had been forced to use worse.

As she washed, Liling tried to imagine what it would feel like to have Valentin fall so deeply in love with her that he would want to kill anyone who tried to take her away from him. Had this Jema woman been blind? How could she not have known? How could she have wanted anyone else?

The water grew warm, and then hot.

The bathroom had grown steamy before Liling recognized the danger and turned off the taps. She couldn't allow her emotions to affect her like this. She had gotten too close to him; she had allowed the sex and the fulfillment of her fantasies to seduce her and make her forget her responsibilities. Valentin wanted her, and for a time she could be with him. Here, while they were alone, while there was no danger of being discovered.

An ache grew in her stomach as she thought of how it would be after they were rescued. The attraction between them was strong. He also felt grateful to her for taking his pain and for helping him to see from where it had come. She now knew his secret: that he could heal himself. In many ways they were exactly alike.

He liked how well they fit together as lovers, too. He would not let her go easily.

She had to leave him eventually. Not only to protect him, but because it couldn't last. Valentin wanted her, but he couldn't love her. He had already given his heart away to Jema.

Liling felt sick, and braced herself over the sink, but nothing happened. And then she knew it was the thought of leaving him, and of knowing he could never love her as much as he had Jema, that was making her ill.

She couldn't leave him, and she couldn't stay. What was she going to do? How could she tell him?

She looked down and saw that the water that had been running down her legs had beaded, unmoving, on her skin. She glanced at the shower and saw more drops running over the edge, across the floor, streaming toward her.

He had found her again.

Steam rose from her body as she crouched, ignoring the icy touch of the water as she pressed her hands to the tiled floor. The droplets on the floor began to jump and sizzle as the tiles turned red. The room was a cloud of steam by the time she rose, snatched up the clean clothes, and walked out.

She dressed outside the bathroom and went to the kitchen. Valentin had put some canned soft drinks in the refrigerator, and she took one out and drank down the entire can, then a second, and a third before the thirst passed. Her stomach surged and she hurried over to the sink.

She vomited until her stomach emptied.

Liling straightened and gasped for air. Something was different; something was wrong with her insides. She tried to drink another can, which made her sick again. As she washed her hot face, the water she hated wet her lips, and she was able to drink and hold down some of that.

Weakened by the bizarre episode, she went out and sat in front of the fireplace. She felt terribly hungry, but the thought of food turned her stomach. She curled up in the strange clothes and stared at the flames.

Fire comforted her like nothing else. She understood its hunger, its greed to consume everything it touched. It was powerful and dangerous, but it could be confined, controlled, made useful. As she had been.

She got up slowly and went back to the bedroom. As soon as she lay on the bed beside Valentin, he rolled toward her and put his arm across her.

Her eyelids slipped down as she drifted off to sleep.

Liling wandered through the dreamscape, watching the gray dullness around her draw and redraw itself. It reminded her of the Magic Board her twin had stolen for her when they were nine.

She had wanted only a book. The priests forbade them to keep anything but Bibles in their rooms, but one of the doctors kept some children's books and toys in a cabinet in one of the hurting rooms. They were worn and tattered—the doctor had bought them at a library discard sale, ten cents a box—and most of them were too young for her. She had been left in the hurting room long enough to unearth a few good ones by Sydney Taylor, Judy Blume, and Laura Ingalls Wilder, and if she didn't make any sound during the testing the doctor would let her take them back to the dormitory.

"I want to read *The Long Winter*," she told her twin. "But Pem took it first."

Her twin thought books were stupid, and told her that, and made her cry.

Liling found the Magic Board, her twin's prized possession, under her pillow the next day.

The Magic Board was covered with silly cartoon stick drawings and was FUN FUN FUN! FOR GIRLS AND BOYS. Made of a thin sheet of cardboard with a thin plastic film rectangle glued at one end on top of a rectangle of sticky gray stuff, it came with a white plastic stylus attached on a black string. Her twin, who loved to draw, had stolen it from the toy cabinet long ago, and had successfully kept it hidden from their monitors.

Liling drew with the stylus on the film, and gray lines appeared as the film adhered to the sticky stuff underneath. Then, when she lifted the film—making a sound exactly like ripping paper—the lines would vanish and she could draw something new.

She carefully etched two pictures on the film, but her twin came over and told her that it was more FUN FUN FUN! erasing them. That ripped-paper sound it made bothered Liling, but her twin loved it.

Unfortunately, the Magic Board was old and well used. As Liling drew the third picture—two stick-figure children in front of a real Picasso of a house next to a broccoli-stalk tree—the lines began slowly erasing on their own from the scarred, ratty film layer. Each time she tried to draw them back in, some of the tree or the house would vanish.

Her twin saw her tears and snatched the board away from her. *Why do you have to be such a baby?*

I want to live in a real house with a mother and father, and you, she said. *Like Laura in the Little House books.*

They're never going to let us do that, her twin said. *We don't have parents. We don't have names. We're nothing.* Her twin tore the board to pieces.

The priests came in and they were both beaten twice, once for stealing, and once for destroying the board.

Liling understood why her twin had become so angry. It wasn't because she had cried. They knew everything that the other thought, that the other felt. They couldn't help but know.

Every time they were sent to a new facility, they were made into a new picture. When they were taken away, it was as if someone ripped the film up and erased them. She tried to be good so they would keep them in one place, but they never did. That was what had made her cry, and had enraged her twin.

Still, Liling couldn't stop thinking about someday finding a home and a family. She built a little house in her thoughts, with rooms for a mother and father and her and her twin. They would have a big dog to run and play with outside, and flowers all around the house that their mother would tend. They would eat delicious home-cooked meals at a small table with a red-and-white-checked tablecloth, and at night their father would read them bedtime stories, and their mother would kiss their brows and tuck them in.

The daydreams annoyed her twin, and then the bad trouble happened.

The doctors had grown upset with them, but instead of

punishing them more often, they gave in to her twin's demand to go above and play in an empty meadow. The twins knew how to play soccer and baseball, but they had never been above for longer than it took to move them.

Liling loved being aboveground. Everything was so green it almost hurt her eyes to look at it. Wildflowers dotted the meadow where they brought them, and she went from blossom to blossom, drinking in the colors and gently touching the soft petals.

Her twin didn't care about flowers, and brought to her the dented aluminum baseball bat and scuffed ball the doctors had found for them.

Come on, her twin called out, swinging the bat and tossing the ball at her before running backward. *Pitch one to me, and don't throw like a girl!*

Liling pitched the ball, which fell short of the mark. That was when her twin swung the bat into the head of the monitor watching them, and then the other one who came running.

We have to run away, Lili. Her twin grabbed her hand. *Hurry.*

They ran together. They ran across the meadow and through the woods. They ran through a small town and down a long road, until Liling's breath burned in her lungs and her legs felt like lead.

I can't run anymore.

You can't stop. They'll catch us.

I'm too tired. She looked down as a bug bit her arm, and she saw a dart in it. Her mind filled with bees and she fell down. *Run. Run.*

Her twin fell beside her. *You run . . . like . . . a girl.*

When Liling woke, she was back in one of the animal cages they used for punishments. Her twin was gone. Seven years would pass before they came together again. Being separated made Liling retreat into her daydreams. The doctors could do terrible things to her, and often did, but she stayed safely in her fantasy world.

Liling's breathing slowed as she fell deeper into the dream. She could stay here, in this place, and no one would find her.

Not even him.

The girl's water came to Kyan that morning from an old spring-fed lake. There were other traces accompanying it: cheap soap, a man's semen, and the tiniest tang of copper. When he had tried to send his power through the channel to read her, it had recoiled on him. She had cut the connection, but she could not destroy the trail.

He had her now.

It took him the entire day to follow her water inland, through a series of rivers sometimes only just deep enough for the boat. He knew the water, and it guided him along a safe route. He stopped one last time to refuel and, using a map and some sign language, confirmed the location of the lake.

"They don't mark the names on the map anymore, not for the ones out in the reserve, but that there's Ghost Lake," the dock attendant told him. "Lotta open land, but some good deer hunting out that way."

"Yes." Kyan folded the map. "Good hunting."

He purchased some bottled water and returned to the boat. When he was downriver far enough not to be heard, he went down into the cabin. Melanie lay on the bed, her wrists and ankles bound, a strip he had torn from the sheets gagging her. Her eyes widened when she saw him, and she began to struggle against her bonds.

"I am not untying you," he said, removing the gag from her mouth and holding a bottle of water to it. "Drink."

She took in a mouthful and spit it in his face.

"You are going to *jail*," she told him, her voice rasping out the words. "I swear to *God*, the *minute* I get away from you I'm going to bring *every* cop in Florida after your *sorry* ass and have them *lock* you up until *doomsday*."

"They will not find me." He offered her the bottle again, but she turned her head. "You are thirsty. Drink."

"You are an *ass*hole. Fuck *off*."

Her anger made him feel slightly ashamed. She might be a poor, ignorant soul who became easily intoxicated, but she had been helpful to him. He had been intimate with her. "If you are hungry, I will make you food."

"If you touch me again," she replied, "I will puke in your face."

He would give her time to calm down, he decided, and retied the gag. "I am sorry I had to do this, Melanie. It is almost over, and then I will release you. I would let you go now, but I don't know if she speaks Chinese."

Melanie glared at him and rolled away onto her side.

Kyan touched her rigid shoulder before retreating to the helm.

He made his way into the Ocala National Forest, watching the homes and businesses disappear and the land turn wild and untouched. Black bears watched him from the safety of the trees, and deer ran from the sound of the engine. Alligators floated in the shallows, their indifferent eyes blinking as he turned on the deck lights. Moths and mosquitoes came to fly at the bulbs, their shadows making them look as big as birds.

He turned off the lights and the motor before he entered the lake, and used the water itself to guide the boat to a small launching pier. Once he had secured the lines, he went below to get the American girl.

He used his pocketknife to cut the ropes on her ankles, but left her wrists bound and her mouth gagged. "We are here. You will do as I say and you will not get hurt." He took her arm and led her onto the deck.

She looked around, flinching as she saw the ghostly outlines of the submerged plane. She did not resist or try to run as he lifted her onto the pier and walked her down to the tree line. She was clumsy, though, and fell on the wood, and slogged through the brush with heavy feet, disturbing the branches and snapping twigs. The noise she made increased as they approached the cabin, until he stopped and tied her hands to the lower branch of a black olive.

The tightness in his chest and throat made it difficult to speak.

"I will come back for you." He could make himself understood without her. "Whatever happens, do not be afraid."

She shook her head, trying to say something as she strained against the limb he had tied her to. Kyan ran his hand over her bright hair before he turned and walked toward the cabin.

Clouds covered the moon, and lightning began to leapfrog from one black cloud to the next. The only sound Kyan heard was that of the generator behind the cabin. The ground seemed to quiver under his deck shoes, making him stop outside one of the windows. Through the glass he saw into a bedroom. A naked man lay next to a small body wrapped in a quilt.

Kyan put his hand to the window, and the glass cracked under his palm. He didn't have to see her face to know it was her. He could smell her water on the air. He could feel her dreaming, as he had dreamed of this moment.

She does not want to see you.
She says you frighten her.
She refuses.
She laughed when I asked her.
You disgust her.
She wants nothing to do with you, Kyan.

The air hummed in his ears as he reached for the bottom of the window. The crack in the glass began to snake out in three different directions, releasing a small trickle of air from inside the cabin.

Air tainted with the blood of a *maledicti*.

So this was the final betrayal. She had turned her back on their teachings and given herself to the demons. It made sense that she would sell her worthless soul for the pathetic wealth and power the Darkyn wielded. It also explained why her trace had been contaminated with the blood of the evil ones, and why she had survived the crash of the plane.

This was God's work, as the priests always said. The Divine One saved her so that she could be delivered into his hands and receive the justice that she so richly deserved.

He would tell them that she had gone over to the demons. He would bring them her head. That would please his masters.

Kyan backed away. He did not want the window to shatter and give away his intentions. Nor could he allow the man inside to be forewarned and use his power to protect the girl. Instead, he went to the back of the cabin. The door there was not locked, but in a moment of inspiration he reached up and knocked against the wood.

As footsteps approached, he reached down and drew the copper dagger out of his ankle sheath.

Chapter 17

The knock on the cabin door roused Valentin, who slid out of bed and pulled on his trousers. When he smelled the human, he felt a surge of tremendous relief. Someone had seen the plane go down; someone had come looking for them.

As he opened the back door to greet their savior, an Asian man lunged at him, knocking him back inside.

Long black hair flew around the human's snarling face as he thrust a copper-bladed dagger into Jaus's shoulder.

Valentin held him off by wrapping his hands around the man's throat and cutting off his air, but the intruder jerked the dagger out of his flesh and lifted it to stab him a second time.

All around the cabin, glass shattered as the windows exploded outward. Wind came streaming through the broken panes, blasting at the two men so violently that it pushed them apart and knocked the dagger out of the intruder's hand.

"Who are you?" Jaus demanded, circling around as he clutched his wounded shoulder.

Lightning flashed, striking so close to the cabin that the

subsequent boom shook the walls and window frames. Pieces of glass left in the panes fell out and smashed to the floor.

The intruder scanned the room and snatched a butcher knife from the block on the counter.

"You will have to do better than that, priest," Jaus said softly as he moved, putting the table between them. "They're made of steel."

"So you, *maledicti*." The intruder threw the blade on the top of the table. "No need weapon."

"Indeed." Jaus bared his fangs. "Neither do I."

The intruder whipped his head to one side, and a blast of lake water came through the window, a solid stream that knocked Jaus into the wall.

The intruder straddled him, clamping a hand around his throat and pinning him to the wall. His other hand flattened against Jaus's chest, where it became an icy, immovable weight.

"You." Hatred flared in the intruder's narrow black eyes. "You turn her."

A sensation as if another Kyn were feeding on him made Jaus look down. Beads of blood popped out all over his chest.

"See, demon." The man smirked. "Your water mine."

"Stop it!" a woman shrieked. "Get away from him!"

Jaus saw a tree limb swinging through the air toward his face and instinctively ducked, pushing his attacker toward the blunt club. A young blond girl smashed the wood into the side of the Asian's head, sending him to his knees.

Before Valentin could say or do anything, the girl launched a vicious attack of her own.

"Tie me up to a fucking *tree*?" she screamed, raising the branch to bring it down over the top of his head. "Leave me

out there for the fucking *bears* to chew on?" The branch
cracked as she struck him a third time. "I don't fucking *think*
so."

The Asian man fell over and went limp.

The woman holding the tree branch dropped it, and
Valentin saw that her hands had actually been tied to one
end. He went to her and quickly released her bonds.

"Thank you," he said.

"You're fucking welcome," she snarled, and gulped in air,
visibly trying to compose herself. "Sorry." She kicked the
unconscious man. "I'm just *really* fucking pissed off at this
guy."

Jaus knelt down to check the Asian. He was still breathing, but a number of large bumps were swelling on his head.
He looked up at the girl, who was panting and still trembling
with rage. "This man, do you know him?"

"I thought I did. By the way, I'm Melanie Wallace." She
leaned over to spit on the back of the Asian man's head.
"He's insane."

"Stay here, please, Melanie." Valentin lifted the man over
his shoulder and carried him out of the cabin.

He looked through the back window to see the blond girl
collapse into one of the kitchen chairs before he jerked the
unconscious man's arm up to his mouth, sinking his fangs
into his forearm.

He took the blood he needed to heal the wounds the man
had inflicted, nothing more. He considered saving himself a
great deal of trouble and snapping the man's neck, but three
things stopped him: His attacker had the same exotic type of
features and almond-shaped eyes as Liling, which made
Jaus assume he was also Chinese. He had used the Brethren
term for the Darkyn before he had stabbed Jaus. And while

he was human, he had some Kyn-like talent over the wind and water.

He decided to keep him alive long enough to interrogate him. *Then* he would snap his neck.

Valentin picked up the long, limp body and carried him under his arm into the woodshed. There he used some of the cords binding the firewood to tie the man's wrists and legs. After bolting the door to the shed from the outside, he removed the hatchet from the chopping stump next to it. If the man somehow worked his way out of the ropes, Valentin didn't want him using the hatchet for a second attack.

Satisfied that the intruder was as secure as was possible under the circumstances, Valentin returned to the cabin. There he found the girl sitting at the kitchen table with a wet dish cloth pressed to her wrist.

"I owe you my life," he told the blond girl as he closed the door behind him. "I am Valentin Jaus."

"Pretty name. Nice to meet you." She gave him a tired smile. "And I apologize for dropping in on you like this, dude, but it's not like I had a choice." She glanced to the back door. "Did I crack his skull open?"

Valentin shook his head.

She lifted the dish cloth and inspected the livid red marks on her wrists. "Let me catch my breath, and I'll give it another shot."

"It is not necessary," he told her. "I tied him up and locked him in the woodshed."

"It is so necessary. That guy is crazy. He kidnapped me, you know? With a gun and everything."

Valentin knew the Brethren had no hesitation in using humans to further their cause. "Who is he?"

"He told me his name is Kyan," she said. "He didn't say much else. I thought for sure he was going to feed me to the alligators or some gross serial killer shit like that." Her voice trembled, and she buried her face in her hands. "Oh, God."

Valentin gave her a few moments to compose herself before asking gently, "How did you come to meet this man, Melanie?"

"He doesn't speak English very well. Think, like, totally slaughtering it? Anyway, he hired me to come on his boat and translate for him." She lifted her hands, showing him her palms. "Dude, I am so sorry about this. I had no idea he was, like, a killer psycho wazoo or whatever he is. Honestly, I thought the guy was just a tourist." She shook her head slowly. "I can't believe I *slept* with him."

He prepared a drink for her while she told him about the trip she had taken with Kyan downriver, and how when she had tried to quit he had abducted her at gunpoint.

"Then he stopped here, and I saw the lights on in the cabin. He must have figured out that I was making noise, like, to warn you, so he tied me up to a tree and left me out there." She nodded toward the tree limb on the floor. "He didn't notice the branch was broken, so I hung from it and swung back and forth until I broke it off. Then I was like, 'Hey, a club,' and I came after him."

Jaus admired her ingenuity. She seemed quite young, and yet she had responded to the situation like a trained soldier. "Did this man Kyan tell you why he was coming here?"

She shrugged. "I got the impression he was looking for someone. And, dude, do you know you have, like, a humongous plane sitting in the bottom of your lake out there?" She jerked a thumb toward the broken window.

"Yes." Jaus realized he now had two human females to look after, and a Brethren operative who could kill them all. Was this the man whom Liling had feared so much? "Unfortunately, I landed it there."

"Maybe you should, like, retake some flying lessons." She cringed as thunder boomed outside the cabin. "Can you call the cops now and have them come out here and arrest him?"

"There is no phone here," he told her.

"Damn. I really want to see his ass hauled off to the county lockup." She rubbed at the red marks on her wrists. "And I was nice to him because I thought he was cute. What a jerk. I am so, like, *never* watching *The Matrix* movies ever again."

Jaus went to the window and checked the skies. The storm rolling in from the south looked dense, and the wind was rising. "If you are hungry, Melanie, there is some food in the pantry. I am going to wash up and dress."

She gave his chest a weary but sweetly lecherous look. "Don't do it on my account, dude."

Liling heard someone singing an old Chinese cradle song, and slowly emerged from the dream. The room she lay in was dark, but flashes of light briefly illuminated a young, smiling female face.

"You're awake. Hey." The blond girl tucked a pillow behind Liling's head. "I heard you calling for someone. You okay, sweetie?"

She spoke in a combination of Chinese and English, which Liling found as surreal as her presence. "I'm all right. I speak English. Who are you?"

"My name's Melanie," the blond girl said. "I just got here. Is that German dude, like, your boyfriend?"

"He's Austrian." Liling wondered what Valentin would think of her calling him a boyfriend. "He's simply a good friend."

"With benefits, I bet. Does he have a brother?" Dimples appeared in her cheeks. "He's, like, *totally* hot."

Liling couldn't help smiling back at her. "How did you get here?"

"I was kidnapped, sort of." Melanie launched into a rambling account of a Chinese man who had lured her onto his boat and taken her downriver. After she finished relating the details of her ordeal, she added, "I think Kyan was looking for you, because he kept saying 'she.' And I don't think he knew you spoke Chinese, or he wouldn't have dragged me out here."

Kyan. He had found her.

Liling looked over as Jaus entered the room. "Valentin, where is Kyan?"

"He is tied up in the woodshed." He looked down at Melanie. "Miss Wallace, would you excuse us for a moment?"

"Sure." Melanie didn't move, and then she smacked her palm into the side of her head. "You want *me* to leave; got it. I'll just go hang in the kitchen, then."

Liling grabbed the girl's wrist. "Where did Kyan leave the boat?"

The girl described the pier on the other side of the lake. "I know how to drive a boat, if you guys want to get out of here."

Liling saw Valentin glance at the windows as he gauged the conditions outside. She had to tell him about her and Kyan, and why they had to leave at once. At the same time, she didn't want to alarm the young girl.

"The storm is growing too strong," he said at last. "We will have to wait until it passes."

"Fine with me; I hate lightning. And you want to be alone, so let me get out of here." To Liling, Melanie said,

"Are you hungry, sweetie? I can make you some soup or something."

"No, thank you." The thought of eating food made Liling's stomach turn. When the girl departed, she sat up, holding the quilt over her bare breasts. "We must take the boat and go now."

"We will, after the storm passes." He sat down beside her on the bed. "You look pale again."

"I feel strange." Talking made something inside her mouth hurt, and she touched her lips. "When we crashed, did something hit me in the mouth?"

"No." He spanned her jaw with his hand. "Open for me."

Cringing a little, she parted her lips, then closed them in embarrassment as she felt a trickle of something warm run down her chin. "Ugh. I'm drooling."

"No, you are not." His hand tightened. "Open again." As soon as she did, he put the tips of two fingers in her mouth and rubbed them against a sore place on her palate. It was so sensitive the slight pressure made her flinch.

When he drew his hand back, his fingers were stained with blood.

Why was she bleeding? "I don't remember cutting my mouth on anything."

"You didn't cut it. Your teeth did. You are growing two more now. They are your *dents acérées*." He got up from the bed and dragged a hand through his hair. "How can this be?"

"Valentin?"

He turned his face away for a moment, his shoulders rigid, and then regarded her. "Liling, I don't know how this has happened, but you are changing. You are no longer human. You are becoming a *vrykolakas*. We call ourselves the Darkyn."

The last word stole all the breath out of her lungs:

Darkyn. If he had punched her in the stomach, she would not feel as shocked. "No, I can't be that. I'm human. I can't change into a demon."

"We are not demons, *Geliebte.*" He reached down to take her hand in his. "We were human once, like you. We are still like humans in some ways."

"But it's not possible." How could she explain to him what she was? She shoved her fingers in her mouth, and pulled them out again to stare at the clots of blood. "You're wrong, Valentin. I'm sure they're only fever blisters. When we go to Atlanta, I'll see a doctor."

"We are not going to Atlanta," he said quietly. "As soon as I can arrange transportation, I am taking you back to Chicago."

The pain in her mouth doubled, making it hard to speak. "You can't do that."

"I will protect you from the Brethren, *Geliebte.*"

She backed away from him. "If you take me back the priests will find me. Now that they know I'm alive they'll never stop hunting me. They'll hurt you to get to me."

As soon as she said that, she recalled that he was one of the *maledicti*, and if what the priests had taught her was true, he could not be harmed or killed so easily.

That's why he didn't drown. She changed tactics by saying, "They could find where you and your friends live."

"*Geliebte*, they already have tried." His expression changed, grew gentle. "The pilot who hijacked my plane didn't know who I was. He had been sent to abduct and murder you."

All of this had happened because of her. Liling curled up, pressing her forehead against her knees.

The priests had taught her about the *maledicti*, how evil they were, and how the order had been formed to fight them.

They had wanted her to do the same. Now Valentin was telling her that he was Darkyn, and everything she knew about him directly contradicted the teachings of the priests.

It seemed almost funny that she might become one as well. Was it revenge, or some sort of twisted justice? Did he even know what she was?

"Did you do this to me?" Liling asked him without looking at him. "Make me like you?"

"I did not intend to. I would never curse you or any human with my fate. I cannot explain how it happened, only that my blood must have mingled with yours . . . and then . . ." He trailed off as if unsure of how to explain it.

She raised her head. "You can do this to a human being and you don't know how it works?"

"Our blood is poisonous; we know that," he admitted. "It is why we never try to turn anyone. No one had survived a change for centuries. But in these last few years, there have been a few who didn't die. Other women. You must be like them somehow."

Liling went cold inside. He didn't know what she was. He might not believe her if she told him. It didn't matter anymore, not now that Kyan had found her. "Whatever is happening to me, it is not your fault. I don't blame you. But you must do something for me now."

"Anything."

"Kill me."

He drew back. "Anything else."

"You must." She saw in his eyes that he wouldn't, felt it in the shift of tension in his skin. "Very well." She climbed out of the bed, holding herself with her arms. The door seemed so far away as she hobbled toward it.

A cool hand touched the back of her neck, holding her back. "Why do you want to die?"

"I want to live." The pain inside her body was nothing compared to the agony in her heart. "But I can't. Not like this. He is . . . Even if I get away . . . you'll despise me."

"Never." Jaus spun her around and pulled her into his arms. "You will live. You will live for me, do you understand? Whatever it is that frightens you, we will fight it together. I promise you."

Liling closed her eyes as he brought his mouth down over hers, and felt something punch through the sore place on the roof of her mouth. He used his tongue to stroke the sharp points that had come down into her mouth, and she tasted blood, both his and her own.

He lifted his head. "You must take more of my blood to complete the transition. Then you will be stronger, more like me."

Liling's stomach surged. To take his blood, she'd have to bite him. "I can't do that."

"You must." He tilted her face back, making her look at him. "However it happened, I did this to you. It is my blood that runs in your veins. You are my *sygkenis*. You belong to me now, Liling. You must let me take care of you."

Liling's teeth throbbed, and as wretched as she felt, a deeper, hotter rhythm of empty longing echoed between her legs. The press of his body, the feel of his penis, long and thick and straining under his trousers, called to the need inside her. She moved, intending to put some space between them, but her body had other ideas. Suddenly she rubbed against him, seeking, inviting.

"You see." He filled his hands with her hair. "You feel it as I do. You know me now." He kissed the place just under her chin, sliding his mouth up to her ear. "Do you want me inside you when you bite me?"

She couldn't speak. He asked too much of her, and she

wanted to agree, to surrender, to do exactly as he wished. If she did, she suspected that she would never be able to leave him.

Valentin caught the lobe of her ear between his teeth, biting down until she quivered. "You were made for me, for my pleasure. I will give you everything you desire. Do you want me?"

She struggled against him, pushing and then pulling at him.

He would not relent. "Tell me."

"I want you. Yes. I want you inside me." She was begging, and she didn't care. She needed this; she needed him. He would keep her safe. He would answer her longing. He would fill the hollow places inside her. She wanted him to do that. She wanted to feel him so deep inside her that she could never take another breath again without feeling him there.

"If I take you, there will be no more talk of dying." He sounded furious now, his fingers tightening against her scalp. "Do you understand me?"

"Yes."

His eyes were changing, the pupils splintering, the pale blue glowing with fierce passion. "I am your lord now. Your master."

Something melted inside her, perhaps the last of her resistance, perhaps her heart. "You are."

"Who am I?"

"You are my master."

She allowed Valentin to guide her head to his throat, and there she kissed the smooth skin with her lips. She knew what he wanted, but she waited, tormenting him as he had her.

"Liling." His hand clamped on the back of her neck. "Take my blood."

Her mouth opened, and the unfamiliar teeth stretched, aching and eager for what he offered. She could feel his blood rising, pulsing under his skin, coming to her, luring her, until with a soft sound of defeat she bit down, driving her fangs into his flesh.

"You did not tell me there would be alligators," Rain complained as he shouldered his way through a tangle of palmettos. One of the fan-shaped leaves sprang back and slapped him in the face. "Or that I would be molested by vengeful weeds."

"It was your nose that led us down this path." Farlae stopped and scanned the area before them. "The alligator did not bite you. If you keep complaining, however, I will."

"No, you won't," Rain predicted gloomily, and filled his chest with the damp, chilly night air. "When we find Jaus, I will ask him to reward me with a place among his *jardin*. He will make me his seneschal, and give me leave to collect all of the tin windup toys I wish."

"*If* we find Jaus before I throttle you," Farlae corrected, "we will radio the major and he will send the helicopter, and we will return to the Realm. Then I think I will throttle you anyway."

Rain stopped and turned. "I am twice your size, and I love you. Rather more than my collection of windup toys."

"Of which you never tire," Farlae said. "God help us."

Rain continued as if he hadn't spoken. "I have done wicked things with you for years that, should I ever die, are going to be the reason our heavenly Father sends me to burn in hell for all eternity. And you liked them, or you would have surely cast me aside for another. So why are you always bullying me?"

"If I did not," Farlae said, "we would be back at the Realm playing strip Monopoly instead of finding Suzerain Jaus."

Rain's broad, plain face crinkled into an enormous grin. "When we get back, you can be the thimble."

The two men moved deeper into the marsh, stopping occasionally to check the air. After another hour of searching, Rain muttered something and crouched, filling his cupped hand with water and bringing it to his lips.

"There is oil in that water," Farlae warned. "It will make you sick, and I will not kiss you until you wash your mouth out with soap." He looked again, and narrowed his flawed eye as he saw the subtle coloration of the pollutant. "That is not oil. It's petrol, but not like any I've seen."

"Jet fuel." Rain brought his wet hand up to his nose and breathed in, and then tasted the water again. "Humans, three of them, but not like humans. Two females and one male. And Jaus." He plunged forward, dunking his head into the shallow water before lifting it out. He pushed his dripping hair back and pointed. "Some distance that way."

"Some distance?"

Rain fiddled with his radio. "Ten miles, perhaps fifteen. There is blood; one of them is injured. Which button do I push to call the major?"

Farlae took the radio from him and clamped a hand around Rain's strong neck before he brought his mouth down and gave his lover a slow, deep kiss. "You," he said, "are brilliant."

Rain gave him a smug look. "And I didn't even have to use soap."

*　　　*　　　*

Pain washed the darkness purple, then red.

Kyan had not felt such sensations in decades, not since his training in the catacombs. Even then, the brothers had been careful not to administer too much pain. Enough to chastise, but not enough to enrage.

Even then, they had feared him.

He opened his eyes to colorless darkness and took stock of his physical condition. He had several painful contusions on his scalp, thanks to Melanie's fury with the tree branch. Two spots of heat burned on the inside of his right arm, confirming that he had been used by the *maledicti* for blood.

He would survive the head injuries, but the loss of blood was a more serious matter. It had left him weak and unsteady. He needed to replace the lost fluid as quickly as possible, for it was the only thing that would restore his balance and strength.

The smell of resin and wood dust filled his nose. His hands and legs were tightly bound with old, dry rope. The wood against his back had been seasoned, stripped of all moisture. The earth beneath him was bone-dry. As weak as he was, it would take him forever to gather what he needed to revitalize his body, heal his wounds, and escape.

The sound of a bolt sliding made him look up, and the door to the shed opened. The American girl stood in silhouette, looking in at him.

"Release me."

She came in and closed the door behind her. "You really *are* crazy if you think I'm going to do that."

She was angry with him, of course. "I am not deranged. I am trying to protect you."

"Protect me?" she echoed, incredulous. "You pointed a gun at me. You kidnapped me. You tied me to a tree. Then you stabbed that nice man." In English she added, "You fucking idiot."

Kyan had to make her understand how much danger she was in. "That man is not nice. He is a killer."

"Like you'd know, right?" She came over and tugged on the ropes around his legs and arms. "Don't start celebrating. I just wanted to make sure you can't get loose and hurt anybody."

Kyan tried again. "The man inside the cabin is not human."

She smirked. "Yeah, I thought his chest was pretty godlike myself."

"He is a demon, a real demon," he insisted. "He will take what he wants from you and leave you to die."

"Dude, please," she said. "He, like, untied me from the branch and made me some Gatorade."

Kyan strained at the ropes. "He is deceiving you. That is how they trap their prey."

Now she snorted. "Right, I'm going to believe that coming from you, Mr. Honesty."

"You have to believe me," he said. "He will kill you if you don't execute him first. Find the dagger I used on him. It will be in the cabin somewhere. You must stab him in the heart with it. If you cannot do that, thrust it into the back of his neck. It is the only way you can kill his kind."

Melanie laughed. "Oh, man. I did hit you on the head too hard."

"I am not joking." He had to convince her, and the only way to do that was with the complete truth. "The man inside the cabin is a vampire. He lives on human blood. There are no others here for him to feed on besides you and me. Can't you see? He will have to use us as food, or he will die."

She gave him a strange look. "Really."

"Melanie, please. I know I should not have abducted you and tied you to the tree. That was wrong. But I am trying to save your life now."

"Maybe you're wrong," she said. "Maybe he's not a vampire. Maybe he's a werewolf who's going to, like, rip out our throats and take a bath in our blood." She tilted her head. "If I turned into a werewolf, do you think my fur would be blond?"

"Melanie."

"If you're truly this crazy, I shouldn't be making fun of you, I guess. I am sorry I hit you." Rain rattled on the roof of the shed. "I'm going back inside. Good night."

Before Kyan could say another word, she left, locking the shed door behind her.

Kyan closed his eyes and concentrated. Tiny drops of her saliva hung in the air, his to command. He gathered them together and sent them out through a crack in the shed to join with drops of rain pelting the ground. He created a thin stream of water and funneled it after Melanie as she ran back into the cabin. He sent the stream under the door and dispersed it, surrounding her with a mist too fine for her to see. His water entered her body through the fluid in her eyes.

He couldn't read her, but he could see, hear, and smell what she did. He watched her take a can of soup from the kitchen cabinet. He heard the sound of a moan, and smelled blood. He heard her light footsteps as she walked down the hall. The scent of blood grew stronger as she opened the bedroom door a few inches. He saw with Melanie the girl and the demon on the bed, their bodies locked together in a passionate embrace. He tasted the sex-drenched air, and watched the girl sink her teeth into the demon's throat, his blood spilling into her mouth.

Now that she saw it with her own eyes, Kyan thought, satisfied, she would do as he had told her.

Melanie did not return to the kitchen; nor did she look for his copper dagger. She slowly walked out into the rain and moved away from the cabin, heading toward the pier and Kyan's boat.

Chapter 18

Valentin held his woman in his arms, their bodies still joined. He couldn't remember taking her, but the scent of sex told him that he had.

"Valentin." She nuzzled his throat, and then stopped. "What am I doing?" She started to laugh helplessly.

"What Kyn do when they discover their life companion." He stroked her back, pressing her hips a little closer so he could settle himself in deeper. Her body surrounded him in a tight, wet clasp like an endless kiss. "We will be doing this quite often until we have completed our bond."

"I have fangs. I drank your blood. And you drank mine. You are vampires, just as they told us." She sucked at her top lip. "You made me into a vampire."

"We are *vrykolakas*, not vampires," he said slowly. "My kind were once human a very long time ago, and then we changed. We believed it was a curse, but now we think it may have been a sickness. Perhaps we will never know."

He told her how the Darkyn needed blood to survive, but how they had learned not to kill the humans upon whom they depended for their nourishment. He also warned her about the individual talents each Kyn developed to help lure humans and protect themselves.

Hearing that, she seemed to withdraw a little. "What sort of talent do you have?"

She was his *sygkenis*; he couldn't go on deceiving her. "My own is truth. It is impossible for humans to lie to me when I touch them."

Her black eyes took on a shrewd gleam. "You've been using that on me, haven't you?"

"A few times." He fingered a strand of her hair. "Liling, I never meant to infect you with this curse, but now that it has happened again, there is a bond between us. It will change both of us."

"Again?" She frowned. "You did this before?"

"I changed another human." He braced himself, but the usual waves of sorrow and loss did not come over him. "Jema."

"Yes, Jema. I didn't know I had until she was with Thierry." He traced the outline of her lips. "You do not wish to be with anyone else, I hope."

"I don't." She kissed his fingers. "What about you?"

"After I lost Jema, I never intended to get involved with another human woman. I never dreamed it would happen again like this." He looked into her eyes. "I will do whatever I can to make you happy, Liling. I hope you will come to trust me."

"If we are going to try to be together, there are some things you should know about me." She drew back. "The truth, if I haven't told you already."

"I will not compel you against your will again," he said. "You can tell me when you are ready for me to know."

She untangled herself from his arms and separated their

bodies, sliding away from him to sit on the edge of the bed. Staring at the rain sheeting the window, she began to speak.

"I lied to you when I told you I wasn't an American," she said. "I am. I was born somewhere in California. My mother died in childbirth, and my twin and I were turned over to the church. We thought the men who raised us were Catholic priests, but they only pretended to be. They have many names—the Light, the order, *Les Frères de la Lumière*. They call themselves the Brethren."

"Do you know they are the mortal enemy of the Darkyn?" he asked.

"You are the ones they call the *maledicti*," she said. "They taught us about you. They claimed you were cursed by God for leading unclean lives, transformed into demons, and sent back to earth from hell so that you could torment the faithful." She sighed. "I did not believe you really existed. Now you tell me that I am becoming one of you. They told us so many lies, I hardly know what to think."

He hoped he could convince her that they were not the monsters the Brethren thought they were. "Why did they teach you about us?"

She glanced at him. "They raised us in special places away from the outside world. They called them orphanages, but they were more like prisons. In those places, they did things to us." Her voice faltered. "Things that changed us."

"How?"

"I don't know. I was only a child, and they never talked to me about it. They injected us with drugs. They used machines. They put things in the food. Sometimes it made me very sick. Once I nearly died." She hunched her shoulders. "I didn't have it so bad. Some of the others, they died. And they did worse things to my twin."

Valentin controlled a surge of outrage. "How long did they have you?"

"Sixteen years. I was fourteen when they told me what they expected me to do for them. They were going to make me pregnant over and over, and force me to give my babies to them. My sons would be trained to fight the demons, and my daughters would have more babies for them. They were already doing it to some of the older girls in my unit." She shuddered. "They never made a sound, even when the priests came to take the babies."

He put his arm around her. "Did they do this to you?"

"They tried, but I wouldn't become pregnant." She sounded ashamed.

"You were raped." Every Brethren responsible was going to die a messy death beneath his blade.

"No, that wasn't the way they did it." Liling wrapped her arms around her middle. "They gave me an injection with a needle. Every month they made me go to the breeding room. It was so cold in there. They made me sit in a chair that went backward, and put the syringe up inside me. I had to stay there for hours after they did it . . . but I never got pregnant. My belly stayed empty."

Another form of rape, Jaus thought, but he felt a little better to know that she had not been used over and over by the Brethren. "Did they tattoo you with the red swan?"

She touched her shoulder. "That was my designation. They never gave us names. Names would have made us seem more like them." Her mouth hitched. "When I told Mrs. Chen, it made her so angry. She named me Liling."

"You said you have a twin."

"I did. They separated us when we were nine, after we tried to run away," she said. "Seven years later, some of the doctors wanted to bring us back together. We were special, not like the other children. When I was sixteen, they transferred us to the same facility. Only something went wrong. The way they changed us, the things we could do . . . We could not bear to be near each other. They called it 'the effect.' And that wasn't all."

Valentin looked down to see her fingers digging into the mattress.

"At first people around us became sick," she continued, her voice dropping low. "Some became seriously dehydrated; others got pneumonia. Then machines would break or catch fire. I never did any of it deliberately, Valentin, and I don't think my twin did, either. It just happened. The last time was when my twin came to get me so that we could run away again."

He could feel the pain rolling off her in waves. "Tell me what happened."

"A storm came. The biggest one I'd ever seen. Like a hurricane, only a hundred times more powerful." She hesitated. "I don't remember too much about that night. There was a tornado made of fire and water, and then a terrible explosion. It leveled the building. Everyone there—everyone I knew—died."

"But you survived."

She nodded quickly. "I hid in a small room with no windows. Some things fell on top of me. When the storm passed, I escaped." She looked at him. "I killed all those people, but I swear to you, I didn't mean to."

"The storm killed them, not you." He pulled her onto his lap. "You do not have it in you to harm anyone."

She rested her cheek against his shoulder. "I've been hiding from the Brethren and my twin ever since that night. They're still hunting me. They're using my twin to hunt me. If I don't run away, terrible storms come and people die."

He kissed her. "You cannot blame yourself for changes in the weather, *mein Mädchen*."

"Oh, but I can," she said softly. "That's what went wrong with us, with what they did to us. What they called 'the effect.' We each have our own power, my twin and I. But when we're near each other, when we're together, we create those storms."

"We have located the crash site, my lord," Jayr, suzeraina of the Realm, reported from her *jardin* in central Florida. "The plane appears intact, although it is presently at the bottom of Ghost Lake."

"Assemble a rescue team and send them in to retrieve Jaus and any survivors," he told her. "Be prepared to accommodate the needs of the humans."

"As you say, seigneur. I will report back to you as soon as our ground team has retrieved the survivors." Jayr ended the call.

Michael turned and found his arms filled with his *sygkenis*. "What is this, *chérie*?"

"A great big thank-you hug." She reached up, pulling his head down to hers, and kissed him passionately. "Plus a bonus kiss." She grinned, delighted. "You found him."

"Jayr's contacts in the Civil Air Patrol found the plane," he corrected. "But the news is very good. Jaus cannot drown, so even if he is still on the plane, he is mostly likely alive. Now, how is your brother?"

"Agitated all to hell that he has to stay in bed, but sleeping." She heaved out a frustrated breath. "Wilhelm told me that you were able to locate the orphanage John described."

"Yes. Although it is now used as a private Catholic adoption agency, not an orphanage." He saw the indecision on her face. "It is only forty minutes away. You and I could go there tonight and see if we can find some evidence to give to John about the months you were kept there."

Her eyes softened. "You would do that for me?"

"My love." He lifted her hand to his lips. "I would crawl naked over burning copper for you."

Alex kissed him again.

That evening, Wilhelm drove them out of the city and north to a small town near the lake. Saint Benedict Catholic Adoption Agency had closed at five p.m., and the small parking lot appeared empty.

He inspected the property. "Wil, stay with Alexandra in the car."

"Excuse me." His *sygkenis* glared at him. "I did not come here to sit in the damn car while you have all the fun breaking and entering."

Michael sighed. "Wil, stay with car and be prepared to leave quickly."

After checking the location of the building's alarm sensors, Michael carefully rewired the leads and entered the building through the back door. The cool air of the interior smelled of beeswax and lemon, but there were no sounds of occupation.

"It looks like the main office is over here," Alexandra said, pulling him toward a hall behind the front reception area.

Michael helped her search the office, and several others, but they found only current records of placements and adoptions. It wasn't until they checked a closet used to store boxes of records that Alex discovered stacks of very old medical records.

"These date back quite a ways; there might be something in here." She carried a stack into the main office to drop them on the desk. She turned on the small green-shaded lamp by the telephone and began sorting through the files. "These are pediatric medical records for kids who were adopted the same time John and I were. Standard stuff." She straightened and then peered at one label.

Michael looked over her shoulder. "Did you find yours?"

"No. I found Samantha Brown's." She thumbed her way down the stack, then stopped at another tab. "Nicola Jefferson. What the hell . . . ?"

"Their names are fairly common," Cyprien said. "It could be a coincidence."

"Names that just happen to be identical to two of the other three human women besides me who have survived the change to Kyn. At the former orphanage where my brother and I stayed." She yanked the files out of the stack. "Coincidence, my ass." She opened the file and began to read.

Suspecting that she would be reading for several minutes, Michael decided to inspect the rest of the building.

The agency appeared to have nothing to hide, except for a few secretaries who had candy and tranquilizers stashed in their desks. Michael was about to return and suggest they take all the medical records with them when he saw a bookcase filled with religious texts. He wouldn't have given it a second glance, except that the titles on the spines were all in French.

He removed some of the books, which were covered in dust and obviously had not been handled in years. As he replaced them, he pushed one too far and it bumped the back of the bookcase with a thump.

To his ears, a very hollow thump.

Michael reached along the back edge of the bookcase until he felt hinges, and then checked the other side. He found a recessed latch and pushed it. The bookcase swung slowly outward, revealing an open doorway and a set of stairs leading down.

He went back to the main office. "Alexandra."

"This has got to be the same Samantha Brown," she murmured. "They transferred her down to a foster care program in South Florida when she was just a baby." She looked up. "What?"

"I have found a hidden door," he told her. "It leads to a basement level."

She came around the desk and followed him out to the bookcase. "Wow. I thought they had these things only in the movies."

"The Brethren have a flair for the dramatic." He reached in and flipped a switch, turning on the stairwell light. "I am going down first."

"Of course you're going down first," she said. "You're the guy."

The stairwell led to a small room with boxes and tables draped in sheets. He lifted one to see a collection of empty glass vials and a tray of needles. Under another were some older microscopes and specimen containers. "Perhaps they performed physicals here, in the basement."

"They were doing other things down here, too." Alex said, her voice strained. She stood in the doorway to an adjoining room.

Michael went over to join her and looked in. The room's walls had been painted gray, and twenty single beds lined each side. The beds were identical to the ones they had seen at the mission in Monterey.

"My brother's not crazy," she said, her voice low and hurt. "He's right. The Brethren kept us down here and did something to us."

"We do not know that you and John were brought to this area," he told her. "We need more facts."

She walked in and inspected the bed frames. "No numbers or letters, but maybe they painted them over."

Michael helped her search the laboratory area, but aside from outdated medical testing equipment they found nothing of consequence. He took her back upstairs, keeping her cold hand in his.

"Don't be upset, *chérie.*"

"I'm not upset," she said tonelessly. "That security guard behind you is, though."

"You want to hold it right there, buddy," a rough voice said.

Michael turned to see a middle-aged human pointing a gun at him. "I am so glad you found us," he said, holding his hands up as he moved toward the guard. "My wife and I thought we would be locked in all night."

"Oh, please." Alexandra stared at the guard, and the hall filled with the scent of lavender. "Put down that weapon, you moron."

The guard lowered his gun.

"This is why the NRA needs to be disbanded." Alex went over and snatched the weapon out of his hand, removing the clip before shoving it in his holster. She looked into his eyes. "You will wait here and do nothing until we're gone. Then you will go home and forget us. Clear?"

"Clear," the guard murmured, smiling at her.

"You'll also resign from this job and get one that gives some meaning to your life," Alex continued. "Like work with underprivileged kids. And you will get rid of all of your guns. Including that one you keep thinking of using to shoot your brother-in-law, Dave."

"Meaning," the guard agreed. "Kids. Guns."

"Come on," she said to Michael, walking down to the office. She handed him the files and unplugged the laptop sitting on the desk, tucking it under her arm.

"There is probably nothing on the computer," he told her.

"Probably," she agreed. "But they're insured, and it's a better model than the one I've got in the lab." She gave him a curiously guarded look. "When we get back, I need to go into the city and see someone about these medical records. Alone."

If Michael had learned anything about his *sygkenis*, it was when to let her go. "As long as you come back to me."

Alex didn't reply.

Chapter 19

Kyan pulled the water under his control back from Melanie and the cabin, and brought it to the woodshed. He sent it into the ropes binding his limbs, coating them with it rather than soaking it into them, so they wouldn't swell. The water acted like invisible hands, untying the knots until his arms and legs were free.

His head spun as he stood, but the dizzy sensation passed and he kicked out the door of the woodshed. Once he was outside, stinging sheets of rain saturated and revived him. He took a moment to turn his face up and drink from the sky, and then scanned the area. The girl and the *maledicti* were still inside. They would not be going anywhere. He had to find Melanie and secure her before he dealt with them.

He ran past the cabin and followed Melanie's trail down to the lake.

Once he eliminated the girl and her demon lover, Kyan decided, he would take Melanie back to China with him. Independent as she was, she would resist at first, but there were ways he could use to persuade her. The island he lived on in the South China Sea was small, and the house he had built on it simple, but it was in his power to give her anything she wished. No one would ever spit at the sight of her again, and he would no longer have to live alone.

She was standing at the helm of the boat, Kyan saw as he approached the pier. The rain had soaked her clothes and plastered her bright hair to her skull. He was prepared to call out to her when he heard her speaking in rapid Chinese.

"Yes, I can confirm the ID," she was saying in a brisk voice that sounded nothing like her own. "He is not going to be a problem." She listened. "Of course I can. Do I have approval? Fine. What about the *maledicti*? I don't think a recovery attempt is wise. His allies will be arriving soon."

Kyan blinked the rain out of his eyes. Melanie was speaking to one of his superiors. She was holding a satellite phone exactly like the one he used in the field to contact Rome.

She was an operative, like him.

"I'll call in when it's done. Remain in the light, brother." She switched off the phone and stepped out from under the canopy.

He walked across the pier, meeting her at the edge. "Why didn't you identify yourself to me?" he demanded.

"So you could dust me like that guy in Atlanta?" Contempt changed her face and made it seem older. "Oh, yeah, I was going to do that."

"You are a terrible operative," he ranted. "You became intoxicated. You had sex with me."

"I pretended to get drunk to have some fun with you," she corrected. "Like the sex, it was good exercise."

"Fun? Exercise?" She was insane; he was convinced of it.

"If you don't blow off steam now and then, this job gets really old," she said. "Besides, sex and bar fights are more fun than aerobics. Anything else?"

"You should have told me," he said bitterly. "I could have used your help with the target."

"She was never my target, Kyan." Melanie smiled, but this time her dimples didn't dent her cheeks. "You were. And I'm sorry, but I have to finish my mission." She raised a gun and fired.

The round struck him in the face and sent him over the edge of the pier into the lake.

The sound was muffled by the storm, but Jaus knew gunfire when he heard it. It sounded as if someone had fired a pistol down by the lake.

"Stay inside," he told Liling as he quickly dressed.

She pulled the quilt around her. "Be careful."

As Valentin emerged from the cabin, Melanie stumbled up to him. She was dripping wet, and she carried a gun in her hand. She was sobbing.

"Melanie." He grabbed her shoulders to steady her.

"I had to do it," she said, her voice shrill with hysteria. "It was Kyan. He got out of the shed. He was going to set fire to the boat."

"You shot him?" Jaus asked.

She nodded frantically. "He had the gun and he was going to shoot me. I struggled with him and it just went off. I think I killed him. He's in the water. Please, can you come and see if he's dead?"

Valentin looked out at the lake. The surface churned violently, as if it were boiling. "Go inside, child. There is nothing you can do for him."

The storm suddenly intensified, and lightning began shooting down out of the pitch-black clouds and striking the trees all around the cabin.

"We have to get out of here," Melanie shouted, stumbling away from him and running toward the pier. "I'll start the boat. Get Liling, and hurry!"

Valentin ran toward the cabin. Halfway there, a bolt streaked down, striking the propane tank on the side of the house, causing it to explode. Another struck the roof, sending shingles flying like shrapnel in every direction. Yet another bolt landed behind the house, and Jaus heard another explosion. Two more strikes hit the cabin from either side. A huge ball of fire erupted inside the structure, tearing the roof off the cabin.

Rain and wind screamed, but not as loudly as he did. *"Liling."*

As fire exploded all around her, Liling wrapped the quilt around herself tightly and went down on her hands and knees. Black, dense smoke filled the air, and the cabin itself shuddered, as if it meant to come down around her. She crawled across the floor and out into the hall, but flames blocked the cabin's back exit. She changed direction and made her way to the kitchen, cringing as the fire shot across the ceilings and down the walls, greedily consuming everything in its path.

If she didn't get to a door soon, the heat would cook her alive.

The fire was blazing out of control by the time she reached the kitchen and stood up. The thick smoke made it impossible for her to see, and the heat pressed against her from every side. She knew it wanted to devour her, and it would, very soon, unless she did something.

She wasn't afraid of death or fire. What she feared was never seeing Valentin again. And for all that life had taken from her—her parents, her freedom, her twin, Chen Ping— she was not going to give up the man she loved. Not when there was still a chance.

We only just found each other. This can't be the end. Not yet.

Something inside her rose and blossomed, something she had not felt in many years. It filled her like sunshine, like the scent of a thousand gardens. It didn't want to run away, or huddle and hide. It wanted to touch the fire. It knew the fire; it called to it.

Flames raced up the quilt and set it alight.

Acting on instinct, Liling lifted her hand, turning it as she felt the heat from the burning quilt touch her skin. Illness, disease, and infirmity weren't so different from fire. Both could become infernos that burned, scalded, and shriveled. The flames from the quilt jumped to her hair and burned it away, but she felt no pain. She knew suffering, and how to remove from the bodies of others; that was her gift, her power. Valentin's blood had done something to that, had awakened the part of her that she had tried so hard to escape. But what she had feared as a child now came through her as power, vibrant and absolute, and invaded every cell in her body.

Although it seemed impossible, she knew the fire was, like pain, hers to control.

A pocket of cool air formed around Liling as she focused, drawing on the outrageous heat building around her, the same way she had drawn on the suffering of others. She no longer had to channel it into herself, not now that she could feel the tiniest parts of it. She could change them, or disperse them.

The quilt stopped burning, and then the flames around her began to dwindle and then died away.

She walked out of the kitchen and into the hall, where the smell of gasoline from the generator that had exploded was thick. She sensed the burning gasoline as she might the symptom of a disease, and sent out her power, using the fire feeding on the fuel to take it apart and render it harmless.

When the hall stopped burning, she went back into the bedroom and extinguished the flames she found there.

All of the windows had been broken, and through them air rushed in, eager to defeat her efforts and reawaken the flames. She pushed it back out simply by thinking about it. Wood smoldered around Liling as she moved through the cabin, tending to each of the lightning-born fires. One by one they winked out, until there were no more to burn.

Her skin tightened for a moment as she looked at the black ruin around her. This was what they had wanted her to do. To destroy instead of grow.

Take, not give.

She walked out of the front door of the cabin, the burned remnants of the quilt still wrapped around her. Rain whipped at her, furious and cold. Then Valentin was there, his hands and face burned.

"Liling."

He reached for her with his scorched hands, and as soon as he touched her she sent her power into them, taking away his pain, healing the blackened skin. She put her lips to each burn on his face, smiling as they shrank and disappeared.

"I am not hurt," she assured him.

She didn't realize her hair was gone until he ran his hand over her exposed scalp. The ashes of her hair fell like black snow to the ground. He took the quilt away and looked all over her. He didn't believe her.

"Fire can't harm me." She turned her face up to the rain, allowing it to wash the soot from her face, and then looked at him, to show him. "I'm sorry you were burned."

"I couldn't get to you. The flames were too hot." He took

off his own shirt, draping her naked body with it. "How did you stop it?"

"Fire is like pain." She heard a rapid thumping and looked up to see a helicopter battling the vicious wind. "Your friends are here."

The helicopter rocked as it descended out of the sky to make a bumpy landing in the clearing beyond the cabin.

Melanie crouched behind a tree, the wind tearing at her clothes as she took out her phone and dialed her American contact.

"Hightower."

"Wallace," she said. "The target has been eliminated."

"What about the red swan?"

Melanie looked over at the couple in front of the cabin. "Still alive. Your little ugly duckling doesn't burn. She's with one of the *màledicti*, and his people just got here." She looked up at the sky above the helicopter, and smiled as a funnel cloud began to form over the aircraft. "I'll take care of them."

"No. You have to follow them and find the vampire's stronghold," Hightower said. "It's somewhere here in Chicago."

Melanie frowned. "That's not procedure—"

"The order comes directly from the Lightkeeper," he told her. "Track them to the nest and report back to me as soon as you have the location."

Melanie switched off the phone and sighed, then watched the lovely funnel cloud draw back up into the sky. Tossing the phone into the lake, she ran out of the woods and hurried toward the helicopter.

*   *   *

Alexandra walked into the waiting room. It smelled faintly of bubble gum and antiseptic, but there were no patients running around as usual. The sight of the small colorful chairs, unbreakable toys, well-read magazines, and a play area shaped like a boat made her smile a little as she went up and tapped on the small glass window.

The receptionist slid it open and frowned at her. "May I help you, ma'am?"

"Is the doctor in?" Alex switched her briefcase from one hand to the other. "I'd like to speak to him for a minute."

"I'm sorry, ma'am, but Dr. Haggerty isn't seeing patients today." The receptionist opened her appointment book. "I can fit you in next Friday afternoon. What's your child's name?"

"I don't have a kid. I just wanted to . . ." She knew why she'd come here, but she didn't know what she wanted. "Thanks anyway."

Alex walked out of the office and put on her shades. The center courtyard of the medical building had once been an empty rectangle of gravel, ash cans, and a couple of pathetic shrubs. Someone had transformed it into a tiny garden with flowers, ferns, small trees, and a reflecting pool.

The pool drew her like a magnet. Alex stood at the edge and looked down at the orange, red, and white koi swimming lazily just beneath the surface. Something fell from her face and dropped on the surface, creating a small circle that slowly expanded over the koi.

"Alexandra?" a man called, his voice tentative.

She turned and a moment later found a shabby lab coat in her face, and long, tight arms closing around her.

"It is you." Dr. Charles Haggerty set her at arm's length and then hugged her tightly again. "What are you doing here? Where have you been?"

"It's a long story." She smiled up at his shocked face. "How have you been, Charlie?"

"How have I *been*?" He turned his head away, laughed once, and stared at her, angry now. "Alex, you closed your practice, farmed out your patients, sold your house, wouldn't return my calls for weeks, and then vanished off the face of the earth for three years, and now you're back and you want to know how *I've* been?"

"Things happened. Some bad things, and I . . . I had to get away." That was a brilliant encapsulation of her life since growing fangs. Charlie Haggerty had been her lover, and she had abandoned him without a second thought. "I'm sorry. This was a big mistake."

"Shut up." He seized her hand and led her over to one of the wrought-iron benches, pushing her down on it. He didn't sit, but paced a short line in front of her. "When Grace called me that last time, I was done with you. I really was. I have a life, Alex."

"I should have called you myself." She ducked her head. "I got caught up in something, Charlie. It became this huge train wreck and I couldn't jump off, and I couldn't make it stop."

He glared at her. "They didn't have any phones on this train?"

She plucked a flower from the gardenia planted next to the bench and cradled the large white blossom in her hands. "It got better, but then I knew I couldn't come back or get anyone else involved. I only came here today to see if you would read over some old pediatric files for me. I'm missing something."

"You came here for a *consult*?" he asked, incredulous. "Are you fucking kidding me?"

She lifted her shoulders. "That, and to tell you I was okay and to see if you were."

"I'm fine. I'm married," Charlie said bluntly. "Very happily married. Her name is Kimberly. She's a special-ed teacher. She's tall and stacked and the sweetest, most patient woman I've ever known." He watched her face intently. "She's also pregnant. Our baby is due in June. It's a little girl."

"She sounds wonderful. You'll be a great dad." Alex forced herself to her feet and held out her hand. "Congratulations."

"You bitch." Charlie slapped her. "That's for not calling me. For making me think you were dead." He grabbed her and pulled her into his arms and gave her a hard, passionless kiss. "And that's for walking away from what we had. You should have been the mother of my child, Alex. *You* should have."

She shook her head, unable to speak.

Charlie swore and pulled her close, stroking his hand over her hair. "Christ, that was supposed to make me feel better." He looked down at her stricken face. "I knew you weren't in love with me, Al, but I fell for you anyway. Hard. It took me a year and a couple dozen bottles of Jack just to get over you."

"I'm sorry I hurt you," she said tonelessly. "I'll go."

"Took a lot of nerve to come here and face me, didn't it?" He glanced down at her briefcase. "Come inside and I'll look at your files."

Alex silently followed him out of the garden, through the office waiting room, past the curious eyes of the receptionist, and into his office. Instead of certificates and awards, framed photos of smiling children, most with visible handicaps, covered the walls.

She took the medical files out of her briefcase and handed them over. "These are the records I found. They were put together about thirty years ago. They look like standard medical records, but there's something odd about them and I can't figure out what it is."

Charlie thumbed through the first one. "It's a pretty basic chart. Intake exam, height and weight, vitals, labs ordered, visual assessment." He read for a moment. "Sounds like a peds nurse prepared them; nothing wrong with the notations." He put the first one aside and opened the second. "Where did you get these?"

"I found them at an old Catholic orphanage."

He went to the third chart, and then flipped open the first. "Funny. The nurse had all three kids on a normal immunization schedule, but they were also given DNA tests. That was insanely expensive back then. Maybe they were looking for relatives. There's a weird notation here, too: 'V. microinjection.'"

"What does that mean?"

"Nothing. That's got to be a mistake," he told her. "The nurse just wrote it wrong."

Alex saw more than puzzlement on his face. "What is it, Charlie?"

"It's ridiculous. Microinjections were used only back in the seventies and eighties." Charlie turned and took a manual from the bookcase behind his desk. "Yeah, here it is. They'd extract a one-cell embryo at the pronuclear stage, inject the male pronucleus with a genetically engineered plasmid. Then they'd implant the embryo, let the female give birth, and the offspring would express the foreign gene from the transplanted plasmid." He looked up at her and chuckled. "In mice, Alex. Not humans. Jesus."

He wasn't making her feel any better. "Why would you do something like that to mice?"

"Gene transfer. Geneticists don't use the procedure anymore; it's risky and inefficient. I remember my dad ranting about it when some articles about the research were published in the medical journals. He called them 'Hitler vaccines.'" He glanced at the chart again. "A few hotheads were playing around with some ideas on using microinjections to create recombinant DNA. Scared the crap out of everyone who had a brain, until the government finally stepped in. It's illegal now, unless you're working with corn or sheep or something innocuous. Even then, it takes years and a truckload of authorizations from the FDA."

"Okay," Alex agreed, "but what if they did it to these kids? What would have happened?"

Charlie laughed until he had to wipe his eyes. "God, I've missed you. Sweetheart, what you're talking about is genetically engineering human beings. We can't even get stem cell research approved."

"You said there were some hotheads back then who wanted to do it," she pointed out. "Maybe they tried this shit. Maybe they tried with these kids."

He stopped smiling. "No way. For God's sake, Alex, this was thirty years ago. Practical genetics was in its infancy back then. Even if they had tried, they wouldn't have known what they were doing."

"What if they tried?" she persisted.

"*If* they could extract a pronuclear human embryo, and *if* it survived the mechanical insertion of the plasmid, and *if* it could be reimplanted, and *if* the plasmid integrated the foreign genetic material successfully into the DNA, then yes, they could have pulled it off. But it's not therapeutic. It's Frankenstein stuff." At her blank look, he added, "We didn't know enough about DNA in those days to do something like this. The kids would have been born with two heads or one eye."

Alex nodded and got to her feet. "Thanks, Charlie. I appreciate it."

He collected the charts, but before he handed them to her, he sighed. "If you don't believe me, find one of these kids and profile their DNA and their parents'. If by some snowball in hell's chance someone did successfully fiddle with their genes, it'll show when you compare the comparative results."

"I would, Charlie," she said slowly, "but all of these kids are orphans, remember? No parents."

Charlie walked her out of the office and to the limo waiting in the parking lot. He eyed it and whistled. "Very nice ride. You traded up."

Alex took one of his hands in hers, the left hand, and she gently rubbed her thumb over the plain gold wedding band he wore. "I loved you, Charlie, but I wasn't in love with you. I missed you, though. And I apologize for what I put you through after I left."

"Al." He curled a hand around her neck. "Wouldn't it be great if we could go back and do everything all over again?"

"We can't, and it's for the best." She made a face. "I'd have made you a terrible wife. Doctors should never marry doctors. And if we'd had kids, they probably would have come out with two heads or one eye."

He gave her a startled look. "Alex, you never said this was about you."

"It isn't anymore. It's about my brother, and trying to keep him from going off the deep end, and . . . another train wreck in progress." She stood on tiptoe to brush her lips against his. At the same time she concentrated, and the air around them grew heavy with the scent of lavender. "Charlie?"

"Hmmmmm?" He looked at her, dazed.

Alex took in a deep breath. "I want you to forget about me now. Be happy with Kimberly and your new baby. Be good to them, the way you were to me."

"Forget," he repeated. "Happy. Good."

"Good-bye, Charlie." Alex got into the limo and sat back, closing her eyes. She wanted to cry, but all she felt was numb. "Take me to Jaus's."

"Are you sure that is where you wish to go?"

Alex turned to look at Michael. "You were supposed to let me do this alone."

"I did. You did not say anything about the ride back to the hall." He eased his arm around her. "He seems like a very nice man, your friend."

"He is. But he's not you, and now that I've doused him with *l'attrait*, he'll probably never think of me again." She gave him a wobbly smile. "Don't worry, baby. I'm still yours."

"I know that. Just as I knew that what you did for your friend was not an easy thing." He rubbed his thumb against her soft cheek. "Sometimes you have so much courage that you terrify me. And you make me so proud. *That* is why I am in the limo."

"I'm glad." She snuggled against him.

Chapter 20

It took six hours to return to Chicago. When they arrived at O'Hare, Valentin directed Wilhelm to escort Melanie Wallace to a hotel.

"As soon as we have confirmed that there will be no danger to you," he told her, "you can return to Florida."

"My parents live in Ohio," she said. "I think I'll rent a car and go spend spring break with them." She smiled and gave him a quick hug. "I really appreciate everything you've done for me, Mr. Jaus."

Valentin took Liling directly from the airport to Derabend Hall. Lights blazed from every window, and every member of his guard lined the long drive, each holding a blazing torch. But when the car stopped at the front of the mansion, everyone stood back, and only one man came to the car.

Gregor walked slowly, dignity making his lined face look stern, and stopped to bow low before Valentin. "Welcome home, my lord."

"It is good to be home, old friend."

A tear wound its way down the *tresora*'s wrinkled cheek,

and then he stepped forward and embraced Valentin like a son.

"You cannot fly anymore, master," the elderly *tresora* told him. "My heart will not stand the strain."

"I was not worried." Jaus kissed Gregor's brow. "I knew you would see to everything."

"Oh, Wilhelm handled the emergency and the visit by the seigneur and the search for your plane flawlessly," he told Jaus. "I mostly sat in my room and cried like a baby until they found you." He beamed at his grandson before adding in a low voice, "I think it is time the boy took his place among your household. He will serve you well."

Valentin shared a smile with Wilhelm. "He has been trained by a master." He turned to Liling. "Liling, this is my *tresora* and very good friend, Gregor Sacher. Gregor, may I present my *sygkenis*, Liling Harper."

Sacher's jowls sagged, and then tightened as he produced a wide grin. "My lady." He offered her a stiff bow. "You are very welcome here." He looked over the cap and clothes she had borrowed from the search-and-rescue team. "May I escort you to your bedchamber so that you may freshen up and rest a bit?"

Liling glanced at Valentin, who nodded, then smiled shyly and took the old man's arm.

Alexandra Keller appeared and hugged Valentin. "A *sygkenis*, huh? Whom you found after you crashed the plane in the middle of nowhere, or before?"

"She was on the plane with me," he told her, and turned to take Michael Cyprien's hand. He found himself pulled forward and hugged again. "Such affectionate greetings. I shall have to disappear more often."

"I told Gregor that if you even *drove* near an airport

again, I'd fly up just to personally kick your ass," Alex informed him.

Valentin laughed. "Perhaps I will buy a railroad." He turned to Michael. "If you have a few moments, Seigneur, we have much to discuss." He glanced at Alexandra.

"You don't have to have anyone whisk me off to the gardens this time, Val," she told him. "I've got a patient to check on." She kissed his cheek and whispered loudly, "But I get to meet the beautiful life companion later, right?"

As the three walked into the mansion, Wilhelm removed two suitcases from the trunk of the limousine. He took the one containing Jaus's ruined clothing out to the trash bin behind the garage and emptied it into one of the cans. A splash of water startled him for a moment; then he chuckled and shook his head before returning to the main house.

The can rocked slightly as the water inside it defied gravity, streaking upward and over the rim. It gathered in a large pool next to the can and streamed, unnoticed, through the seams and cracks in the stone-paved drive.

Archbishop Hightower was so upset that he couldn't eat, sleep, or rest. He went out into the church and ignored the pain of his swollen legs and aching back as he knelt before the altar railing, folding his hands. He did not pray.

Prayer was for the weak. He had to think of how to explain the girl's death to D'Orio.

"Your Grace." His housekeeper appeared, a tray of his favorite sandwiches in her hands. "I don't mean to interrupt you while you're communing with Him, but you have to eat sometime."

"I told you—" He stopped as the shouted words echoed in the empty sanctuary. In a more moderate voice, he said, "Forgive me, Mrs. Murphy. I will have something later."

"I'll leave them in your office." She glanced around. "Father Cabreri still hasn't returned? Would you like me to stay?"

"No, go home to your husband," he told her. "I will see you tomorrow."

"Good night, Your Grace."

Hightower brooded another hour after the old woman left, and then retreated to his office. He sat down on the love seat reserved for visitors, reaching over with a grunt to take one of the sandwiches from the tray. He munched on the smoked ham and imported Swiss as he considered what D'Orio would do when they failed to deliver the girl.

He couldn't give her to Rome, not when the cardinal remained ignorant of the red swan's true ability. She had been living free for years; even after the years of conditioning the odds that she would behave obediently were next to nothing. He didn't regret the careful editing he had performed on her reports, however. She had been one of his special lambs, and if she hadn't faked her death and escaped, her abilities might have helped propel him to his proper place in the order.

Still, there were others, and for all his machinations D'Orio would never be able to cope with the coming apocalypse. When the proper time arrived, August knew he would have no trouble taking over control of the order.

The desk phone rang, and Hightower almost fell over trying to grab it. "St. Luke's."

"I planted a locator on the *maledicti*," Melanie Wallace said. "I have the address of his stronghold. There are dozens of *maledicti* there."

"You are to remove the girl and bring her to me." Hightower saw Cabreri in the doorway, out of the corner of his eye, and waved him in. "My men will exterminate the nest. Give me the location."

"I can't bring the girl to you. The *maledicti* have turned her," Wallace said. "She is contaminated now and of no use to us."

They had turned her? Hightower's mind raced. "What I do with the red swan is none of your concern. Where are you? Tell me."

"Good-bye, Your Grace," the girl said, and hung up.

"Wallace? Wallace!" With a curse he threw the phone across the desk. He turned to Cabreri. "I want you to trace that call. Don't just stand there."

Cabreri tried to speak, and then fell forward as an electrical sound buzzed in the air. The double prongs of a Taser protruded from between his shoulder blades.

"Carlo doesn't feel like talking right now." Cardinal D'Orio came into the office, followed by a dozen Brethren in street clothes. He passed the Taser in his hand to one of them before walking to the desk and helping himself to one of the sandwiches. "I always loved ham and cheese. My mother would forget sometimes and pack it in my lunch on Fridays. The nuns would snatch my sandwich and strip it off. I always thought they waited until we went back to class and then ate it themselves."

"Your Eminence." Hightower's eyes went from Carlo's inert body to the cardinal's placid expression before he recovered and rose to his feet. "I had no idea that you were in America."

"How many?" D'Orio asked.

"Your Eminence?"

D'Orio sniffed the glass of iced tea Mrs. Murphy had left on the tray before sipping from it. "Not enough sugar. I've been doing a little research on your archdiocese. Imagine my surprise when I discovered just how much funding you've spent on the care and feeding of poor little orphan children over the years. So how many have you used for your own experiments, August? A dozen? Twenty? Fifty?"

Dazzling red lights occluded his peripheral vision, as if the fires of hell were closing in on him. Sweat poured down his face. "I don't know what you mean, Your Eminence."

"You'll tell me now," D'Orio said, "or you'll tell them later." He nodded toward the men waiting by the office door. "But first they'll hang you from some very nasty meat hooks and show you what happens when you attach jumper cables to a man's testicles." He dusted off his hands and the front of his robes with a napkin.

Hightower glanced down at Cabreri. "If Carlo has been involved with some misuse of our funds, I will of course investigate immediately—"

"August." D'Orio sighed. "Your pathetic power play is over."

Hightower felt as if a crushing weight had landed on his chest, and the heat became stifling. "I serve the Light," he gasped. "You won't torture me."

D'Orio pursed his thin lips. "I'll do anything I like to you, and we both know it. Now, I'll ask you one more time: How many?"

Pain streaked up Hightower's arm, eating at it from the inside, and then he understood what it was. "Carlo doesn't know," he said, with no small amount of satisfaction. "No one does but me. You'll never find them."

D'Orio looked bored. "If you think that, then you're a fool."

Hightower pressed a hand to his chest, gasping in one last breath. "Wait . . . wait until . . . he comes. . . ." He pitched forward and fell on top of Cabreri.

Air whistled slowly from August's lips as men shouted and pounded on him with their fists. He closed his eyes as the pain radiating from his arm became the hell that consumed him.

After Valentin's elderly manservant assured himself that Liling was comfortable with her bedchamber, the private bath, the many lovely garments he had stocked in the closet, and the bottle of bloodwine he poured for her, he withdrew.

The room had been decorated in pure white, from the snowy carpet to the frost-colored walls. A crystal vase with a single red tulip it in was the only spot of color in the room. Liling took a moment to gawk at the luxury of her surroundings before retreating into the bathroom to clean up.

She took off the ball cap and shook out the short mop of hair that had grown back on her scalp. Her hair grew quickly, but not this fast—another change she would have to grow accustomed to. Valentin had told her that the hair of a Darkyn sometimes grew as much as a foot a day, and still it seemed like a miracle that she wasn't completely bald. As she undressed she discovered that patches of soot still blackened her skin, so she made use of the shower.

Once she had finished in the bathroom, she wrapped a large blue towel around herself and went out to pick something to wear from the closet. She chose a simple ivory dress and matching slippers, and placed them on the end of the bed.

"Lingerie," she muttered, looking around the room. She nearly dropped the towel when she saw Valentin leaning against the closed door. "Oh. I didn't know you were there."

"I came in while you were in the shower. I thought I might join you, but then you came out." He looked at the towel. "Take that off."

She glanced at the windows overlooking the lake. Sacher

had opened the curtains, so anyone in the right place outside could look in and see her.

"Liling."

Her mouth dry, Liling slowly pulled out the end tucked between her breasts and let the towel fall to the floor.

His cool eyes moved over her as he inspected her from head to heels. "Come here."

Ignoring her jumping nerves, she walked across the velvety white carpet toward the door, stopping in front of him.

"Turn around."

She pivoted, showing him her back, and felt him come up behind her. He didn't touch her, but leaned forward to put his mouth by her ear.

"Are you weary?" he asked, his breath stirring her hair.

She shook her head.

"Do you wish to be left alone?"

Biting her lip, she shook her head again.

"Go and lie on the bed," he told her. "Facedown."

She heard the click of the door lock as she walked over to the bed and did as he had instructed. She turned her head to watch him as he moved around the room, closing the curtains and turning off the lamps.

She tried not to squirm, but her skin crawled with anticipation.

"Be still." He was standing over her now, looking down, watching her.

He might be immortal, but this waiting was going to kill her. "Valentin."

"Some Kyn masters know what their *sygkenis* is thinking," he said softly. "Even when she says or does nothing to betray her thoughts to him. Their bond is that strong. It seems that is the case with us, for I knew what you were thinking as we were flying to O'Hare."

She had been terribly nervous about getting back on another plane, but Valentin had been at her side every moment, either holding her hand or with his arm around her. During the flight she had kept the fear away by remembering what they had done in the back compartment of the other plane.

And he had known, and had held her hand and said nothing.

Liling felt his fingers stroke the curve of her hip, and arched into his touch.

"You loved how we were together," he said quietly. "It excited you to surrender yourself to me like that. But I did not have time to do all things I wished." He bent down, putting his mouth to the small of her back and running his tongue up the length of her spine. He pinned her down with his body, stretching her arms out. "Now we have eternity together, *Liebling*, and I have you completely at my mercy."

His dark, silky words should have terrified her, but Liling only shivered with delight.

Jaus wedged his hand under her, pulling her hips up an inch from the bed. With his other hand he opened his trousers and guided his penis between her legs. He prodded her slick folds with the stiff head, pressing against her but not penetrating. She wriggled her hips, trying to entice him to give her more.

"Liling," he breathed against the back of her neck. "This is what I was thinking of on the plane."

He pierced her body with a single thrust, pushing deep as he jerked her hips up, his hands holding her in place until he had forced her to take his entire length. He shifted one hand under her, sliding it between her breasts before he brought her up and back against him, her shoulders to his chest, her thighs spread wide over his.

He kissed her shoulder as she writhed on him, and put his cheek against hers. "Put your hands on your breasts."

Liling groaned, her hands in fists against her thighs, and then forced them to open and pressed them over her breasts. The stiff, distended points of her nipples seemed to scrape her palms.

Valentin pushed her hips down, working the head of his cock an inch deeper. "Squeeze them." When she did, he flexed inside her and began to thrust back and forth. "Harder. Like that. Yes. Does that feel good?"

She didn't know if he meant the subtle, maddening strokes of his penis or the way he was making her torment her own body.

"Yes," she gasped. "I love it. I love you."

His body tensed, and then he brought his hand down between her thighs. He caught her clitoris between his thumb and forefinger and gently squeezed the stiff little bud once, twice, three times.

Even as Liling felt her climax budding, he said, "No. Do not come yet. Wait."

"Valentin."

"You will wait." He took one of her hands from her breasts and pushed it down. "Touch yourself. Rub it while I fuck your pretty little cunt. The way I wished to every minute I held your hand."

Liling knew he watched over her shoulder; she could not fool him by pretending. She brought her middle finger to rest against her clit and rubbed slowly.

"Faster," he said, working himself harder inside her.

She flexed her finger, stroking herself with more vigor. Her clit sent a ripple of red-hot sensation through her groin.

"Harder." He put his hand on top of hers, holding her and forcing her to do his bidding. When he felt her hips twist and shake, he quickly withdrew from her and inserted her finger and his own into her vagina.

"Please," she begged, needing him inside her, and then she felt him rubbing his cock against the sensitive ruck of her bottom.

He pressed in there, not quite entering her but stimulating her unbearably while he fucked her with their fingers.

"Now you will come for me, *Liebling*," he said, his voice hoarse. "Come on our hands."

As if he'd released her from some unseen restraint, Liling came with a wild cry and felt his penis jerking and twitching against her bottom as he spilled his semen between her buttocks, rubbing it into her with long, luxurious strokes of his shaft.

He brought her down gently onto her back on the bed and lay beside her, his hand caressing and fondling as he stroked her breasts, belly, and thighs. Little quakes of pleasure, like climax aftershocks, shook her as his touch kept them shimmering through her body.

"I love you." She looked up at him, her mouth soft, her eyes damp. "I think I always have. I just needed to see the real you."

"As I needed to know you." He smiled, a warm and beautiful smile, as if she had offered him a miracle. "Now we have found each other, *Geliebte*."

Chapter 21

"And that's all I know," Fort Lauderdale homicide detective Samantha Brown, the *sygkenis* of Lucan, the suzerain of South Florida, said. "Sorry I couldn't be more help, Alex."

"No problem, Sam. I knew you were just a baby when they sent you south." Alex tapped the end of her pencil like a drumstick against her notepad. "One more thing: Did they ever tell you why they sent you all the way down to Florida for foster care placement?"

"Not that I remember. Wait, yeah, there was this one weird notation somewhere in my DCF jacket. Let me look." There was a shuffle of papers as Sam checked her personal records. "Here it is. It's just a scribbled note by the CW caseworker in Chicago. Says I had allergies when I was a kid. They had to give me a bunch of injections."

Alex thought of what Charlie had told her. "What are you allergic to?"

"That's the weird part. Nothing. Not even penicillin." A wry note entered her voice. "Maybe I was allergic to Chicago."

After Alex hung up the phone, she carried her notes from

the sitting room into the bedroom. "Any luck with rooting through the laptop?"

"I have not found any records on it that relate to the orphanage or the Brethren." He closed the device and turned to her. "Did Samantha offer any insight?"

"No. She knew she was born in Illinois and sent down south when she was a baby, but that's all. Nothing in her records to speak of, except a note about allergies she doesn't have." She flipped a page. "The very tough phone call today was Nick, once I tracked down her and Gabriel. They're over in Paris, looking for some missing Kyn and generally fucking with the Brethren."

Cyprien nodded. "Nicola is still not comfortable talking to us."

"Richard's wife killed her parents. She's entitled. But she likes me. Thing is, she didn't know she was adopted. Shocked the hell out of her, too." Alex made a face. "She said she has her mom's papers stashed at her farm, and she's going to go through them as soon as they get back to England."

Michael regarded her with a patient expression. "If you confirm that Nicola was also adopted, what will you conclude from that?"

Alex started counting off points with her fingers. "One: None of us remembers being in an orphanage in Chicago. Two: All of us are female. Three: We each had some strange ability before we made the change from human to Darkyn."

"Samantha has an ability?"

"Yeah, and it's worse than mine."

"How bad could it be?"

She looked at him. "If she touches the blood of murder victims, she has a vision of how they were killed. Front-row seat to murder."

Michael grimaced. "That is worse than yours."

"What it boils down to is that we were all different before the Kyn ever messed with us," Alex said. "I'm superfast with my hands, Nick can find pretty much anything, and Sam never has to rent slasher flicks. Not what you'd call standard human operating systems."

"There is only one problem with your theory," Michael said. "Jema did not have a talent before she changed, and she was not adopted."

"Bitch just ruins everything, doesn't she?" Alex shook her head. "I still think there's a connection between us; I'm just not seeing it. But it could explain why the four of us survived the change from human to Darkyn when no one else has since the Dark Ages."

"Five."

She frowned. "I missed someone?"

"I spoke to Jaus," Michael said. "Liling Harper was human when she got on his plane."

"Well, hell." She tossed her notepad on the desk. "That blows my theory." She glanced at the calendar. "Hang on; they were only out there a couple of days. It took the rest of us weeks to make the change. How did she do it so fast?"

Michael moved his shoulders.

"You're a lot of help." She helped herself to a stack of the medical records they'd stolen from St. Benedict's. "I'm going to take these over to the lab and let John go through them."

"Is that wise, considering his condition?"

"There's nothing in them that would send him tearing off across the country, and I think I can stall him from trying to do anything else." She felt grim. "If all else fails, I'll need to borrow some manacles and chains."

*   *   *

Her brother was out of bed and fully dressed when Alex walked into the lab.

"I'm sorry, sir, but you can't discharge yourself without filling out the proper paperwork." She saw blood dripping from the dangling IV needle. "You did a nice job ripping out your line. What are you going to do now? Go and play with a chain saw in a bathtub filled with oil?"

He gazed at her steadily. "Cyprien told me you found another dormitory and medical files at Saint Benedict's. I was right."

"I was coming to talk to you about it." She didn't like his color. "Will you get back in bed before you pass out again?"

"I'm fine." He sat down on the bed. "What were they doing to us?"

"They gave us standard pediatric physicals," she told him. "The kind you give kids before you place them in a new environment, like foster care or with adoptive parents. Height, weight, BP, that's it."

"There has to be more." He grabbed the medical files from her and started flipping through them.

Alex leaned back against a table and decided it was time to sell him her phony theory. "Speaking as a physician, here's what I think. We were probably being used as part of some sort of clinical control group. Fifty to sixty kids would be about the right number."

He jumped right on that. "A group for what?"

"Different types of testing," she said. "Control groups of that size were very popular back in the seventies and eighties. Researchers would begin by testing fifty to a hundred random individuals who were healthy and disease-free. They graphed the results of each test, charting them by number of subjects and test values. It's how they determined the curve of normal frequency distribution. The largest number of identical test values was the norm by which all subsequent values were measured. It didn't hurt the kids. They were just randomly tested."

"That can't be right," John said as Michael came in and joined them. "Why would they test kids all from one place?"

"They didn't know any better," Alex said. "It was probably easier for them to use kids from one region. Their test results would have been flawed by certain factors the researchers didn't consider, like environmental contaminants and even geographical location." She gestured toward the window. "People who live in the mountains, for example, have higher levels of hemoglobin than people who live in the city at sea level. The body produces more red blood cells at higher elevations to compensate for the oxygen deficiency in the atmosphere. That sort of thing."

"Why use only orphans?" John said.

"The doctors wouldn't need parental consent, for one thing," she told him. "They might have taken kids from the same region for another reason, like compiling ratios of sentinel phenotypes among the poor." She saw the look John gave her. "Sentinel phenotypes are individual traits researchers use to track things like newly emerging diseases and recessive mutations. The traits manifest physically, either in the patient's outward appearance or in their lab results. Hemophilia, muscular dystrophy, and cancer are all sentinel phenotypes. They're statistically evaluated, so they would need a control group." And if he didn't start buying her lie soon, she was going to run out of fake theory.

John folded his arms. "That proves they were looking for something specific. Something abnormal."

Alexandra sighed. The problem with her brother was that he was no dummy. "All it proves is that they could have been simply testing us and using our results as a baseline for the really sick kids."

"Then why not test normal children? Why lock up the kids and have them sleeping next to a lab?"

"We don't even know for certain that they were locked up, John," she reminded him. "Hell, Charlie and I did a study a few years back on phenylketonuric mothers who gave birth to mentally retarded heterozygous children. I was able to prove that, thanks to too many cousins marrying each other, eleven percent of the population in a small town in Idaho carries the defect. I had two hundred people, including fifty-odd kids, staying at a study clinic for two weeks while we profiled their DNA and mapped out familial connections. It's a very specific type of study." She paused, caught up in her own lie for a moment. "The orphanage doctors wouldn't study a control group for something like that. Sentinel phenotypes can't be predicted among random groups of children unless . . ."

John imitated one of her favorite gestures by rolling his hand.

Everything Charlie said came rushing back to her. "Unless they knew the parents were carriers."

"I need some water." John walked into the bathroom.

"What does this mean, Alexandra?"

She gave Michael a blank look. "It means I'm a great liar, and my brother may be right."

He thought that over. "You do realize how dangerous it will be to proceed from here?"

Alex felt as if he had wrenched her out of a smothering cloud. At the same time, she wanted to hit him. "I don't think I have a choice now."

"The truth about what happened to you and John when you were children may also reveal how you, Samantha,

Nicola, Jema, and Liling survived the change," he pointed out.

"Which will then give me some idea of how I can change us back," she snapped.

He nodded. "But in the process, you may learn the exact method of how to change a human into Kyn."

"That's why we're not going to write down or otherwise share the information," she told him. "No more giving my research to the vampire king. And you're my failsafe. If things get bad, you're going to make me forget it."

The lines of tension around his mouth disappeared. "You would trust me to do that?"

"Baby, I'm counting on it."

John came out of the bathroom, his hands clapped over his ears. "Alex." He groaned and sank to his knees. "Something's wrong. Outside. Something's happening— you have to stop it."

"Stop what?"

His tormented eyes met hers. "Something terrible."

Liling felt Jaus relax beside her and go still as he fell asleep. She waited a little while, watching his face and wondering whether she had the strength to do this.

Love, she decided, would not be denied. Like Valentin, it demanded everything. And if she loved him, if she meant more than simply saying the words, she would have to give everything for him. If she didn't, he and his friends would die, just as all the people at the facility had.

She slipped out of the bed, arranging the pillows under the linens before she went to the closet. She dressed in the first things she put her hand on, a flowered, floaty shirt and a white blouse. She pushed her feet into a pair of pale green slippers and silently left the room.

She had felt his power growing steadily all night. Even when she was making love with Valentin, it had been in the back of her head, a silent invitation, tugging at her, trying to lure her outside.

Now it was swelling out of control, like his anger, creating a hum in the air inaudible as yet to everyone but her. If they had been far from water, it would not have frightened her as much, but Valentin's home sat next to one of the largest lakes in America. She knew that if she did not stop her twin, he would use the almost-endless supply of water to destroy the mansion. As strong as he was now, the end result might kill hundreds, even thousands of innocents and devastate the entire area.

She couldn't let him do it again.

No one detained her as she walked outside and down to the lake. She stopped only to stand for a moment in Valentin's gardens, to run her fingers over the pure white petals of his camellias and let the scent permeate her senses. It frightened her now to think that she might have gone her entire life never knowing him. But she had found him at last, and what they had shared had been real and enduring. Love worth protecting, love to stand and fight for.

If need be, to die for.

Valentin dreamed of the night that he had lost everything.

"Durand." He stepped into Thierry's path and raised his battle sword.

"Get out of my way, Jaus." The tall, angry man looked over him and then turned, breathing in deeply. "Jema. Where are you? Come to me now."

Valentin froze. Thierry called to Jema as if he had the right to her. As if she belonged to him. But she was his. "You cannot have her."

"She's already mine." Thierry lifted his sword. *"Can't you smell her on me?"*

He didn't feel his heart break. He felt his sanity snap. *"No."* He lunged.

Thierry parried the attack and returned it with interest, slamming his blade into Valentin's so hard that sparks flew between them.

Valentin had studied blade work his entire life, both as a human and as a Darkyn lord. He trained every single day. And so he attacked with every ounce of skill he possessed, determined to separate Durand's head from his shoulders, because that was the only payment he would accept for what Durand had stolen from him.

But the man he fought was not a practiced swordsman. He was the man who had been left behind to hold Castle Pilgrim until the last Templar had escaped. The man who alone had fought his way through a gauntlet of five hundred Saracens to reach freedom. The man who had left five hundred headless, armless, and lifeless bodies in his wake.

Durand does not dominate on the battlefield, the Kyn said of him. *He makes it his charnel house.*

"Jaus. Durand." Michael Cyprien stepped into the room, a human dangling between his hands. *"Lower your swords. Now."*

Jaus was in a cold, killing rage, and ignored the seigneur's orders. Thierry did as well. They circled the room as their swords clashed, slid, and danced, moving in patterns too swift at times for the blades to be clearly seen. They circled and sidestepped, gradually working their way into the ballroom, until they were battling in the center of the floor.

"Thierry, please stop this."

Valentin saw how Jema's voice had distracted Durand,

*and when the other man turned his gaze away from their
blades, he took advantage of the opening and lunged.*

"No!"

*Jema appeared, seemingly out of thin air, directly be-
tween Valentin's blade and Thierry. There was no time or
space to prevent what happened next. Valentin's rage became horror as he saw her step into the thrust, but it was too
late.*

*His sword pierced Jema's abdomen and came out the
other side of her body.*

*Thierry bellowed and brought his sword down on
Valentin's arm. The razor-sharp steel sliced through flesh
and muscle and bone as if they were made of butter. Valentin
staggered, his eyes fixed to the stump that healed over as he
watched. Thierry caught Jema's waist and pulled Valentin's
sword out of her body. It fell to rest beside Jaus's severed
arm.*

Valentin opened his eyes, his hand moving to touch the
scar encircling his arm. Carefully, so as not to disturb Liling,
he got out of bed, pulled on his trousers, and went to open
the curtains.

The moon's grin had widened, casting a wide net of ghost
diamonds onto the lake. Just after the surgery Alexandra had
performed to reattach his arm, he had stood here, in this very
spot, watching the woman he loved embrace another man in
the snowfall. It was then that his heart had turned to ice, and
he had thought he would never warm again.

Until Liling, and her touch burned away all of his sorrow-
ful yesterdays.

A part of Valentin would always love Jema. She had long
been a dream that had made his lonely life bearable. But
now that he had Liling, and real love that was not only wel-
comed but returned, sunlight filled his heart.

Full circle.

Storm clouds where there had been none before blocked out the moonlight. Jaus looked down as a small figure stepped over the seawall and walked down to the water. The lake began to churn in an ominously familiar way, and the air itself seemed to crackle as lightning began slicing through the sky.

Jaus pressed his hands against the glass, and then went over to the bed and jerked back the linens. Only pillows lay in her place; Liling was gone.

He went back to the window in time to see a column of water rising in front of Liling. It darkened and contracted and solidified into a man, the Asian man named Kyan who had attacked him at the cabin in Florida. He had the ability to control water as easily as Liling manipulated fire.

Valentin didn't wait to see what would happen next. He turned and simply ran.

Kyan gathered himself from the lake and rose from it, returning to the human form in which he had been born. The first time he had melded himself with his element, it had been such a glorious thing that he had almost not returned to his own body. But being water simply was, without thought or intention, and the order had taught Kyan that he needed more than that, that he had a responsibility to protect the helpless from the demons preying on them.

The girl stood on the shore, watching him change, seemingly as calm as he was furious. She smelled of sex and blood and flowers—the perfume of a demon's whore—but no fear colored her scent.

She needed to be reminded of who Kyan was.

He lifted his arms, drawing from the storm, luring and concentrating the water-laden clouds into the sky above him.

Around him, the lake water began to boil as it sent several whirling spouts up into the clouds, feeding them with water and power.

The girl mirrored his movements, and behind her the torches lining the seawall flared, shooting showers of sparks that fell like orange rain all around her. Some fell on the hedges of camellia at the edge of the garden, but she glanced at them and the embers died.

As before, the air between them began to ripple and stretch, changing as if in response to the two forces about to collide.

"You are not welcome here," she said to him, the air distorting her voice into a resonant echo.

The skin all over his body seemed to feel the words. "You speak Chinese."

"It was all we spoke for the first sixteen years of our lives," she told him. "They only used Chinese with us. They refused to teach us English so that we couldn't communicate with anyone outside the facilities. Or did they take that memory from you, too?"

Of course she would attack the Brethren. He should have expected it. "You are a liar."

"We were born here, in America." She said it in English, and then switched back to Chinese effortlessly. "That's why you can understand what they say, but you can't speak the language. We were punished if they caught us using any English words we overheard. Only rice and water for three days in the isolation room."

He shook his head. "The priests were kind to us. They brought us here from China. We would have starved if not for them."

"They took us from our mother. They may have even killed her in order to steal us. I have tried to find records, but there are none." Sympathy softened her eyes. "I will tell you everything I remember. They did not have time to tamper with my mind."

"You believe I would listen to your lies? Do you think you can control me so easily? I know what you have become." Rain began to fall, soaking them both. "How could you go to him? How could you let him put his filthy hands on you?"

She wiped the rain out of her eyes and glanced back at the golden-haired man behind the wall. "I love him."

He didn't need to use his mouth to speak to her. *Then say good-bye to your lover. You can't run away from me this time.*

I don't wish to. She moved toward him, and the space between them became crowded with seething shadows as the air thinned and seemed to tear. *If you insist, we will end this tonight.*

"Don't take another step, either of you." Melanie Wallace appeared, guns in both of her hands, and stretched out her arms in either direction, pointing them at Kyan and the girl. "If you do, I'll shoot."

The girl lowered her arms. "This is between us," she told her, never looking away from Kyan. "Move away before you get hurt."

Melanie turned her head. "Boys? A little help would be nice."

Two men in dark clothing came out of the shadows behind Melanie. They both held automatic weapons, one pointed at Liling, the other at Kyan.

One shouted a prayer in Latin as he raised the machine gun and began shooting at Valentin and the others standing behind the seawall.

Liling flung a hand toward one of the torches, pulling the

flames from it and sending them in a concentrated, blue-white stream between the assassin and the Kyn. Bullets, partially melted, began dropping onto the rocks.

The other man fired directly at her, but Kyan sent a column of water from the lake, blasting the weapon and the bullets he had fired away. It slammed into the assassin, driving him into the concrete side of the seawall, where he fell to lie soaked and unconscious over the edge.

The girl regarded Kyan with surprise. "You defend me now?"

"Your life is mine," he snarled. "No one else takes it."

Melanie made an exasperated sound. "Men, always like dogs in the manger." She fired at him.

Before the bullet reached him, Kyan dissolved his form into a pillar of water. He saw Melanie fire her other weapon at the girl, who cloaked herself in a column of flames.

Kyan shifted back into his human body, and sent two streams of water to blast the guns out of the American girl's hands. "Melanie, leave us alone."

"Liling." The *maledicti* was running toward the flames.

The girl stepped out of the flames and smiled at the demon before she shook her head. Kyan saw two more of the Darkyn grab the golden-haired man and pull him back.

Kyan summoned the storm, and turned once more to face his sister.

Chapter 22

Liling knew from the growing violence of the rain and the rising wind that she was running out of time. The lightning went wild, striking the water and the land all around the three of them.

The bright white flashes illuminated Kyan's face in snatches, like a strobe. His black hair, as long as hers had been before the fire at the cabin, seethed in the wind around his stern face. She was not surprised to see he had grown into a tall, strong man. Even when they were little, Kyan had been bigger and broader than she. No one would ever imagine the two of them had once shared the same womb.

Looking into his eyes, however, was the same as looking at herself. Except there, too, was a distinct difference. Tiny sparks of wild energy crackled in Kyan's black eyes, making them look as blue as the swan tattoo on the inside of his right forearm.

This was her brother, her twin. The keeper of her childish secrets and the mirror of her lonely soul. The angry boy she had loved with all her heart, and the deranged man she had feared more than any other. If she couldn't drive him away, she would have to break her promise to Mrs. Chen. She would have to give pain, not take it away.

She would have to kill him.

The lightning danced, splitting around them into a glittering, moving web of light. One thin tendril of electricity shot into the center of the space between Kyan and Liling, striking Melanie on the arm, making her scream with pain.

Kyan reached out to her at the same time Liling did, trying to draw the lightning away from the girl. The web collapsed around Melanie and formed a strange, dark current that leaped between Kyan's and Liling's hands, impaling Melanie in the center.

The next thing Liling saw was a corridor of light around her. She realized at once that she did not occupy the place physically, but her thoughts were so strong and focused it was the same as being embodied. She could feel Kyan there as well, near the other end. He seemed as bewildered as she was.

As soon as her brother became aware of her presence, hatred turned his thoughts turn cold and unyielding. *What have you done to her? Where is this place?*

Melanie is all right. Liling could feel the girl acting as a sort of conduit, but the energy pouring through her was not harming her. *We must have created this place together with our abilities and our minds. The way we did with dreams when we were children.* She reached out to him with her thoughts, feeling the light intensify as she drew closer to the essence of his soul. *Kyan, I will not allow you to kill again. You can have my life, but you will not harm the one I love.*

How can you love him? Bitterness darkened his rage, feeding the twisted snarl of his emotions. *He is a demon.*

No, Valentin is a good, kind man. She withstood the violent backlash of his angry, wordless reaction to those words until it subsided. *The priests lied about so many things. These Darkyn, they are like us. They have abilities like us.*

He blasted her with a new wave of anger, this time cold with contempt. *No one is like us.*

Why are you so angry with me? she demanded. *Why do you want me dead? I know they brainwashed you, but you must remember something of us. I was never your enemy.*

You left me. You left me to them.

Images of what had happened to him during the seven years they had been separated as children flooded through her mind. No wonder he hated her. He thought she had kept him away, had abandoned him deliberately. That was what they had told him, that she didn't want to be with him. They had made him believe that she despised him.

Now she would have to give pain, not take it from him. It was the only way to make him see the truth.

No, brother. The priests wouldn't let us be together. She opened her own memories of what had been done her, and how she had wept for her twin. The terrible loneliness she had endured. The punishments they had given her for begging to see him, for refusing to obey the bells, the priests, and the doctors, and then for the many attempts she had made to escape so that she could find him. One year, the first year after they took him from her, she had lived on almost nothing but rice and water, locked away from everyone in a small six-by-nine-foot room.

Liling showed him everything, every thought, every agony she had suffered. She poured her pain into him, forcing him to accept it as she had been made to accept their separation.

Kyan's thoughts became confused. *But I came for you when I could. I resisted, the same as you did. I came to take you away from them, and you summoned the storm and tried to kill me.*

It was not me. The storm came because of what they did to us while we were apart. The doctors went too far. She recalled all of the conversations she had overheard, the reports she had surreptitiously read. *The treatments cause us to generate all this power when we are together. But we can't control it, and it makes the storms come. That is why we had to stay apart. Why we can't be together now.*

The terrible loneliness inside her brother's soul became an abyss of anguish that yawned between them, but it was answered not by Liling, but by a third presence.

You've hurt him enough, Melanie said, coming to awareness between Liling and Kyan, creating a defensive barrier with her own thoughts. *Leave him alone.*

Liling reached out to her, and felt a terrible recognition as the girl's conflicted thoughts flooded back over her. Melanie had been raised like her and Kyan, at a Brethren facility in another part of the country. She had been born to a young mother, from whom she had been taken at birth. Moved from place to place, she had been subjected to the same treatments and punishments. She had not escaped, and like Kyan had been trained as an operative to use guns, blades, drugs, and even her own sexuality as weapons. For most of her life she had traveled the world on behalf of the Brethren, assuming different identities in order to carry out her missions.

Beneath all of the coldness and discipline and blunted emotions, Liling felt the remnants of a sad and silent little girl. It had been the little girl who, despite her orders, had not wanted to kill Kyan. But the Brethren had given her no margin for failure. If she had not killed him, she would have been executed herself.

Liling poured herself around Melanie's presence, using her ability to remove pain from her soul. As she removed the poisonous influences the Brethren had inflicted on the girl, she felt Melanie retreat into herself, as wounded and confused as Kyan was.

When she had removed the last of the girl's pain, Liling turned her attention back to her brother. *Now do you see the truth of what they did to us?*

It can't be undone, can it? Kyan thought, and then answered his own question. *What they did changed what we are.*

Only our bodies, our abilities. They can never take who we are away from us. Liling embraced his devastating sadness and deep sense of betrayal, and tried to remove it from him, but the connection between them was growing weaker. *Kyan, the Darkyn are not evil,* she thought while she could still reach him with her thoughts. *The Brethren deceived us about them as well. You must get away from the order and never allow them to control you again. Take Melanie away, somewhere they can't find you.* She used the last thread of the connection to pour her love for him through it. *You will always be in my heart, brother.*

Liling was pulled back into her human form as the violet current of energy disappeared. Melanie fell between her and Kyan, unconscious. Liling looked over at her brother, who nodded.

As Liling carefully retreated, Kyan came forward and picked up Melanie, carrying her out into the water. He stopped and turned back.

"I won't forget this," he said. "Or you."

"I am with you, Kyan," Liling said softly. "Even when we're not together."

Her brother took one last look at her, and then he dove under the surface of the lake, taking Melanie with him.

The rippling energy distorting the air gradually dissipated, and above her, the skies cleared. Liling turned to find Valentin standing behind her.

He searched her face. "He came to kill you, but you faced him alone, without me. Why did you not wake me?"

"He is my brother. I had to try to heal him first. I couldn't allow him to harm you or your people." Suddenly feeling more than a little ashamed, she looked down at her hands. "I didn't want you to know what I am, not this part. It's ugly and frightening. I thought if you knew what I can really do—how I give pain as easily as I can take it away—that you wouldn't want me anymore."

"Mein Mädchen." He laced his fingers through hers and drew her to him. His mouth touched hers gently before he looked into her eyes. "You are my fire now."

Liling moved into the curve of his arm and walked back with him to their home.

"Did you see the way that girl juggled fire?" Alexandra said to Michael as they watched Jaus and his *sygkenis* disappear into the mansion. "Before we leave, I have got to get a blood sample from her."

Michael glanced down at the melted copper slugs on the blackened, scorched rocks where Liling had stood. "I would not recommend boiling it."

Phillipe met them inside the mansion and handed an envelope to Alex. "These are the reports you wanted, Alexandra. In French and English."

"Thanks, Phil." She carried them toward the lab, stopped, and turned back around. "John's probably sleeping. Want to go to our bedroom and read stuff in French for me?"

He put his arm around her waist. "As long as I can do other things in French to you later."

"Lecher."

He nodded. "And proud of it."

Back in their room, Alexandra separated the contents of the envelope and handed a stack of papers written in French to Cyprien. "Phillipe got me copies of the arson reports on those *jardin* the Brethren burned out." She skimmed through the translated reports. "These say the police never recovered any bodies from the scene of the fire. Same on yours?"

He studied the original documents. "Yes. They must have been removed and buried by the Kyn's human servants in that area."

She shook her head. "No, all the *jardin*'s *tresori* fled the area with the survivors. Phil double-checked."

He tried to think of another explanation, but failed. "Someone removed them before the humans could."

"Read the incident report dated October fifteenth."

"One of the local people reported seeing men in dark clothing at the scene just after the fire." He skipped through several paragraphs of nonsense questions from the interrogating officer. "The eyewitness claimed they were looting the property, because he saw them carrying out bags and loading them onto a truck."

"Uh-huh." Alex checked her own translated copy. "Want to guess how big the bags were?"

He looked up from the report. "You believe the Brethren are stealing the bodies of dead Kyn?"

"Why would they want them?"

"Trophies."

"I don't know." She rubbed the back of her neck. "We know the Kyn can survive terrible wounds. Gabriel Seran was tortured daily for years. They even blinded him with copper-tainted holy water, and yet he eventually healed and regained his vision." She scowled. "Although I still don't know exactly why he healed. Anyway, what if they weren't dead? What if they were just really well-done?"

"The Brethren are committed to our destruction, Alexandra," he reminded her. "They would not try to save victims from a fire they set themselves."

"That's it." She took in a deep breath and covered her mouth with her hand, then gestured outward. "What if they're not setting the fires to kill the Kyn? What if they only want to incapacitate them long enough to transport them somewhere, keep them prisoner?"

"C'est impossible." Cyprien did not even want to think of all the Kyn who had been burned to death over the centuries. "We would know if they were doing such things."

"The Brethren haven't burned Kyn since they rounded most of you up back in the fourteenth century, when the church condemned the Templars to death. Phil told me that," she said. "Since then they've attacked with copper weapons, tortured, and beheaded you guys, but that's about it. Or it was, until three years ago. How many *jardin* have they burned since then?"

He thought for a moment. "All of the attacks on the *jardin* in Italy and France were arson. Ten or fifteen, at least."

"All the fires were set during the day, while the Kyn were inside and at rest, right?"

"How did you know that?"

"Remember when I talked to those refugees at the Realm?" she asked. "They all kept describing the same thing: The Brethren attacked them without warning, trapping them inside their homes and trying to burn them alive. Never anything else. No other type of attack. I bet if you check reports for every Kyn-related arson in France and Italy, you'll find the authorities never recovered any remains at all."

"If that is so, it means the Brethren could have captured and imprisoned dozens of Kyn." Michael shook his head. "No. I do not believe it."

"What if I'm right?"

"If you are," he said, his eyes turning pure amber, "then we will find them and set them free."

Alex thought about the wild theory she had spun for John about the orphanage, the theory that she suddenly didn't want to research anymore. "I need to put John in the hospital, somewhere he can see specialists and get the treatment he needs, and where the Brethren can't get at him. Do you think that rehab place where Val hid Luisa has room for one more patient?"

The unnatural lighting retreated into the clouds and died away as quickly as the booming thunder. The Asian girl who had made the fire dance walked back up the shore to embrace Jaus. John could see no sign of the other two.

Whatever this confrontation had been about, it seemed over.

The storm over the lake flattened and thinned out until the stars appeared again. The moon, its snide smile beaming down at the city, seemed to be congratulating itself for surviving the near-apocalypse. The wind blew its last, disgusted huff at the lake before settling down into a mild breeze.

John stepped back from the windows and let the curtain fall back into place. Over time he felt as if he'd become a voyeur to the strange battles of the Darkyn, but this one he was sure would defy explanation even among their ranks.

Depression dragged at him. He had no business being

here or watching this. He was human, and Alexandra was not. It was time to accept that, and what was happening to him.

Tomorrow he would not convince Jaus to go with him to meet the archbishop. Hightower, ever eager to spin his web of lies around his surrogate son, would have agreed to meet him anywhere. But John was tired of clinging to the edge of reason and fighting for truth. The truth was ugly and painful and destroyed too much. It had taken John's faith and his peace of mind. It had forced him to ally himself with monsters. Confronting his old mentor and finally learning what the Brethren had done to him and Alex might send him over into the abyss.

He felt his shrunken stomach tightening and sweat running down the sides of his face. He needed a shower and a meal. He walked into the bathroom and stopped at the sink to splash cold water on his face.

He straightened and stared at his pale reflection. The attack had left his eyes with a strange cast; he still looked feverish. He squeezed his eyes shut as pain spread from his knotted gut up through his chest.

He had run out of time.

John knew he couldn't stay in this place, not if he was dying. And from the way she had behaved since discovering his malaria, and the way he felt now, the end was closing in. He had inflicted enough pain on Alexandra; he would not force her to watch him die and blame herself for not saving him.

The confrontation down by the lake had distracted the guards, making it easy for John to slip out of the house. He went to Jaus's massive garage, took a set of keys from the neatly labeled wall rack, and stole one of his Porsches.

John drove north out of the city, stopping once to get directions to the Saint Benedict Catholic Adoption Agency. He parked across the street and watched a pair of patrol cops talking to a worried-looking woman wearing a black dress and a modified nun's veil over her silver hair. When she glanced across the street, John started the Porsche and left.

He realized it was a Sunday when he saw a group of people walking into a Methodist church. The family had four little girls, each wearing a ruffled dress and a flowery hat. More people followed, and John saw why the services were so well attended when he read the small sign posted on the front lawn of the church. It was Palm Sunday, a communion service.

How long had it been since he had prayed in the house of God?

John found a parking spot in the crowded lot, and followed the faithful into the church. All he knew about Methodists was that they liked to sing and eat. He didn't try to sit down in the crowded church, but found a place to stand at the back. The pews filled rapidly, and latecomers had to come and stand beside him.

The sanctuary was beautiful. Potted lilies, honoring the upcoming Easter holiday, lined the aisles and decorated the altar. A three-foot-tall rabbit stood on one side of the altar, guarding a giant basket filled with multicolored plastic eggs. An enormous aluminum cross hung suspended over the center of the altar, but the savior's corpse was markedly absent. Instead, a stylized red flame wound around the cross, a more palatable symbol of the sacrifice God's son had made for the sins of the world.

"Is this your first time here, dear?" a smiling matron in a powder blue twinset and pearls asked him. When John nodded, she pressed a happy-face sticker with the word *visitor* on John's lapel. "We're having a bagel breakfast in the fellowship hall after services," she said. "You're welcome to join us." She moved on to the next man standing.

John watched a young, smiling minister make a remarkably casual entrance with his lay leaders, and the service began with a large choir offering a joyous hymn. The accompanying organist missed a few notes, but the congregation didn't seem to mind. Every person in the church held a hymnal and sang along.

The minister offered prayers, and then a lengthy but energetic sermon on charity and forgiveness. The way he grinned and gestured emphasized his enthusiasm.

"Albert Einstein said, 'We must learn to see the world anew,'" the minister said. "Our Lord God wants us to make the world new. When we are generous, when we forgive, we remove some of the darkness from the world. We bring His word and His light to those who have dwelled away from it for too long."

By the end of the sermon, John felt the pain in his stomach disappear. The congregation stood to pray and sing again, and then the minister invited them to receive communion.

John doubted the eating and singing Methodists gained any more favor from God than the confessing and atoning Catholics. But being here and seeing—feeling—the simple joy of Christian fellowship made him feel like a new man. Perhaps because it reminded him of how much he had sacrificed when he had abandoned his calling.

Something pushed John away from the back wall of the church to join the long line walking up to the altar railing. He felt better, but he had no illusions; malaria had no cure, and he didn't believe in miracles anymore. But for whatever time he had left, he could shun the war between the Darkyn and the Brethren and find a shelter or a clinic where he could work. He would return to a simpler purpose, the purpose that had originally made him become a priest.

He would accept communion today, and dedicate the rest of his life to performing good works among the faithful.

When it was John's turn, he knelt at the railing beside a little girl in a spotless white eyelet lace dress and a straw hat with clusters of daisies around the brim. Like her, he folded his hands together and looked up at the aluminum cross with its stylized flame.

We must learn to see the world anew.

"The blood of Christ," a patient voice said, holding a tiny plastic cup in front of John. From the smell, it was filled with grape juice. John looked up into the young minister's friendly eyes, and saw the gaunt reflection of his own face. He tasted blood in his mouth, and it didn't taste like grape juice.

He didn't belong here.

John shook his head, rising and turning his back as he walked, faster and faster, until he was running down the aisle. As he went, the lilies lining the aisles began to wilt and turn brown.

At the door to the sanctuary, an older male usher intercepted him. "Sir, is something wrong?"

John swallowed blood and bile. "Bathroom?"

The usher pointed to a door on the left in the front hall outside the sanctuary.

John hurried into the empty restroom and made it as far as the sink before he vomited. Blood splashed the immaculate white porcelain and dripped onto the floor. He groped, turning on the cold water and flushing most of the mess down the drain before he cupped his hands and splashed his hot face.

The inside of his mouth felt sore, and with his tongue he

felt two large fever blisters on the roof of his mouth. Touching them brought another wave of nausea that made him double over. He tasted blood and spit another mouthful into the sink; the fever blisters inside his mouth must have burst.

If that was the case, why did they still feel as if they were bulging?

John's arms shook as he braced himself and straightened. In the mirror above the sink, he saw blood running down his chin and dripping onto his shirt. He opened his mouth and tipped his head back, trying to see how badly the blisters were bleeding.

The pupils in his eyes expanded, covering his irises and then the white corneas, until his eyes turned solid black. John couldn't breathe, his lungs as solid as if they had been filled with cement, and then a fresh gush of blood spilled over his lip. He brought his hand up to wipe it away and felt one final, tearing pain.

John parted his lips and watched as two long, white fangs slowly slid from his palate into his mouth.

"Don't go yet, love."

The mortal female didn't resist Robin of Locksley's hold. For this he was glad, absorbed as he became in the texture and warmth of her silky skin against his. From the moment she'd walked into the club, her presence had held him riveted. Many human women had fetching features, effortless grace, or engaging wit, but rare were the ones who possessed all three.

"There's no reason to stay," she said.

Along with her obvious virtues, she had a manner as direct as a man's and as pitiless as one of Robin's arrows. That, too, he found captivating; it had been centuries since any mortal female had denied him anything.

"If you go now," he countered, "we may never see each other again."

She gently eased her wrist from his grip. "I'll try not to let that ruin my life."

Her resistance puzzled him. A small percentage of people were slow to be affected by or were immune to *l'attrait*, the scent his immortal body shed to attract and control humans. But his talent, the ability to charm any mortal he touched, had never failed to sway even the most defiant human.

Perhaps it had more to do with her than him, Robin thought. Everything about her attested to her character, from the dignified set of her shoulders and spine to the clever choice of her garments. A businesswoman, her well-cut dark rose jacket and slim skirt said, one who disdained hiding or apologizing for her sex. The pale pink silk scarf she wore knotted around her slim neck suggested that equally delicate lingerie lay beneath the lace confection of her cream-colored blouse.

Then there were her legs, which could be called only superb. Robin imagined easing the thin straps of her heels from her feet and sliding the shimmering stockings from those long, curvy limbs. He might have done so, had she succumbed to *l'attrait*. Bespelled by his scent, she would not have been able to leave his presence or resist any request he made.

The woman's obvious intelligence and confidence indicated a very strong will. Perhaps she could not easily be swayed by anything, even his Kyn talent.

"It is getting late," she was saying.

Robin knew he should let her go—such humans as she were dangerous to the Kyn—but found he could not. Not until he further tested her remarkable restraint. "You will never know, then."

"Know what?"

He took her hand again, lifted it, and brushed a kiss across her knuckles. "What *my* stratagem was."

The intimate gesture seemed to amuse her. "So tell me before I leave."

Robin wondered how she would react if she knew that he'd deliberately sent the brunette call girl over to distract the last inebriated male who had pestered her at the bar, or that he'd cleared everyone from the tables around him to create an oasis of calm in the noisy club. An oasis for *her*.

"I have endeavored to keep you from discovering"—he turned her hand and touched his lips briefly to the thin blue veins on the inside of her wrist—"that I came here for you."

At last gratifying surprise rounded her cognac-colored eyes slightly, revealing the glints of fawn and gold in her irises. A moment later it was gone. "Seeing as we've never met, I doubt that."

"In life, perhaps not." He admired the play of the light cast by the mirrored ball over the strands of fiery hair she'd tamed into a smooth twist at the back of her head. "There are other worlds. Other lives."

She studied him just as closely in return. "I don't believe in quantum theory, past lives, or reincarnation."

"Nor do I." Slipping into the old way of speaking was dangerous, but he didn't care. "It matters not, as long as you will stay."

"I don't know you," she replied, her tone remaining maddeningly reasonable, "and I never pick up strange men in bars."

"I'm Rob." He gave one end of her scarf a playful tug. "Tell me your name, and we'll no longer be strangers."

"It's Chris." Her head turned as the music slowed, and the humans gyrating on the dance floor embraced and began swaying together. Without looking at him, she added, "I really can't stay. I have to go into work early tomorrow."

As she made her excuse, Robin could hear a wistful note

in her voice, and saw a glimmer of envy in her eyes as she watched the other mortals dancing.

She might not want him, but she wanted to dance.

"Then we shall not waste another moment." He laced his fingers through hers. "Stay for this song, Chris. Stay and dance with me."

She regarded him for the space of ten heartbeats before she turned and led him toward the crowded dance floor.

Robin enjoyed many of the freedoms of this modern era, but none so much as the dances which permitted a man to take into his arms and hold close any woman who gave her consent. During his human lifetime, such scandalous contact would have resulted in the instant ruination of the woman's reputation and an immediate end to her partner's bachelor status, if the woman's father didn't demand other, more lethal forms of satisfaction.

Once on the dance floor, Robin guided her around to face him, encircling her waist with his free arm while lifting their entwined fingers to hold her hand over his heart. She was tall for a woman; if she moved two steps closer, she could tickle his mouth with her curly red eyelashes or kiss the hollow of his throat.

Chris did neither of those things, but stepped back until several inches separated their bodies.

Undaunted, Robin spread his free hand over the gentle curve of the small of her back, where a delicious amount of body heat permeated the thin material of her dress to caress his palm and fingers.

"You feel very warm," he said, bending his head so that his breath stirred the smooth strands of hair coiled above her ear. "Are you uncomfortable?"

"I'm fine." Chris did not press herself against him, nor did she strain away as she followed his lead. She maintained that respectable distance between them as she danced. She did not look up at him, however, but kept her eyes on the band's gray-haired singer as he crooned the words to the gentle tune.

"It's a pretty song, isn't it?" she asked. "I think it was the only hit Spandau Ballet ever had."

"Spandau Ballet." He'd heard of many dance troupes, but never that one. "I cannot say that I am familiar with them."

"Before our time," Chris said. "My mother loved this song." Her shoulders tensed and her voice changed, growing crisp and impersonal again. "How did you know what I was drinking? Did you ask the waitress or the bartender?"

"Neither." She guarded herself better than a Scotsman did his purse, while asking questions better left unanswered, Robin thought. He decided to tell her the truth and see what she would make of it. "I could smell the ginger ale on your breath."

"You couldn't have done that," she told him flatly. "You were sitting at least ten feet away from me."

"Alas, I'm cursed with a sensitive nose." He took in the scent of her on a slow, deep breath. "You also smell of rain, herbs, honey and . . ." He bent his head close to her mouth. "Maraschino cherries. Did you steal them when the bartender wasn't looking?"

"No, he put two in the first drink he made for me." Her fine cognac eyes grew wary. "That's quite an impressive trick."

He moved his shoulders. "It's nothing."

"I washed my hair with rain-scented shampoo and conditioner today," Chris said, "and I drank a cup of herbal tea with honey."

He grinned. "So I was right."

"I did all that," she continued, "when I got up this morning." She waited a beat. "Seventeen hours ago."

Robin's smile faded as her words invoked an image of her

in his bed, her pale skin and auburn hair glowing against the dark sienna of his silk sheets, her arms open and welcoming. Unless he found some way—and quickly—to lay siege to the fortress she had built around her heart, he would never see her there.

"If this is a practical joke, it's a good one," Chris continued. "Did Hutchins put you up to it?"

"I don't know anyone named Hutchins." He could barely speak as primal need surged through him, lodging in his groin to swell and harden his cock while demanding that he find some manner through which to turn the fantasy into reality. Feeding earlier had lent him a certain measure of control he might otherwise have lost in this astonishing rush of desire for her, but Robin did not trust himself. "I am not joking with you."

"You're not." She sounded uncertain now.

Robin couldn't jest with her, not with the urgency of his hunger pounding inside his head. He could not tolerate another moment of this. He had to have her. Tonight. *Now.* He kept a suite of rooms at the hotel where he frequently used willing females. The only thing that kept him from sweeping her up into his arms and carrying her off to the nearest elevator was the sound of her voice, asking him more questions.

"Do you know a fair-haired man who wears a lot of red?" She nodded toward the other side of the dance floor. "There's one over there staring at you."

Robin glanced over to see his seneschal, Will Scarlet. He made a simple gesture behind Chris's back, and Will scowled but retreated into the crowd.

"Pay no heed to him." He noticed the other couples staring and smiling at him, and realized how badly his control had slipped; somehow he'd flooded the entire dance floor with his scent. No wonder Will had come to see what the matter was. Soon every occupant of the bar would fall under his spell.

Except one, it seemed.

Robin peered down at the woman in his arms to see whether her pupils had dilated, but the dark color of her eyes made it impossible to tell. "How are you feeling?"

"This is nice." She sighed. "I don't want to go home."

At last, her fortress was crumbling. He didn't know whether it was due to his talent or to *l'attrait*, and he didn't care. He tugged her closer, fitting her body to his and pressing his aroused flesh against her belly. She did not pull away, and indeed the movements they made caused her abdomen to rub lightly over the ridge of his erection.

Robin gritted his teeth. "What if I ask you for more than a dance, love?"

"You can ask." She emphasized the last word oddly.

Robin knew women, delighted in them. He had spent several lifetimes enjoying their company, learning their ways, and recognizing their wiles. He knew the subtle changes arousal caused in their voices and their bodies, the tantalizing signs that showed their interest in a man.

Although Chris was perhaps the most reserved human female he had ever encountered, and she possessed great skill in masking both her true thoughts and emotions, he did not doubt now that she desired him. No mortal he touched had ever resisted his charm for long. Not even this stubborn wench, who had wanted nothing to do with him but five minutes ago.

Fool. Inside Robin's skull, his father's angry voice shouted across seven centuries. *You only want her because you cannot have her.*

The scent of bergamot thinned as Robin's self-disgust grew, and gradually the other couples on the dance floor lost interest in them. When the song ended, he released Chris and stepped away from her, breaking all physical contact. As long as he didn't touch her, his talent could not influence her decisions. As soon as he left, the effects of *l'attrait* would rapidly dissipate.

And he would never know her, and that was how it would have to be.

Robin bowed to her. "I thank you for the dance."

Chris began to say something, and then hesitated as if choosing her words.

"It's all right, love. This is not your doing." Because he couldn't help himself, he added, "My home in the city is on the penthouse floor of the Armstrong Building. It is that unsightly tower of black glass and steel at the end of the street. Do you know it?"

She nodded.

"Good." At least he could offer this much. "Come to me there, whenever you wish."

"Come to you? Rob—"

"Listen to me now." He felt his *dents acérées* emerge into his mouth, fully extended and aching for a taste of her flesh. He slid his hand to cup the back of her neck and pressed his cheek to hers, using his talent to enforce his words. "I want you, love, more than I can say. But it must be what you want. When I am gone, when your head clears, then you must choose to do as you wish. Nothing more. Do you understand me?"

"Yes, but—"

Robin pressed his scarred fingers against her lips. "You know where I will be. I do not sleep until after dawn." He put his mouth to the back of her hand, careful not to let her feel the sharp tips of his fangs. "I hope that we meet again, my lady."